VIRGIL'S
GHOST

Also by Irving Weinman

TAILOR'S DUMMY

HAMPTON HEAT

VIRGIL'S GHOST

A NOVEL BY
IRVING WEINMAN

FAWCETT COLUMBINE
NEW YORK

A Fawcett Columbine Book
Published by Ballantine Books

Copyright © 1989 by Irving Weinman

All rights reserved under International and Pan-American Copyright
Conventions. Published in the United States by Ballantine Books, a division
of Random House, Inc., New York, and simultaneously in Canada by
Random House of Canada Limited, Toronto.

LIBRARY OF CONGRESS CATALOGING-IN-PUBLICATION DATA
Weinman, Irving, 1937–
    Virgil's ghost : a novel / by Irving Weinman.
        p.   cm.
    ISBN 0–449–90445–8
    I. Title.
PS3573.E3963V5   1989
813′.54—dc20   89-90885
                                                              CIP

Designed by Beth Tondreau Design/Gabrielle Hamberg

Manufactured in the United States of America
First Edition: January 1990
10   9   8   7   6   5   4   3   2   1

To my lovely children
Zoe and Michael

Lo pianto stesso li pianger non lascia,
e 'l duol che truova in su li occhi rintoppo,
si volge in entro a far crescer l'ambascia;
che le lagrime prime fanno groppo,
e si come visere di cristallo,
riempion sotto 'l ciglio tutto il coppo.
   —*Dante,* Inferno, *XXXIII, 94–9*

Tears in that cold place
prevent their weeping; grief lies
frozen on each face
in balls behind the eyes:
tightening mask, ice agony,
impacted crystal cries.
    —*Author's translation*

BOOK I

In the middle of the night, Schwartz woke to find himself in a damp bed, his side of it. On hers, his wife slept peacefully and dry, undisturbed by the images that sweltered him.

He sat up, propped on his hands with the sheet stuck to his stomach, and reconstructed the police funeral he'd attended two days earlier. Funerals were always the worst of it, yet he'd never before memorized details like this endless "poem" read by the young policeman's mother.

> *It feels like only yesterday that I showed you with joy*
> *To your father in the hospital and said here is our darling baby boy.*
> *And I remember how you would look up at me with such big black eyes*
> *That I knew that when you grew up you would be so good and wise . . .*

She'd kept forgetting how he died, asking why the casket wasn't open.

Schwartz licked his lips. He was thirsty, damp and dry; he was out of bed walking naked to the bathroom in the dark. Why was it still so hot in early October? The hallway smelled of dead leaves.

He splashed his face and drank lukewarm water from cupped hands. In the mirror he saw his face drip water. Yesterday that other face he saw dripped sweat. A white face, the whiteness made Schwartz notice the man crossing Worth Street at Center. A wet face, his thinning hair pasted flat, the man stepped off the curb and began to die of a heart attack but kept walking, slanting toward the tool bag he first carried, then dragged. The woman next to Schwartz understood. They were going toward him as the man collapsed at their curb, one gray gaberdined leg still in the street.

In the mirror, Schwartz the atheist saw himself rock back and forth at the basin as if reciting prayers for the dead. The dead, the dead were crowding him.

He'd lifted the leg from the street and slowly turned the man. Such white gray skin. The woman who wanted to help was black, a smooth mid-brown. And Schwartz? The back of his hand on the basin was a yellow brown pink sort of olive-drab white. He'd told the woman he was a policeman and looked to the building across the street—DEPARTMENT OF HEALTH, HOSPITALS AND SANITATION. Schwartz said, "Over there. Either they'll restore his health in a hospital or, if he's as dead as I think, they'll come with a garbage truck." Then he apologized and ran to call an ambulance, but one more decent person now disliked police.

And the dead face as they covered it: the furrowed brow and downturned mouth showed more chagrin than pain, as if dropping dead in public was another, if the last, embarrassment.

But neither this random death nor the young policeman's

had been the final straw. He'd left that humiliated camel broken in the sand months ago and gone into the desert on foot. Sitting on the side of the bed, he looked down at his feet. Toward what oasis? Where? Why still so hot?

"Len? Len, what is it?"

"What?"

"You're talking to yourself, rocking on the edge of the bed."

"I've . . . Karen, I've quit the police."

"What?" Karen sat up. "I knew it. You shit. I knew it. Would you get me some coffee, please?"

He set her coffee on the bed between them and held the glass of soda water to his mouth so that its bubbles hissed wet under his bottom lip.

"Nothing to say? You end a career of eighteen years without mentioning it to me and now you sit communing with seltzer?"

"Club soda. Sorry. I'm confused."

"You're telling me! Telling me sooner would have helped."

He lifted his knees so that the sheet billowed and slacked. "I'm clear about quitting. It's telling you that has me confused."

"We've been together . . ." Karen lifted the cup with two hands. "After twenty-one years I suppose I should know you couldn't. But I hate it, having to tell you what it is you can't tell me."

She left the bed, cup in hand, and switched on the air conditioning that neither could sleep with. Schwartz watched a wave of dark hair shade her forehead.

Karen sat cross-legged on the sheet and pulled her long blue T-shirt over both knees. "You quit because you couldn't live with the police anymore."

"Yes."

"And you still feel guilty because of Jake? It's . . . Look, you took that damned cocaine bribe to put Jake through college, you beat the investigation five years ago. You keep saying you've done your penance. And now you're back onto real cases, so . . ."

"But you don't know how Gallagher—"

"Yes I do! I know you think he uses your guilt to manipulate you. Oh, damn it, I know! You've told me all I'd ever want to know about that relationship, every damned permutation." She stopped, looked down and sipped the coffee.

She shook her head. "And you still sit there silent as seltzer, excuse me, club soda. Well, it's not Gallagher and it's not the police and it's not Jake, since he's at New Haven. So why isn't God in his heaven and all right at home and at Homicide? Because you haven't told Jake."

"No, he couldn't cope."

"He could. It's you who can't cope. You're rationalizing your own fear. You know you have to tell him . . . Good lord, why do I waste the breath? I've said all this before."

"Karen, I quit because I couldn't stand being manipulated through my guilt into corners and compromises that I'd never otherwise . . . Yes, *because of my guilt.* There's so much guilt that I feel I can't be a cop, don't deserve to be a cop. But I really am sorry I hadn't the courage to tell you. I was afraid you'd talk me out of it."

"Really? May I ask you some questions *now,* if it's not too pushy? Has your resignation been accepted?"

"The commissioner accepted. But Tom got me to make it a year's leave, during which time I can return at rank."

"Well, that's something."

"It's no big deal, even though the mayor himself had to

okay it. They threw me a laurel as I crossed the border; I won't take them up on it."

Karen shrugged. "You're a poet of self-deception. You chose to leave the Republic, and they've been good enough to give you a return pass. And just where is it you're going? What are you going to do?" She looked at him and bit her bottom lip.

"Don't worry. I'll probably make better money. I'll—"

"Money? Did I say money? Oh, damn you, have I ever complained about *that*? What kind of a monster-woman have you projected onto me?" Her cheekbones pushed out as she clenched her jaw. "Well?"

Schwartz turned. The air conditioner rattled. "I'm setting up as a private investigator."

"You're joking! Oh, God, you're not joking. Oh, Len, Len, I'd still be furious for your not talking it over with me, but if you were saying you had to quit to finish your doctorate, or to write a book, or something like that, I'd understand. But to quit for . . ." Karen looked into her coffee. "You could do so many worthwhile things: crime journalism or . . ."

"Or what? Here are the facts. I'm not twenty-one, Karen, I'm forty-three, and all my experience is in this field. You don't go from police inspector to market analyst or professor of juris-prudence or sculptor. Of course, you can go from police inspec-tor to store detective or maybe even trainee salesman at Barney's."

"But you're going to private eye? A private dick? Don't give me that look: I'm not being snobbish. Len, it doesn't even have the moral compensation—that's your term—the moral com-pensation of public service." Karen gave a small, unsmiling laugh.

"That's what I'm saying about the police: the job has lost its morality. I'm immoral, forced into immoral procedures.

Karen, Jesus, it's like death. But on my own, well, the actual work of a private investigator is similar to police investigation, and—"

"Are you serious? Hanging around hotels to photograph unfaithful husbands is similar? Fifty dollars a day is similar?"

"Husbands or wives. And it's closer to five hundred a day."

"Oh, well, naturally *that* makes it splendid. But why stop at five hundred? With your drug contacts you could make a lot more . . . I'm sorry."

"Are you?"

"For that, yes. But you're making such a mistake and you're too pigheaded to admit it."

"I've taken an office down on Flatbush Avenue Extension, and there'll be an ad in the next Yellow Pages."

Karen crouched on the bed and shook her finger. She jumped off, paced, turned and pointed. "How long? How long have you been making all these plans without saying a word to me? Weeks? Months?"

"Months. I'm sorry. I was wrong not to tell you. But, Karen, there are advantages. I choose my jobs, my methods; I choose my hours. I don't have to be away on weekends or be on call at three in the morning. And with my background there was no problem getting the license, so—"

"License—that's what you take. It's another marriage license!" Karen turned and snapped off the air conditioner. "That's bigamy. I hate it. I'll leave."

"No. God, no! Please listen." He stood, but Karen pointed him off. "We'll work it out. Give me a chance to—"

"I've given you a chance for five years. *I* need a chance now. *My* life, *my* career. Or maybe you think art history is trivial, sissy woman's stuff compared to peeking through keyholes."

"Stop it, Karen. It isn't—"

"No!" she said. She was shaking her finger as if it were a

sword. "You give me a chance. A chance? You wouldn't even mention this. And for months, months! No, either I stay here or you stay here, but as long as you're . . . Damn! I can hardly bring myself to say it. As long as you're a private investigator, we don't live together. You can't do this to someone you really live with, damn you. Call it a trial separation. It can't be worse than the trial you've been putting us through for the last five years."

He looked across the bed, a Sahara. "We should see a counselor. We have to compromise."

"No! We can't compromise this. Look where we are, Len. My God. Len!" Karen was walking toward him with open arms.

Schwartz held his wife. His tears ran into her hair. It would be all right now. "We'll work this out."

"Not this, Len. We won't."

He said, "Don't be silly."

And she wasn't. At five in the morning he lay in the guest room, the table fan on the desk alternating its hot, tiny breeze left to right, right to left over his chest. They'd worked out a trial semi-separation. He'd stay away during his working week, returning to Karen and Park Slope on weekends. That way . . .

It would be terrible. Schwartz switched off the light, shut his eyes and tried to tunnel back into the small, receding darkness.

Schwartz sat behind the desk in his newly painted office looking to his right through partition windows into the outer room where an assistant should have been. To his left was the door to a narrow back room with a cot and a cheap clothes rack and the cardboard chest of drawers he'd bought at A&S. A small humming refrigerator had been left by the former tenant; a stall shower dripped in the adjoining washroom.

He could see to the glass in the entrance door and the back of the dark blue sign made by the print shop across the hall. He'd first considered hand-painted lettering, but with that had come so clear an image from fiction that he could still envision the letters ꓤꓱꓧꓛꓤA ꓷИA ꓱꓷAꟼꓢ vaguely Cyrillic on the frosted glass. But this glass was clear, with three steel bars across it, and the letters said L. SCHWARTZ, PRIVATE INVESTIGATIONS.

Taking the order, Carl the printer had asked if he wanted

a logo, a magnifying glass or something, and looking into the start of Schwartz's snarl had continued, "No, I guess you want it plain." Now Schwartz had it plain: an empty office, a silent phone.

His one call, half an hour earlier—at which he'd jumped and then forced his heartbeat to slow down and his voice to sound ham casual in answering "Good morning. L. Schwartz, Private Investigations"—had been from his new ex-boss Tom Gallagher, calling to wish him bad luck. "You're right. I'm a hell of a sore loser," said Gallagher.

"We'll see, Tom. But thanks for the thought, anyway."

"I can't believe you're going through with this, you damned fool. The best goddamned mind in Homicide and you jump off . . . Ah! And listen, Lenny, if you think you can count on me or the department to help this half-assed PI career of yours, you're dead wrong."

"I still have friends over there," Schwartz said, "better friends than you've turned out to be, Thomas, in the pinch. I'm busy now. Good-bye." He kept from slamming the receiver.

A lie. He hadn't been busy then, he wasn't now. He looked straight ahead to the opposite wall with its Matisse poster. A Mediterranean room, the shutters open to a palm tree in white light. And in the foreground, the table with its orange plums and spotted pomegranate. Below, in splashed blue handwriting, *Travail—Joie.*

Work, joy. Damn! What had he done? Gallagher was right. It was . . . What?

It was the door opening, two people, real people coming in. Work! Joy! Schwartz sprang to greet them.

He bobbed about, not exactly bowing, hearing his babble concerning the assistant not yet being in. He found himself so nervous that he didn't focus until he'd blustered them to the inner office, when the man said, "My name is Carter Hayes. This is my wife, Irene. You *are* the Leonard Schwartz who's been a police detective?"

"I am." A hundred express questions went through his local mind.

He was setting a second chair before the desk. Mrs. Hayes sat down with an inaudible "Thank you." Then Mr. Hayes sat and now Schwartz knew it was his turn, so he sat behind his desk and looked at his first clients and immediately disliked them. He found them a handsome but unattractive couple, he with his neat white hair and small blue eyes and short nose over thin, dour lips that reminded Schwartz of a certain dean of men at Harvard with a genius for humiliation; she, perhaps ten years younger in her mid-fifties with the female version of his looks that proclaimed, "I am enormously subservient to my husband and enormously proud of it."

"What can I do for you, Mr. and Mrs. Hayes?" Schwartz asked, hearing their name as some cruel fraternity initiation.

Carter Hayes folded his hands across a knee in the manner of the dreadful dean. "It's difficult to know where to begin, Mr. Schwartz."

Schwartz nodded, hoping the small upturn of his mouth signaled benign concern rather than avarice.

"Six months ago our son, Virgil, died. We want you to investigate his death. He was a brilliant young mathematician and could have been . . . Well."

"I'm very sorry," Schwartz said, noting no emotion on the father's face. Mrs. Hayes sat looking down; there had been a slightly larger intake of breath from her. Schwartz twiddled a green pen over the blank yellow legal pad. "How did your son die?"

"That's precisely what we wish you—"

"Carter," came the small voice from Irene Hayes.

"Mr. Schwartz, the coroner's report says Virgil had AIDS.

Virgil couldn't have had AIDS. Whatever his shortcomings, Virgil was not a pervert. We hope that your investigation could prove that."

Schwartz shook his head. "I don't think I could be of any use. Your son died six months ago, and the coroner's report said, I take it you *meant* it said, of a disease or diseases related to AIDS. On a question of medical expertise, I wouldn't be able—" He stopped, seeing Irene Hayes's hand come up timidly, finger raised. "Mrs. Hayes?"

"You see, Jimmy—"

"That's all right, Irene," her husband interrupted. "She called our son 'Jimmy.' I thought his given name 'Virgil' was fine. Virgil James Hayes. He was found in the East River. His body . . ." He turned toward his wife. "Excuse me, dear, but it is necessary. His body was painted and he was badly mutilated. The report gave the immediate cause of death as probable misadventure. By 'misadventure' I found, not easily, I assure you, I found they meant some sort of monstrous activities I know my son could never have been part of."

"They said that he had advanced terminal Kaposi's sarcoma," Irene Hayes said to the lap of her navy blue skirt, "as well as other diseases, and that suicidal or . . . or that other sort of behavior was sometimes a result of the depression associated with AIDS."

"Oh?" said Schwartz. "But I still can't see how I can help." Schwartz doodled on the pad, a figure eight on its side, thickening loop over loop. He narrowed his eyes at Carter Hayes. "This was six months ago, yet when you came in here you asked if I was the Schwartz who had been a police detective. My resignation has only been official for a week. Who told you about me? Why?"

Carter Hayes didn't blink. "I promised not to divulge his name. Mr. Schwartz, we've been battling for six months to get the truth. And finally, a few weeks ago, I don't know why—"

"Because he took pity on us, Carter," his wife said, looking up for the first time.

As if "pity" were a word only slightly less distasteful than "AIDS," Carter Hayes continued. "For whatever reason, sir, a former colleague of yours was good enough to tell us, unofficially, that he felt there was something strange about the coroner's report but that the police couldn't help. He suggested that a private investigator with a good police background and connections could possibly help, and he mentioned you."

"All right, Mr. Hayes. We don't have to name the person; he must have known I'd figure it out. You give me your address and phone number. I'll speak with this former colleague, and if there seems a possible error or cover-up or miscarriage of justice, I'll take the case. If I do, I'll need full statements from both of you. But I'd better make this clear: I won't take your money to make up lies for your homophobic conscience, Mr. Hayes. I think it's a bad conscience."

His hands still folded on his knee, Carter Hayes pushed in his elbows and stiffened his arms. He swallowed once, a small swallow, considering the pride. "Very well, Mr. Schwartz. There seems no other recourse."

He'd make it easy for them to refuse. "My fees will be five hundred dollars a day, plus my expenses, plus expenses for my assistant." And for good measure he added, "And it might run ten, twenty, or even forty days, if it runs at all."

"I'm prepared to pay your fees for however long it may take, Mr. Schwartz. As to my motives displeasing you, I believe that whatever yours may be, they'll serve to prove what we know to be the truth about our son. You may have different values, sir, but it's Mrs. Hayes and myself who have to live with our memories of Virgil, and so I would ask that lectures in morality, from either you or us, should not be part of any arrangement we come to."

So this was the marketplace, thought Schwartz. He nodded as he rose, taking their address and phone number. He showed Irene and Carter Hayes to the door, noticing that they were very well dressed. The brooch at the top of the woman's plain blouse was one large sapphire.

As he closed the door on the Hayeses and the noises from the print shop, Schwartz felt as if he were stuck in a vast marsh, muddied by bubbles of depression. Work and joy? Or was it work that made you free? By his desk, the source of that wisdom came to him in German and he shuddered.

He remembered a coin from his childhood, a one-franc piece from Vichy, France. His father had translated, explaining why "Liberty, Equality, Fraternity" had been replaced by "Work, Family, Country." How tinny-light the coin was; how fascinated he'd been by its shoddiness. He'd given his small collection to Jake, explaining the coin to his son as his father had to him. Did Jake still have the box of coins? He dialed Santini. Work would free him, anyhow, from thought.

Santini wasn't in his office or lab, so Schwartz left a message for the doctor to call back as soon as possible. This was where it started—the polite obliteration of working relationships. He saw across the mud flats of his desk that Santini wouldn't be given the message for hours, wouldn't get back to him for days, by which time—

The phone rang under his hand. "Schwartz, private investigations."

"I like it, Len. Only the last name. Tough yet somehow learned," Santini said, laughing.

"That was quick, Gerry."

"I was blipped on my blipper, and when I heard it was Sherlock Hammer, I picked up the first phone."

"A safe one?"

"No, nothing over here's safe for you, at least not until

15

Gallagher stops roaring and cursing you for nine generations. Listen, I can guess what you're calling about. I have to be in Brooklyn this morning, so why don't I drop by to say hello first, say, in ten minutes?"

"Ten? Without a department chopper, even you can't make it over here that fast, Juan Fangio."

"That dates you. I'm pretending I don't understand. See you in ten, my old African explorer."

Schwartz hung up the phone and smiled. One short call could unswamp him, float him out into . . . Who could tell? But he felt clear, felt he had direction. Work. Joy. Coffee. Did Gerry take it black or milky—coffee mated? Family, work. Gerry liked mud espresso, but they didn't have that across the hall, where he was sharing coffee with Carl and the print shop. Despite Carl's constant references to this end of Flatbush Avenue becoming so up-market, "almost like the Heights," he was delighted having an ex-cop around.

Carl's wishes made him lie like a real estate agent. The area was still seedy: Schwartz listened to the siren blaring closer. Then he smiled and ran downstairs in time to see Santini U-turn from across the street through four lanes of flabbergasted traffic to a screechstop at the hydrant.

He leapt from the car, shaking his wristwatch. "Eleven minutes! Eleven from Police Plaza, over the bridge and through downtown Brooklyn to fabulous Flatbush Avenue Extension. Ta-da!"

"Gerry, you're supposed to analyze corpses, not create them," Schwartz said, holding both arms out to the sallow, handsome man.

"Well, business is slow, but never Santini," he said, hugging Schwartz at the curb. He stepped back, his hands on Schwartz's shoulders. "Fantastic! You look less like a private eye than you did a cop, and you never looked like a cop."

Schwartz scuffed his shoe on the pavement. "Aw, gosh."

"Len, it's good to see you, *amico mio.* I never got to spend any time with you these past months, and I know how the ca-ca was dropping on you, from on high."

"Verily, yea, even from City Hall. But here are the fruits of that manuring—your sending me custom."

Santini ran his hand through his hair. "Well, you'd better not get your hopes too high. I don't think there's much here." He looked up. "Is *this* your office building? I've seen nicer shooting galleries."

"Nonsense. This is Numero 1-B Flatbush Avenue Extension. And what would you know, growing up in Cobble Hill?" Schwartz opened the door and nodded Santini upstairs.

"Cobble Hill? That's real estate hype. I'm a good Italian kid from Red Hook. And don't tell me about today; when we were growing up it was you Eastern Parkway kids who were ritzy."

"Here it is," said Schwartz, opening the door to the office. "How the ritzy have fallen. Want some coffee?"

"No, thanks," Santini said. "Hey, this is fine. You have an assistant?"

"Not yet. My hiring policy depends on what you have to say. Let's sit in here."

Santini sat, stretched out his legs and looked around. "Yes, very nice. A Matisse on the wall. And what's back there? Storage?"

Schwartz shook his head.

"Bad, is it, Len?"

"Does it show?"

"Yes, you're Mr. Manic-Depressing. Your smiles are too big, and you look at a door and it's like you've fallen down a well."

"Into a swamp. That door leads to my little bedroom—refrigerator suite."

"Ah. You and Karen."

"My fault. Gerry, I couldn't tell her until last weekend that I'd quit."

Santini sighed, took off his poplin suit jacket and threw it over the back of the chair. "That's lousy. What's happened to you? I thought you were so close."

"This last year . . . Oh, shit, Gerry, I can't begin . . ."

"You don't have to. I've sort of guessed what the last four or five years have been for you and . . . Jesus," he laughed, as Schwartz's head hung lower, "why am I being so nice? I've been lusting after the lovely Karen for years. She's far too good for you. What she needs, you know, is a fellow Catholic, I mean, another lapsed Catholic fellow. We could elapse, elope, share an ex-communication and eternity flitting around after each other's tail . . . Hey, Len! This is supposed to cheer you. I love you. I can say that because I'm a macho Italian male. We get a special dispensation for telling guys we love them without having to be gay."

Schwartz looked up. "Thanks. Maybe if I succeed at this . . . Anyway, tell me about the Hayeses, my creepy potential clients."

"All right, but I don't know much. It was your friend Simp the Wimp who did the honors."

"Simpkin?"

"Simpkin, Simpkin. You must be the only one in the department who liked him."

"No, not liked. I don't know, I never felt I wanted to make fun of him. He's gone to some government job, hasn't he?"

"A very fancy admin job with the Public Health Service. He started last month. As a matter of fact, it was at the awful going-away party we had to give for him that we began talking about tough calls. You know, causes, times of death, shoptalk. We were swapping stories and he capped them with this one in his whiny, finicky Mr. Science voice, about a body he'd been called out to. It had been fished out of the river. It was mutilated, painted and had signs of what could have been AIDS-related Kaposi's sarcoma, making everyone work fast and fearfully. There were further complications because the body had obviously not been in so long and its lividity looked—"

"Lividity?" asked Schwartz, then remembered. "Oh, the blood settling and discoloring the skin after death."

"Right. So there was lividity looking like bruising, and real bruising and mutilation marks, and mutilation marks looking like the sarcoma, and to make a long and messy story short, it was technically as tough a call as you could have. Of course, Simp didn't mention names or dates, so nothing clicked at the time. But about a week or ten days later, when the message from the Hayeses landed on my desk, Simp being gone, I remembered back a few months when I'd heard about a denied exhumation request involving an AIDS victim whose parents refused to believe it was AIDS. A bit weird. And this message referred to that. I wondered if this could be the case Simp had described. At that point, I guess it was just curiosity. So I agreed to meet them, Mr. and Mrs. Hayes. And then, when they told me—"

"What did you think of them?"

"Personally, I thought they were cold, unloving shits who only wanted to rest easy with the memory of a straight son. But it also occurred to me, once I was sure this was Simp's case, that there *might* have been a mistake, given those circumstances. And I guess there was something moving about Mom Hayes, those eyes downcast all the time like she was holding some tremendous pain. And even his stiff upper-lip psyche . . . Well, what with the already refused exhumation, I knew they wouldn't get diddly-squat from the department, so . . ."

"You thought of me."

"Yup."

"Maybe I should check with Simpkin first. Then, if he thinks—"

"Len, Len, do you want to succeed at this PI business, or do you want to do charity work? If you think it's worth going back to Simp the wimp you should do it on client's time, not your own."

"You're right, Gerry. And where'd you get so business smart?"

"Are you kidding? I may be in public service, but I'm also a card-carrying member of the AMA—you know, All Moneys in Advance." Santini stood and draped his jacket over his shoulder. "Do it. Take them on, find out from Simp and go—or not—from there. Now I've got to go to my Aunt Anna down on Court Street. Would you believe she'll trust only me as her doctor? When I tell her I'm more used to corpses, she says, 'At's okay. I'ma feel like a corpse.' She's eighty-four and going strong. Well, family, what can you do?"

Schwartz opened the door and put his arm around Santini. "Yeah, family. Family."

"Len. Jesus, make it up with Karen. And you'll feel a lot better once you start working at this job."

"Sure. Thanks, Gerry."

"Stay in touch," he said, running down the stairs. He stopped and looked up. "I haven't looked at the file on this, but maybe I can get it for you."

Behind his closed door, Schwartz pulled at his lip. Work, family? Gerry, fraternity? Karen, equality? And should he look for an assistant now? Maybe that funny guy he'd used down at Brighton Beach? Should he call the Hayeses?

Santini's siren faded down the avenue. Schwartz recalled the other side of that Vichy franc. Over the words *Etat Français*, where *République Français* had been, two sprigs of wheat flanked a nasty double-headed axe.

Hi, Karen. Just calling to say I have my first clients. Karen? Hello. I've taken on an assistant for what looks like a major . . . major lie," Schwartz said, ending rehearsal, realizing the show would never run.

He stood with his back to the desk, looking out the window over the roof of the Chicken and Shrimp House. Across the avenue, the lights from Junior's restaurant gleamed brighter than the still brilliant day.

But it had, damn it, been a good day. The potential clients, then Santini, then the clients becoming actual. And Abrasha Addison! Schwartz sat down, tilting back in the secondhand Naugahyde as he had when calling Abrasha's "private" number in Brighton Beach.

This number was a phone booth at the corner of Brighton Sixth and Brighton Beach Avenue. It was generally answered by

Abrasha, who invariably said he wasn't Abrasha but if you left a number, Abrasha might get back to you. And when you asked who this was, Abrasha would say, "This is *another* Russian hustler," and hang up, calling back immediately without bothering to change his voice.

"Abrasha?"

"Inspector, my friend?"

"Yes. Listen—"

"Of course. But please, you call me right back so I don't have to fool with quarters." And he hung up again.

Schwartz called back. He'd used Abrasha several times to get difficult street information; he was irritating, unreliable and good. "Abrasha?"

"Hello, yes, a much better line. What is up, Inspector?"

"What is up is that I'm not an inspector. I'm a PI and want you to work with me. What do you say?"

"Impossible. Of course. Certainly. Is an honor. Lenny I can call you?"

"Sure. Abrasha, this is a real business. I don't even know if you're licensed."

"Of course. Certainly. How much?"

"How . . . Oh, I thought as I get paid, a per-case basis. I could do a hundred a day." Schwartz heard the intake of breath.

"A whole day, eh?"

"Plus expenses."

"Oh, well, not so bad, plus expenses."

"You're naturalized, right?"

"Addison."

"What?"

"My full name. Abrasha Addison."

"Addison?"

"Not Yarmolinsky. A new name. I tell you legally, deed poll."

"Why Addison?"

"Why? I'm standing downtown in deed poll office with some wise guy hears my accent, asks me if I know 'Stalin' means 'man of steel.' So I say maybe, but I not steal. Then he say maybe I'm Addison? So I say why he interested? He say he isn't, is just a spectator. So I say anyway okay. I take name Addison because Addison was great American inventor."

"Ah, yes, Addison's electric limp."

"What? Look, I get over to your place but not before five or six."

"Yes, fine. It's 1-B—"

"I know, I know. For weeks is big street talk."

Schwartz had hung up laughing. Abrasha was naturalized and he had no PI license, but that was just a matter of posting a bond. Addison was his new name? Yarmolinsky hadn't been his old one. It was Abraham Resnick, and no use trying to keep anything from him.

Now, at half past five, Schwartz heard the chirpy "Tap, taptaptap tap-tap-Tap-Tap!" Abrasha's black, bushy head popped in through the door. "Inspector? Schwartz? Lenny! Is fabulous space! My desk out here?"

"Hi. What's all—"

"Oh, these flowers," Addison said, throwing an enormous bouquet of dyed baby-turquoise carnations on Schwartz's desk. He set down a big paper bag and rummaged. "You know, start of business best wishes, like Chinatown. Odessa, too. And in bag is some vodka, shnodka, some little snacks to celebrate." He pulled out a half gallon bottle. "Never mind how mad at you is Deputy Chief of Detectives Gallagher. Spilt milk. Blood under the bridge," Abrasha said, holding out a strong hand in front of a shy smile.

Schwartz shook his hand. "Thanks. I'll find something for the flowers. They're very . . . That's a lot of flowers. They're really very . . . kind. And for the—"

"You have some ice, some freezing here? Back in here is what? Toilet? Fridge? Bedroom? You have some trouble at home is none of my business, boss."

"Absolutely none of your business. There's some ice back there," Schwartz called. "Has the street talk mentioned how many ice trays?"

"Boss, don't be silly. Someone see you buying this real shit paper furniture at A&S. Same price I could get you from Coney Island friend some deco, be sensational. Ice, glasses, and I shove flowers in toilet here until we get this place shipshapely."

"Speaking of which, Abrasha, you'll have to change your Volga boatman image. No more yachting cap. Get a haircut, wear shoes or sneakers with smaller holes. And you have to wear some sort of grown-up jacket. The Minnie Mouse sweatshirt won't impress the clientele."

"So. Here, a drink. *Santé! Prosit! Dasdarovnaya* and *l'chaim!* Partner!"

"Senior partner, please. Your very good health, Addison."

"You give me a thousand advance, I'll get clothes as boring as you."

"I'll give you two hundred and you come in looking sharp tomorrow morning. All you need is a haircut. You have a warehouse of everything stashed in Brighton Beach. Do you have a gun license?"

"Of course, certainly."

"You don't. Want one?"

Addison laughed, nodded yes and said no. He was a few inches taller than Schwartz, around five-ten, five years younger and forty or so pounds heavier. He dug something out of greasy paper from the bag.

"Tremendous meat knish, boss? Boy, you damn smart. I'm apologizing and from now on I'll tell you almost entirely whole truth." He stood, leaning over the desk.

"No knish, thanks."

"Okay, there's herrings, here, pickle peppers—"

"Sit down, Addison. Listen, we have clients who want us to prove that a coroner's report was wrong. They've tried, unsuccessfully, for an exhumation order. They want me—us—to show that their son didn't have AIDS; in other words, that he was not gay or bisexual."

"But could be Haitian hemophiliac and, serious, now plenty hetero have AIDS."

"Right. But there are extenuating circumstances. If there weren't, I wouldn't touch the case. Virgil Hayes, the son, was taken from the East River. He could have drowned, but he'd been severely beaten and mutilated, so it could have been murder. But he had AIDS-related symptoms and there was some idea that if it wasn't a bizarre suicide, it was half-consciously a death by exposure or self-mutilation. The depression of the illness."

"Is horrible. But why you take such a case?"

"Two reasons. First, they were sent by Gerry Santini. You know him. He's a good forensics man. The second reason is that Gerry heard of the case, or is sure enough it's the same case, from a former top coroner-pathologist who filed it and later told him it was a difficult call."

"A moot call, yes," said Addison.

"Gerry thought there might have been a miscall, but since official ranks are closed, he sent the parents to me."

"Because you most brilliant, outstanding and—"

"Before you get to 'mediocre,' thanks. So I think there's

enough to go on without accepting the clients' reasons. Santini will try to pull the file for me, and I'm going to try to see the retired doc. He's working for the PHS now."

"And what I do?"

"You can start digging around in Virgil Hayes's life. I couldn't get much from Carter Hayes, the father, but here it is. Virgil was an only child, twenty-eight at the time of death, last April. He'd been a brilliant mathematician at Cal Tech. The father should know, because he's a retired administrator from the Brookhaven Labs. But they hadn't seen each other or spoken for three years. Why, he wouldn't say; he insisted it was personal and 'irrelevant.' Whether this estrangement is also true of the mother, Irene, I don't know. It's very much his show; she's very much under his thumb."

"Irina is nice name. Boss, there must be money? Vodka?"

"No vodka, thanks. Yes, money. They have no problem paying for this investigation, even though I warned them it might take time. And a few months after Virgil's death they sold their Huntington house and bought a very pricey East Side apartment. Private money. Hayes told me he moved closer to the police offices he was mostly sitting outside of, every day. Well, he's one cold fish, but I think we can tell him pretty quickly whether there's a chance to reopen his son's case. Any ideas?"

"Sound scary, the body from river like that. I hear talk of such sickness going on with AIDS."

"Yes, there are terrible sicknesses associated—"

"No, is how such people with nothing to lose or so sick they not understand and taken for exhibition, snuff show, you know, murder."

"You're crazy, Addison. Pour me a large vodka and keep talking."

CHAPTER 4

Stuck in Friday's rush hour on the Verrazano, Schwartz shifted the Volvo and considered Simpkin's phone enthusiasm. They weren't friends; Schwartz had done no more than refrain from teasing the police lab's senior pathologist, and Simpkin, without saying so, was grateful.

To other ordinarily decent men, Dr. Armand Simpkin was irresistibly "The Simp," or "Simp the Wimp," or even "Wimple the Pimple." It wasn't just his looks—short and pear-shaped, the little close-set eyes behind thick lenses, the shapeless smudge of nose and nothing chin. No, it was his personality that isolated him from others, an ineptness almost stereotypically the "scientist as jerk"—rude, mannerless, unsocialized.

Schwartz checked directions. Up there, between Emerson and Todt Hills. He was happy to meet away from Simpkin's Public Health Service office or his own Flatbush Avenue chambers. And

Simpkin, happily, seemed to think Schwartz was still with the police.

Typical of Simpkin to want to live in the middle of nowhere. Schwartz looked at the car clock: almost an hour, so far. He loved the car clock. It was everything he wasn't: it was serious and accurate and Swedish.

The middle of nowhere was becoming splendid. Grand old trees and houses to match. Out to the left, as he climbed, a bay view opened sensationally.

Poor Simpkin. When Schwartz had been in college, his type had been called "tools." They tooled away monomaniacally at studies, their slide rules—the tools' tools—dangling from their belts, those young ungainlies he'd passed in halls and quads at Harvard and Chicago, ugly ducklings who'd end up ugly ducks.

Schwartz parked before the house number cut in stone. Poor Simpkin? Schwartz rechecked. Yes.

Fourteen Ridgeway Court was a massive red-stone ranch house–hacienda. No, prehacienda fantasy—Mayan plaqued, landscaped with sands and spiny pines. Here in the staid heart of Staten Island it was shock-exotic. Simpkin in this? This looked like Frank Lloyd Wright, a desert joke played on the East Coast that loved him too late.

Schwartz's shirt pulled away sticky from the seat back. He slung his jacket over his left shoulder and crunched up the yellow and black pebbled drive. He rang. A deep chime sounded. It could be Santa Fe in summer. Strange.

"Hi."

Stranger. Clearly the wrong house.

"Hi," she repeated. "Inspector Schwartz? Armand's expecting you. I'm Betty, Armand's wife."

Schwartz stared at a twenty-three-year-old gum-chewing blonde in a tight red T-shirt and in tighter red shorts and out of any old issue of *Plaything* or *Pentup*.

"Hello. I was expecting Dr. Simpkin . . . I was . . . Thank you, Mrs. Simpkin." He stepped past her, turning sideways as if the wide doorway were very narrow.

"Call me Betty. We've been married for a year. Armand's first wife died about three years ago. You know?"

He nodded, then shook his head. "No. I'm sorry. I mean, I didn't know." He knew nothing whatsoever, following Betty, except that there'd be trouble if he didn't stop watching those bouncing tight red buttocks. He looked at the walls. It was a gallery of pre-Colombian art. And there was a fountain in that room. Where was Betty from? A Western accent? Simpkin rich? They turned down another grand corridor.

"Rose, his wife, inherited this place from an aunt. Great, isn't it?" asked Betty.

"It's very," Schwartz said as Betty swung open a carved door leading off the halls of Montezuma.

"This is Armand's study. He's in his collection room, back there. Armie? Armand? It's your friend from Homicide."

Before the door opened, Schwartz had worked it out. Simpkin had bumped off his first wife (he couldn't quite picture her but had her looking a lot more like Simpkin than this wife) for the house and art collection. Then, after a deep mourning period of about three hours, Simpkin had gone on meditative retreat to Las Vegas where he'd found Betty Boop, set her up here in Taliesen Staten Island and quit the department. Poor Simpkin?

Simpkin came in, ending Schwartz's crazed case history.

"Hello, Leonard. Thank you, Betty," Simpkin said to his disappearing child bride.

"Hello, Armand." Schwartz shook the hand that felt like flounder. "How's the new job?"

"Satisfying. The Public Health Service requires more administration than the police laboratory, but I find it interesting."

"Nice people to work with?"

Simpkin blinked. "Everyone treats each other respect-fully. I'm head of the section. So there is none of that foolishness there was at the police department. How are things there?"

"Oh, much the same: loud, rude and generally ham-strung," Schwartz said, seeing no suspicion from Simpkin. "And how's federal pay?"

"An improvement. They took my police work as time-in-grade and gave me a GS-19, if you know government service grading. Do you wish to sit?"

Schwartz wished to. He looked up at painted beading tying the bookcases to the frieze of colored stone above.

"I can keep up the house on this salary. My late wife, Rose, inherited it from her aunt. It's a Frank Lloyd Wright house, though I don't mind. It's very comfortable. The art collection was also her aunt's. I've made an addition, back there, for my own collection. Now, Leonard, what can I do for you? Please sit down. Do you wish to have something? A glass of water?"

They sat in deep square armchairs facing each other.

"No, thank you, Armand. Well," Schwartz began, hoping to continue the deception without actually lying, "I was wonder-ing about a case Gerry Santini mentioned, a possible suicide or misadventure that you said was a hard call. An exhumation re-quest by the parents was refused just before you . . ."

Simpkin nodded. Sitting in his brown suit, he looked like lumpy chocolate pudding. "I remember. The parents kept pester-ing. Hayes was the name. Yes, we didn't like the ambiguous report, but we decided against the exhumation. Since it had been so problematical immediately after death, it was going to be im-possible all that time later. Santini is competent. He'd know. What is your interest?"

"Gerry felt bad about the parents and sent them to me. I

didn't like their motives—at least what Mr. Hayes said they were. But, well . . .''

"Oh, yes. They wanted to show that their son wasn't a homosexual. Personally, I don't think that is a bad motive, but the fact is, the record does not say he was homosexual. The other evidence might support such a surmise, but that is not the same. You've read the file, of course."

Schwartz leaned forward past the slabs of light oak under his arms. "I haven't actually gotten around to it. I thought I'd first talk to you, Armand, because if *you* found it difficult, I knew *I* wouldn't be able to understand it at all." Now he was lying by half-truths and flattery; lying by telling complete lies might feel more honest.

"Hmm," said Simpkin. He shut his eyes in thought.

Schwartz waited and imagined bouncing Betty. No one had known Simpkin had a first wife.

Finally, Simpkin said, "I could show you the difficulties of the Hayes case right here. You know I appreciate your attitude toward me all these years. But, Leonard, you might feel bound, as a high-ranking officer, to report it. I don't, therefore, see how . . . Is this amusing? Why is this amusing?"

"It's amusing, Armand, because you feel you can't confide in me, thinking I'm a police officer. I've held off telling you that I'm no longer with the police for fear you wouldn't confide in me."

"Yes?" Simpkin smiled. "Explain," he said, the smile sinking back into the tapioca face.

"I'm a private investigator now. For a number of reasons, some of which you may know—but, then, you were never one for office gossip—I, too, have had my fill of the folk at Police Plaza. Anyhow, Gerry sent the Hayeses to me knowing they couldn't get any action from the department. The rest I've told you, except that whether I continue investigating this depends on what I learn from you."

"I see. Very well, but I am still going to ask for your word not to tell the department what I show you."

"Of course."

"Thank you, Leonard," Simpkin said, not so much rising from his chair as seeming to pour himself up. "In here."

It was a long, narrow room, windowless and brightly lit. One side was a laboratory. The other was a bank of labeled drawer cases. It looked like the sort of place in which an insect collection might be housed.

"This is the addition I've made to the house," Simpkin said, closing the door. "Over the years I've kept my own records of the more interesting cases. Copies of the reports and some material evidence—a shred of clothing, an extra biological sample. Never anything necessary for the record, but it is, you see, breaking regulations."

Simpkin went to a desk at the end of the lab table and began operating a computer. "Cases are cross-indexed by name, date and category: type of crime, if criminal, and by type of injury, cause of death. You know, axing, barbiturate, carbon monoxide. These correspond to case numbers you see there on the drawers. I'm working on a textbook of pathology based on these cases." He squinted at the screen. "Yes, here: four-two-one-six."

Simpkin crossed to a stack, looked down and pulled out a drawer. "Here it is. Do you want to see the report?"

"No, not now. I'll be able to get a look at the department's file if I go on with it."

"This should explain," said Simpkin, bringing out a large envelope and a small, capped glass vial.

Schwartz moved to the table, where Simpkin had laid out two large photos.

"Do you know what these are, Leonard?"

"Yes. Microphotographs of cells. They seem fuzzy."

"That's correct. Technically they are very poor. That is one of the problems here: technicians working with samples from known or suspected AIDS victims are gloved and masked, which makes for lack of precision handling and observation, and they are sometimes very nervous and work too fast. The results are then not at the proper standard for serious scientific investigation. Nonetheless," Simpkin said, pointing, "this is clear enough to show the large whitish area of the tumor between epidermis and dermis, down here. Though it's not clear, if you look carefully in the white area you can make out these shapes—here, here, which are the typical spindle cells of Kaposi's sarcoma."

"There? I can't make it out," Schwartz said, peering at the photo.

"It takes a trained eye. Besides this, there was the typical immunosuppressive range of infections in the laryngeal and respiratory tracts."

Schwartz lifted his head. "So that's it. He had AIDS."

"No, it isn't that clear, even to me. First, as you see, this is technically poor evidence. And because of particular circumstances, I did not get to see this under the microscope myself. And with a corpse, we couldn't run an HIV virus check." Simpkin pulled out another photo from the envelope. "Here, this demonstrates another aspect of the problem. This is unpleasant, Leonard, but you have probably had to look at as many of these as I have."

"Show me," Schwartz said.

Simpkin placed the photo on the counter.

"God," Schwartz murmured, "I heard he was painted, but blue with gold veining, like lapis lazuli? And beaten and . . ."

"Yes. This is why the report is long and complex. You see

why the lab technicians were nervous. We were lucky to find positive identification. And this," said Simpkin, picking up the vial, "is—"

There was a knock on the door.

Simpkin frowned. "Yes?"

"Sorry to interrupt, Armand. There's a call from Washington. I asked if you could call back, but they said it was important," came Betty's voice.

Simpkin looked at his watch. "Washington? Very well. Excuse me, Leonard."

Alone, Schwartz picked up the vial, looked at its contents and looked back at the photos. Then he went to the door, opened it, looked into the study, closed the door again and went back to the table.

How wrong could this be, he thought, as he took out his handkerchief and unscrewed the cap. There were lots of small blue and gold flakes inside; Simpkin wouldn't miss a few. Besides, Simpkin really shouldn't have any of this: it was a little ghoulish. Tilting the vial, tapping its base lightly, Schwartz moved two flakes to the edge and shook them onto his handkerchief. He capped the vial and set it back by the photos. Then he folded the twice-stolen specimens into the handkerchief and slipped it into his jacket pocket. Footsteps.

"Leonard," Simpkin said, entering, "I'm sorry. I'm going to have to make some phone calls."

"I understand. Armand, what's in that vial?"

"Skin samples. As you see from the picture, they were not difficult to get. Well, I hope I've been of some help to you," he said, putting the photos back into the envelope and returning it with the vial to its drawer.

"You have. Thanks very much. I see why it was difficult and why the exhumation wasn't in order. I'll tell Hayes to stop wasting his time and money."

"I think that would be the most logical advice," Simpkin said, moving with Schwartz through the study. He held open the hall door. "I must call now. Best of luck, Leonard, in your new career."

"You, too, Armand."

"Thank you. Betty will show you out. Betty?"

Schwartz shook Simpkin's fish-finger hand and walked down the hall beside Betty.

At the front door, she touched his arm. "Want to see something?" She smiled, chewing her gum. Her eyes were bright and empty as a blue Nevada sky.

"Sure," he said.

"Over this way."

She walked before him in the warm early evening and made him think of bees. No, of B's. Bouncing Betty. Blonde Betty, Beautifully Ball-Buttocked Betty and Big trouble and Better not.

She stopped by a wooden bench beneath a maple. "Isn't this good?" she asked, her T-shirt red as the leaves. She turned, swinging an arm out.

Before them it was certainly good, a sweeping panorama of water and flying bridge and ships moving in and out through the narrows and, beyond, the towers of lower Manhattan and Liberty's torch. He said, "You have a beautiful home."

"Don't I?" she said, her chewing gum cracking with enthusiasm. "Armand's terrific. Isn't this a gas?" She fell back onto the bench with both arms outspread.

"That's what it is," Schwartz agreed and said good-bye.

At the drive he looked again at the amazing house and then at the amazing new bride. Betty was still on the bench, looking out over New York City as if owning it all. A gas, he thought, starting the car. But was it laughing gas or carbon monoxide?

The car clock said 6:10. Private enterprise: you fooled yourself and your customer for the right price. No, he'd taken the case for pride, showing off for Karen like an adolescent. The pop songs of his adolescence had warned of "foolish pride," but then he'd been too busy showing off to pay attention.

And now home-for-the-weekend-only. It was only 6:15 and 38 seconds, time to take the ferry and relax. He'd arrive at 7:30, not early, to show her . . . He was at it again. But wasn't any pride proper? When was it foolish and when *amour propre*?

He parked and ran up to the second deck to see the ferry pull out from St. George. It was still so strangely warm for an October evening, but the heaviness of inland was here broken, lifted from the open waters of the upper bay. No case. Back there was Simpkin in his surprising house with a private police lab and

Betty, the Juicy Fruit kid. How she'd looked out over the city!

Schwartz turned, hoping to see that brave new world.

The sky's deep blue had darkened to a purple pinked by city lights when Schwartz walked through the door in Park Slope.

"Hello, darling," Karen said, standing in the hall, her hand over the telephone. "I'll be right off."

Schwartz smiled as she went back to her call. He felt a slight depression. Nonsense, he felt fine. He put his hand out as he passed her. She raised hers so that their index fingers touched, side along side.

Halfway upstairs he turned and watched Karen's black hair moving as she nodded, talking to her publisher, Bob. She sensed him there; she looked up and went silent in mid-sentence.

She opened her mouth as if to call him or smile, but it became a stammer. "Oh, sorry, Bob," she said turning away from Schwartz, "I'll think about this and get back to you by Monday. Yes, he is. I will. Bye."

She put the phone down and looked up again with a bright, failed smile. "Hello from Bob. Gin and tonic?"

"Yes, please." His hand went to the bannister. "I'll have a quick shower and be right down. It's good to be . . ." He turned back up the stairs.

He had the quick shower and was right down, and though he felt it was good to be here everything in this living room, solid with books and paintings and music, was now falling away between them in a landslide silence.

"No," said Karen, when he tried to tell her. "It's you, five days away from home, trying to make me relent. And if I did, as things stand, I mean, we'd be back at each other's throat. Don't you think?"

He said yes, though her throat was so beautiful a place to

be back at. But he wasn't going to quit what he started, even though this first case had come to nothing. He didn't say that; he said there'd been one short job and he'd put some money in their joint account. She nodded without asking how much. They were sitting on the couch, not touching.

"We both—" he began.

"Yes. I think we—"

"Maybe we'd be better with other people," he said.

"Yes."

So they'd walked down to Seventh Avenue, found a place they hadn't eaten in for years and were embarrassed by the happy diners around them.

Back in the house, Karen grabbed Schwartz and hugged him tightly. He pulled her into the living room and they made love on the sofa. Afterwards, they stepped over their shoes and underpants and jackets, each feeling, both said, as if the lovemaking had happened only for the other, then agreeing it hadn't happened for either one.

What happened on Saturday and Sunday, aside from household business, was a sad hanging around each other, a tentative touching, then a breaking off to hang around.

"We're polar opposites," he said at one hanging point.

She said, "If we were, we'd stick together. It's our likeness that keeps us apart."

"Our pride?"

"Yes, but I need mine, after what you've . . . considering," she said.

She didn't bring up his work and she was too hard at work on her book to answer more than, "Oh, you know. All right, I guess. I don't know. All right." And, no, she hadn't seen anyone. Well, Bob, one evening, about a lecture tour he'd thought up.

By bedtime Sunday night, they felt exhausted, as if they'd

spent two days hovering inches from each other in midair, heavy hummingbirds. They lay down; they didn't touch.

It seemed hours they'd lain awake, and they had to work tomorrow. He wouldn't ask if she could sleep. It was so hot.

Schwartz thought of the ferry back, of the judgmental, lidless eyes of Liberty looking past poor huddled masses to where Long Island flattened neatly green, as if the words between the lines read,

> . . . *Give me your rich,*
> *Your well-heeled surgeons yearning to make more,*
> *Your cocaine colonels, inside traders,*
> *But leave your losers on the third world shore . . .*

Or, at least, beneath that straight accusing brow, this—

"The phone. The phone's ringing, Len. I know it's for you."

He picked it up without turning on the light. "Yes?"

"Inspector? I mean, sir?"

"Malinowski? Do you realize what time it is?"

"A quarter past eleven. I'm sorry—"

"Only quarter past eleven? Oh. I didn't want you to call me 'sir' when I was your boss, let alone now that I'm a mere insomniac."

"Sorry. About an hour ago I finished checking something out for you, through Dr. Santini. The file on Virgil Hayes?"

"Oh, yes, thanks. When can I have—"

"There's no file, sir. Nothing at all. Nothing in the computer, no hospital records, nothing but the death certificate."

Schwartz didn't bother asking if he were sure. Bob Malinowski was the most wonderfully, boringly thorough officer he'd ever known. So he said, "Maybe we could find out who was on that case, even for the short time it was active."

"We've already tried that. No one remembers, or no one's come forward."

"Probably the same no one who wiped the file. Thanks, Bob."

"Should I know what that was?" Karen asked.

"That was some more deposits in the joint account."

She said that was nice and he said yes. They said good night again, held hands and then let go.

CHAPTER **6**

No," said Jack, the tall, stooped black waiter at Junior's, "I don't mind *fressers.* It's *shlumpers* I mind—and bad tippers." He put two more bowls of pickled tomatoes and cucumbers, two of coleslaw and another large basket of bread on the table without bothering to look at anyone. "Let me know when you're ready to order, gentlemen. Take your time," he said, walking off, looking at his watch.

Pignatelli stuck his fist into the pickle bowl and came out with two green, dripping half-tomatoes which he shoved into a pumpernickle roll. He put half the stuffed roll in his mouth. The half he tore away dripped pale green tomato seed onto the white-on-white shirt lying on the horizontal plane of his stomach.

Piggy Pignatelli was one of the city's great fatsos, the kind whose belly hung down both sides of his crotch into the thighs of his size 70 trousers.

41

Schwartz didn't like looking at Piggy, but he was the man for certain areas of information. Addison knew Pignatelli and had arranged the meeting, telling Schwartz, "Maybe he weighing six hundred pound but is still hard to see."

"Hey, Brasha," Pignatelli said to Addison in his smooth, deep voice, "I got a good deal on furniture for you. New deco, two grand for at least ten thousand's worth. But you gotta go fast for it. Over in Astoria."

"Maybe," said Addison, smiling at Schwartz. "We talk later."

Schwartz ran his finger through the water condensed on his glass. New deco. When would Piggy say something to the point? Piggy was now into coleslaw. He lifted it with his fingers—red, white, green and dripping, a shredded Italian flag. He flopped it onto a slice of rye bread, folded it in two and dropped it into his mouth.

Schwartz looked sourly at Addison. Addison shrugged.

"Hey, Schwartz," said Piggy, making another slaw-bun as he chewed, "you hear the one about George Burns and Diana Ross?"

"Yes, Pignatelli, from a Jew. So it was only sexist and racist. If you tell it, it gets to be sexist, racist and anti-Semitic."

"You're off your rocker. It's a good joke." He dropped the new piece in his mouth, a continuous, autonomic process. "So you guys gonna order? They do a good mixed platter here. But the cheesecake's overrated. Not bad, but overrated."

Schwartz had no appetite. Addison said he'd have iced tea. "You know if they make it from bags or that crap powder?"

"Bags I think. Hey, Schwartz, get Jack's attention. I'm starving here. You gotta beg these fucking waiters. So what do you think of this heat? Some fucking heat wave, huh, since fucking June into fucking October? They say the beaches are still crowded. I don't go. Maybe I'd go if they got me in for a swim

with those fucking whales they got down at the Coney aquarium."
He laughed, a rumble from under flesh mountain.

"Beluga," said Addison.

"You having caviar? It's okay here, with the cream cheese
and the bagels," said Piggy.

"No, whales."

"Brasha, they don't serve whale here." Piggy rumbled
again. "I know where I can get you some whale meat. I don't like
it. Too fatty."

Schwartz asked, "Do you—"

"Where's Jack? I'm fucking famished. Get Jack, will you?"

"Do you have something to tell us, Pignatelli?"

Pignatelli held a pickle near his mouth. "Yes, potz. I can
do some asking for you." He pointed the pickle at Schwartz. "For
a grand. Five and five." He bit off half the pickle.

Schwartz said, "Four hundred, two and two."

Piggy crunched. "Fuck yourself. Hey, Jack! Jack, I'm dying
over here! Schwartz, you can't deal like that no more. A big cop
can bargain; a nothing private dick pays going rates. Eight, four
and four. No less, potz."

"Ready to order, gentlemen?" asked Jack, looking at the
ceiling.

"Yeah. Gimme that mixed platter of yours: brisket and
tongue and pastrami and turkey and some corned beef, but easy
on the corned beef. Put on more tongue. Two platters. Got that?
Two. And a couple large Cokes and then a cheesecake. What you
got?"

Talking to his pencil stub, Jack said, "Plain, cherry, blueberry, pineapple."

"Cherry. Cherry cheesecake. And bring me more of this
stuff here, and bread."

Addison said, "And for me a real iced tea, no powder."

"One real iced tea," repeated Jack, making it sound like

"one real big jerk." "So that's two mixed platters, two large Cokes, a piece of cherry cheesecake and one real iced tea."

"No," said Piggy, "a whole cherry cheesecake. A small one. After the platters. And I'll have the coffee then. Oh, and this skinny guy's paying."

Jack turned away saying, "Very good, gentlemen."

Schwartz said, "Five hundred, two-fifty, two-fifty. And you feed yourself. You're a big boy now, Piggy."

Addison kicked Schwartz.

Schwartz stood up. "The federal government couldn't afford to pick up your food bills." He moved the remaining bread out of Pignatelli's reach.

Pignatelli looked across at Addison. "Tell your boss two things. First, tell him he can go shove it up his ass. Second, tell him who my friends are and how he's made a big mistake trying to get tough with me."

Addison stood. "Sure. Very sorry this doesn't work out, Pignatelli, my friend. But I will get back on this furniture."

"It's gonna be gone in a day. So you get back fast if you want action."

Addison chased after Schwartz through the door and into the street. "Where you go so fast off the bat handle, boss? Jesus, why you go against the lights across the avenue you kill us? Ah, shut your horn!" he yelled at a car swerving to avoid them but sticking to its steady twice-the-speed limit.

Schwartz stopped in the middle of Flatbush Avenue and turned to Addison. Car drivers were honking, swerving, swearing, doing everything but braking.

"You gonna kill us, boss!"

"No, I'm going to kill you, Resnick, Yarmolinsky, Addison, whoever the hell you are with your sleaze friends and fat furniture deals and deli pigs making it so clear they're in with at least two leading Mafia families! What do you think, Abraham, that I'm just another black marketeer hustling the back streets of Odessa? Or do you think I don't mind jerking around my clients just because they're powder-iced-tea goys paying us good money?"

Schwartz found he was holding Addison by his jacket, a new, respectable poplin. The lights had changed; pedestrians crossing their way gave them a wide berth. Schwartz let go and crossed to the concrete peninsula before the Chicken and Shrimp House and sat on a concrete bench by a sleeping drunk. Addison stood before him.

"Addison, I'm risking a lot. My marriage, for one very big thing. And I didn't take you on to increase the risk."

"I understand. I am sorry. I understand you are very moral man, Lenny. But this is not so moral job, finding out things when people want keep them secret. Even, maybe, when you're police officer is not so moral job."

Schwartz looked up. Addison was right, of course. Beside him, the drunk sat up groaning.

"Man, you got a dollar help me get it together?" he asked, his eyes still shut.

Schwartz stood. "All right, Addison. Sorry. Go back there and try. I want to find out if there was any connection between Virgil Hayes and the snuff-show world, if such a world exists. Deal with Pignatelli. Should we take his threats seriously?"

"Don't worry, boss, I make it up with him. We find out. But, Lenny, that fat man want, he have us chopped into *cutlyeten*, we end up two mixed platters across the street."

"Oh, man," groaned the drunk, his head in his hands.

"Okay," Schwartz said, "you fix it. I'm going to the office to figure out what next. Oh, and Addison, as Jack the waiter would say, give this gentleman a dollar."

Upstairs, Schwartz thought that the best idea for "what next" might be a serious nap back there on his mean mattress.

He'd bother Simpkin later for his file, without scaring him by mentioning that the original one was missing.

He sat on the edge of Addison's desk with the mail in his hand. He dropped the bills for Addison to sort out and opened the plain white envelope. Inside was a single sheet of stationery bordered in green with a long-tailed bird, also green, on a branch between white blossoms. Camellias? Audubon? The handwriting was small and tight:

> *Dear Mr. Schwartz,*
>
> *I find this difficult to write, as Carter would not approve. However, I know that like me, he now depends solely on you to clear our son's name. I am therefore giving you the following information.*
>
> *Someone who could be very helpful is Jimmy's (Virgil's) former girlfriend. Her name is Ann McCarthy. It has been several years and I have no address, but the last phone number I have for her is 522-8351. I believe it is a Brooklyn Heights number.*
>
> *I would add that Carter did not mention her because he did not at all approve of her for Jimmy. But I know he was not purposely trying to be obstructive. For reasons which I am sure you will appreciate, I ask you please to treat this letter in strictest confidence.*
>
> *Sincerely,*
>
> *Irene Hayes*

Well, Schwartz thought, this solved the problem of what to do next. He dialed the number.

"Hello. Whole Earth."

"Hello. Is an Ann McCarthy there?"

"Who?"

"Ann McCarthy. This is the number I was—"

"You have a nerve, you sick bastard!" The phone slammed in Schwartz's ear.

He wasn't jerking around the Hayeses. Were they jerking him around? What did he actually have here, besides two flakes of blue skin and the nauseous memory of Pignatelli's mid-afternoon snack?

What next? It was time for a serious nap.

C H A P T E R 7

When in the late sixties stores like Whole Earth began springing up in Brooklyn Heights, locals wondered what the neighborhood was coming to. Now, twenty years later, the same neighbors signed petitions to save those stores with their sacks of brown rice, packs of brown sandals and racks of recycled books that explained why plain grains and holey clothes, so overpriced, were vital. For the neighborhoods were now threatened by frozen blight—the destruction of the inner city by ice cream stores.

Whole Earth, between Gladya-Licke and Tofutti Tutti-Frutti (Tofu to you), was down three steps, just off Montague on Hicks. Schwartz opened the door. Pottery chimes clanked flatly. Ah, yes, the unmistakable aroma of ecology—sandalwood and sandal sweat.

Schwartz passed between racks of wool somethings, stopped and looked at a tag. Beneath the good news "You now own an unwashed woolen garment," it told the purchaser never to wash it. It was either a skinny poncho without a neck hole or a long sock for a victim of elephantiasis.

"Can I help?" asked the man who'd come up the aisle.

"What exactly is this?" Schwartz asked.

"Peruvian knit trousers," the man said, taking the garment and shaking it so that two hairy legs rolled out.

"Oh. I see. The legs were stuck up in there so I couldn't figure out . . . Interesting. How much?"

"They were two-ten, but they're on sale at one-twenty, a very good price. Want to try them on? They'd fit."

"Unwashed Peruvian wool knit trousers, eh?" said Schwartz, itching not to buy them. "No, I don't think so." He smiled. "Actually, I called yesterday. I think I may have spoken with you. You or whoever seemed offended when I asked for someone I'm trying to locate, Ann McCarthy."

"Are you the police?"

"No, no. Just a private investigator. My name's Len Schwartz."

"I'm John Myerson. Hi. I wish the police were looking for her. This is my store, and my office used to be the coordinating center for a number of local antinuclear groups: Mobilization for Survival, Anti-Nuclear Coalition, you know. Now the center's moved to its own, bigger place." He stopped and smiled. "How do you feel about these things?"

"Oh, I'm for nuclear disarmament, no nuclear power. My wife and I . . . We . . . I've been on some marches and demonstrations. Not recently."

"And you couldn't find Ann McCarthy's number?"

"Not the right Ann McCarthy."

"I can see why she wouldn't want to be listed. There are still a lot of us who feel betrayed by her. She . . . You really don't know?"

49

"No, I don't know anything about her."

"Well, Ann worked with us for about four years. First she was part-time, when she was at NYU, then she became the full-time administrator. She was very good, seemed very dedicated. And then, about two years ago, she disappeared from here and so did our records. All our records! A CIA operative. Terrific, isn't it!"

"How do you know she was CIA?"

"What else could it be? One or two people have run into her since, and of course she denies everything, claims *she* was threatened and scared away and that 'they'—CIA or whoever from the government—cleared out the files. But it's too obvious."

"I see. Would you know where she is?"

"No. But I've been told she's now the administrative side of Henry Hawthorne Smith, you know, the artist who moves those things around buildings and mountains."

"Good. Thanks. Oh, did you happen to know her boyfriend when she worked here, a guy named Virgil or Jimmy Hayes?"

"Yes. Jimmy. He was a scientist, a physicist or mathematician. I met him here, about three years ago, and I saw him with Ann at some marches and demos. Later, Ann told me she'd broken up with him. That was just before . . . Damn it! It still gets me so mad. Of course, it wasn't the first time something like that happened. We've had harassment, but nothing like that, not from inside."

Schwartz thanked Myerson and asked if he could make a donation.

"Sure. There." he nodded toward the desk lined with boxes, jars and cans.

Schwartz put twenty dollars into the Anti-Nuclear Coalition box. Then he saw a picture of two swimming whales. They weren't as big as Pignatelli but a lot cuter. He put in five dollars and left.

At the phone booth on Montague Street, Schwartz looked up Henry Hawthorne Smith.

The answering machine had a Southern accent. It said, "This is Henreh Hawthowan Smith, ahtist of conceptual events. On Octobah eleventh, at noon, the Great Golden Ball will be rolled up to Grand Ahmy Plaza in Brooklyn and through the Soljah's and Sailah's Memorial Ahch as a Southern boa's act of reconciliation with the Union. This event is in paht funded bah the New Yohk Council for the Ahts, the Brooklyn Museum—"

Schwartz took the phone from his ear and looked out to where he might grab a bite of lunch. Ice cream, ice cream or ice cream. He'd eat later. He listened again.

". . . efellah Fund and Exxon. Theyah's a li'l beep comin' on up after which y'all please leave your message, heaya?"

Schwartz hung up and looked at his watch. Twelve-ten. And eleven! The little date window said eleven. Today! Now. Ten minutes ago!

Fifteen minutes later, Schwartz was driving up Flatbush, saw the crowd and parked just far enough from a hydrant.

It was an event of some clout, lanes rearranged and streets detoured. But moving through, Schwartz found much of the crowd composed of photographers, arts journalists, camera and sound crews and men and women with folded arms who frowned and then spoke to other men and women holding microphones or makeup.

And just beyond, the focus of their concern, an enormous golden ball, probably fifteen feet high, rolled slowly with stately squeak and grand metallic clatter through the Memorial Arch. Having pushed closer, Schwartz saw that its means of propulsion was magic-wand power. That was, anyhow, the effect achieved by the man in the wizard's hat and the black robes decorated with golden suns and moons and planets—Henry Hawthorne Smith— who held before him two rods of gold with which he pushed the ball. Yet the rods were so slender and the ball so vast that it did seem strange. And strange and sad was the absence of children to enjoy it.

Schwartz searched for someone who could be the wizard's administrative assistant. There, that tall woman in the white . . .

He worked his way toward the other side of the arch. "Hi, Karen. Hi, Bob."

Karen's surprise was a smile and then an earnest nod. "Darling," she said, and kissed his cheek.

He shook hands with Bob Childs. "What brings you out to this circus?" he asked.

"Really a duty," Bob said, his brown hair falling over his round face as he shook hands. He pushed it up with the back of his forefinger. "I chaired a grant committee involved and so . . . This isn't my favorite thing, but it's good, as conceptual events go."

"What's the concept here?" Schwartz asked Karen.

She chose to answer the question as if it pertained to the golden ball. "Oh, I don't know. The magic is everyday Brooklyn, the strangeness, the scale, the gold. I think the ideas are supposed to come to the viewer later."

"I see. More an eventual concept than a conceptual event," said Schwartz.

Bob laughed. Karen explained that since Bob was so close to the house, they'd met and were headed back for a working lunch.

"Do you have time to join us?" she asked, her particular smile signaling "Please don't."

"No, thanks." He looked at Bob. "I can't go home because

I'm a private detective. I mean, I'm busy working now so I can't join you."

Despite his boyish looks, Bob Childs was a totally sophisticated New Yorker. But Bob blushed.

"Ah," Schwartz said, "you've heard. I see. Well, besides, if it's a working lunch, I'd only interrupt. Well, you're Karen's publisher, her editor, and now I hear you're setting up a lecture tour."

"We're talking about it," Bob said. "It pays well."

"I'll bet. Karen, Bob's such a Renaissance man it wouldn't surprise me if he went with you, became your fine arts roadie."

"Oh, God, Len," said Karen.

They followed the ball in the crowd as it rolled back toward Flatbush Avenue.

"Speaking of roadies," Schwartz said to Bob, "would you—"

"Stop it, Len!" Karen said.

Bob put his hand on Schwartz's sleeve. "Len, forgive me, but I'll make one short statement. I think you were wrong and I think Karen is wrong. That's it. Oh, and I'm her publisher and editor and, if Karen agrees, her tour agent and I'm honored to be. And her friend. And that's all."

"I was *going* to ask if you knew Smith's assistant, Ann McCarthy, and could point her out. But thanks for all the other."

Karen had turned her back and stood, shoulders rising and falling with angry breaths, looking out toward Prospect Park.

"There she is," said Bob, "behind Henry. Tall, in white, with the black sash. There."

"Right. Thanks. I'm sorry, Bob. Karen," he said, putting his hands on her shoulders. She shrugged him off. "I am sorry. Us private eyes are a crude lot. But we're also a sorry lot."

She nodded. Bob shook hands. Schwartz watched them

walk across toward his so-close house, three days away from *him*. He turned and followed the golden ball.

"Ms. McCarthy?" he called.

The tall, woman turned. "Yes? Oh, didn't you get a press release? We've been . . . You are from UP, aren't you?"

"No, PI—a private investigator trying to find out about Virgil James Hayes."

At the name, the woman's knees bent and her shoulders hunched. Had she long ears, they would have lain flat back. She turned and walked with long strides to the front of the ball.

"Ms. McCarthy," Schwartz said, hustling up beside her. "Ms. McCarthy, I realize this isn't the time, but can I please see you later on this?" He walked sideways through the crowd to keep up with her.

"No," she said, composed now and merely annoyed. She stopped with the ball at the start of the slope down the hill. Her light brown hair swung over her eye and she pushed it back with a long, thin hand. "I hadn't seen Jim for two years before his death. I told the police what I know, and that's all."

"The police? Who—" He broke off, having to duck the video camera swinging by his head. When he came up, Ann McCarthy was standing near her boss, as near as was safe, for he was having some trouble with his five-ton toy. But no, it was part of the act, this fine battle of control, the delicate balancing of two massive forces, gravity and the ego of H. H. Smith.

And what did this nonsense cost, for thirty minutes and four hundred media people and a few onlookers? Schwartz counted the extra police. At least a quarter of a million, all in all. A goddamned golden ball and back there in Brownsville little kids went hungry. Smith was the wizard of wastefulness!

And McCarthy wouldn't talk? McCarthy was pleading the Fifth? Screw this. Schwartz shouldered to the front.

"Ms. McCarthy!" he shouted, leaning back against the

push of the crowd. Here and now was very good. Local, maybe national TV. He'd embarrass cooperation. "Ms. McCarthy, about the police and your boyfriend's corpse!"

She turned at a whisper from Smith, now leaning into his rods, obviously doing the impossible in keeping the ball from rolling down the hill.

"Please!" she called to the crowd. "For your own safety, please step back."

Seeing two policemen come to help, Schwartz began moving slowly away when in the small of his back a shove like a cannonball shot him out arms forward, flying into the ball. He smashed against it, bounced off, fell, his eyes shut. He pushed up to one knee hearing the screams, "Behind you! Behind you!"

Smith wasn't there. Schwartz looked over his shoulder to see gold turn to shadow. He knew he should stand before starting to run but the sound frightened him to run first, so that he fell flat, knees scraping as his legs churned the road. The screaming became great tearing squeaks of metal. The clanking steel was over him; his right ankle was caught. The sound was swallowing him, crushing up his right tendon. No use. He shut his eyes. Let it happen fast, he thought, not this slow, tearing, scraping death-squeak.

But it was staying only on his right ankle, and the clack was now a small creak.

"Is all right, boss. No good ball heavy as . . . Uh! Oi! I get you out. Come give hand here! Uh! Help!"

Schwartz opened his eyes to find Addison bowed over him, his arms propped palms down on the street, his back bent against the ball. Blue police trousers appeared on either side. Everyone grunted. The ball rolled off.

Addison sat beside him, breathing hard. "You can move? You okay? Alive? Where it hurt you? Ai, my back! You bleeding but not serious, scrapings only."

"I'm okay. Addison, you saved my life. Damn, Addison, you did! Ouch! It's okay. My ankle's only stiff. I should move around. Ouch!" Schwartz sat up and saw a black and gold triangle. The wizard flattened? No, Smith was back there in full press conference. A golden opportunity.

"I help you up," said Addison, groaning himself as he stood.

"We'll need a . . . Inspector!" said the police sergeant, recognizing Schwartz and saluting.

In no mood to update the man, Schwartz said hello and it was a stupid accident and he knew Sergeant Cronin would help keep everyone, especially the press, away from him. And in return he'd promise to say nothing about the shoddy crowd control. And the sergeant obliged.

Addison went down the slope with the limping Schwartz. They found some empty curb space by a hydrant and sat down.

"You know, Addison," Schwartz began.

"I know. You are pushed. And you are pushed by one great pusher because when I see you by big ball and starting with yelling to stand back, I watch that crowd and I still don't see who do it. And when you fall, everyone else typical staring, having good time thinking you be crushed to death."

"It sure as hell wasn't a random push. Now I can feel it all down my back. A foot? A head butt?"

"Who knows? But is good thing I'm up here in lunch break seeing this American nonsense art bullshit."

"Indeed, Addison. How can I thank you?"

"You not get mad I tell something?"

"No. What?"

"Your car here, it's got ticket."

Schwartz looked. "It's all for art, Addison. If not fixable, that ticket's tax deductible. We've got lots to talk about. But first, what can I do to thank you?"

"You want really do something for me?" he asked, rubbing his back as they stood.

"Yes. Anything."

"Okay, you take me in this terrific new ice cream place, here. They got a rocky roadway knock your tongue out."

CHAPTER 8

What had infuriated Schwartz with the police was the intricate hierachy that made him deal with delegations, congresses, constitutional conventions. Now he was solely in charge. And on his own was he working better?

Absolutely not. There were clients with conflicting stories and secret messages and massive repressions of facts. There was Pignatelli to keep harassing for sleaze information, expensive five and five information. And to pass such an expense on to Hayes he'd have to cultivate the chutzpah of a medical accountant. (He'd once received a call from the hospital asking for his blood type. He'd said AB positive. The hospital said thanks and hung up. This appeared three days later on the bill as "Hematology Research" and cost eighty-five dollars.) But, like with Piggy, you couldn't dicker with monopolies. You paid through the nose, the vein, the aching ankle.

Schwartz walked across the office. It wasn't just the ankle, it was the noise that angered him. Racket in the hall, trucks pulling up. Of course that was Carl, the printer, taking deliveries of paper or supplies, so you couldn't complain.

He'd lost his idea. Where was he? Yes, out of control. What else angered him? Ann McCarthy was what. Without a badge, how did you get people to talk who didn't want to? If you flashed your PI license at them they couldn't talk for laughing.

Schwartz was dialing Simpkin when Addison came in. "Where have you been?"

"Looking after business with Pignatelli."

"Good. I'm just about to call—" Schwartz stopped. Addison was hanging around the door, not closing it but blocking the gap. "Come in and shut the door. There's such a racket out . . . What is it? Carl bringing in new presses?"

"No. Is . . ." Addison lifted his hands in a gesture both supplicating and celebratory. "Is terrific deal, of course, but needs storing just one, two days."

"Storing? What?"

"Few pieces terrific furniture. If I could store here while place at Brighton Beach gets emptier."

"Furniture? You've been looking after our investment in Pignatelli by buying his stolen furniture in Astoria?"

"No, is terrific. Look, just go on work. Don't lift even your fingernail. Just a day, two at most, fit here okay."

"Fingernail? All right, for God's sake, bring it in and let's get to work."

"Great, boss. A few pieces, is just. Hey, you see us on Channel 7 news last night?"

"No, but my wife, who has the television at home, called . . . Never mind that. What's out there?"

Schwartz went to the door and looked. It was not a

mountain of furniture. "A mountain" would be an exaggeration. It was a New England hillside of bad furniture.

Schwartz gave Addison a withering stare. Addison weathered it. Schwartz went to the window.

"Addison, I can't see Flatbush Avenue. Everything out there has turned blond mahogany. Fake blond mahogany, Addison, and the man is still unloading."

"You like? I give you a couple pieces for nothing, gratis," he responded cheerily from inside Schwartz's office where he was stacking furniture.

He finished, with Schwartz's help, two hours later. As he said, it didn't take up that much room. Schwartz's desktop, for instance, was free of furniture so that he could answer a phone call from Pignatelli.

"Hey, potz, guess what?" came the bass over the line.

Addison had made it to his own phone through the dim-lit trenches of curved stretchers.

"Tell me, Pignatelli," Schwartz said. "I pay you to tell me."

"It's gonna be cheaper than I thought."

"Explain."

"It was a five and five deal, but you're gonna save that second five hundred."

"You're not delivering? Only two days in and you're sure?"

"Yeah, potz. What are you gonna do about it?"

"Pignatelli, I'm not fighting you now. I'm not suggesting anything rash like you using artificial sweetener in your coffee with your cheesecakes. I'm saying you have a reputation. That's what you have, why you get paid well by me or whomever. If it gets around that . . . Wait, are you shaking me for more money?"

"No," said Pignatelli. "And you're right, it's no good for my business reputation. But it wouldn't be fucking worth it, not for ten thousand, not for anything. Understand what I'm saying?"

"I understand. But for my five, could you tell me if the doors closed because of the event in question or the person? In your opinion."

"I don't know. But for your five I'll tell you to stay the fuck away from this if you like living, potz." Pignatelli gave a belly laugh and hung up.

"So much for your great contact," Schwartz yelled to the general area of imitation wood where Addison spelunked.

"Never mind, boss, temporary back-set. Listen, for five hundred I give you quarter share in this stuff, we both do well. Well?"

Schwartz slowly raised his head.

"Okay, okay, you no want, is none my business."

"I do not, Addison. And it is your business. This will all be out of here by tomorrow afternoon at five or you will. Be out. On the street. Again. This is no longer a serious office; this isn't even a serious furniture store. But I'm remaining calm. I'm going to show you how one *should* conduct this business. A quiet, rational, productive phone call. Watch, listen, learn."

Schwartz dialed. "Hello? I'd like to speak with Dr. Simpkin. For the rest of the day? Thank you, I'll try him at home." He looked in his notebook, a smile on his face, and, without looking at Addison who had tunneled back to listen at his phone, dialed again.

"Hello? Mrs. Simpkin?"

"Hi, yes, this is Betty. Who's this?"

"Len Schwartz. We met last Friday. You showed me the lovely view?"

"Oh, yeah. Sure, hi. Hey, I saw you on the news last night, Channel 5. You okay?"

"Yes, Betty. Hi. Fine, I'm fine, thank you. Is Armand there?"

"Sure. Want me to get him?"

"Yes. I'd like to speak with Armand. Thanks. Please."

"Sure, wait a sec."

Schwartz glanced through the partition where, among the seatbacks, he saw Addison nod to him and make a "nice going" sign, a circle of thumb and middle finger.

"Hello?"

"Armand, how are you?"

"Hello, Leonard. I'm fine, very busy. What can I do for you?"

"Well, it's turning out a bit trickier getting to that information than I thought. So I'd like to take up your offer to see it out there."

"What information was that?"

"You know, in that insect collection of yours."

"I don't have an insect collection, Leonard."

"I know. The insect *file*. Armand, for God's sake, I'm trying to be discreet. The Hayes file."

"Oh, Hayes. We talked about that case, of course. But there's no file."

"What do you mean?"

"I wouldn't have case files, Leonard. That's police department property."

"Come on, Armand. I won't mention it on the phone, but, come on, stop joking."

"I do not joke. Leonard, I really don't know what you're talking about."

"Jesus, Armand, this line isn't bugged," Schwartz said, unwilling to turn Addison's way. "Four-two-one-six. That was the file number off your computer index."

"I'm sorry, Leonard. Either you are joking, a rather silly joke, or you're very overworked and should take a few aspirins and rest. Really. This sort of thing can happen when you're over-tired."

"Okay. Armand, can I come out and see you?"

"No, I think not. There's no point. I've told you all I know. The file will be with the department."

"Ah, but it isn't. It's vanished."

"Strange. But *I* certainly don't have it. I never had it, Leonard, nor any other case file. My professional advice would be to rest. Then you'll remember it correctly."

"Rest. Yes, all right, Armand."

"Good-bye."

Addison, putting the phone down in unison with Schwartz, yelled, "What kind no good stinking pathologist liar this Simpkin?"

"Very funny, Addison. Let that be a lesson to you in effi-ciency. It took me just three minutes to wipe out ten days' work. Is that you coming up through Mock-Mahogany Gulch?"

"Never mind, boss. Be of faint heart. We keep plugging along a finger in every dike, we pull out some plums."

"And say what a good boy . . . Good-bye, Abrasha. Take the rest of the day off, all eight minutes."

Addison tapped his shoulder. "Don't be silly. I go now to sell this furniture, move it out tomorrow morning, lunch is latest. But is too disgusting crowded you sleep here tonight. You come to Brighton Beach, then we have nice dinner—Georgian, Uz-becki, Moldavian—what you want. I have good extra bed."

"No, thanks. Some other time. I can squeeze through to the bedroom. Now I have to think. The textbook would say the same force that pushed me out pushed Simpkin off. But Piggy's Mafia veto doesn't fit with Simpkin. Maybe I'll come up with something."

"Okay, boss. I see you tomorrow and promise have good news."

"Sure. Good night."

Alone in the heap of junk furniture, Schwartz took a new yellow pad from the desk drawer and wrote the word "Piggy" on it. By the word he put a large X. From the X he drew an arrow to the right and placed a large question mark at its point. He moved his green pen to the next line down and wrote "No. Not if it can be avoided."

This was a stupid waste of time. He dialed.

"Karen? Hi."

"How are you?" she asked.

"Lousy, missing you. Can I come home tonight?"

"We should stick to our deal."

"Your deal."

"All right, our agreement on my deal, then."

"But it's Thursday, just one—"

"Are you working tomorrow?"

"Damn, you're . . . Yes, I'm working."

"Then no, please."

"What about meeting for supper? The Heights or that Italian place you like near Pratt?"

"No. And I'm staying home alone and . . . It's just not fair, talking about it like this, now."

"Yes, I see. Okay, sorry. See you tomorrow."

"Yes. Len? You promise you didn't get hurt? It looked so awful on TV."

"No, I'm okay. My ankle's a lot better."

"You'll call Jake?"

"From home, tomorrow. With your encouragement I'll explain our—arrangement. Bye."

"Bye."

Maybe he'd go up to that Italian restaurant. No, it would be maudlin now that Karen had refused. He could call Carter Hayes and discuss . . . No, he hated Hayes. Besides, Hayes wanted only good news, saying in that small, steely voice, "Positive information only; otherwise a brief weekly statement, Mr. Schwartz, to save all our feelings." Hayes was certainly a miser of his feelings. Not his cash. In Schwartz's wallet was his very good Bank of New York check for five thousand. And next to it in a stamp envelope were two blue-gold flecks of his son.

Schwartz took a new sheet and wrote "Simpkin" at the top. Then he wrote "police," drew an arrow and wrote "Public Health Service." On the arrow line he wrote "AIDS" and tapped his pen on the arrow head until he knew that nothing would come of this and the office was too hot and smelled of some foul varnish from the stolen furniture his crazed assistant had bought from his failed informant.

Schwartz dropped the pen and decided to try out the ankle. He put on shorts, a tee shirt and an ankle brace under his sweat socks.

It felt better than he expected. He ran north through the mess of roadways down along the edge of the Navy Yard and then west into the warehouses between Manhattan and the Brooklyn Bridge. Pilings, pillars, high-up strips of orange evening sky, a Piranesi paradise. It always came to him down here that John Roebling, the designer of the Brooklyn Bridge, was Hegel's favorite pupil. What could it mean? He ran back across Cadman Plaza and by Fulton Street with a throbbing ankle and no dialectical insight.

Upstairs showering, he thought about how red Manhattan had looked from Fulton Ferry, a city blushing, a city with plenty to be ashamed of. He should take it easy on his ankle.

Still, it wasn't that bad. He dressed and walked back up Fulton Street and had red snapper at Gage and Tollner's. And when this, too, didn't cheer him, he knew things were bad. He returned and, avoiding the wilderness of furniture, slid into the narrow bedroom and turned on the light.

A few loose pieces of paper on the bed, his diary with notes and his wallet. The whole case. Yes, and the letter with the pretty bird from Mrs. Hayes. He put it all into his trouser pockets.

The damned chemical smell of the schlocko furniture out there was killing him in this illegal, windowless bedroom. He opened the jammed bathroom window to its full four inches and kept open the adjoining door so that the bedroom could flood with the city's fresh warm car fumes.

One more review, he thought, folding his pants over the chair, putting the glass of cold seltzer on the floor by the bed. If he fell asleep thinking of the case, maybe he'd concentrate, freed from the wisecrack distractions of consciousness.

He woke with the light still on at midnight. He turned it off and got under the sheet.

It was a dream with Jack the waiter from Junior's. But it was at Gage and Tollner's. The red snappers on the tray were flipping, red, on fire. The waiter was fatter, was Pignatelli waddling with a stack of cheesecakes just from the oven, steaming. He set one on the table for Simpkin. The restaurant was red. Simpkin dropped the cheesecake into the bowl of a huge gold pipe and lit it with a bunsen burner. It melted to a river that Schwartz looked into. In its reflection the city was burning. Smoke was black-brown between waves of flame. It was too hot. Too much smoke.

Schwartz sat up coughing, then took a deep breath and retched. Pulling the sheet over his head, he sat up and felt his way into his trousers and loafers. He touched the hot door to the office as he fumbled in the dark.

Schwartz pulled the sheet away from his head and opened the door. A flame shot in. The heat hit him in the face and knocked him back onto the bed. Yellow brown smoke filled the room. He gagged. He vomited smoke, pulled the sheet back over his head and lurched coughing to the bathroom. Through the sheet he saw pale fog. There was a roaring. He dropped to his knees, and pushed the sheet into the toilet bowl and pulled it dripping over his head.

Window. It was jammed. A chair. He plunged back into the bedroom and caught at a nearby chair. The wet sheet was too hot, steaming, burning his shoulders and ears. He felt his way back with the chair legs before him. He swung once, coughed, swung twice. Nothing. A third time the glass was breaking. Two more times, glass breaking and the break of the inner wood frame. But he couldn't breathe. No more breathing. He dropped the chair. The sheet. He shut his eyes, pulled the sheet off and wrapped it steaming around his hands. He pushed them through the window, coughed, made the space bigger, breathed, breathed and pushed his head through and looked down.

Fifteen feet to the flat roof. He gagged. He jumped, crashed, coughing fresh air. His ankle hurt. The burns weren't bad, but he felt pieces of glass now in his neck and shoulders.

Schwartz crawled coughing to the edge of the roof, over the Chicken and Shrimp House entrance. Fire trucks, hoses, a ladder swam before him until the burning tears closed his eyes.

A voice was calling, "Anyone else up there?"

Schwartz coughed. Eyes shut, then open, then shut again. He called back, "Just me. The arsonist's probably gone by now." He coughed. "Can I come down on this?"

"No, you have to let me get up there and help."

The fireman was rule-bound but right. Schwartz found he was shaking so he couldn't have held the rungs.

They took very good care of Schwartz, the firemen and some ambulance people. All the glass came out, the cuts were cleaned and bandaged, his breathing pronounced good; they even strapped his ankle. He insisted that he keep on his own pants though they smelled like last night's barbecue. And after they learned he was a "recently retired detective inspector," the fire chief, Billy Whalen, insisted the blanket over his shoulders be replaced with a new blue sweatshirt with NYFD SOCCER across it.

By three in the morning, the fire was under control. Looking at the building, it seemed to Schwartz that they'd fought the fire by beating it out with axes. Carl's print shop was basically intact, but there'd be little business there until the roof and stairway were rebuilt.

By four, when Carl arrived, Schwartz felt that he'd destroyed Carl's life and kept apologizing for bringing ruin, not protection, to the building. Carl, well insured, was philosophic. He wondered about Schwartz.

He thought. "My lease is okay. There's insurance to replace any office . . ." Schwartz couldn't bring himself to say "furniture."

So what had he lost? Some clothing, a bottle and a half of seltzer and his trust in Addison.

Then Chief Whalen took him aside to say they'd found what looked like traces of a firebomb around the mail slot in the ruins of the office door. It looked like a professional arson job.

"Would it have worked if all the furniture hadn't been there?" Schwartz wondered.

Whalen shrugged. "Don't know. Maybe. But not like this. You were damn lucky to get out."

Yes, Addison. Addison, he thought later, sitting in a spectacularly uncomfortable plastic bucket seat over his fifth cup of coffee in the Chicken and Shrimp House, now a smokehouse but still in business. Addison was strong enough to have catapulted him under the golden steamroller. Ah, but Addison had saved him. Why do both? He'd leave that, for now. Addison had known of the explosive furniture being there *and* had asked him to sleep at Brighton Beach. That pointed away from intended murder. But it still pointed at Addison.

At eight, Schwartz called Addison's phone booth. "Oh?" he said, "This isn't you, Abrasha? Well, tell your friend he needn't worry about removing his furniture from his employer's office. The office has just been burnt down, his employer has somehow managed to escape and the fire department has removed the few remaining bits of Addison's art-drecko."

"I'm there in a little while. Wait," said Addison, dropping the usual guise.

There was little point in calling Karen. He'd tell her tonight, at home.

Schwartz bought newspapers and kept reading the same headlines and forgetting them. He hadn't the heart to push on into the texts. Earthquakes, fires, torture of Indians in Guatemala, leaking reactors and the usual censorship from South Africa where no news was bad news.

By nine the fire department was gone. Schwartz was sitting in the concrete peninsula park when Addison appeared, smiling.

"Why are you smiling?"

"If I smile, you smile. I lose all that furniture but show you it doesn't matter."

"Addison, did you set the fire?"

"You serious ask me this?"

"For insurance? Have you pulled some insurance scam with that furniture?"

"No! I lose it all. You are crazy!"

"Why'd you ask me to sleep in Brighton Beach?"

"Because office last night a terrible place full of my furniture. You do me big favor, so why not I ask you sleep my place? Look, boss. Look. I bring you this."

Addison placed a cheap gray suitcase on the concrete slab in front of them and snapped it open. New underpants, socks, shirts, a pair of trousers, a sweater appeared in Addison's hands. "What you think? Just your sizes, Lenny. No? Look, is first drawer quality. Bloomie's, Abe Strauss, good stuff. Huh?"

"Very nice. Damn it! Addison, what the hell's happening?"

"Burnout, who knows? Not fatso Pignatelli himself, of course, but maybe who he ask. Maybe same who push you? We work it out."

"From where, Addison? That burnt showroom of ersatz? Should we set up out here, the world's first private investigators as bag ladies?"

"That's more like. You witty again. Art-drecko. Hey! Remember I promise yesterday good news?"

"Yes. Don't tell me you have good news. No, go on, try. I dare you."

"I got great new office for us! From a friend still have lease. Cheap, cheap. And is downtown Manhattan, right in middle of anything! Ready right away. On Warren Street."

"Addison—"

"Is break we need, maybe. Yes?"

"Addison, how is it you happen to have arranged new premises the night the old one goes up in flames, the night you ask me not to sleep in the old premises?"

"Boss, you are still angry and in shock. Otherwise you understand you speaking circumstantially off the top your hat."

"Maybe. Maybe I'm just worried by the fleas in your bonnet."

"No, boss. Expression is 'bees in my bonnet,' idiotmatically."

"Of course, Addison." Schwartz thought, why not take an idiotmatic look at this place on Warren Street, so much closer to police headquarters and Simpkin's PHS office, and exactly that much farther from Park Slope?

"So? We cross to Manhattan?"

"Why not?" Schwartz said. He remembered the city red across the river, burning.

BOOK II

The weekend turned out sadder than the first. Schwartz thought that calling Jake at New Haven before leaving the office on Friday would raise his spirits and so raise Karen's, but telling his son of the new arrangements in and out of Park Slope had been a flat, nervous affair. Schwartz heard his own voice as a cold autumn monotone against the actual weather—hot and blue preposterous October. Jake's understanding had been chilling, except for his lapse from the cool when at the close he said, "I love you, too. Dad, you two better make it up." Schwartz had said, "Sure."

But when he told Karen that he'd called and explained, he heard in "That's good" only her relief in having one less battle to contend with. Or maybe her mood came from his prior news, that his minor injuries resulted from a fire in his building and a window he'd stood too near, her bitterness rising from his need to lie to keep her from some seamy, violent truth.

This mood pulled down the weekend despite the frenzy of repeated lovemaking (which by Sunday Schwartz thought of as "clutched fucks") with Karen's eyes squeezed shut afterwards, her face turned to the side so that the tears fell to the sheet and from her other eye ran over the bridge of her nose in a straight, shiny line. And it had never felt so hot, not in brownout hundred-degree heat waves as in this unseasonable, powdery high-eighties autumn when he'd say "Karen, Karen" as he lifted off her, his chest wet, her breasts wet, black hairs off his chest on her like question marks. At her name she looked up and pulled him down tight onto her, and her fingernails raked his back and bandaged shoulders until he cried out and made her stop.

They tried to talk about it, once, on Saturday afternoon, each with a pillow on the lap, sitting naked on the edge of the stripped bed, damp sheets balled on the floor and Purcell from the Met over the radio.

Schwartz said, "Falling. It's like we're suddenly slipping out of our own hands."

Karen pulled the pillow to her stomach. "No, it's not sudden. We've been walking on this edge for years. Now we've gone over, grabbing . . . I don't know, roots and bushes on our way down."

"We'll have to get back up again," he said quietly.

"We can't. We, I think we'll have to see where, how we are when we land. I don't . . . What's this part, now?"

Schwartz listened. "Where, I think where Dido first learns—"

"Oh, another woman who's found he's done her wrong. Another man . . . You all just *have* to go off and found Rome or a detective agency or fool around in boats."

"Or write nice music."

"Or found a detective . . . Yes, nice music. It's a change from all that honey-heavy nineteenth-century opera."

"That's the joke about how to make Milton Cross."

"Angry? Oh, Milton Cross. I thought you meant, you know, Milton, *Paradise Lost.*"

"Was it?" he asked.

"Lost?"

"Paradise."

She dropped her eyes. "We didn't need paradise."

He looked at the fading tan line on the side of her thigh, at the dark cream flesh above, at the black wisp of her pubic hair along the hugged pillow. Insatiable, his lust and its despair.

On Monday morning he sat in his dusty two thousand square feet of Warren Street rented so quickly by the amazing and shifty Addison. He'd pulled his own trick on Friday, amazing Addison by getting the telephone turned on immediately, no real trick if you knew the right person at New York Telephone, the person thinking you were still on official police business. And so what? They were boys at play, comparing the size of their clouts.

Addison came in full of cheer and bullshit and a bit of real news concerning a mathematician friend of his at NYU named Braverman who'd heard of V. J. Hayes as a good mathematician who'd dropped out a few years back. Addison was having him write for information to a buddy in topology out at Cal Tech who'd known Hayes pretty well.

Schwartz gave him a grudging "Okay" and sent him out to find or take photos of everyone, starting with their Upper East Side clients; if he could get a look at their mail, so much the better. When Addison tried to sell him an "undercover Minox like mine, I get you cheap as hell," Schwartz told him to get the hell out so that he could concentrate on annoying Simpkin and marveling over the office.

"I'm going without listening to such sarcasm. Oh, bed and other things be delivered later today. So be a terrific room and office for you." Addison added, "You poor fellow," and closed the door.

The poor fellow smiled. He'd found that Simpkin could get a sharp talking-to for building his private case collection from the department's public one, but it wouldn't be worth the embarrassment of prosecution. All he could hope for was to scare Simpkin into cooperation by a little leaning, creating a scene at his sacrosanct PHS office. He went to the window and looked across the street at other cast-iron buildings whose store signs, at his second-floor level, read DISCOUNT, FIRE SALES and DAMAGED GOODS.

Crossing the plaza, Schwartz glanced at the renamed federal building—the Jacob Javits Federal Building—and was struck with the idea from childhood that it was somehow more wrong for a Jew to be a Republican. How hemmed in he was by childhood ideas. Never mind; it was time to needle Simpkin.

Inside the door marked "Public Health Administrator," the woman behind the counter asked if she might help.

"Yes, I'd like to see Dr. Simpkin, please."

"Do you have an appointment?"

"No, I don't."

"Who shall I say?"

"Len Schwartz. A former colleague. Thank you."

"If you'd like to take a seat," she said, "I'll be right with you."

He took a seat by serious waiting-room reading: PHS publications and professional journals with titles like *Studies in Melanoma* and *The Pancreas Review*.

"Mr. Schwartz? I'm sorry. Dr. Simpkin is in conference. If you wish to make an appointment, I could put you through to his secretary."

"No. I think I'll wait. When will the conference finish?"

The receptionist, a slim black woman in her forties, gave him a please-no-nonsense look and said, "Please wait."

"Dr. Simpkin will be in conference for at least another hour. But I'm afraid his schedule is booked then, too." She held the receiver.

"I'll wait. It's a matter of some urgency."

"You could leave a message."

"No, no. It's not anything I'd want to leave in writing. I'll just wait, settle into a copy of *Impetigo Today* that's caught my eye." He returned to his seat.

She said, "You won't be able to see Dr. Simpkin, but if you feel you have to wait, please suit yourself." She turned to the desk behind her.

Schwartz felt he had to. He felt he had nothing else to do. He felt foolish, fooling himself for five hundred a day. But the fire hadn't been a dream. Nor had the visit to Simpkin's house. He'd wait.

Schwartz pulled out a magazine on radiology. He thought of his Uncle Maurie, lifetime CP member, funny guy and general pain in the ass. He'd passed sad warnings to the child Schwartz when, through Arbiter Ring insurance, he'd been an early recipient of radiation treatment.

It was, he'd told his seven-year-old nephew who stood by the bed in the scrubbed Lower East Side project mesmerized by the lively, wise-cracking skeleton before him, a plot. Radiation was a bosses' plot. Aunt Celia, Maurie's wife, sobbed in the next room and made to tear out her hair, perhaps an act of empathetic magic corresponding to Maurie's radiation baldness.

"It's not enough these bastard capitalists have to threaten us all with their A-bombs. They have to use this *dreck* in hospitals to get rid of progressives. Give me cancer, straight cancer. You hear, kid? Straight cancer, no radioactive chaser."

He leaned forward and shouted, "You hear, Ceely? Straight cancer I could cope with! I'd die with my hair on!" And then Uncle Maurie fell back weakly and Aunt Celia wailed with new strength.

Schwartz glanced down the office corridor. Nothing, no one. He flipped through the journal. Radiology. The pictures reminded him of something, probably from childhood. A quarter to two. He'd give it another half hour.

He'd thought Celia and Maurie hated each other, always yelling, fighting, so unlike his parents. But then, five or so years after Maurie died, he'd one day overheard Aunt Celia talking to his mother about how she still missed Maurie, how crazy about him she'd been, how she'd screamed when they made love so that she'd blush to see the neighbors in the hall next morning. His mother said, "Of course they didn't hear, darling. They were asleep."

Aunt Celia said, "Maybe when we started, but not after-wards!"

Then he'd heard the two women laughing and then laughing and crying.

"Becky, I'm dying, I miss Maurie so," Aunt Celia said.

And she had, or anyway died two years later. Two? No, a year before his mother died. So he would have been thirteen, fourteen?

Before him was a radiology photo that he couldn't through the blur make out.

He sucked his breath in with surprise. Not just "died." Aunt Celia committed suicide! What shocked Schwartz was the persistent loss of this memory, a memory trying to commit sui-cide.

"Mr. Schwartz?"

"Yes, sorry. Yes?"

"I said, Dr. Simpkin's secretary called to say he can see you now. Third door down on your right."

He nodded. Of course Simpkin had to see him. The denials had been some telephone paranoia. The door said "Division of Preventative Health Services" and beneath it, "Dr. Armand B. Simpkin, Director."

Inside was another serious assistant who smiled, picked up the phone and said, "Mr. Schwartz to see you." She put it down and said, "Please go in."

This was more like it. He felt the coming battle of wills and wits, the curtain rising in the little theater of innuendo. He passed through the inner door saying, "Hello, Armand."

"Mr. Schwartz, I'm C. Richard Weiss, Special Programs Director."

It was a firmly un-Simpkinish handshake. Schwartz didn't like it. He introduced himself as "L. Maurie Schwartz, but you can call me Len." He didn't like the tanned bald head, neat charcoal suit, the natty round-collared pink shirt with its pin under the tight knot of the rep-striped tie.

Weiss pointed to an armchair. "Please," he said, returning to Simpkin's chair behind the desk. "I believe," he said, folding his hands, "we owe each other explanations." He smiled into Schwartz's flattest stare. "Armand is a fine administrator, but as you know, he doesn't cope well with personal confrontation, so he's asked me to step in, as I happened to be around."

"Are you his boss?" Schwartz asked, trying to understand what beside the "C. Richard" pomposity he didn't like.

"Not exactly. I suppose you could say his superior. I've been apprised of the facts and, to the extent they're accurate, it seems to me you are hounding the man without cause."

Schwartz looked at Weiss's hands on the desk. "What did he tell you?"

"He spoke of your distinguished police career and he said

you're now a private investigator. You've spoken with him at his home concerning a case for which he was pathologist-coroner. You represent the deceased's parents who dispute the cause-of-death findings. Is that right, so far?"

What was so unpleasant about Weiss's nose and the way his cheekbones bumped out? "Yes."

"Armand said he'd discussed what he knew with you and you'd seemed satisfied. But later you called and asked to see the case file you claimed he had. When he said he had no such thing, you accused him of lying. Am I putting this too strongly, Mr. Schwartz?"

Through the slats in the blinds, Schwartz saw slivers of the county courthouse portico. "No, that's close enough," he said. There was something about Weiss's eyes, those ovals . . .

Weiss shrugged. "I reassured Armand that even if he had been silly enough—I said 'overenthusiastic' enough—to take copies of police files for his own research, he wouldn't be in any serious trouble. What's your opinion?"

Schwartz found himself appreciating the man's approach—inviting the prosecutor to witness for the defense. "There wouldn't be much fuss if the files were closed cases, not with Armand's former senior position. But file copies and especially material evidence from *open* cases would be different, possibly an obstruction of justice. You can appreciate the distinction."

"Certainly. In theory," said Weiss.

"Of course. This case is closed, at least for now. Besides, I suppose you believe that Simpkin never did have a copy."

"Yes. And it's not only his word. I've been to his home, I've seen his research setup. There are no files there, as he says you claim." Weiss's smile was poised between concern and challenge.

"Oh," Schwartz said, "you've seen that big mock Tudor place of his on Staten Island?"

"I'd hardly call a Frank Lloyd Wright house 'mock Tudor,' Mr. Schwartz."

If the man was bluffing he was bluffing well. Why all these thoughts about Uncle Maurie? Weiss looked nothing like him.

"Mr. Schwartz, if you could tell me what your problem is with Armand, I'd like to help resolve it, if possible."

"Why not? My promise of secrecy to Armand doesn't apply now. Look, I had no axe to grind with Armand until my ordinary questions met with extraordinary results: files wiped from police records, an attempt to repair Flatbush Avenue using me as road fill, and another to make me the entrée at a midnight weenie roast. So I don't see how I can keep from continuing to pester old Armand on this, even if I think he was probably correct in his findings on my clients' son."

"Maybe I can be of help, after all," said Weiss, opening a drawer in the desk. He placed a plain white envelope before Schwartz and sat back.

Schwartz made no move for it. Damned if he'd play someone else's . . . Himself! That was it! But for the baldness, C. Richard Weiss reminded him of himself. Face, expression, height, build. They could have been—no, not twins, but brothers. And this was why he found Weiss so unpleasant?

Weiss cleared his throat. "Of course, I couldn't get the actual autopsy report on Virgil Hayes at such short notice, but as you'll see in the envelope, a copy will be ready for you to pick up by six this evening at the VA hospital, on First Avenue, you know, just south of Bellevue."

"Why the VA? Hayes wasn't a veteran."

"Let me explain." Weiss laughed. "I have the feeling that if I don't, you'll chase after me, too. All right, my job—Special Programs Director? Our top-priority special program now is AIDS research and education. I liaise between Washington and major incidence and research centers and I coordinate various

PHS agencies working in the field. When Hayes was pulled from the East River, Armand thought what he observed was curious enough, scientifically, to immediately notify this field office, and as I happened to be here at the time I thought I'd see, firsthand."

Schwartz nodded. Did Weiss really look so much like him? He left the envelope alone.

"It was on my recommendation that the autopsy was done at the VA rather than at Bellevue or anyplace else. We were close; the body had been brought out on a nearby pier, I think Pier 70. I thought we'd get more immediate and better access to path labs at the Federal VA hospital and so maybe get better results. You know we need all the real data we can get. Armand agreed and I arranged the lab use, but as you know, it was a complicated case and the work was rushed, for technical and other reasons, so that the results, unfortunately, weren't useful for our research purposes, though adequate for certification as AIDS-related death."

"And that's it?" asked Schwartz, looking at the envelope. Weiss didn't look *that* much like him.

"Yes, it is. And I can't think you're suggesting that any of this is connected with the events you mentioned." Weiss smiled the intelligent person's embarrassment at police stupidity.

Schwartz wouldn't disappoint him. "And that's it?"

"Yes. I certainly don't know more details. But the VA file I've cleared for you to see may give them."

"I'm sure," Schwartz said. "I'm grateful for your time. Could I impose on you a little more?"

"No imposition, but I don't have much time. On the other hand, I wouldn't want Armand to feel that I hadn't been fully cooperative."

"Thanks. I wanted to ask if you knew Armand before that night in April when Hayes was found."

"Yes, as a senior police pathologist."

"Oh? And did you know that he'd applied for his current job?"

Weiss said, "I certainly did. I knew of the vacancy coming up and recommended him to apply."

"And you mentioned visiting his house. Was that before or after April?"

"After. It was late May, maybe early June. I felt I wanted to get to know him a bit better before I made a final recommendation."

"So his new job was up to you?"

"No. I was recommending him to the assistant secretary's office. There was also a board involved."

"Speaking of boards, Dr. Weiss, did you know of the Hayes's request for exhumation?"

"Armand told me. He was concerned and wanted my view, since I'd known the case originally."

"And you concurred that a new autopsy would be even less clear?"

"That's right."

Schwartz rose and took the envelope. "I could drop the case now, if it wasn't that I understand the difficulties of that autopsy because I saw photos of the state of the corpse in Armand's possession. And I also understand why he'd want to deny having the files. Thanks for getting this VA report."

Weiss opened the door and they shook hands. "Mr. Schwartz, I appreciate your tact in not referring to why I might wish to support Armand's denial."

"Nothing at all. By the way, how did the young Mrs. Simpkin strike you?"

Weiss laughed, bringing veins into relief across his forehead. "Frankly, the whole improbable setup out there struck me as pretty wonderful. Take that any way you want. Good-bye now." Smiling, he shut the door.

He does look like me, thought Schwartz. But balder. Balder like Maurie. Suicide. Virgil's? Aunt Celia's?

Schwartz recognized this thought-hopping as a symptom of failure. A small cover-up for Simpkin. He'd go to the VA hospital. He'd go through the report, he'd go through the motions and then he'd go close the case.

CHAPTER 2

Schwartz hadn't the heart to go back to the emptiness of Warren Street. But by now, Addison and his balalaika bandits had stuffed it with cheap furniture. Well, he hadn't the heart to go back to the fullness of Warren Street. And he couldn't, for five hundred a day, just futz around, even in these last few overpaid hours. He owed it to his clients to sit in City Hall Park and think.

Finding a bit of bench relatively clear of pigeon shit, he sat down and reflected on the mystery of things. There was none: everything was clear. The plane-tree leaves were placidly committing suicide, jumping off branches. The ordinary signs abounded in brown grass: "Danger: Rat Poisoning in Progress." Progress? Tell that to the rats.

The rats. No mystery—Simpkin had second thoughts on the wisdom of confiding his secret collection to an ex-policeman. He'd gone to Weiss for counsel and was told to deny and get rid of everything. Weiss probably supplied the shredder or took it all down to Washington, where used shredder lots were appearing, the current wisdom being "better shred than read."

What remained? The fire? The fire could have been one of those old Brooklyn Family Traditions, otherwise known as having Pignatelli ask the wrong burning question. And the golden shove could have been the fire's early warning. And there was nothing strange about Ann McCarthy's reluctance to revive the painful dead and buried past, especially now that she'd turned over a new golden leaf.

Dead and buried. Aunt Celia. With the tip of his loafer, Schwartz turned over a leaf at his feet. Golden with pale green spots, both sides.

After Maurie died she'd sometimes stay with them, on the couch in the alcove off the living room they called "the study." One night, that last year of her life, Schwartz had woken thirsty and walked down the hall to cup his hands under the tap. He stopped. From the bathroom a wedge of light lay across the hall. The tap was running. Through the angle of the open door he looked into the bathroom mirror and saw Aunt Celia naked. He stared. It was the first time he'd seen an adult woman naked. His mouth, already dry, went drier. His heart beat on his eardrums. He kept moving his eyes from the large brick-colored nipples to the hair under her stomach. He'd seen photos of women, but she wasn't like those photos. She was . . . He'd stopped breathing there at the edge of the light. She was throwing water at her face now; the drops ran to her big breasts and down to wet the puff of light brown hair that thrilled him so that his guilty heart went bang-bang and he could hear a clicking from the back of his throat. She was so beautiful, angry at herself in the mirror, splashing herself all over, and she couldn't see him going cold behind the yellow wedge of light.

For years from that night (he was twelve, thirteen) she

became his secret image of sex. When she stayed with them, he tried to keep awake and sometimes did, but she was never up or the bathroom door was locked. If he fell asleep those nights, he woke next morning with a misery: that door *had* been open while he slept. Celia (for now she was Celia) *had* been naked at the mirror, the drops of water glistening on her belly and into that hair which he thought of in a mix of street slang and Hebrew school as her "burning bush."

And his secret sadness at her death (that same year, the next?) was that he had taken the image of his aunt in vain and she had killed herself. And later, when he learned the truth of her grief—the married man, her awful abortion—it was still his own guilt. Still later, he understood it was his own jealousy which would have no rivals in guilt. Sexual longing, ignorance and early sorrow—the stuff of his problems.

Was there still some adolescent set that ran from his lust fixation through his aunt's death and then through that next year's death of his mother? His mother's death, the final sign of his guilt (although by then he was a card-carrying atheist), as if looking back to the thin edge of the wedge of light he saw it came, not from the bathroom bulb but from God's single burning eye.

And why was the image of God cyclopic? Maurie! That was Uncle Maurie, years before, holding up a dollar bill. "See, kid, this is their god. Moolah-worship. See the eye on the pyramid? Know what the Latin means? Never mind *their* grammar; it's the parasitic capitalist's credo, *out of one buck, many.*

That certainly took. When he was eleven or twelve taking Latin, Mr. Pinders had given his class the exercise of finding Latin in everyday Brooklyn. Schwartz had stood up in class the next day with a dollar bill, had proudly read *E Pluribus Unum* in the Uncle Maurie translation and was made to feel more of a fool than the kindly Pinders would have wished.

Mr. Pinders, Uncle Maurie, his mother, Celia, sex and

suicide. And he hadn't told Karen he was quitting his job. He was lucky she'd still see him on weekends. Schwartz kicked over a new leaf. It looked like the old one. He'd take the IRT uptown and think away the only remaining problem, Carter Hayes.

Schwartz had managed to choose rush hour, had managed to catch one of the few old, un-air-conditioned trains left, and, really tricky, the one with the stuck-shut windows. He walked unhappily on Twenty-third Street, his trousers sticking to his thighs, his underpants clamming his crotch.

His next diversion from thought was over the beer at the bar he went into to cool off and kill the half hour before six. The elderly man in old tweed sitting next to him insisted Schwartz was Irish. Schwartz resisted the insistence. The man, who at times called himself Farrell and at others Carroll, went on to tell Schwartz of a Jewish Lord Mayor of Dublin and in his enthusiasm for the man made him sound so vile that Schwartz finally admitted his Irishness, at which point Farrell-Carroll said, "I might be drunk, but I know when a man's pullin' my leg."

"Sorry, Mr. Farrell."

"Carroll's the name."

"Sorry. Carroll. Listen, what would you think if, say, when you were a kid, say, a very beautiful aunt of yours killed herself, and afterwards—"

"A sin and that's all there is to it."

Schwartz considered the likelihood of in-depth therapy at this hour, a quarter to six, from this quarter, three sheets to the wind. He threw two quarters on the bar and left.

Twenty minutes later he'd come down from the VA hospital's records office with a large envelope and sat in the lobby reading its contents. This took him two minutes. There were no photos, no microphotos. This reminded Schwartz of something, but he couldn't remember what. What? There was a copy of the death certificate. There was a two-page, tampered-with report of far less detail than in certain issues of *The Advocate.*

Schwartz decided he'd run back to Warren Street; the shoes weren't the best, but his clothing couldn't be sweatier. He ran off. It was a jog, but he'd been a competitive runner and hated the idea of "jog"—like walking the dog with yourself as the dog, like changing a sport to a slog, like throwing a lance like a log. He liked to rhyme and run. It kept a rhythm, gave him fun. The case, the case, the case was done. In the old days, weeks ago, when he was stymied, then he'd go to Gallagher.

There. All you did was think the name and all rhyme fled. The hell with Gallagher. Yes, but in the department he'd tell Gallagher he was stymied, struck out, stumped (Gallagher taking exception to the last term upon Schwartz explaining its English cricketing origins, Gallagher a passionate Irishman wondering why there couldn't be an adequate term from the great sport of hurling, Schwartz asking like what? and Gallagher suggesting they get back to work.)

Schwartz turned west at Houston. The loafers weren't too bad, but the clothes were so sweat-drenched they'd have to be set on fire. No, he didn't mean that.

And Gallagher would review the case with Schwartz in so corny a manner—not merely textbook, but as if the key might lie in retyping one particular day's report in triplicate—saying that there was nothing more to do until something new "turned up." And between them—

"Are you all right, sir?" asked a young woman jogging on West Broadway of the crazed man running in the poplin wetsuit and flapping loafers.

He picked up his pace. And then, he thought, between them they'd work something out through Schwartz's frenzied insistence that something new never "turned up," that "turned up" was a time-serving, old-fartist attitude and through Gallagher's more and more stodgy obviousness until Schwartz, just to agitate him, would say the stupidest thing and Gallagher would consider it seriously, make a logical variation, which Schwartz would then instantly turn into an elaborate scheme, which Gallagher would laugh at and simplify. Something like that. Sometimes. They were—

Should he push it, these last three blocks? Not with the ankle in these loafers.

They were a very successful team. But then there was everything impossible else. He wouldn't think of Gallagher whom he sure as hell could use now.

He looked up the stairs. Come on, just one flight. Yes, but a very long one with high risers. At the door he felt awful. The part that wasn't exhaustion was apprehension of the horrors Addison had deposited within. Schwartz turned the key and said "Oh," out loud.

It was better than marvelous; it was, as Addison would say, adequate. Good rugs, two good desks, an answerphone! The space had been divided off by wooden bookcasing and shelving units, and behind, Schwartz careful not to drip on anything, a platform bed with new linen, bedside table with a radio and big fan, a chest of drawers and a clothes cupboard. And new towels in the funky shower room. Yes, Schwartz thought, stripping off, Addison had outdone himself, must have somehow fallen into a den of good taste.

Out of the shower with a towel around his waist, Schwartz went behind the old repair shop counter. A small fridge and freezer, a stove and a coffee maker. And Schwartz saw the Matisse print.

Where could Addison have found it? The one that burned had been the only one Schwartz had seen like it, aside from the place he'd found it, the little *affiche* shop, with Karen, on Rue Bonaparte where it came out by the Seine. They'd stood, flipping through the prints . . . "Adequate," Schwartz said.

And of course there'd be . . . He took the vodka from the freezer and poured it into a heavy glass. Frozen, the vodka poured like heavy glass. A septuple? Why not. It was just after eight, time to call the Hayeses, call off the Hayeses. Addison mentioned a few small tracking jobs he'd been putting off. Okay. But this should be done with music. Schwartz went back and turned the radio on low to BGO. Oh, yes, Lester. A little bit of Pres brought everything to cool, blue suede perspective.

Schwartz lifted the phone. Oh, the answerphone. He pushed a button. A whirring, a short beep and "Three-two-one-six, hello boss is what we spend fix up the place. You like? If no is all refundable and we can go upmarket jiggedy-jog. Maybe I'm back there tonight with pictures from Upper East Hayes. Suggest, boss, anyhow you take a look before what next. Also got more bad news from a contact I hope you should never meet who says we no way find out snuff showing even if you still have friend in vicious squad. So like song go, do nothing till you see from me. And so long, boss."

Schwartz put the phone down and had another drink. The vodka was good but it was going to his sex, a sad waste. He put on underpants, jeans and a jersey and sat on the edge of the bed in the fan wind. How many years ago? Twenty-two? He'd sat on the edge of the bed with Karen in that tiny Chicago apartment. Not the first, it was after the second time they'd made love and he told her how before, with the others, not that there'd been so many, he wasn't trying to . . . Anyhow, he'd had to picture this aunt of his, the first woman he'd seen naked, when he was an adolescent. He meant, the image would come to him and then, sort of, have to come to him so that he could. Come, he meant. What he meant, anyhow, he must sound like such an asshole, was that it wasn't like that with her, not last time, not this. He was, like, *with* her when he was with her, if she knew what . . . She pressed his hand. She knew what. They were married six months later.

Twenty-two years ago when he loved her, Yeah, Yeah, Yeah, Yeah.

Shit, what was there to do but get fish soup in Chinatown?

Later, back from Bayard Street's anonymous, bustling jollity, which Schwartz thought was probably a white man's mistaking the Chinese there more likely crying "dies irae" and "oi vay" as they twisted by each other in the street, he walked around the loft impressed by Addison's transforming work. Three-two-one-six was very good.

Addison came in. Schwartz hugged him. "Addison, this is wonderful."

Addison nodded, smiled, put a satchel briefcase on his desk and opened it. "Wait," he said, laying out the photographs. "You think wonderful now, wait till you look these." He stepped back.

Schwartz looked. He moved the desk lamp closer and looked again. The photos showed white blobs against black blurs. Some of the blobs had squiggling on them. "You're right. I've changed my mind about how wonderful you are. What is this stuff?"

"Stuff is enlargements of Minox baby photos. You know how hard to get photos U.S. mail in foyer fancy apartment house? These, look, I show you there. See, 'Carter Hayes, 246 East—' "

"Where? Where?"

"Boss, right here and in corner say 'Bank of New York.' See?"

"See? I've seen flypaper more legible than this!"

Addison's round face furrowed like an angry soft toy. "I tell you what each one say. You such a hard man. I risk, you know this federal offense can get me Sing-Sing-Sing? Okay, so this you don't see don't kid me is from Bank New York. This to him it say Princeton Alumni Association. This from—"

"Hunger."

"What?"

"A dated expression. Worthless. Zilcharoonie, Addison. Diddly-squat and *rien de tout. Panyemayish?*"

"You polyglot all over me, but you still wrong. I see. This—"

Schwartz clamped his hand on Addison's wrist. "This is enough. You're a great interior decorator, but the case is closed. There's nothing here, even if I were dopey enough to believe you, that—" Schwartz stopped. "What's this?"

Addison passed him a small bundle of mail. "Is just as backup because I'm aware of your such skepticism. I stole mail."

"You stole the mail. And we've been looking at . . . I don't want to know how you stole it. I don't even want to know why. I only want to know you'll steal back there to return it."

"You don't want even to look?"

"At what? My client's bank statements?" Schwartz threw the envelope on the desk. "News of the class of '42?" The envelope dropped onto the first. "A magazine subscription to *American Opinion*? *AMERICAN OPINION*?"

"What is, Lenny? Is something?"

"A nasty something. It's probably nothing, but it might mean we should hang on here a while longer. This little mag is the diseased organ of the John Birch Society. Do you know—"

"Sure, sure. Some Ukrainians take this. Is bad stuff. This society like to find émigrés from USSR. So what mean?"

"I don't know. Not even a real hunch, but at least something's turned up, as an ex-associate of mine would say. Good work, Addison. But get this mail back."

"Sure, boss. And here I got photo of Hayes and Mrs. coming out."

"Addison, I can actually see them. Features. Eyes and

noses. I don't know what use it is, but it's terrific."

Addison put his hand to his forehead and said, "Thank you, boss. You get me faint with damned praise. So case is not closed?"

"Let's say the case is altered."

S chwartz walked toward the club he'd been to once before, but that was as a police officer, backed by the whole department. Now, all on his own, he hoped it wouldn't come to a fight with Cal Anderson, the camp thug giant who owned the club. But if he survived this encounter, he might have a lead, though he was going less on a hunch than to avoid using an even more frightening source of information.

Under his arm, Schwartz felt the heaviness of his hated gun, a feather to his fear. When, last winter, Anderson had been a semi-suspect in a case, Schwartz had to lean on him hard enough, the weight of a full detective team thrown in, so that his S&M club had practically closed down.

Here it was now, at daytime just another garage door on always inelegant Eleventh Avenue, with the small sign STICK 'EM UP CLUB. And behind the door the night entrance with a sign whose graphics disabused any from thinking the club entertainment was cowboy music. Schwartz bent through the street door. And back behind a door studded with studs spelling "Studs" was good old Cal, who'd probably beat him to a pulp for auld lang syne.

He pressed the buzzer, prepared to invent a doorphone story, but the door buzzed back and opened. He'd play Detective Inspector.

Inside was as red and black and bad as he remembered: wall manacles that weren't only decor, the mattressed dining booths. Someone was mopping the floor. And there over the bar, the same awful photos: Cal—jutting naked.

"Hi. I'm looking for Cal Anderson," Schwartz said to the old geezer propped like a mopstick behind the bar.

"You're looking *at* Cal Anderson."

"No, you're . . ." said Schwartz, despite that same high tweety voice.

"You happened to catch me right in the middle of a remission."

Schwartz swallowed. "I'm—"

"—the same small shit cop who hassled me last February. Schwartz, wasn't it? What now? Want to beat me up? You probably could, now. Just. Know what I regret, sweetheart?"

Schwartz shrugged, looking at a head full of dark holes: cheek sockets, eye sockets, and over the brow ridge two craters.

"I'm only sorry, now that I know what's happening to me, ducks, that I didn't make a mess of you, you fag-bashing fuck. I mean, some major disfigurement to that straight, tight little person of yours," he said, bracing himself on the bar with twig arms from which his wasted tendons shook like cut wire.

In the dim light Schwartz couldn't tell if the dark red bruises on Cal's arms and neck were anything like Virgil's in those photographs. Pity and terror. Schwartz felt sick.

"Anderson," he said, "you might be interested to know that we got that killer—and he wasn't gay. He was as screwed-up a hetero as you'd like."

"Surprise, surprise," said Anderson. "Is this what you dropped in for?"

"No. You have a couple of minutes?"

"I'm busy. I'm starting a final inventory before selling the place—at a huge loss. But you know medical expenses; so do the harpies, don't they, and they offer shit. Know what I used to take in here at the peak, in the early Eighties? Eighty to ninety thousand—a week. *Pas* fucking *mal*, huh, detective? Now I'm clearing three, three and a half. Probably ten thousand a week gets ripped off by my loyal staff, now that I'm not here to watch. And I need at least five to break even."

"But all that money you made?"

"Oh, my dear! Gone with the wind—sex, drugs, and rock and roll. What am I doing? You see how feeble I've become, talking to a cop like this? So what do you want?"

"Some information you might have."

"Not anything *I've* been up to. I've been such a boringly good, sick boy, taking my medicines on time."

"No, nothing like—"

"Well, then, I'll end my fucking days—no, those are already over. I'll end without becoming the sweetheart of Precinct 9."

Schwartz put his private investigator's license on the bar. "I've seen the light and quit the fraternity."

"Well! That's different, even if you haven't come over to the sorority. So what is it you think I know that you don't and want to, hmm?" Anderson asked in a voice so high camp it made Capote's sound like George Schultz.

"Snuff shows."

"You *are* a dark little horse, aren't you!"

"A case I'm working on."

"Oh, I believe you, ducky, though thousands mightn't."

"Do they still go on?"

"Snuff shows? They thrived, throved? flourished, if one may say so, in the late seventies. Not that there were so many then, and most were cons. Others were gossip. You know, the usual New York head-fuck. But there were some. Then you people—your former boyfriends in dreary blue—came down *très, très* hard. But such is inhuman nature that I think they would have kept going. Want a drink?"

"No. No, thanks."

"Think I'll contaminate you? Come on, you big sissy. Look, you can open the whole prophylactic pack of untouched plastic glasses. I'm having a pre-lunch tipple of . . . wait," said Anderson, slowly bending, opening a door and bringing up the bottle. "Krug, 1959. Would you believe it? No one gets this little beauty in the inventory. Do the honors?"

Schwartz took the bottle, realizing that Cal, who less than a year ago did one-arm curls with a hundred and fifty pounds, now found a champagne cork hard going.

The cork banged and flew. Cal clapped and Schwartz filled two tall plastic cups.

Anderson said, "Let's not toast. This is good. What I like about great champagne isn't only the taste but how the color looks like good, strong . . . But then, I'm talking shop again. Where were we, ducks? Yes, your interest—snuff shows. I think what stopped them was some mad internal warring between producers. Burnings, even a bomb planted. I mean, it was getting so that entire *audiences* were getting snuffed! Well, a teensy *exagéré*, but that's more or less what stopped it all."

"Could there have been one last April?"

"April? Oh, that's when I'd fallen ill. I mean, fallen down fallen ill. I cracked a bone, so for me it was April in plaster of

Paris. There could have been a show, but there was no talk of one, and we're such gossips, us big girls."

"I'm going to ask you an awkward one, Anderson."

"Pour another and ask away. I find I take the grand view these days." He raised his cup. "These last days. No, that wasn't a toast. Mm. Good."

"Great champagne," Schwartz said. "Would you know if AIDS victims have lent themselves, I mean, have been used as snuff show victims because either they're suicidal or . . ." Schwartz was unable to finish.

"Oh, tacky! Tasteless!" Anderson was laughing in shrill tee-hees from his gaunt height. "I can't resist. I just don't know, ducky-pie. I can tell you that *I* wouldn't. Oh, look, darling, the only people who'd want to be snuffed would be crazy or drugged or both. Well, there certainly are lots of people in those categories. But not these medicinal drugs. Not . . . One's simply too weak. Anyhow, one *heard* that the best snuff shows were always surprises. You know, a boyfriend or girlfriend thinking they were just part of an ordinary group sex show or that someone *else* was getting it? You can imagine, can't you, the begging and screaming *then*? But I see I'm offending you, you straight old drake."

"Yes. Well, if you do hear anything about . . . something like this last April, here's my number. And thanks for the drink and the time, Anderson. I hope . . . I . . ." Schwartz found himself folding the entire money contents of his wallet into an AIDS support collection box on the bar.

"Sure," Anderson said. "If you don't hear from me by Christmas, ducks, you won't. Oh, here's a good one!" he called to Schwartz who stood in the door. "Because of this location, I used to be known as the Hudson Rock. Now I'm just known as Rock Hudson. But don't *you* tell it; it would be anti-gay." He gave a short "tee" and fell silent.

When the door shut, the warm, oily air from inside the

garage door filled Schwartz's head so quickly that he couldn't make it to the outer door but lurched to a dark forward corner and threw up. What justice? His moment's sickness? Cal's fatal one? He blew the sour champagne out of his nose.

CHAPTER 4

He hadn't learned much from Anderson. Back at Warren
Street, Schwartz sipped lightly sugared tea, ate a dry cracker and
finally felt well enough to check the answerphone.

A woman from Sheepshead Bay named Saltzman wanted
him to follow her husband, "the bastard, to get the goods on
him" but left no address or phone number. Fine.

Next was Addison: "Boss, this is you-know-whom landed
on certain island. Going to you-know-what to you-know-who."
Finer.

Then Karen! But Karen said, "Oh, Len, the talk at the
Corcoran seminar? Well, it's on, so I have to take the Friday
afternoon plane to Washington. I'll get back Sunday evening.
And I've had to put the Volvo in for servicing. It's been acting
funny and they had a cancellation. Dave says to call him at the

garage for details. And give me a ring if there are problems. We have an answerphone now. Bye." Finest.

He called Henry Hawthorne Smith, whose li'l ol' machine told him, as part of its current magnolia-scented ad, where he might find Ann McCarthy.

Half an hour later, Schwartz crossed the gallery-sized hallways into the air-hangar-sized Tower Gallery in time to see Ann McCarthy supervise the final touches of white paint on the huge, empty white walls and scratch a buttock through her jeans. Schwartz saw this scratch as an omen of normal behavior and told the man sitting at the entrance desk that he was with Ann. He walked over.

"Don't tell me," he said. "The roof slides open and H.H. brings down the Graf zeppelin, successfully, this time."

She turned around and recognized Schwartz with a pulling down of her long nose and an "Oh, no. How'd you find me?"

"The corn pone answerphone, but I promise to be nice, not pushy. And speaking of 'pushy,' I think you owe me answers to at least the easy questions."

"Look, I'm sorry about what happened. But it wasn't our fault. There were plenty of witnesses, Mr.—"

"Len Schwartz. I'm ready to drop the fifteen-million-dollar lawsuit if you answer. And you don't want me to keep pestering you, which I'll do, just for a few questions. Not even remotely scary questions. Please? Please?"

"Wait a minute," she said.

She ran to the painters, who were folding up their drop cloths. The way she walked and the set of her head when she talked was very . . . Virgil must have had something besides a promising math career to have attracted such a . . . What the hell was he going on about? He was a seriously unhappy married man whose wife understood him too well. Besides, Ann McCarthy was probably six feet tall.

"All right, Mr. Schwartz," she said, trotting back as the painters left. "I can give you five minutes. Let's get out of the paint smell."

"I'd like to call you McCarthy, McCarthy," he said, following her up the stairs and out onto the wilted remains of a roof garden.

"I don't mind, Schwartz, but you're using up your five minutes. Over here?" She sat on a faded deck chair beneath a lion's head wall fountain whose dry roar topped the notice "Conserve Water. City of New York."

Schwartz sat on a hot wooden bench.

"Isn't this a marvelous space? It's going to be a great show. Do you have a question?"

"Yes, to the first. If you say so, to the second. And was Virgil Hayes gay?"

McCarthy laughed a convincingly behind-scratching sort of laugh. "Jimmy? No, he wasn't!"

"How do you know, McCarthy?"

"I lived with him for two years, Schwartz."

"But a man can be bisexual and . . ." He looked at McCarthy and decided McCarthy would know. "Okay, but you lived with him for two years: you worked in Brooklyn Heights and he was at Cal Tech. McCarthy, are you confusing roommate with pen pal?"

She picked up the pink husk of a rose in her long, constantly moving hands. "I went out to Pasadena when I could. But Jimmy was here a lot, then. I mean, at Princeton between terms and in the summer. And out on the Island."

"With his parents at Huntington?"

"No. A little."

"McCarthy, what a face you pulled. Why doesn't Carter Hayes like you?"

"I don't know, Schwartz; no taste. Look, what's this all

about? And your answer will be deducted from the three minutes."

"I'm sorry. I haven't even told you. Carter Hayes wants me to prove that his son wasn't gay."

"Prove? That doesn't make sense. Who says he was gay?"

"The circumstances of his . . ." Schwartz sighed. "McCarthy, what do you know about Virgil's—Jimmy's death?"

"He killed himself." She dropped her eyes to the rose in her hand. "Drowned in the East River. Isn't that . . ."

"Not really. I'm very sorry to have to tell you this. Yes, he was taken dead from the East River, but he'd been mutilated, and his body had been elaborately painted."

"Oh, dear God." She looked at Schwartz. "Jimmy," she said to the rose.

"There's more. He'd been terminally ill with a number of symptoms pointing to AIDS-related diseases, and that's what his father wants disproven. Look, McCarthy, I'm not on the case in support of Carter Hayes's bigotry but because there are several strange circumstances surrounding the official recording of the death, not to mention some very weird aftermaths."

She rolled the pink rose with her thumb. Dry petals fell from her hand.

"Jimmy's father is a shit. I was never good enough for his son. But Jimmy dying like that . . . Jimmy wasn't gay or bi or a junkie. There was something very innocent about Jimmy. When we met, he was twenty-three and a virgin. It was . . . In some ways he was completely lacking in imagination, but the wonderful part of that was his inability to lie. It was infuriating sometimes; no guile, no tact, no little white kindnesses, but no lying. So I know he was heterosexual and faithful. And after we broke up, which was just a personal thing, I don't know, but . . . Yes I do. His personality couldn't change like that."

"Was Irene Hayes also set against you?"

"I don't think so. She really loved Jimmy, but she was so under that damned man's thumb. Wait a minute, Schwartz."

She pulled a red bandanna handkerchief from her jeans and wiped the tears. "God, this. Now this when I'd about gotten used to the sadness of the death I believed. Well, it's way past your five minutes, Schwartz."

"Sure. Oh, a tiny question."

She stood and turned into the bright sun. "If it's tiny."

"Did you know that Carter Hayes was a John Birch member or, at least, supporter?"

"No. But it doesn't surprise me, the extent of his shittiness."

"And Jimmy, was he politically involved with you? I mean—"

"No more questions."

"Why does it scare you? Who's gotten to you? What have you been told?"

"That's three more questions, Schwartz. I stopped four questions back." She let the remaining petals fall from her hand, then lifted her hand to her nose. "Almost no smell now, but enough to tell you what it was."

"I can smell a metaphor. Thanks. I'll follow quietly," he said as they went back in. "So what's Henry Hawthorne going to bring in here?"

"Nothing."

"Well, install, then?"

"Nothing."

"Come on, McCarthy. What event, happening?"

"This is it, Schwartz," she said, pointing to the solid white emptiness. "The people, the critics. Imagine the opening. The drink, the dress, the talk, photographers from *Time*. Don't you see?"

"Ah, the opening of the nonevent as event. Both emperor and citizens naked in new clothes. Nice publicity stunt, McCarthy."

"A complex work of art, Schwartz."

Schwartz looked hard at McCarthy and thought he saw a very small grin. "Yes? Well, is it for sale?"

"Of course."

"I see. You can have this opening event in another place, for a price. But so could I."

"No one would come if you did, Schwartz. And if no one came, it wouldn't be the same. You see, it's complex." McCarthy was rubbing her hands.

Schwartz hung on. "You have this opening and then close up."

"No, Schwartz. The show runs for three weeks."

"So what am I having now, McCarthy, a preview?"

"Oh, you don't understand." She pushed her hair back. "Now, this is just what you see—an empty, all white gallery space. The *show* only exists from the opening. Well, I have to go."

"McCarthy, I'd like to hang around for a few minutes and think of what you've been saying."

She looked at the desk man who held up five fingers. She turned to Schwartz and gave him a sad shake of her head. Then she ran out.

Schwartz walked to the middle of the enormous floor and sat down. Whitewash. A coat of paint to make emptiness into substance. Henry Hawthorne Smith in a wizard's robe, doing well from an iron ball painted to look like gold. Wizards, tricksters, alchemists making gold from base metal. Was McCarthy's parting sadness at Schwartz's dullness or at Virgil's death, or was it just more bad magic? And where did it leave him?

It left him hugging his knees in the middle of twenty

thousand square feet of white empty floor, knowing where he'd have to go for information. He shivered in the heat.

The man at the desk asked Schwartz if he'd like to be put on the gallery's mailing list.

On Friday morning Schwartz made up photosheets with Addison, who reported that his NYU friend told him a letter was coming concerning "old VJ."

Later, Schwartz called his clients and told Irene Hayes that he'd found a cover-up (omitting part of it was her husband's) and that her tip on Ann McCarthy had been helpful. She seemed cheered, agreed to send a photo of Jimmy by messenger service, and then stuttered some excuses for not meeting with Schwartz without her husband. An hour later the photo was delivered along with a large check and a small note from Carter Hayes: "Received your message. Please continue," a note so moving as to rush Schwartz out to deposit the check and withdraw pay for Addison and money for himself.

Schwartz then typed the report and challenged Addison's expenses of $246.50 for the fifty-cent trip to Staten Island.

Addison argued that $243.20 was the necessary rental of the
Lincoln so that he'd be able to take Betty Simpkin's photo incon-
spicuously "in such swank neighborhood where even hermit lives
in Hermitage and, besides, Mr. Hayes is paying." Schwartz, feeling Addison's cuteness wear thin against the hard edge of his
hustling, wrote him a check and suggested that in the future he
clear any proposed expense larger than a subway token. Finally,
he wished Addison a nice weekend, after lying "No" in answer to
"Any other leads, boss?"

At 5:30, in running clothes, the case materials in a back-
pack, Schwartz was halfway across the Brooklyn Bridge trying to
ignore the clumpy gothic arches, when the prospect of the weekend without Karen overcame him like twenty pounds of iron on
each ankle. Over the slope of Flatbush Avenue, the sky was per-
plexed, a messy spread of color.

Schwartz said "Hi" at his door to Susie going in two doors
down with her baby and shopping bags, agreeing that his work
had kept him away a lot these days and asking her to say hello to
Mark.

In the front hall he said "How" to the Baskin Indian,
which didn't know or wasn't saying, and the stairs pulled on his
ankle. The ankle was overreacting to being home. It would do it
no good. See? She wasn't here, so it could lie on the big bed and
throb itself to sleep alone. It was foolish talking to his ankle: it
wasn't interested. He sat cross-legged under the shower and
rubbed the ankle. It would have none of it.

Dressed, he opened the drawer where Karen kept her
underwear like folded flags: white for surrender, pink for flesh,
black and tan for civil war. How much still was, after all these
years, lust? How much was love? Was he having a mid-lust crisis?
Why did he stand here staring? And what was this strange thirst?

It was thirst. He shut the drawer and went downstairs for
a drink.

The note on the refrigerator door told him there was a beef stew to heat. It ended with four X's. He saw the pot of guilt stew, took the tonic and sliced a lime, filled the tall glass with ice and headed ginward.

He drank half, filled it again and had to have piano music. He went through the tapes, the records. Why so much Dvorak? He always wondered about it, not sure if he wanted less Dvorak or more not-Dvorak. He sat in the armchair in the silence.

With Jake away, the house was too big for the two of them, certainly for the one of him. Jake would never really be back to stay again. The house could be sold. Forty-five, they'd bought it for in '69. It had been so overpriced. Now—what had Ed said? Ten times that?

Such money. Karen was on the brink of real money. Had he quit to keep up, so she wouldn't outpace his cop's salary? Had it come to that jerkiness?

Shit. He'd heat the stew, eat the stew, forget the case and go to bed. But tomorrow and Sunday? There was . . . No one, he didn't have many friends. What cop did? Gallagher did. No, Gallagher's were professional acquaintances, butter-up buddies.

Schwartz stood at the stove eating stew from the pot. Karen had good women friends. She claimed he made friends with women more easily than with men. It was true. Due to childhood, he thought, sticking another beef chunk with his fork. He'd hung around so much with his mother. Dad he got to know later; he was always on the road organizing the out-of-town unions until she died.

Mother was remarkable. Off they'd go to the Brooklyn Museum, the Met, the Frick; off to the best of them all—the Natural History; off to little concerts, plays. Sometimes with Aunt Celia. Celia. She was really a beauty. Somewhere he had a photo of Mother and her at Coney Island just before the war. The Seigel sisters, skirts blowing, hair blowing, laughing. As a child he'd thought "the seagull sisters."

Where was it? Schwartz was squatting at a bookcase in the dining room, the stewpot in his hand. Where was that photograph? It used to be . . . He stood and looked around. Who the hell needed a dining room? This place was made for servants, a hundred years ago.

He set the pot on the round mahogany table. Should he light a candle? And what would the candle be for—Shabbos or champagne? Mother would tell him about Shabbos at her parents'. Dad, an orthodox atheist, wouldn't have it. But that year or so after Celia died, Mother had lit the candles Friday nights, said the prayer quietly. Little wiseass that he was, he started to interrupt her that first time. But his father had pulled him back, taken him to his study and told him that his mother had every right to "comfort herself this way," just as years earlier he'd let her send Schwartz to Hebrew school. The other kids went and Schwartz was curious. But he'd quit after . . .

The teacher had hit him, slapped his face. Mr. Abrahms. "Mar" Abrahms. Pulled him to the front of the class by his ear and slapped his face hard. And the next day Schwartz's father had walked into the middle of the lesson and called Abrahms a fascist coward. Kids whistled, hooted, except the goody-goods with their neat little half-smiles, Abrahms breaking a ruler between his own twitching hands as Father dared him to take a swing at someone his own size. Scandal, shame, delight!

Nothing was left in the pot but sauce and one large potato. Some carrots had fallen onto the table. What did he need to comfort himself? A shrink? Maybe. Maybe they should see a counselor.

He wiped the table. He washed the pot and fork. Oh, yes, the new answerphone. He could play with that until bedtime. He pressed the button. "Lenny, this is Tom Gallagher. I'm gonna be around your way tomorrow, Saturday afternoon. Thought I'd drop in. So if I don't hear from you, I'll see you then, after lunch."

Schwartz sighed. Gallagher thought he could just pick up . . . Schwartz went up to bed humming a Bud Powell tune. He laughed, recalling that its title was "Celia."

In the middle of the night Schwartz turned, woke, sat up and rubbed his eyes in the dark. It really hadn't been a dream. It was a thought. The waiting room. Something about a waiting room. What? He couldn't think. He remembered that Gallagher would be coming tomorrow and went back to sleep.

Running in the park in the morning, Schwartz thought the weather was finally changing. The damp came off the fallen leaves in what smelled like autumn must. But by half past seven, coming home, he smelled heat wave—the city as a low, unventilated attic.

An hour later, Molly, Karen's mother, called.

"Oh," she said, "I thought Karen wasn't leaving until later this morning. Well, how are you?"

"I'm—"

"This is silly. You're terrible. Karen's terrible. Why don't the two of you see someone?"

"I've been thinking of that."

"Len, Karen mightn't thank me for telling you this, but she calls and cries over the phone, and it's not only anger. She misses you. But she's so stubborn."

"Molly, we're both confused. I have to work some things out. This is really my fault."

"Don't be too hard on yourself. Nothing will change then. You know I love you, Len. I love my daughter more, but you and Jake come a photo-finish second."

"Thanks, Molly. That's nice to hear. How's autumn in Boston?"

"Beautiful. Sunny and crisp like it should be. Are you still having that New York Indian summer?"

"A Calcutta Indian summer. We're dry and dusty and high-smelling down here. Molly?"

"Yes?"

"Thanks. I need to figure things out, but I want to . . . Thanks. You coming for Thanksgiving?"

"No, you're all coming up here. And I expect everything resolved or at least resolving by then. Do you hear, Len?"

"Yes, ma'am. I can't see where Karen gets her stubbornness."

"No, dear, I haven't a clue either. Good-bye. Much love. Good-bye."

Maybe he should write to Karen in order to clarify things? But, oh God, writing to the person you're living with? Weekends. Why didn't he just go down to D.C. and turn up at the Corcoran and whisk Karen off to dinner and dancing and bed? Why? Because she was probably booked. For dinner, he meant, only for dinner. Besides, he could imagine the embarrassed silence from Dr. Hammacher Schlemmer, Viennese professor of Sienese painting, when he answered "Private dick. Used to be public."

So, instead of taking the shuttle, he took the shammy and washed the windows.

Mark came by as Schwartz was standing on the bow windowsill.

"There you are. Susie said she saw you."

"Hi, Mark. How's the window look?"

"See-throughable, in a glassy sort of way. Hey, what's your opinion on all the windows here with police supporter stickers? You're one of the few houses without."

"Well, I'm the thing itself, aren't I? Anyway, they're depressing. Proclamations of paranoia. What are you doing these days?"

"Into another book. Boring. Me, I mean, not the book. The book's impossible."

"Sounds nice."

"Yeah," Mark said. "So your professional opinion is those stickers don't work?"

"They don't change burglary rates. Maybe they make the people who put them up less afraid." Schwartz pushed open the window, crouched and put his legs inside.

Mark waved. "You're one weird policeman, Mr. Len. Come over for a drink sometime, you and Karen."

"Thanks, Mark. I will. We . . ." Schwartz waved back from behind the closed window. He couldn't tell the neighbors of his private eyeship. Was he ashamed or was he protecting their peace of fantasy—their living police sticker, the "Warning, Bad Dog" sign on the fence, when inside was an aging cocker spaniel?

After the windows, he dusted, he vacuumed, he polished furniture. He'd have made someone a nice husband. He even looked out back at the small, wild yard. It snarled at him; he'd attack it some other time.

Noon. He went down to the liquor store to get Irish whiskey for Gallagher and resisted Frank's offer of one called "Celtic Twilight" as sounding too like an evening with Lady Gregory at Boston Garden (Frank taking down the Jameson with a handshake). But he fell victim of his own literary sentimentality, buying the tequila whose label showed a cactus under a volcano.

Anyway, what was wrong with getting in what Gallagher drank?

"Nothing," Tom said. "I don't want anything to drink, Lenny, thanks. Well."

"Well, we've been through handshakes at the door and mutual agreement at the stinkiness of the weather, for the season. We've sat down, comfortably, I hope, and I'm able to say you don't seem to have aged much in the three weeks or so since I last saw you."

"I'm not even gonna take offense at that, you sonofa-bitch," said Gallagher, stretching his legs, running his hand over his chest. "Oh, and I'm—I mean it—I'm sorry I said 'sonofabitch' because this is Karen's house, too, and I know how she feels about that word and she is such a good woman."

"I know."

"No, you don't, you sonofabitch! Jesus, no, you don't. You treat her like shit! I hate this cool act. You can kick me out of here and never see me again, but damn it, not before I tell you a thing or two!"

"Tell away," Schwartz said, shrugging.

"All right. Lemme calm down," he said, pulling his sprawled legs back tensely. "She's called me, told—"

"Called you?"

"Are you gonna let me talk? Jesus D. Christ! She's called me, talked to me about it. I been over here—"

"Here? You've been here?"

"Yeah, here, here. Will you—"

"Sorry. It's just . . . Go on," said Schwartz.

"Well, she's told me. That's all. How you didn't even tell her. Are you nuts? This is a woman you don't . . . Listen, you've always come on to me as having—I don't say a perfect—but, you know, all this feminism stuff, an . . . an equality. Jesus! And you didn't . . . I'll tell you, I may be the chauvinist pig you say, but never in a million years would I do something like that to Kitty. Jesus, Lenny, Karen was in tears. That strong woman in tears, I'm telling you."

"What else did she say?"

Gallagher pulled his shoulders back. The plaid of his shirt stretched tight. His voice was quieter. "She didn't tell me what you're afraid of telling me—the bribe, which of course you never took, because . . . No. She talked about your career problems. She's so damned loyal to you. And she talked about her career taking off and the pressure that may be putting on you—and her. For someone so miserable, she talked very sensibly."

"And you're going to say you can't see what she sees in me, but—"

"No. Hey, I'll have a drink. You got any Jameson?"

"I'll see."

When Schwartz returned with ice and glasses and lime, Gallagher stood at Karen's rolltop desk.

"You know," he said, taking the glass, "Kitty and I have always liked Karen a lot. We don't—me especially—understand a lot of what she does, art history, but she's a good person. Funny and warm and we love her. And I'm raising this glass to you two. Get it together, Lenny. If you don't, if you split up, I promise you I'll chase you and find you and with these two hands I'll beat the shit out of you."

"I don't know that I should drink to all of that, Tom, but seeing how it's you, why not." Schwartz drank back his tequila and sucked the lime, thinking maybe the lime should have come first. "Does this mean Karen wants to stay with me?"

"Sure it does. Why the hell do you think I'm here now? I mean, I guess it took Karen to get me off my high horse," Gallagher said, frowning, shuffling about as if on a high horse. He sat again.

Schwartz sat on the other side of the ice and two bottles. "Thanks, Tom." He thought that if he could tell Tom—Tom knew about the bribe, but if he could *tell* him, then maybe he could tell Jake. "Tom—"

"Listen, Lenny. I gotta tell you the truth. No games. The department needs you. Of course, it's my own career that I'm thinking of. Also, I mean. I'm taking another Jameson because I see nobody drinks it around here but me." Gallagher dropped in an ice cube and half filled the glass with whiskey. "I'd put water in this, but you know how the city's trying to save water. Ha! Listen, you know I'll beg you if you want. To come back. You know?"

"Jesus Christ, Tom! Don't beg me for anything. You beg me, and I promise I'll find you and beat the crap out of you with these two hands and these two feet and maybe some hired help. So let's just, uh, not . . . Well, what's happening at headquarters?"

"The word—keep this to yourself—the word is that our beloved commissioner is soon saying good-bye. My money, if I were a betting man, would be on Don Phillips."

"And your heart?"

Gallagher leaned forward so that his wide black belt disappeared under his belly. "It might interest you to know that Don Phillips is the best chief of detectives I've ever served under, and I think he's the best choice for commissioner and I know how you think I'm such a bigot, but I think his being black would be a damn good thing for the force and this city. What do you say to that?"

"I'm not surprised, Tom. You've always been the sharpest politician in the department. You know, I send my boy to Yale on some good stock investment, and everyone assumes I'm guilty of taking drug money. You, on the other hand, have a Riverdale condo, a Westhampton beach palazzo—Westhampton, for Christ's sake—and that place in Jersey you own, and everybody thinks you're Mr. Germ-free." Schwartz swirled the tequila around the ice and drank it. He'd forget about the lime.

"You're not going to rile me with that, Lenny. You know we rented Riverdale until we had a chance to buy it cheap. And Westhampton was—well, there was Kitty's inheritance and a big mortgage and some luck, and the Jersey place cost nothing when we were married, but I'll tell you it's trouble now. I want your advice, as a matter of fact. But to finish what we're talking about: I have my own problems with department housecleaners. But the difference between us is that I can get on with it because I know I'm a good cop, whatever they think. I really am. You really are, Lenny, but you think you aren't because . . . You know. Well, you've served this city very well. Despite all that other, and I'm not here as your father confessor. *Slainthe!*" said Gallagher, tipping back his whiskey.

"I want your advice on a problem," he said after smacking his lips. "It's driving Kitty and me crazy. You know Patsy, our oldest?"

"Sure. I saw her and her husband last summer, at your Labor Day party."

"Right. Well, you know we let her and Mike live in the Jersey house for a low rent, for really no rent, these past two years, what with him having trouble finding the right job. It's been tough. Anyhow, now he's landed this very good engineering job and wants to buy the house, bit by bit, at market price from me."

"Don't you want to sell it?"

"That's not it. I don't need to sell it, but, you see, now Patsy's pregnant and not working, and Mike wants to buy the house. And Patsy's talked with Kitty and me and wants the house to be hers."

"Are they okay, Patsy and Mike?"

"Sure. That's not the problem. I tell Patsy that in law, if anything did happen, they'd split it fifty–fifty. I also tell her that if anything did happen I'd break her neck and she'd be excommunicated and I'd never speak to her again. I do that just to remind her I love her. But Kitty says I should have given Patsy the house outright for her wedding. Well, that would have been a tax mess and, besides, it would have spoiled her. But if I give her the house now, I piss Mike off; he feels, you know, unmanly or something, in Patsy's eyes. But if I sell Mike the house, Patsy feels I'm some kind of unfatherly sexist shit, not to mention Kitty's feelings."

"What about letting things go on as they are?" Schwartz asked, his nose on the tequila, his eyes on Gallagher, his mind in Cuernavaca.

"Then everyone's pissed. The kids own nothing, Kitty thinks I'm selfish, I continue losing money—not that it's a big deal, but the kids can afford more. So what do I do?"

"First, you pour another Jameson. Good. Then—you really want my advice?"

"Yeah. Cheers."

"Cheers." Schwartz tossed it down. "Brr. Then, if that's the house they want, you give it to Patsy and tell Mike he can buy his half on time from her, monthly payments. A formal contract, even. Patsy has her security and dignity, and so does Mike. And you've done the right thing by Kitty, too."

"That's not bad. Some small problems, but not bad. Very nice. I didn't think you'd . . . I never—"

"I know, Tom. You brought it up to show me I'm not alone in having woes. Maybe then I'd talk about, oh, I don't know—cocaine bribes, or something."

"Jesus!" Gallagher pushed out from the chair. The whiskey bottle fell off the coffee table and rolled to his feet. "You . . ." He stopped to pick up the bottle. "It's closed. There's no stain. You know, you got more macho uptightness than me, Mr. Liberated Liberal. You're so defensive, you're offensive. You're arrogant." Gallagher went back to Karen's desk. "You think I wanna know so I'll have something to hold over you? You ain't so smart. I have more on you now because you're so wound up worrying I believe you took the bribe."

"Just what Karen says."

"Lenny, you went through that investigation. You paid your dues for three, four years afterwards."

"For five."

"Whatever, five. And now, frankly, I don't give a shit. Don't tell me. What I want is for you to come back to the department. Sure, things go on, and I know I'm a good cop. But of a kind. You're a good cop of another kind and we work good together. But I'm not gonna bore you. You don't want me to go on, I won't. Just to prove it."

"Prove what?"

"I don't know, to prove whatever. It's true that right after you left I was so pissed I didn't want anyone inside helping you make a private career. But then I thought, hey, what am I doing? Not only was he a good partner and a pal, but that's no way to get him back."

"There is no way to get me back."

"Sure, okay. So I know Malinowski and Santini are helping you, and I'm not standing in their way. I'm not gonna interrupt my staff's work for you, but little favors from others—okay. So what's it like, this case, this PI stuff?"

"Frustrating. I have to relearn everything because I don't have a team of experts or labs or a fat databank at my disposal;

"Yeah. What's this about the Simp?"

"Just something involving someone he did the honors for. Some problems getting him to tell me about it. Nothing, really."

Gallagher smiled. "I thought you were his great and only buddy."

"No. I was just the one who called him 'Simpkin.' "

Gallagher scratched at the side of his jaw. "And how's the money?"

"Okay."

"Come on, come on. I'm not asking you about your con-fidential case. What's the money?"

"Five hundred a day plus expenses."

Gallagher stared. "You're not kidding? Jesus D. Christ!"

"Tom, I've always wondered what the 'D' stood for."

"What? I don't know. Dear Christ! That's a lot of money."

"Oh?"

"Don't get me wrong. If you were a big or established agency, that would be the going . . . What I mean is, your client must want you, and I mean *you,* badly."

"Well, yes. As an ex-senior cop . . . You think there's some sort of setup in that price?"

"No, not if your client has the dough and wants you. No, maybe not."

"Maybe? Oh, that's very reassuring. Well, out of that I give an assistant a hundred. So."

"Who do you have?"

"Addison. You know, we've used him a few times."

"The crazy bastard from Brighton Beach? Can you con-trol him?"

"No, he's a pain in the ass. But he's good."

"Yeah. But you watch it. The whole thing sounds . . . Ah, forget it. I'm just jealous and want you back. Hey, how the hell can you drink that junk? I had some once. It was like meths."

"Ah, well. The ex-British consul and I are made of Sterno stuff. Tom, you ever hear of someone in Public Health named Weiss, C. Richard Weiss?"

Gallagher shook his head. "No. What I wanna know is, what are you gonna do about you and Karen? I want to know, Kitty wants to know. The Kerry Association wants to know."

"Very touching, especially as Karen's people are from County Mayo. I think I'm going to try to succeed at this case, in this new job."

"Oh. And what happened to the idea of public service? For eighteen years I've heard that idealistic bullshit from you every day."

"Maybe I've found it *is* bullshit."

"Bullshit! You mind if I have a cigar?"

"Yes, I do."

"You're as bad as . . . Saturdays I have one, *outside the house*! Look, if you don't mind hearing it from a thick mick: if you think doing well as a private eye or brain surgeon is gonna fix things between you and Karen, you're one very stupid smart hebe."

"You are neither 'thick' nor a 'mick.' I am not a 'hebe.' I'm also not smart, like you say. You're right that I have to regain Karen's trust. You're right that I . . ." Schwartz stopped because the tequila was at the back of his head, pressing its cactus fingers deep into a needle numbness. "Dumbness, Tom."

"Huh?"

"It's just come to me after five years."

"What's up? That stuff getting to you?"

"No. This is . . . I can't tell you, but now I *know* why I can't. It's terrific, actually. Isn't that terrific? I mean, you'll have to take my word for it." Schwartz was up, walking to the window behind Gallagher.

"Terrific, Lenny. You should switch to whiskey. Scotch if you don't like Irish, but something, you know, American."

"Tom," said Schwartz, looking out at two kids walking up either side of the street, throwing a football back and forth over the parked cars, "it's helped, your coming over."

"Good. Mind you, I don't know exactly what I'm gonna report to Karen. But I'll say you feel encouraged."

"When are you speaking with Karen?"

"Wednesday. She's coming over for dinner. I hope I can make it, but Kitty will give her your message if I can't."

"I'm glad she's seeing you and Kitty. I thought she . . . I don't know."

"Thought she got too big for the Irish cop and his wife?"

"Something like that, not to mention the Jewish cop and his life."

Gallagher put his hand on Schwartz's shoulder. "She's okay and so are you. And I'm glad to hear you still know you're a cop."

"Ex-cop. Fine rising private investigator. Drop over at my office. It's on—"

"Yeah, yeah. Warren Street."

"That doesn't mean you should leave."

"No. It's . . . Jesus, it's after four and I still have to pick up something for Kitty. You okay?"

"Okay. It's you who have to drive. I don't. Couldn't if I wanted to. Not that I'm incapacitated, but the car is. Incapacitated. The car is also not drunk."

"Well, that makes three of us. Take care, Lenny."

"I'll see you to the door."

"Great house you got. Great *home*, if you catch my meaning."

"Subtle as it is, Thomas, I think I caught it. Thanks." Schwartz watched Gallagher go down the street toward his car, steadily enough.

Steady enough. Schwartz would have to be. If he started calling today, continued tomorrow, maybe he could set up the meeting. And yet he'd come so close to telling Tom: it *took* coming so close to make him realize why he couldn't. He was afraid. It made him feel wonderful. Not moral cowardice. All this time he hadn't told Tom about the bribe because he feared for his and Karen's and Jake's life. Because if Tom knew, they'd know he knew. As it was . . .

In the living room, Schwartz poured a large tequila and

put on a Bud Powell cassette. Terrific. As it was, they still owed him. Wouldn't that be their thinking? He could learn what they thought, very clearly, maybe even next week. They'd do him the favor or they'd kill him.

It had a sort of off-beat logic, like Bud playing "Un Poco Loco," like this one more tequila in memory of the ex-cop, he meant ex-consul.

CHAPTER **6**

Schwartz woke on Sunday feeling the tenderest top holes of his skull, his eyes and his temples, imploded onto cactus needles.

Between the first and second phone calls, he took a cold shower and iced down his forehead. Between the second and third, he found the hatchet and rake; he didn't dare set fire to so dry a backyard. When he'd hacked through to the weed hillock (matto grosso under the Brownstono) he found it based on an ancient, forgotten box spring. A cave-in somewhere behind his ear accompanied the pain as he pulled up the creepers.

How many days had he spent out here this morning between eleven and two? He left the yard in two pyramids of trash; one in a biodegradable state, the other a Reich of garbage that would last a thousand years.

The third phone call came at four when Schwartz was again in the shower. It gave him the same address he'd known five years ago, the same shock to think it was the neighborhood he'd grown up in. It gave him a meeting tomorrow at four.

He was still on the bed, the damp just soaking through the towel, when he heard Karen in the hall. She went into the kitchen. The groan would be her looking through the window. Here she came. She'd say, "What's happened out there?" and he'd say, "By next weekend, we'll have the basis of a garden."

"Len?" she called. She came in. "Len, hi. What have you done to the yard?"

"Do you want to divorce me?"

Karen opened her mouth. "Oh," she said. She began to cry. She stood with her hands to her eyes, shaking her head, crying.

He went to hold her. "I had to hear it from you. I heard it from Molly on the phone and from Tom who came over yesterday. Shh." Her back, under his patting hand, heaved and sank. "Shh. It's all right. We can . . . They were very sweet, Molly and Tom."

"I don't . . ." Karen said and choked. She coughed and went to the box of tissues by the bed. Her tan skirt had a large damp stain from Schwartz's towel. "I haven't bawled *this* much, have I?" She looked up with a smile, but when she met his eyes she started to cry.

He went to her.

"No, the towel." She pointed.

He dropped the towel and held her.

"I hate to cry like this. It's so weak, so . . ." she cried. "What are we going to do?"

"Maybe we could see someone. Let's just . . . Shh. I'll stay."

Karen pulled her head back. "It's wrong. It wouldn't help. You could, the way I feel you could seduce me to let you stay. Don't. Please. Don't." She pulled herself hard into him.

Early the next morning, Schwartz woke and looked at Karen sleeping, an arm fallen back, her hair fallen half over her face, the sheet fallen away from her breast. He could stay. They'd make love all morning. But then . . . What? She'd feel . . . He kissed her and left the bed.

At the bottom of the Warren Street stairs he again became depressed. Was this his office? His loft? Maybe it would cheer him to name it like a grand West Side apartment house. The Elba, the St. Helena?

By any name, the place had been broken into—carefully. Certain too-neat replacements showed someone had been through everything. Addison, arriving ten minutes later, agreed with Schwartz that someone could only want to know what they'd found. Schwartz said luckily that was very little and had all been at home with him. They agreed it could have been done by or on behalf of anyone involved.

Addison wondered if that extended to Schwartz's police contacts but swore he was only joking when he saw Schwartz's pained expression. He suggested that Schwartz relax by doing some "trans-incidental meditation or chapati yoga."

Schwartz declined and set up a very tight work schedule for Addison: accounts in the morning and Ann McCarthy in the afternoon. "Be tough with her, in your cutest nonviolent way," said Schwartz, thinking this was as good a lead as any to keep working on and that it would keep Addison from tailing him.

Schwartz killed time, fidgeted. The case was making him a whiz of a fidget, a maniacally busy do-nothing. If Addison only knew.

At five to noon, Addison announced he'd be finished with the bookkeeping in five minutes.

"How can you work so exactly?"

"What exactly? I'm screwing around like you, make thirty minutes work go two and a half hours. You think in Odessa we don't learn good American business practice?"

Schwartz wished him a nice two-hour lunch during his thirty-minute lunch break. And with Addison gone he could concentrate on this very risky meeting, but all he could come up with was not to carry a gun. He set the alarm, lay down on his bed and slept like a baby, or a madman, for three hours.

The subway train was full of messengers and hand-delivery men. No motorcycles, no trucks here under Metropolis. Here the cargo moved by hand and foot, by human pack animals, *untermenschen*, under the city. He couldn't describe it. America needed a Brecht, an Eisler to describe it. But America had Brecht and Eisler. It had them investigated and kicked out.

If he got out here at Bergen he'd be home in ten minutes. Home. Or here at Grand Army Plaza. Kicked out of his home. Three more stops.

Schwartz got out at the second, Franklin and Eastern Parkway. At least he'd have time to clear his head.

But how could it be clearer? Nothing stayed in there. A thought would come in, look around, think "Is this *Schwartz's* head on its way to see *Montanares*? No, thanks!" and flee without noticing the doorman who worked only for tips.

The tip was: Flee. Get the hell out of your old neighborhood while . . .

There was Bobby Abelman's old house and what's-her-name, Marcia Wax's. The childhood map still intact. The synagogue—Kehileth Yisroael—now the Universal Baptist Tabernacle. And next to it, the same shutters but half off, the front porch where Stu Mirski's father had caught them smoking and believed he'd morally persuaded them to go to the police and turn themselves in, actually a softer option then letting Mr. Mirski tell their fathers.

But at the corner of Nostrand his childhood deserted him and he thought of Montanares's necklaces. Ten years ago, Juan

Montanares had been running extortion loan offices, and what hung from the chain was a heavy chunk of gold. Five years later, he'd moved up to much bigger and riskier drug money, and a very large diamond had been set into the gold so that the effect was of a little sun within a molten, baroque cage. During their negotiations Schwartz had looked at the trapped light, unable to look Juan in the eye.

Schwartz crossed the crowded avenue and went into the loading alley between the fruit-and-vegetable and yard good stores. A big Korean kid was dragging sacks of potatoes from a small truck into the side door as Schwartz squeezed past.

He found the buzzer in the hallway. The wooden door opened. He went in. It shut. The inside of the door was steel. Schwartz kept his eyes down.

"What are you carrying?"

"Just my best wishes," said Schwartz, as he lifted his hands, feeling hands pat him and slide quickly and thoroughly.

"You can go up."

Schwartz went to the top landing, looking down at his feet on each plank. The guard at the top frisked him again, again well. The guard opened the door.

"Through there."

The same faint smell of bananas and garlic and decaying greens from five years back came to him in the hallway. The place was a rat trap, a rival trap, a police trap or a Schwartz trap, if he weren't careful. This door was in the next building: there were probably exits back here into two different streets, but this was the only way in and out that he knew. He entered the small, plain, air-conditioned office.

"I'm here to see Juan," he said to the blue silk suit behind the desk.

"In there. You're expected," it said from behind gray shades.

Before he reached the door it opened.

"Lenny Schwartz! Very nice. Come in, get out of the cold," said Montanares, shaking Schwartz's hand.

The inside office was sealed. The windows were one-way metal-stripped glass with bars outside. The heating was on. A large wooden ceiling fan slowly churned the air, which was in the high nineties and steamy. Two men in short-sleeved white shirts sat behind two desks flanking the central desk to which Montanares went, indicating the deep leather chair to Schwartz.

"You remember Julio and Roberto?"

He certainly did. He nodded, they nodded back. Everything was the same, except that Montanares dressed less flashily; the bauble hanging from the chain was tucked into the tan silk shirt under the dark jacket.

"I have to tell you this is no surprise, Lenny. I knew you'd come. I've been expecting you, somewhere back here or here," Montanares said, tapping his head and then his chest.

"You look good, Juan, considering the strains of your business. Do you still wear that diamond?"

"This?" said Montanares, running his finger under the chain. "This is different." He pulled it up and held out a cross, three inches long and two wide. It was made of four emeralds.

"Very grand," said Schwartz.

"Three hundred and fifty years old. It's a present from a Colombian associate. Colombia is the land where the emeralds grow." Montanares tucked the cross back in, smiling.

He would have been a conventionally handsome, large-eyed and perfect-toothed ladino-mestizo but for the high arch of his left nostril and leftward pull of the end of his nose, which gave his face a gentle and good-humored turn. "I wear this," he said, "but I don't flash it. I'm more careful these days."

"You were careful back then."

"Not as careful as you, Lenny. You taught me. That

seventy-five grand we settled on disappeared so fast and so well that to this day I don't know how you did it." He raised the fingers on his hand; they had fewer and plainer rings. "And I don't want to know. Good market investments and your son in a fancy college. That's good. You should be pleased."

Schwartz felt the top of his left foot itch. Sweat. He rubbed it with his right. "It was in my interest to take very good care of that money."

"Sure, sure. You earned it. You kept your word. We know. We watched. You don't know, or maybe you do, how many policemen break their promises, get greedy, get scared, try to lean on you for more and more, try to turn you in. And lots of them try both." Montanares shook his head. There were smaller echoing headshakes from Julio and Roberto.

"A list of their names would make interesting reading, but that's not why I'm here, Juan."

"I know, Lenny. I know a lot. You're a private eye, private *investigator* now. As I say, we watched you. All this time they leaned on you and you said nothing. You're a man of your word. It must have been tough. And we would have helped, but you wouldn't come to us because you're proud. I respect that, too. We've been impressed. That's so, isn't it, Roberto?"

"Yes."

"Julio?"

"Yes."

"I'll also tell you this, Lenny. Five years ago I paid a good price for your favor, but it came at a very important time. My business would have developed anyway, but not so smoothly, not with everything *intact*, without that help from you. Now you've come to me and I'm glad to see you. I owe you. Can I say it fairer?"

"Very fair, Juan."

"Wait. Before you say anything, I want to tell you something else, right up front. I hope what you want is a real business relationship. Heh, Lenny Schwartz. You know me as a man who doesn't lie. In three years with me you could make a million dollars. At least."

Schwartz smiled. It was the open, benign expression of Montanares's face that angered and frightened him. He scratched his thigh to steady his shaking right hand. No wisecracks, no insults. "Thanks, Juan, but I'm doing all right." There. Better. If this sentimental smiler felt insulted, he could butcher Schwartz's family and make him watch. "I'm here because I'm drawing a blank trying to get a little information, and I want to ask your help."

"I'm listening."

"I'm trying to find out about the death of a client's son last April. He could have died of AIDS, it could have been suicide, it could have been a snuff show. I want to know about the snuff show—not the organizers. I'm not interested. I'm trying to clear up a confusing coroner's report. It could have been a snuff show from the way the body was painted—dark blue with gold veining all over—and the injuries, which could have come from clubbing and whipping, maybe impalement. So it would have been an elaborate show, last April, the sixth to the eighth. I only want to know the circumstances of his death, his condition, how he got there. Here's a photosheet of him and of the other players I'm aware of."

Montanares nodded to Julio, who came around his desk, took the sheet from Schwartz and sat down again.

"Oh, I tried to find out through Pignatelli, but he got his fingers slapped for asking and I think I got burnt, too. So I'll understand if you don't want to bother." There, that was his best hook.

Montanares was quiet. The other two were always quiet. The fan spun quietly.

It was hot. Sweat ran down the channel of Schwartz's spine. The damp spread along the elastic of his underpants. This was an awful place, awful company. He was awful for being here.

"Lenny, this would be a big favor, but not because of the Italians. They've had it too easy for too long. Italians go to Atlantic City for a weekend of blackjack, they think they're living dangerously. They're soft." Montanares pulled out the emerald crucifix and looked into it. "I think we understand each other, Lenny, because we're alike. You're what, five or six years older? In good shape, I see, but your face has aged too much for five years. You got bad worry lines. Your eyes blink too much."

He paused and then went on. "Never mind. I'll tell you why this is a big favor. Seven or eight years ago, when the heat came down hard on these shows, the people involved, who were always very high-strung, became crazy. It was, you know, one of those pet peeves the police sometimes get. There weren't so many convictions, but a number of people managed to die while in custody. One way or the other. So these days there are very few real snuff shows, and the ones that go get kept very quiet."

"Juan, if you can't, you can't."

"I didn't say that. I owe you. I'm just explaining why it's a big favor. And I wouldn't do it for any other policeman or ex-policeman. Right?"

"Right," Schwartz nodded. "Thank you, Juan. How long do you think it might take?" Schwartz heard his voice as if it came from the wall behind him.

"Days or maybe weeks. Not months. That's all I can tell you. It's been very nice seeing you."

Schwartz stood and shook hands with Montanares. "Thank you. Good-bye, Juan."

"Good-bye, Lenny. Lenny Schwartz, heh. It's been very nice. Hasn't it, Julio? Roberto?"

"Yes."

"Yes."

"We'll be seeing more of you, Lenny," were the words Schwartz shut the door on, walked through the cool office and down the dark hall with, went through the door and across the guarded landing with, and down the stairs and past the downstairs guard with and was buzzed out, out with those words into the thickening dust-light of the alley.

Montanares said they were alike; Montanares would be seeing more of him. Montanares didn't lie.

Schwartz bought a pound of emerald granny smiths from the store. He took one from the bag and crossed the avenue. He rubbed the apple on his pants.

Juan was right. Schwartz had just done the worst thing in his life. Wrong; taking the bribe from Juan had been the worst. This was second worst—another killer five-year plan. And for what, stupid vanity? The case? But what would he do even if he were to learn about a snuff show?

The apple was too sour. He threw it in a garbage can. He stopped a young boy and offered him the bag with two apples.

The boy backed off a step and frowned. "My momma tell me don' never take nothin' from no stranger man, specially no white man."

"Your mother is absolutely right," said Schwartz to the boy. "Sorry."

An old, heavy black woman tapped his arm. "Sir, you givin' them, I'll take 'em. Guess I'm *way* pass gettin' in trouble takin' anythin' from any man!" She thanked him, laughing.

He should have, he thought, for gallantry, argued the point with her. He wanted the sweetness of her laugh. He went into a store called "Dixie-Whip" and came out licking a long, swirling puff of flavored cold vegetable fat. This he couldn't give away. If he tried offering sweets to passing children he'd probably be arrested. Very fitting. He glanced at the gutter but couldn't add to the ghetto filth he needn't live with.

So he walked with the cone, holding it farther and farther out in front of him as it dripped faster. He felt guilty about the filth. He felt guilty about his own prissy bourgeois guilt. Gutter filth was nothing to his own.

He was half running along the grass verge of Eastern Parkway. He stopped and squatted by a pile of leaves and set the cone inside it. He used some leaves to wipe his hand. The leaves powdered. The palm of his hand was dry leaf bits and sticky Crisco. It served him right, supporting a firm that cheated its poor black clientele. "Dixie-Whip"—the name was mean and Klannish.

He stood looking at the peeling, set-back house. Marcia Wax's. Marcia Wax! Oh God, his first feel of a woman's breasts. A heavy twelve-year-old's plump buddings. Marcia. What had they felt like? Wax. Like soft wax. There'd been a chant. What had they chanted, the cruel bastard boys, he, too?

> *Marcia's wax!*
> *Marcia's cracks!*
> *Something, something*
> *With Ex-Lax!*

This was the sort of thing he remembered. He wiped his hands together. Both now stuck with leaf-grease. Let him try to remember something better—some Virgil or Pliny or Cicero—and his mind went blank.

He stood in the middle of the broad, broken sidewalk stretching out his arms, unsticking his fingers, and called, "I'm sorry, neighborhood, I let you down."

A teenage boy was walking by with a blaster to his ear. "You go for it, man," he said pleasantly.

It seemed a sensible suggestion. Schwartz went for it via the Lexington Avenue Express to Warren Street, thinking and trying to remember. But all he managed was *sic transit gloria corona* Heights—*corona altumi?*

CHAPTER 7

"Addison," he asked, coming in, "do you know Latin?"

"I got my own problems."

"What?"

"I catch this Ann McCarthy, who is, believe me, a fabulously sensational looker, boss, at the foolish, terrible empty art show, you should excuse me, Malevich does for once is too much seventy years ago. Nothing on nothing, this show should be."

"Art later, Addison. Ann McCarthy now."

"Sure. I show photos without saying nothing. She says yes, identifies Virgil Jimmy and ones of parents and not know the Simpkies and of course know her old boss, but when this one she sees of the man looking like you but bald and better dressed—"

"On, Addison!"

"Of Weiss, her face change and she say no, but she mean she's scared. So I get strict, tell her to tell truth in her own defense. She finally say this man is police officer who questions her last April when Hayes dies."

"Weiss? No. This photo? What's it mean?"

"Ah, but I say name 'Weiss,' she say definitely not name. Name, she not sure; Williams, Wilson maybe."

"Why should Weiss pose as a policeman to ask Ann McCarthy questions? What questions?"

"She's saying routine, like real cop asks. When she last see? If anything she know make Hayes sad? She's answering me straight, but I tell you she still is scared plenty and isn't saying some things. Hey, maybe Weiss not even a real official?"

"I've checked. He's definitely known in Public Health, listed on federal record."

"Boss, I got something else for us. Letter finally come from Cal Tech to Braverman, Braverman give it me. I give you digest?"

"Digest away."

"Okay, is colleague saying this V. J. Hayes very bright, hardworking mathematician. Very abstract. He goes to institute at Princeton in summer and holidays for maths. So, four years ago starts going with girlfriend—this Ann—and becomes very more political. Is marching, is on sitting-downs, standing for antinuclear movement, nonproliferations, and saying everywhere West and East Coasts to nuclear power no, thanks. By two years later spends less time at Cal Tech and tells his colleague sometimes is chased and attacked for knowing too much. But about what, is not saying. Anyway, this colleague thinks VJ going nuts and then disappears for year and a half or so and then finding out he's dead."

"Two years ago Ann McCarthy supposedly got scared off the antinuclear movement. That's when she says she split up with Virgil. Maybe what he was into—real or imagined—scared her off.

Addison, what do I pay you? It's too little. One-fifty a day from now on."

"Thanks, boss, for terrific raise. Is still too little, but thanks, boss. I enter right away in good bookkeeping. Here's letter."

Schwartz took the five pages of single-spaced typing. "Does your friend Braverman have a copy?"

"No, he gives this first, ask we make a copy I give him back."

"We'll do no such thing for a while."

"Aha! Boss, you so tricky I could learn from you forever, especially with pay going up. What is now?"

"Now is quitting time. Go home, do the books tomorrow. I want to read through the letter and see if we can come up with another approach. Addison? What's out there?"

"Is big change. Coming is dark clouds from Jersey. Windy, going be cool and wet."

"About time. Maybe we'll get you to see if anything is still out in Simpkin's on Staten Island, this week. On foot, this time. I've already set aside the fifty cents for your trip."

"Good night boss. Keep making jokes perk up your spirits."

Schwartz went to the window. A breeze was blowing, cooler, bringing massed dark clouds, puffed gray and purple. And there below went Addison, scudding through the homeward crowd, a burly cloud in trousers.

Schwartz sat and looked at the letter. So Virgil had become antinuclear. No wonder his right-wing father didn't like Ann McCarthy. But how could that get Virgil painted into a snuff show?

Schwartz rocked back on the spring of the desk chair. Maybe he did need to be part of a big team; maybe he wasn't up to much on his own.

Oh yeah? He certainly was up to . . . well, up to going to a good film tonight. He'd listen to the weather.

The phone rang.

Let it be Karen, lonely in the coming storm, needing his warmth.

"Hello?"

"Leonard Schwartz?"

"Yes."

"C. Richard Weiss. Mr. Schwartz, I've been reassessing this Virgil Hayes matter. There are details requiring clarification on my part."

"So I'm finding, Dr. Weiss."

"That's one of them: it's not 'Doctor.' Could we meet in my office, say on Wednesday, at one o'clock, if that would be convenient?"

"I don't know."

"Room 1045 in the Government Office Building, the Lafayette Street entrance."

"Someone else's office, again?"

"No, it's my office. The PHS was a cover. I'm with the Central Intelligence Agency, Mr. Schwartz."

"More games? What's your story—AIDS is a Sandinista plot?"

"Virgil James Hayes was an agent of the Soviet Union."

Schwartz heard his own breathing come off the mouth-piece. "I'll see you on Wednesday at one."

"Good. We'll clear up everything. Bye," Weiss said crisply.

Schwartz went back to the window. A few first drops of rain hit the sill. Large drops. Dust shot up in the splatter. Good. The wind was colder. Montanares hated cold weather. Good.

B O O K III

C H A P T E R 1

Schwartz stood at the window as the evening rain became a warm summer thunderstorm. On a top-floor fire escape balcony across the street, a young man in blue shorts was shampooing a young woman. She sat on a yellow chair, in white bra and under-pants. His hands were under the lather in her long hair. He threw back his head and smiled openmouthed into the rain. He bent and kissed her neck and spat out lather, laughing. He put a hand over her face, his other on her neck, and pulled her head back to keep the shampoo from her eyes. He bent deeper and kissed her. Her hand stroked his thigh.

Schwartz stepped back from the window. Was voyeurism legitimate practice for private eyes? He peeked out. The man's hands were on her breasts. What was the city coming to? And why couldn't he get there, too?

He changed and ran up Broadway and around City Hall.

In thick rain, the Woolworth Building was a gothic ruin and the tor it stood on. But it was cold, or that couple had warmth he'd lost.

He ran back. They'd gone in from the balcony, and the buildings looked streaky with rain. Schwartz thought of the man's hands on the woman's face, a mask of fingers.

By seven on Tuesday morning, Schwartz was up and again at the window. The rain was harder and the wind had picked up.

He sat at Addison's desk and wrote him a list of jobs. Then he ripped it up and set out the first job in more detail and then the second. Schwartz was still writing when Addison showed up as a Gloucester fisherman, except for the sou'wester hat with union jack design.

"Addison, good morning and don't answer. Here are notes which overdirect you in several tasks. Take your pick. Considering the weather, you might want to start with the indoor jobs. My bad mood, by the way, has nothing to do with your splendid self or spiffy rain gear, which, thanks anyway, I don't want to buy, cheap as it doubtless is. I'll want to confer with you this evening or tomorrow, early. 'Confer' is not a pine tree and I'm leaving. Say nothing, Addison, or only good-bye."

Addison opened the door for Schwartz, stood to attention and, putting his fingers to his mouth, imitated a bosun's pipe so well that Schwartz was obliged to salute.

Outside, the rain had muddied. Schwartz saw it drip brown off his umbrella tips. What was this? Uncle Maurie, whose atheism had never kept him from speaking ill of the Deity, might have said that God had told the wind, "Wash up that dust bowl down there, do it fast, and I don't care where you get rid of the dirty water. New York? Fine. There they won't notice the difference."

Schwartz checked this theory—the dirty rain part—with Sid at the coffee shop.

"Yeah, Lenny, it's filthy. It's disgusting, the color of your bran muffin. Here's your coffee. Enjoy."

Nor could he enjoy the subway with an odor worse than its usual dank of ozone and pee.

Out on Seventy-seventh Street, he huddled into his raincoat, slanted the umbrella across his shoulder and went east.

Now it was a combination rainstorm and sandstorm. When Schwartz turned north he was caught in a downpour and updraft so violent that it rained at him up from the pavement, as if Third Avenue had become a bidet. Up his trouser legs, up under his raincoat, under his chin, a sour, greasy rain. It was a nightmare. He rubbed grit from his eyes like sleep.

Five minutes later, the porter handed him the desk phone. Carter Hayes said, "Good morning. I take it this is quite important, Mr. Schwartz."

"No, I'm dripping on the plastic laid over your lobby's Bohkara just as a joie d'esprit in my morning mudbath."

"Come up. But phone first, next time."

It was one of those small, well-built apartment houses from the 1930s, the Hayes place designed to match, in that style Schwartz recognized from Uncle Maurie–lore as High Anti-FDR.

Irene Hayes immediately directed Schwartz to the sort of bathroom he should have been scrubbed clean for before entering. He sensed the linen hand towels turning up their Northern Irish noses at him, and the plant in the window was holding its little chlorophylled breath with the effort to look artificial. Schwartz refolded the towel so that most of the mud streaks were covered and went to join his jolly clients in the living room.

It was more a sitting room, and there was weak coffee in fine china and Irene Hayes looking from Schwartz's shoes to her husband and back along the Schwartzspoor on the carpet.

"Sugar? Milk?" she scolded.

"Thank you, no," said Schwartz. These folks had swell

manners: they sure knew how to make you feel uncomfortable. Schwartz looked around the room for the bust of Warren Harding.

"Irene, dear," said Carter Hayes, cocking his head.

"Oh, yes. If you'll excuse me," she clucked, rising.

"Mrs. Hayes, you should be here," Schwartz said.

"That's all right, Irene. It won't—"

"It will, Mr. Hayes."

She looked to her husband, who gave a nod.

"I'll probably be dropping the case anyhow, but I wanted both of you to understand why. I thought an unannounced visit might be the best way."

Carter Hayes said, "Mr. Schwartz, what are you talking about? You told Mrs. Hayes only a few days ago how well the case was going."

"No, sir. I said there seemed to be a cover-up. And while that was true, you pay well and I may have been motivated by greed. Now my greed's run out, or there are more cover-ups than I can cope with."

"Oh?"

"Oh, yes," Schwartz said, passing the photosheet of Weiss across the coffee table. "Do you know that man?"

"No."

"You, Mrs. Hayes?"

She glanced at the sheet, looked at her Royal Doulton and said, "No."

"Mrs. Hayes, you're loyal. Mr. Hayes, you're lying."

"Sir, I will not—"

"No, *I* will not be spoken to like this, half-truths and no truths. Mr. Hayes, why didn't you tell me that Virgil was suspected of spying for Russia?"

"I thought, perhaps, you wouldn't take the case if you

knew from the start. I also knew you'd come to it and thought that was something else you could set straight. You see, Virgil was not . . . He wasn't. That McCarthy girl led him to whatever . . ." He slowly turned his cup in its saucer. "Whatever treachery went on was hers. And Virgil was too much a gentleman, too besotted, perhaps, to . . ." He shook his head. The cup rocked in its saucer.

"Carter, please," Irene Hayes said, reaching to the blue veins on her husband's hand.

"No, Mr. Hayes. Ann McCarthy stopped seeing your son about two years before his death. She was scared off, perhaps by what Virgil was up to, perhaps by that man whose photo you won't recognize. I'm not making assumptions about Virgil's guilt or innocence. Look, I have some questions to ask. Maybe your answers won't help the case, maybe they'll confuse me. But I'd better be convinced that they're honest answers, or your bucks stop here, if you'll excuse the allusion to a Democrat. Well, Mr. Hayes?"

"Certainly."

"I take it that means you wish me to go on with the investigation?" Schwartz waited and said, "That was the first question."

"Of course."

"All right. Now, exactly what are you trying to set straight: your son's sexuality or his good citizenship?"

"Both, as I've just said, sir."

Irene Hayes said, "Mr. Schwartz, if it was difficult for my husband to cope with the allegations of Jimmy's having that disease and doing . . . and being . . . cope with that, it was equally difficult for him to cope with the allegations of Jimmy's being a spy."

She spoke with conviction, fingering the jewel on her necklace, a ruby not much smaller than the sapphire Schwartz had seen her wear on their first meeting.

Carter Hayes nodded. "I see that it must have caused you trouble. I'm sorry. But Irene is right: I consider myself something of an old-fashioned patriot."

"Yes," said Schwartz. "Do you consider yourself something of a John Birch Society member?"

"I don't see—"

"And I don't care if you do or not. Answer me, please, Mr. Hayes."

"Yes. And I'm—"

"I know, I know—proud of it. Mrs. Hayes, who has the money?"

Carter Hayes narrowed his eyes.

Irene Hayes asked, "The money? I'm sorry, I don't understand."

"Well, it hasn't been difficult to find out approximately what Mr. Hayes earned, being a federal employee. It couldn't pay my fees, let alone buy this apartment or your jewels. They *are* real, aren't they?"

"They are. I have. That is, Carter has been an excellent provider, but my father was comfortably off and I inherited much of his estate."

"Thank you, Mrs. Hayes. I only wanted to know that this investigation wasn't sponsored by anyone else."

"The fact that we have independent means doesn't prove that, surely," Carter Hayes said with the thin beginning of a smile.

"Very true. That's the kind of logic I was sure you were capable of. I'd like to know more about your work. What exactly did you administer out at Brookhaven?"

"A range of projects involving liaison between civilian and government agencies working at the laboratories."

"What kind of government agencies, besides the Atomic Energy Commission, I mean?"

"There is, for example, a sizable Navy scientific presence

there. Brookhaven is a complex of facilities shared by various educational and scientific institutions."

"During the time when Virgil was alleged to be spying, was there anything special going on at Brookhaven?"

The little smile showed again on Carter Hayes. "Mr. Schwartz, there was and there always is something 'special' taking place at Brookhaven. But, as you must be aware, everything at Brookhaven is classified, and my oath of secrecy lasts my lifetime."

"You had a high security clearance, then?"

"Yes. Even my secretarial staff had high security clearance."

"I understand. Mrs. Hayes," Schwartz said, smiling as he set down his cup and saucer, "even if he had been gay, you'd still have loved Jimmy, wouldn't you?"

"Yes. I . . . I mean . . ." Her cup dropped into her saucer. Tears came to her eyes.

"Of course. I'm sorry. Of course you would."

Carter Hayes said, "Look here—"

"No, let's continue. I understand that Jimmy's behavior changed in those last two years. He showed up less and less at his Cal Tech job, he dropped out of sight. You yourselves didn't see him, you've said. Yet if he felt so haunted or wanted by the FBI or CIA, wouldn't he need help from you? Financial or emotional? Wouldn't he try to make contact?"

"No, sir. Virgil knew what . . . He had a trust fund sufficient for his needs."

"Go on, Mr. Hayes. You broke off, about to tell me— what? What sort of reception he'd get from you? But that doesn't fit your story that your son was merely the dupe of Ann McCarthy. And Virgil wasn't even seeing her by then. It's this sort of inconsistency—from an intelligent man like yourself—that makes this impossible."

"You're quite wrong. I was not going to say anything of the sort."

"Is that right, Mrs. Hayes? I mean, that you *never* saw Jimmy during the last two years of his life?"

"He and his father had such a falling out over . . . over what Ann had made him do, made him become."

"I know. I'm constantly amazed at what one person can make another one do, even against his better judgment. Or hers. But I've spoken with Ann—I traced her through some of Virgil's Cal Tech associates—and she doesn't strike me as having that sort of monstrous power. She strikes me as being very frightened."

Carter Hayes stood. "I don't like any of those implications, Mr. Schwartz. I've admitted being wrong about not telling you of the other allegations, from the start, and I've apologized. I'll apologize again, if you wish. But I will not collude with your evident belief that homosexuality is good or normal or worthy of any support. Nor will I collude with those who for whatever reason wish my dead son to bury someone else's sins."

"You mean Ann's sins, or yours?"

"Don't try to trip me up, Mr. Schwartz!"

"Carter, please don't lose your temper. I'm sure Mr. Schwartz is only—"

"Yes, Mrs. Hayes. I'm only trying to get on with the job you're employing me to do. Or to tell you that because of your own attitudes I can't get on."

"Well, which is it?" asked Carter Hayes, turning back from the wall at which he'd glowered.

"I asked you first," said Schwartz. "And now, for the last time: Mr. Hayes, have you ever seen the man in that picture?"

"Yes."

"Oh, Carter, good for you!"

Hayes gave his wife a short, hard look.

"And so say all of us, Mr. Hayes. I won't press for the no doubt classified details. I think I can get on with your investigation, at least for another day or two. But I'll need more cooperation from you. This has been a start. Well, now I'll return to mud wrestling with the streets."

"I'll see you to the door, Mr. Schwartz," said Carter Hayes, leading the way.

"I think I left a pen," Schwartz said, backing into the sitting room. In a low voice he said, "Call me, Mrs. Hayes. I know Jimmy saw you. Please. You know I can be trusted. Contact me."

He expected what he got—the intake of breath and her hand rising to the red stone beneath her throat.

Out at the door, Schwartz asked, "Isn't that Herbert Hoover in the photo?"

"Yes, sir. And that's my father. He worked under Hoover for a time at the Bureau of Mines."

It wasn't Harding, Schwartz thought, but it would do.

The last of his mud was swirling down the shower drain when the bell rang. Schwartz yelled "Coming! Coming!" even before he turned off the water, kept yelling "Coming!" as he grabbed the towel and bathrobe and did a wet-step, rubbing hop-dance that took him breathless to the door tying his robe.

"Hi. Oh, did I wake you or something?"

It was Betty Simpkin, streaky, soaked, exuding mud and Juicy Fruit.

"No, I was just . . . Come in," Schwartz said, dirtying himself nicely as he took her umbrella and coat.

"Mr. Schwartz, can I use your bathroom, please? I'm so filthy from this yucky rain!"

Schwartz pointed her and rushed to dress. What could she want? Had he left the shower on? Was she washing her feet? His eyes came up through the sweater neck. They saw Betty in a towel.

"I hope you don't mind, but I was so soaked through and there was that nice shower, so . . . You look funny just peeking out of that sweater. Want some gum?"

Schwartz pulled the sweater over his nose. "Mrs. Simpkin, I'm afraid I—"

"Betty."

"—don't have any clothes your size or shape. And the bathrobe's damp. Maybe you can . . . Here are some running clothes. Dry and clean, anyhow. I'll make some coffee and we can . . . Wait! Don't, ah . . ." Schwartz ducked around the room divider.

He made coffee and tried not to think of Betty letting the towel drop like that as she reached for the clothing. But the try focused her image in such lush detail that he decided to trick himself by actually thinking of Betty's nakedness as a way to have done with it. And what was he supposed to have done with it?

"Oh, thanks a lot. I'll get all this stuff back to you."

Schwartz's sweatpants and sweatshirt were too big for her and had never looked so good. "Milk? Sugar?" he asked.

"Please. Lots of both."

He directed her to sit in front of his desk. He sat safely behind it and stared at her. An airhead, but a determined airhead. "What can I do for you, Betty? I mean, besides what I wouldn't do back there when you played drop-the-towel?"

She dropped her eyes. She lifted them. Large, sky blue, clear white. "Gosh. I'm sorry. I thought you'd maybe . . . I thought, you know, that if I was nice to you, maybe you'd lay off Armie."

"Armie? Oh, Armand." Schwartz shook his head. "I'm not pressuring him, Betty. Did he send you?"

"Are you kiddin'? Armie would die. He's . . . Listen, Mr. . . . Can I call you Lenny?"

"Anyone in my tracksuit can call me Lenny."

"I know what you must think. I mean, about Armie and me. You know, like why? Well, he's swell and I don't want his life messed up. He treats me so nice. See, I was a sort of starlet."

At the word "starlet," Betty's eyes snapped shut like a doll's and her head fell. But she didn't say "Ma-ma"; she said, head down, "You know what 'starlet' means. I didn't act much, but I did a lot of sleeping around in L.A., and when it looked like a choice between porno flicks or waitressing, I got so depressed I went back home."

"Where's home?"

"St. Paul. You know it?"

"No."

"It's pretty awful. Minneapolis is sort of the same, but with bars and discos."

"What does this have to do with Armand?"

"Well, he's sick with worry between you hassling him and Choochie hassling him."

"Choochie?"

"Choochie, my cousin. He introduced me to Armie after his wife died. See, I was back in St. Paul hating it. I was dancing in a club, but I had to tell my mother I was a night secretary. I mean, that's the sort of family I come from, see. So Choochie was back in town for a visit. He's something or other, sort of a big shot in the State Department, I think. His folks still live in St. Paul and we've always been good friends. Actually, we used to have a thing when I was a teenager because, you know, he's only a second cousin. So, anyhow, I told him how lousy everything was and . . . Can I have another coffee, please? Thanks, Lenny. Hey, I'm sorry about, you know, sort of trying to fuck you."

Schwartz returned to the desk with her coffee. If only all the others in this investigation were more like Betty. Talkative like Betty; they were all certainly doing the other.

"So he said he knew this guy who was a lonely widower in New York, and one thing led to another and the guy was Armie. I know he's not much to look at, but, I mean, I'm real happy with him, you know? So now he thinks you'll ruin his new career. I mean, he doesn't say much, but I know him."

"I'm not going to ruin his career, Betty. How could I?"

"Well, maybe not so much you, but with Choochie finding out about that stuff Armie had and not being happy . . ."

"Who's Choochie? What does he have to do with this?"

"Choochie Weiss, my cousin. He's—"

"*Weiss*? Do you mean *C.* Richard Weiss?"

"Yeah, but everyone in the family calls him Choochie, not Charlie. You know him? Oh, Jesus, please don't let *him* know I was talking to you. Armie would be so, you know, mortified if Choochie told him I'd been . . ." She reassured herself with two sticks of gum, the second the one Schwartz had declined.

She chewed and chewed. She lifted her shoulders and dropped them in a sigh. "Lenny, have I done the right thing?"

"Sure, Betty. Not that towel business. That was silly, but it's right that you've told me Armand's problems with my investigation. So Weiss introduced you to Armand and helped get him his job. Armand must be very grateful to your cousin."

"Yeah, of course. He sure is."

"Betty, I want you to answer me honestly. I give you my word of honor I won't use anything you tell me against Armand. Is the real problem that Armand had to get rid of that police-case collection of his?"

Betty nodded. "Yes, it all went. Armie almost cried. But Choochie told him he had to. I think he said that someone in a high position like Armie's couldn't have stuff like that around because it really belonged to the police department. You know, Choochie sent a truck around and they worked a whole weekend getting it all out. I helped. Hey, Choochie wasn't doing anything wrong in taking all that stuff and burning it, was he?"

"No, no. Don't worry. Getting rid of that was helpful to Armand."

"Yeah, well, okay, so, but what's gonna happen now?"

"I don't know, Betty. I'll try to keep away from Armand, but if I have to involve him, he shouldn't get in trouble—if he cooperates. So I'm counting on you to convince him, if it comes to that."

"Yeah, sure I'd do that. I think you're a pretty straight guy. Lenny? I wouldn't mind dating you."

"Oh, I'm happily married, Betty. Like you."

"Yeah, I'm happy. But Armie's not . . . But anyway, you're married. That's nice. Any kids?"

"A son, about your age."

"Come on! I'm twenty-five!"

"That old? I thought you were only twenty-two or three. Well. Thanks for coming and talking to me."

"Sure. Oh, I'll mail this stuff back to you. I'll get my things in the bathroom and let you get on with your work."

Schwartz found a plastic bag. "Here," he said, holding it open.

Betty dropped her clothes in. "Think my shoes will look funny?"

"No. I think Staten Island may be ready for high red platforms and my black sweatsuit."

"Lenny, can I ask you, you know? When I was, I mean with the towel . . . Did you, you know, think I was pretty?

"Pretty? Pretty isn't the word for it. Betty, you were absolutely—cute!"

Wide-eyed and chewing, she turned at the door. "Really?"
"Really. I wouldn't kid you. Bye."
She smiled and closed the door.
He'd kid her.

C H A P T E R **3**

In the colder evening rain, Schwartz had bought autumn fruit as if this way he'd encourage the season to act seasonably. He looked at the washed fruit in the bowl. Bosc pears stuck up like stubby rockets from the apples' red glare. And if Virgil were a spy, why hadn't *anyone* told him from the start?

He went out running and returned with bits of blown leaves stuck to his legs and face. He itched. Acid leaves, acid rain.

Stripped, sweating, he checked calls. No calls. He dialed home.

"Hello?" A man's voice.

"Who's this?" asked Schwartz.

"Who's calling, please?"

"Leonard Schwartz."

"Len! Sorry. I didn't recognize your voice. It's Bob. How are you?"

"Okay. You?"

"Fine, fine. I'll get—"

"Yes, please." Schwartz lost the breath he'd gotten back after his run. He forced himself to take long, slow breaths.

"Hello, Len?"

He lost his breath again. "Hello, Karen. I'm naked at the phone here. Sweaty. Breathless. I called you because I want you. Bob answered."

"Should I be flattered by your crazy jealousy? You know Bob's gay."

"It's a cover. Out of Molière. No, Proust. In reverse, you know. Charlus came on as such a ladies' man. I don't want to talk about French literature. I don't trust Bob and, yes, I'm crazy jealous even if you're drinking tea and talking business."

Karen laughed. "Eat your heart out: we're drinking tea and talking business. Come on, Len. What is it, really?"

"Really? It's what I say it is. I want you. Come over here. There's nothing in our agreement that prevents you from coming over here."

"No, that's not the spirit of it."

"I don't want spirit. You don't have to spend the night. Three hours. Bring the Bo Diddley cassettes you like. Three steamy hours. What do you say? I'm cold here."

"No."

"Not even if I shoot an alley cat, to make my pretty baby a Sunday hat?"

"No. And if my diamond ring don't shine, I'm *not* gonna take it to a private eye."

Schwartz said "Oh" and "Well" and "Good-bye."

In the shower he kept picking leaf bits out of the drain. Perhaps Virgil was a Russian spy. Perhaps Virgil was a gay Russian spy. Perhaps C. Richard Weiss was a CIA agent who'd posed as a PHS official to hush up the AIDS-related snuff-show death of the gay Russian spy he'd been chasing, helped by Armand Simpkin, beholden to him for his nice new job and bride, Weiss's cousin. That was the story so far, and it contained at least thirty-seven "perhapses."

Now, apple and pear salad for supper, yum-yum. And for dessert he'd eat his heart out.

Schwartz woke at dawn, put on damp running clothes and went into the cold rain with its oily mud. He came back and called Addison.

"Who speaks?" came a woman's voice.

"I'm looking for Addison. Can I leave a message?"

"This his assist . . . assist . . ." She was laughing. "He tell me say assistant. This his wife. You are Detective Schwartz?"

"Yes. Hi. I didn't know Addison was married."

"Lots of time he don't know, too. We got also three little kids. He don't say?"

"He's very private, Mrs. Addison."

"Resnick. Irina Resnick. He says tell you he's working on many tasks you give him. So he's now out of town until tomorrow. Okay?"

"Yes. Mrs. Resnick, did he mention anything about buying a Bentley for this trip?"

"No. He's taking his own taxi."

"Oh?"

"You don't know too he's taxi driver?"

"I know he's a man of many . . . facets. Well, thank you, Mrs. Resnick."

"Sure. Listen, Mr. Schwartz, Abrasha thinks—how you say—sun rises and sets in your soul. Is right expression?"

"Better than the right expression. Thank you."

What was Addison up to? Everything. Maybe he should pay Addison the three-fifty, take the one-fifty himself and await

Addison's orders? Meanwhile he'd take his laundry to Chambers Street.

"Sid! he said, picking a blueberry from his muffin, "I've got it!"

Sid paused with empty coffeepot in hand. "Don't spread it; this is an eating place."

"Very cute, Sidney, but I still have it. You can put the muffin in one of those bags you've had under the counter since 1946."

Schwartz acted on his inspiration just after nine. "Is this the New York Field Office of the Central Intelligence Agency?"

"Yes, it is. What can we do for you?"

"My name is Schwartz, Detective Inspector, New York Police. I'm to see someone claiming to be one of your operatives, C. Richard Weiss. Could you verify this?"

"Please hold the line."

The voice returned. "Yes, sir. Mr. Weiss is with the Agency. He has a one o'clock appointment with you. And you're no longer with the New York Police."

"Very good," said Schwartz. "And now for fifty dollars, can you tell me the color of my socks and what I've just had for breakfast? Thank you so much. Good-bye."

Okay, Weiss was CIA. So? It was time for some of that intuitive nonsense for which Schwartz had been so feared—at least by his own police force.

He dialed. "Ah, nice to catch you off the answerphone. This is Lenny Schwartz."

"Sorry, cahn't place you."

"I was a little unplanned publicity for your Kallisti stunt. You mistook me for Aphrodite?"

A slow, drawled chuckle. "Ah like yowah erudition, suh. You weren't the fairest, but you were the best spowat. My lawyahs have been expectin' to heayah from you."

"They won't, Mr. Smith. Would you do me the favor of speaking with me—without worrying Ann about it? Dinner or lunch tomorrow?"

"Certainly, suh. All this old Jimmy Hayes business comin' up again is gettin' to Ann. Ah owe it to both of you, but Ah can't do anythin' tomorrow except in the mohnin.'"

"What about breakfast, nine-thirty at the Algonquin?"

"Fine."

"At the round table in the corner, I'll be the one amusing Dorothy Parker."

But Schwartz couldn't amuse himself. For the next two hours he sat at his desk doodling his obvious Rorshachs out of whose curlicues the names "Ann" and "Irene" arose. Blocks became block letters spelling "Ann" and the masts and sails of childish sailboats were I's and A's.

It was half an hour too early when Schwartz tipped back his umbrella to see the tenth floor of the old Federal office building across the street. All he could see up there were sodden drop sheets and yellow rubbish chutes. Was it being rebuilt? Why had Weiss wanted him to show up at the Lafayette Street side?

An umbrella waved from under scaffolding. Weiss? Schwartz crossed the street. "One o'clock, wasn't it, Mr. Weiss?"

"In case you were early I didn't want you to get hurt or lost, with all these renovations." Weiss put a key in the side door.

"Why are we going in through here?"

"Security." Weiss shut the door behind them and said, "I shouldn't be telling you anything and you shouldn't be here."

The hallway was a mess of scaffolding and wiring and pipes. Schwartz ducked, following Weiss to the dark recess of an elevator door. "Then maybe I shouldn't have asked the CIA field office. But they knew."

"Of course. I thought you'd want to check my credentials independently, but I don't want bigger waves than necessary."

"Sure. I've seen the generals and admirals and colonels on TV; I know how your fine Washington minds work. If all this rebuilding is going on, how come no one's working now?"

"Here's the elevator, Mr. Schwartz. After you. It's lunch hour, and I suggest you give me the chance to explain and stop needling me."

The elevator was stacked with cement sacks. The door closed very slowly. A weak lightbulb hung exposed from a cord.

"You deserve all the needling you can get, Mr. Weiss."

Weiss tapped the tip of his umbrella on the elevator floor. He sighed. He pulled his pulled-tight necktie tighter. The elevator took its own unrenovated time.

"Mr. Schwartz, I'm offering to explain a delicate political matter, here. It's not helpful for you to make it so personal."

"Mr. Weiss, everything's personal and everything's political, too. And the personal is political. So my not liking your looks, for instance, is almost objective political theory."

The elevator shuddered and stopped. "Here we are," said Weiss, as the doors opened on more demolished hallway.

Schwartz thought he'd save the Betty–Choochie business. Weiss unlocked another door.

"Sorry for all this inconvenience, but it's all right from here." He led Schwartz through a small front office into a larger office. "Please put your things down here. Have a seat, Mr. Schwartz."

It was a real office and a real desk with one of those phony stone blocks with Weiss's phony name carved in. There was an American flag on a stand in one corner and the regulation chain-of-command photos on the wall, from grim Agency chief to grinning President.

Weiss drew up his chair and ran his hands back from his ears along the side of his skull, as if he were straightening out the memory of hair. He adjusted his shoulders and folded his hands on the desk before him. "For security reasons, I won't be able to give certain details of this matter, just as certain things couldn't appear in the autopsy report. And I realize that the VA report was unsatisfactory. But I feel you need to be put in the picture so that you don't unwittingly stir up things which might be of use to enemies of our country."

"We might not agree on who those are," Schwartz said dryly. "For instance, I think there are a few framed up there behind you."

"Mr. Schwartz, I'm really trying to be decent about this. Your record—the bribe enquiry. I don't want to ask any embarrassing questions. I—"

"Like what, Mr. Weiss?"

"Like questions about the funding of your son's very expensive Yale education, Mr. Schwartz."

Schwartz watched Weiss's hands. Nothing. Weiss was an efficient needler.

"Mr. Schwartz, I think we can at least respect each other as Jews who've risen in fields where it isn't easy to succeed as a Jew."

"Mr. Weiss, I respected you more when you were merely trying to shake me down, before that cheap appeal. Besides, steeped in *Yiddishkeidt* as you obviously are, you know the old saying, 'Where there are three Jews, there are four political parties.' So why don't we get on with this party: tell me a story about Virgil Hayes." Schwartz was watching Weiss's hands. They weren't as cool as the rest of him. They rolled into fists and straightened flat-fingered on the desk.

"Yes. Virgil Hayes began his career as a traitor, as do many in the antinuclear movement."

"Wait, Mr. Weiss, wait. Just the facts, *landsman*, not the John Birch sermon. I feel the most patriotic Americans are antinuclear. But I won't go on about it. I also won't have *you* defining patriotism for me. Right?"

"To continue, Mr. Schwartz. He started in the antinuclear movement first under the influence of Ann McCarthy, his girlfriend of four or five years ago. You may know this. But he soon became more radical than Ann. We became involved about two and a half years ago when Hayes made contact with a Soviet agent we'd been watching, an agent still under surveillance. I can't give you details, of course. Hayes began giving this agent information which threatened national security."

Schwartz held up a hand. "How does a mathematician who goes on peace marches and sits outside the gates of the Shoreham plant *get* any information?"

Weiss pulled at his necktie and sighed. He pointed a finger obliquely. "It's precisely as a mathematician that he obtained information. He managed to break a series of codes pertaining to top-secret government research. By this time, when we contacted Ann McCarthy she was disturbed by Virgil's antigovernment actions, and what we told her was more than enough to make her stop seeing him. If she's told you different, well, that's not our problem."

Schwartz looked at the edge of the desk. If Weiss was lying, he was confusing things very well. If he was telling the truth, he was confusing things even better. "Okay," Schwartz said, not looking up. "Anything else?"

"One more thing. I assume you find Carter Hayes a difficult client."

"I do."

"It's no wonder. The person who tipped us to Virgil Hayes was Carter Hayes, his father."

Schwartz looked up.

Weiss had leaned forward, his right forearm on the desk.

He had an expression of calm concern. "I mean," he said, "his father informed us that Virgil might have secret information. You'll appreciate that I can't divulge its nature or how he came to have it."

"From Brookhaven? I see. You can't say. Well, this makes *some* sense of Carter Hayes's behavior. The man's in a cleft birch stick. He wants his son nailed for spying but cleared of disloyalty to straight sex."

"Something like that."

"Nothing like that, Mr. Weiss. Carter Hayes also wants me to prove that Virgil wasn't a spy or was, at most, a dupe of Ann McCarthy. And you've just told me Ann had nothing to do with this spying business. And I'm left with having your clarifications, like his, just raise more inconsistencies."

Weiss pushed back in his chair, folding his arms and nodding. "I know. We also found it hard working with the man, both before and after his son's death. I'm not trying to tell you your business, but I don't see what you can do. We took over from the police the minute Virgil Hayes was positively identified. It's standard in such cases. You know that."

"Sure, but what about the other business—the AIDS, the painted body, the mutilation? As you say, the VA report you had them give me was more doctored up than Virgil."

"I don't accept that. However, I can tell you that by the time he was under our surveillance, Virgil Hayes had suffered some sort of mental breakdown. Drugs, weird sex, you know. And that's all we know of that aspect of the case."

"Nonsense, Mr. Weiss. You give me a plausible political story, but on Virgil's sexuality you give me glib garbage. What kind of surveillance could you have been running on him to know so little about what supposedly killed him?"

"Sorry. I can't give any details for security reasons." Weiss stood. "Mr. Schwartz, I'm actually not that worried you'd breach our security. What I hope is that you'll now see there's no 'case' for you to continue with so that you'll stop harassing Armand. He certainly doesn't deserve it."

"Mr. Weiss, you now say you're not concerned with me, personally. A few minutes ago you were appealing to our being brothers beneath the missing foreskin. But never mind," he said, standing, "I agree that Armand deserves the best. And you've certainly helped provide it."

Not a twitch. Cool bastard.

"I'll see you out."

He'd try another way. "I suppose Virgil was an even greater security risk being gay and into rough sex."

"Yes," said Weiss, standing at the office door, "there was that."

"Was his contact gay?"

"I can't discuss it."

They stood in the dim hall waiting for the slow elevator.

Schwartz said, "Why did you agree with that nonsense? Virgil's gayness would only be a security risk if he were spying *for* us."

Weiss seemed to purse his lips. Did that count as a gigantic reaction?

"Mr. Schwartz, I suppose I agreed just to have done with a discussion that seems to have led nowhere. So please don't think you can trick me or get tough. If I wanted to, I could be tougher and make you drop your stupid investigation. For instance, your son doesn't seem aware of what's putting him through Yale. But I hope you'll just tell Carter Hayes that it's pointless to continue."

"I know you do."

"Will you or won't you?"

"That's a matter of client confidentiality, the gumshoe version of national security. Ah, the express elevator."

They entered and waited for the door to shut.

Schwartz said, "What do you think of gays, Mr. Weiss?"

"They're not my style, but I wouldn't tattoo numbers on their wrists." Weiss watched the door as it closed.

"The CIA sometimes has people killed, doesn't it? Calls it—I hope you won't call the Anti-Defamation League—'extreme prejudice'?"

Weiss answered with his eyes on the floor indicator. "You've been reading spy thrillers. Most of the time the Agency speaks of killing as 'killing.' It sometimes happens. Not very often, and not to Americans and not in America. But your sort doesn't think much of the Agency, or of the American flag. You spend your time besmirching good men like President Nixon and President Reagan."

The door slid open.

Schwartz stayed in the elevator. "Besmirching? Nixon used the American flag as a fig leaf. Reagan used it as a diaper."

Weiss smiled and pressed the door-hold button. "Let's agree to differ."

"No, Mr. Weiss, let's not even do that. Thanks for your time." Schwartz stepped through the door that Weiss had unlocked.

"I've tried to be helpful, Mr. Schwartz."

"Perhaps you have, in an oblique way," said Schwartz. "Maybe we've been too formal. Why not call me Len?" He turned back to the calm face in the closing door. "And I could call you Choochie."

The door slammed.

CHAPTER 4

What had he meant by calling Weiss "Choochie"? That he knew more than Weiss assumed? That Weiss was lying? Not telling the whole story? None of these. What "Choochie" had meant was to warn Weiss from telling Jake. Who in hell was Weiss that he could know so much? But who couldn't know so much by trying?

How could Weiss know that Jake *didn't* know? Only Karen and perhaps Gallagher knew that. Besides himself. Weiss was guessing. Anyone could. But that such a slimy, reactionary . . .

The door. A very wet Gallagher filled the room. "Lenny, the goddamned drought's over. Jeez, listen, I was thinking up wisecracks humping up those stairs, but this place looks nice. I'm soaking."

It might have been the wet shine of his hair, but he seemed grayer to Schwartz. "Hang up your drenchcoat and welcome."

Gallagher, dripping and stamping, asked, "Am I interrupting?"

"No, no. What do you really think of this place? Is four-thirty early enough for a drink? There's vodka, wine and double-cross Mexican beer. And welcome. I've already said that. You like the place?"

"Easy, Lenny. This place is great. A beer's okay."

"Right. What brings you here?"

"Your invitation. And my promise to drop by. For another thing, it's Wednesday."

"What's Wednesday, for another?" Schwartz asked, coming up with beer and vodka and starting to pour.

"That's when . . . Hey, the bottle's fine."

"No, no. The beer gets poured into a glass so that this doesn't become like some seedy private eye's office. Here."

"Thanks. Tonight's when Karen's coming over for dinner. Turns out I can make it, so I thought I'd see if there was anything—you know, a last-minute message or something, you wanted me to give."

Schwartz dropped his head and gazed into the glass he held in both hands.

"This vodka, Tom—I don't drink as much as you might think, seeing me drink so much, I mean, in between you seeing me drink. No, nothing. Where are you off to?" Schwartz asked as Gallagher wandered away.

"This is, no shit, a nice setup, little bedroom you got back here. You mean you don't drink nothing except when I'm around?" Gallagher called.

"No, nothing to say to . . . no particular message for Karen."

Gallagher came back into the office area, nodded at the kitchen bar and sat on Addison's desk. "Some bachelor pad you have here. Kitty would murder me if I had an office like this."

"Ah, well, that's something you might do. You might refrain from telling Karen what a great place I have. I'm not too happy here."

"I knew it."

"No, Tom, not the work. You know damn well what I mean. Don't tell her that I like the work, either. I don't know. Tell her what you want."

"Sure, buddy, sure. Why don't you get in some real beer rather than this spic piss?"

"Don't worry, Tom, it's brewed by the same beefy Germans who brew it here."

"Oh, I know," Gallagher said, sipping and turning up a smile. "That idea of yours for the Jersey house? Everyone likes it. It's gonna work out."

"Good. Maybe I should have gone into counseling or something."

"Problems with this case?"

"All sorts."

"Jeez, this beer is . . . I gotta use the head."

"Back there." Schwartz thought it would be good to get a fresh viewpoint, any viewpoint at all. Impossible.

Returning, Gallagher said, "You know, this isn't a bad setup. Maybe you could make a success of this."

"Gee, thanks, Tom. That's something like my idea."

"I mean, it's probably a matter of knowing when to let go, you know, with a case like this."

"It's a tough one."

"I was just thinking how the department gets so many damned requests to do things it really shouldn't. Not that we could actually refer calls, but, you know, it could get around about you being over here. You'd get a lot of work and you got the space here to expand into a good-sized operation. Great location, too."

"That would be nice, but first I have to struggle through the case I'm on."

"Why? You're not in public service any more and you're the boss here. Dead ends are dead ends. Go ahead, drop it. Take it from me, you won't regret it."

"Sounds like bribery, Tom."

"But you say you're getting nowhere."

"It's more like I'm getting deeper, or if there are dead ends there are new openings, too. It's like a maze."

"Yeah? Well, be careful you're not the rat running in it." Gallagher picked up a pair of desk scissors and with the thinner blade began cleaning his fingernails.

"Tom? Come on, I've known you too long; don't tell me it's nothing."

Gallagher looked up from his thumb and leveled the scissors at Schwartz. "You're in way too deep. The commissioner has a request from Washington, Lenny."

"Gosh, Washington! Lucky you remembered to tell me this, I mean, among all those other, more important reasons for your visit."

"Be a wiseguy. Look, you know we don't let feds just pick up our jurisdiction, but we also gotta respect theirs. You know that's the deal."

"That's the deal between the police and the FBI or CIA or DEA. I no longer have any such deal, remember?"

Gallagher tossed down the scissors. "I'll tell you what you got. You got even less of a deal. A private eye's a private citizen: *you* pick up federal jurisdiction, you're breaking the law. And they can get you for it and we can't help, except like I'm doing—a friendly warning off in time."

"Of course you could help. It's not clear where the jurisdiction is, here. You could do what you've done before: elegantly tell them to go piss up a rope."

Gallagher crossed to the chair in front of Schwartz's desk and threw himself into it. His right fist came down hard on the chair arm. "The commissioner didn't ask me to do him a favor, Lenny. He ordered me."

"I thought you said Collins was on his way out and your good, good buddy Don was coming in."

"Collins is still commissioner and he still gets to make all sorts of recommendations up and down and sideways as he leaves. Lenny, shit, I'm up there too close, now! And if this Washington type is big enough to shake up this commissioner, he's big enough to shake up whoever's next."

Schwartz looked at Gallagher's square face and gray-eyed stare and saw the frightened career hustler his friend had become. He looked down and asked, "And what are you supposed to do when I refuse?"

"Don't be dumb. You know your PI license can be pulled."

Schwartz shook his head. "Jesus, Tom, is this you? I'm onto what's at least a serious, unsolved crime, probably murder within our jurisdiction, and what also might be gross perversion of justice, here. I don't know, but it could be. And you're saying you're going to pull my license because someone's ordered you to?"

"Wait a second—"

"Let me finish. Jesus, whatever other crap I got up to, I never licked any ass in the department, and I'm telling you, Tom, you're losing everything because you're so afraid of not getting everything."

"Very clever," said Gallagher.

"No, just very obvious. And you know what else? If you go for my license I'll bring a lawsuit, and we both know a dozen good lawyers, let alone the three hundred bad ones, who'd be delighted to do it just for the publicity of you and me and the commissioner and the CIA or whomever. And with a cast like that, how could our mayor resist? And how our newspaper pals would love to jump into that mudbath! No, I'm going to protect myself, and you're not my boss anymore. But you're still my friend and you were the best police officer I've ever seen and you're making me ashamed of you."

Schwartz looked at Gallagher who had a big pride and bad temper. Once, years ago, he'd swung at him. Schwartz, quicker, had blocked the punch; his forearm was in a sling for days. Now Gallagher was slumping, a bad sign, and biting his bottom lip.

The lip popped out, he sat up and sipped some beer. "Okay, pal, you play it your way. But I can't make any promises. I'll pass on your legal plans to the commissioner."

"That's good enough."

"Oh, and Lenny, Washington—the CIA, I think—asked for your records, I was told. No way I could have stopped that, even if I'd known. Which I didn't. I don't know what the hell you're getting into and I don't wanna know. I don't think you know either. Still, if I hear anything, there's no law says I can't let you know."

"That's good."

"I better be getting home to change and think up some lies for Karen about what a great guy she's leaving all alone on Warren Street."

Schwartz watched Gallagher putting on his wet coat. It wasn't the rain; his hair *was* grayer.

Gallagher said, "About that other stuff, buddy, about me making you ashamed?"

"Yes?"

"Screw you."

C H A P T E R **5**

Having passed from the Algonquin's cozy brown lobby into the dining room's white clutter, Schwartz sat on the rounded red banquette in the corner, inhaling smells of coffee and bacon and the waffle-waft of heaven. Lifting the heavy fork brought back the childhood image of the adult-life-to-come: his mother's distant cousin Morton Zeigler from Buenos Aires, via Warsaw and Antwerp, a man "in diamonds" who stayed at the Waldorf and invited his cousin Becky and her little Leonard to lunch ("Your moder iz mine favorite relative, yonk man."). To an already dazzled Schwartz he'd said, "Feel dat linen, pick up de silvervare, yonk man. *Det's kvality!* Det's vat you should aim for in life!" This was his fabled Uncle Morton from exotic Argentina, and for years young Schwartz believed the epitome of a suave Spanish accent was "Det's kvality!"

"Ah you gonna essay that grapefruit with a fowak, suh?"

175

Schwartz looked up. He couldn't see the face beneath the poplin sombrero shading the fawn raincloak zigged with black lightnings.

"Mr. Smith?"

Henry Hawthorne Smith swept off the hat with a bow and straightened with the cloak fallen into his arms. "Yowah servant, suh. Ah'll join you on the banquette, if Ah may."

"Plenty of room," said Schwartz.

Uncostumed, in green Shetland sweater and chinos, H. H. Smith looked shorter and plumper. And younger and older. Younger because of the pale blond hair that fell in a short bowl cut over a large bowl head with plain round glasses which enlarged his pale blue eyes. Older because, as he moved closer, lines appeared furrowed in the brows and pecked under the eyes and mouth. Smith stretched out his hand as he sat, a hard, nail-chipped hand.

"I'm Len."

"Henreh. Ah'm afraid Ah've less time than Ah told y'on the phone."

"All right. I'm interested in what you know about Virgil, Jimmy Hayes—what Ann has told you, I guess."

He motioned to the waiter, who came and took Smith's order.

"This is a fine ol' place. The South's supposed to be full of this sort of place, but it's not. Maybe a few, but theyah mostly like everywhere—sleazy or plastic or pretentious. Well, should Ah just go ahead?"

Schwartz dug into his grapefruit. "Please. I'll ask anything that comes to mind after."

" 'Bout three years ago Ah met Ann when Ah was asked to provide an event at Shoreham nucleah powah station by Mobilization for Survival. Ann was coordination . . . Ah see, Len, yowah surprised those'd be mah politics. Well, Ah put on one of mah Ahmageddons out theyah. An' then Ah saw Ann at a few more like events, once or twice with Jimmy Hayes. He was quiet, but all right, you know. Bright. Maybe half a year later Ah saw Ann at a Soho gallery. Ah'd been rememberin' her. And she was on her own and we went out for coffee and she was sort of shaky. Tole me how she'd been less interested in Jimmy—nothin' about that gay business you brought up with her. Ah suppose Ah was sympathetic—Ah was sure tryin'—and she sort of spilled out her soul to me then. She said how the FBI or maybe the CIA, she din know which, had been harassin' her, ringing her up day and night, askin' what she knew about Jimmy bein' a spy. She said of course he never was; you know them—if you don' wanna nuke folk dead yowah a spy. So they were threatenin' her with three thousand yeeahs of jail if she din' cooperate, but she wouldn't. When Ah asked her what was really happenin', she said Jimmy tole her that he was onto somethin' big and bad goin' on between Shoreham and Brookhaven. But he din' tell her more, said it was too danger-ous 'cause he was bein' bugged and chased 'round by CIA or such. Well . . . Ahh.''

Smith poured maple syrup and ate half-inch-thick pieces of French toast. He drank his coffee, finished the French toast and had another coffee. Schwartz was still on the white rim of his first egg and had four of his five pieces of bacon before him.

"So Ann and Ah became sweethahts and Ah saw she was goin' to have a nervous breakdown if she stayed over theyah workin' in the middle of the movement, so when Ah suggested she come an' work with me she was happy to. Best career move Ah ever made! And from then on, she was left pretty much alone by those people chasin' Jimmy. But folk who din' know the real story thought she'd betrayed them. Hell she did! Ann's too fine to make it harder for Jimmy or anyone else tryin' to undo any of that nucleah huntin' or fission. Those records gone from ol' John's place in the Heights were taken by those CIA-type goons.

An', let's see, about Jimmy. Few months after comin' to work with me, Ann bumped into him ovah in the East Village. Said he was glad she was 'out of the fire,' she said he put it. And he was very strung out, nervous. He tole her he now had enough to put the nucleah energy industry back thirty yeeahs. Wouldn't say mowah. Wished her luck. And next time, well, that was after Jimmy was found dead and this policeman showed up warnin' Ann not to bring up any of this nucleah business because police were told Jimmy was a spy and his Russian contact was still bein' followed so that he'd lead them to others. She tole him he was full of bullshit. And that's it. Ah'll just get a little mowah coffee."

Schwartz showed the photo of Weiss, which Smith recognized as the "policeman." Then Schwartz asked if he thought Ann had told him all she knew.

"Yes, and if not, suh, Ah adore the woman's courage in not tellin' and will not for the world staht in on her, understand?"

Schwartz did. To his questions about Jimmy's parents, Smith remembered that Ann had talked about the father as a bigot, but that was all.

"Did she ever mention anyone else with whom Jimmy may have been involved in this or in whom he may have confided? What's funny?"

"Just that Ah heayah hardly anyone these days takin' such cayah to tuck in his prepositions. Say, there was Sci-Fi."

"What about it?"

"No. Him. Cy Fisher. Ann once said that Jimmy had hung around with Sci-Fi Fisher a few years back. Don't you know him, fellah that ran Conspiracy Books?"

"The one from the sixties? Is he still around?"

"Ah'm not sure."

"Here's one you don't have to answer. That show of yours at the Tower Gallery. It's a joke, isn't it?"

Smith laughed. "Well, what do you think?"

Schwartz smiled.

Then Smith thanked him for breakfast. "Len, don't you just *like* this place, with the coffee that just keeps comin' and the napkin layin' heavy on yowah lap," so that Schwartz had put his chin in his hand and squinched his eyes toward the dining room until it blurred in silverware and crushed-ice coolers and people's voices and the rustle of newspapers being read and red banquettes.

"You awright?"

"No, Henry, not very with the people I love most."

Smith stood. "You take cayah, now," he said and was instantly, magically under his sweeping sombrero and swirlingly cloaked. "Yowah gonna be awright if you take the advice of this charlatan and just tell *everyone* the truth, heayah?"

Schwartz had a hundred things to do, but, pushed back against the deep banquette padding, he sat with his nose in his coffee cup. No hedonist, at least not by Midtown standards, Schwartz was sunk into the Algonquin's solid comforts because Karen was his Irish linen, his heavy silver, his coffee comfort. And Jake. He sighed. Some lukewarm coffee lapped into his nose.

Could you, he wondered, dig into a Forty-fourth Street banquette like a foxhole to hide from enemy fire? "Out of the fire," Virgil had said to Ann as he went down in flames. Well, there was Sci-Fi Fisher to chase up, down or, probably his luck, intergalactically.

Outside, the drizzle had become a mist, the gray dropping between buildings as if their granite were projected into air. He'd walk down to the library for some Shoreham–Brookhaven research.

This was a funny block: the famous Algonquin Hotel and its unsung blood brother, the Iroquois. And here the New York Yacht Club, rococo stern windows in cold light, a club of flying dutchmen going north. And then a club indeed—the always understated Harvard. By the time Schwartz was invited to become a member, he didn't want to. Funny block, a block that made you think of John O'Hara.

And by its end, something else was funny. Schwartz turned left and went into the Bank of New York, where he looked at a mural, turned and walked out again. He crossed Fifth Avenue and continued east. He went into the Forty-fourth Street entrance and out the Madison Avenue door of Brooks Brothers.

Whoever it was was very good, and whoever was more than one. But why? He could get into a cab and they'd all end up outside his door on Warren Street. So it was general surveillance, seeing who and what and where he saw and went.

Well, he'd been thinking of the library, anyhow. He'd continue down Madison to Forty-second, and then . . .

Three of them. Three good people in radio contact could cover anyone: you'd think you were looking at thirty-seven different people going about their business. But you wouldn't know to look. They'd picked him up from Warren Street, of course, and he hadn't noticed until the Harvard Club. No, that's where it had clicked, but it was back at the Algonquin lobby, a wing chair behind a wood-paneled column, and turned away from him so that he hadn't seen anything at all, yet . . .

He waited in the crowd at Fifth and Forty-second and crossed south. Then he waited in the next crowd and crossed to the library. They were good. They had radios. CIA? Should he feel honored? He'd go for a stroll to see how good they were.

Schwartz passed a gentleman offering to play chess. He passed a gentleman offering to play three-card monte. Another gentleman looked past him into the gray sky reflected elliptically up a graceless building and suggested a smoke. Another, seemingly without soft drink, suggested coke.

Schwartz saw a police informant he knew and skipped up the steps to Bryant Park, but Bobby had already twigged and growled out fuzz-warnings to his associates.

"Bobby, my man," said Schwartz.

Bobby dug his hands deeper into the pockets of his army jacket. "Come on, Schwartz, I'm always good to you death-squad mothahs."

A good sign, that "death-squad"; at least someone in town still thought him a cop. "I want your professional opinion, Bobby."

Bobby looked at the side of his sneakered feet and spat. "What, someone sell you some recreational oregano, man?"

"Very funny. Bobby, you have good antennae. I think I'm being seriously followed. What's your sense of it? That's all I want to know."

Bobby hunched. Then he squatted so that Schwartz looked down on the brim of the fatigue cap turning and on the long black fingers tapping the gravel. Then he stood.

"Yeah, there's something all around the park, for sure."

"Thanks, Bobby."

"Mothafuckah, you know what would of happen if *I* went to Harvard like you?"

Schwartz turned. "What's that?"

"Shiyit! I would of been an *educated* dealer."

Schwartz waved his fingers over his shoulder. Bobby with Harvard would have been worse than that; by now he'd have been chairman of the International Monetary Fund.

Schwartz decided to go west and take them (Weiss and Co.?) into crowds and out of crowds. And maybe see.

His first variation on a straight-walk theme was bravura at Times Square, where after walking to the corner of Nathan's and

Forty-third, he ran back to Forty-second and dropped down into the IRT entrance long enough so that one of them would have to go down under with him, which, at this point, would be the one west across the square. After one minute, Schwartz walked back up and crossed west. Dodging the traffic wasn't fun, but it had given him the space to see one of them in the brown raincoat at the IRT entrance. They were good, but he was better.

He walked the theater block to Eighth Avenue without bothering to look. One would already be ahead across Eighth, another would have hung back at Times Square, and the third (he hoped for three; he really was worth three) was free-floating the area, a fast operator ready to move inside, up or down. That's how he would have done it.

The block ended pornographically: live acts, skinflicks, the videos and magazines, small sleaze boutiques and dildo department stores. And in the street before the parlors hung the hoi pornoi, the girls and boys in skirts as skimpy as single shingles or dressed for the scramble in ball-turret pants.

Halfway to Ninth Avenue, Schwartz saw Weiss back on the other side of the street; he'd turned as if talking to an unhappy hooker. Their first mistake. Schwartz crossed the street as Weiss turned into a doorway to receive the radio message that he'd been picked out and was being watched.

So Schwartz stopped watching and walked on toward Tenth, deciding that going left into Dyer wouldn't gain him anything; they'd have him boxed between Ninth and Tenth. He walked to Tenth, crossed and hailed a cab.

There was just enough traffic to do it. He opened the door, put a few dollars through the cash window and said he was only passing through and the cabby should drive himself up a block. He went out the other side, crouching low in the slow-moving traffic. He saw the other cab start at Forty-first Street. It was an old trick.

But not a good one. He saw the other cab's door thrown open as he took off running for the corner of Forty-third. Lights were flashing down the block. A firehouse. Sirens. He made it past just as the first truck pulled out. Over his shoulder, wheels and chrome and hoses, booted bodies jumping on, he saw the CIA make a bad second mistake in the form of C. Richard Weiss pointing a black man his way.

At Eleventh, Schwartz turned uptown and ran fast for three blocks. The black man was a good runner but a bad tail. He must have been the free-floater. By the time Schwartz got to the car salesrooms he'd decided to slow down.

This was getting silly. He'd embarrass their side and get back to work. He turned down Fifty-second and sprinted down the side of Clinton Park so that he was rounding the corner of Twelfth just as his tail turned off Eleventh.

Cars whizzed by Schwartz, but there were no people around down here. He'd simply turn and walk past his tail and make fun of him. Here he came, now.

Schwartz stepped out smiling. He said, "I thought—" but stopped because the gun was up so fast under his chin.

"Get the fuck up against that wall, you fuck! You make one fuck move and I'm gonna shoot yo' fuck ugly face over this stone!"

Schwartz asked, "What is this?"

"Shut up, you fuck! This is a stickup, fuck! So shut the fuck up and keep yo' fuck hands up on that wall except you drop yo' wallet an' whatever else you got right here slow behind you and you even fuck think of lookin' back you dead meat!"

Was it just a random stickup? Schwartz was no longer sure if this was the man who'd been following him. Marvelous. He'd run into a junkie holdup. His left hand was throwing out keys and his wallet and a pen and his notebook. Not his gun. The man was too jumped up to frisk him. His right hand stayed up on the stone wall ledge. One big stone was loose.

"There," he said. "That's it. Take the cash, but could you please leave the cards and the stuff you don't—"

"Shut the fuck up, fuck!" came the voice from behind and below.

Schwartz spun to throw the stone down at the voice, but the stone stayed on the wall. In his momentum Schwartz's open, empty hand met the rising stickup man in a little slap to his left cheek. Horrible, an old lady could have done better with a small handbag.

For a second the thief was puzzled. "You nuts, you fuck? You turn back there or you die."

The gun was an old .45, so huge it would have been dangerous filled with raisins.

"You stay the fuck right there. You come round this corner, you gonna come right into some bad fuck shit bullets," shouted the thief, and left Schwartz with his hands back on the ledge.

It was all so stupidly humiliating. Schwartz pulled and pushed himself up, found a hole in the fence and ducked through. He stayed back from the edge, sprinting along the park fence to a gateway, where he dropped behind the stone and held his breath. If the thief were stupid enough . . .

Schwartz saw a hand and threw his body behind his right arm, so that all his weight went into the side of his right palm as he snapped it over the man's collarbone creasing two inches into the bottom of his neck.

The .45 hit the ground just before the stickup man. His tongue was sticking out, his mouth was open, contorting, unable to get air. His eyes were popped with the shock.

Schwartz picked up the big gun. The thief was in some

trouble. Schwartz slapped his face hard, and the knees jerked toward the chest and hoarse groans began, a sign that Schwartz wouldn't have to explain manslaughter. When Schwartz found his wallet and other belongings in the pocket of the lumberman's jacket, the thief was only beginning to approach consciousness.

Should he call the cops? No. Of course this man was somehow working for Weiss. It was a private matter, but, damn it, he wanted this bastard to know what it felt like being robbed, how much more it took away than money.

Schwartz thought: off with the heavy jacket that kept you warm and dry. Then off with the shoes and socks, that solid base you went on. And his trousers, because being robbed made *you* ashamed.

The man's eyes focused. "Hey, fuck, what you doin'?" He coughed and put his hands to his throat but found the space already occupied by what had been his .45.

"Get up," said Schwartz.

"I'm gettin'." The man stood. "I didn't mean no . . . " He coughed, bent, repeated. "I didn't mean no . . . " and coughed again. His underpants were torn.

Schwartz said, "I see you have some hand-modified bad bullets in here. I saw one of these .45 dumdums in a man's gut once. Looked like they were excavating a new tunnel to Jersey. I'm only going to ask you each question once. Were you paid to follow me and stick me up?"

The man nodded. Urine was spreading yellow over the front of his underpants.

"Who? Speak very clearly."

"Guy name Brown. I don' know him, I swear. Paid me two-fifty before and gonna give me two-fifty more and, he say, some crack when I give him what's on you."

"Who's Brown?"

"Man, fuck, I swear I don' know. Guy's some big-shot

white man, all I know. Fuck. You saw me with him, back there where them fuck fire engines comin' out."

"Okay," said Schwartz.

"Man, fuck, what you gonna do with me?"

"Give me your shirt."

"Oh, man, fuck, it's cold."

"Give me the shirt off your back," Schwartz said, lowering the .45 level with the thief's intestines. "Good. Now drop it on the pile with the rest of your things. Now get down on your knees and make a good, tight bundle of those things in your jacket."

Schwartz took out his own gun and emptied bullets from the .45 magazine as he directed the man to first fold over the jacket sides and then fold up its bottom. Schwartz backed to the curb, crouched and threw the bullets down the sewer grate, speaking to the bent brown back in front of him about keeping the sides and bottom tight inside of the arms as he tied them. The .45 stuck on the sewer ledge. Schwartz told the thief that if he even twitched as though he might turn, the west wind off the Hudson would be blowing through his neck, and he reached down and in with his own gun to knock in the .45.

Schwartz thought how foolish it must look. He was lying with his cheek along the curb and his right arm down a sewer, while ten feet in front of him another adult male crouched naked in fouled underpants, coughing, afraid of being shot in the back yet hugging himself, despite such doom, against the cold wind.

"Mr. Thief, I want to see you right here," said Schwartz, picking up the bundled clothing, "when I turn that corner."

He did. At over one hundred yards they exchanged stares that neither could see of such pure hatred that they skewered the air.

On Eleventh, Schwartz found a construction hopper and dropped the bundle to the bottom under pipes and broken wall-board. Now the thief would know what it felt like. Schwartz walked on in a daze of righteousness. By Fiftieth Street he realized he was being followed again by a black man in underpants, hugging himself and alternatively running and hopping and consistently screaming, "Fuck! Fuck, man, gimme my clothes!"

Schwartz slowed down by a car showroom window. The thief caught up with him. Schwartz pulled his gun and made the thief turn and lean into the window, hands over his head. Inside, the salesman showing the Buick didn't appear to notice.

"Hey, man, you win. But my clothes, man. Fuck! I gotta have my clothes. I ain't got clothes, like I ain't got nothin'! You know?"

Schwartz held his pistol to the back of the man's head. There was a strong, bad smell. "You are going to stay right here until I'm out of sight. You have no clothes now. You have nothing now. You've been robbed."

A man came out of the showroom, smiling. He glanced at the clothed white man about to shoot the naked black man, said "Hi" and walked away.

So did Schwartz. The last thing he heard was, "It ain't fair! Fuck! I ain't nothing without them clothes. You stole my . . . Like you stole my . . . "

But what it was he thought Schwartz had stolen he didn't know or didn't say or Schwartz couldn't hear.

Schwartz was on the downtown IRT with his head between his knees, breathing deeply. By Thirty-fourth Street, in the cool, rocking car, his adrenaline abated. Thought began. What had all that been about?

The robbery. Weiss had counted on Schwartz's ability to pick up a tail, had been clever enough to do it not quite cleverly enough so that . . . Weiss had counted on Schwartz's vanity. That clever bastard had studied Schwartz's records well. But for what? A shot in the dark? The notebook had nothing in it that Weiss didn't know or couldn't get. The wallet?

Schwartz took out his wallet. Two hundred dollars. Not money. Credit cards, Social Security, Blue Cross. No. Brooklyn Public Library, voter registration. No, no. Photo of Karen holding Jake as a baby. No. And this?

What, stamps? He looked in the small shiny envelope. The gold-blue chips of Virgil Hayes's skin. Simpkin must have told Weiss about leaving the room while the vial was on the table. What was it? What was it? What was it? he thought, as the train banged and rocked.

Brookhaven, Shoreham. Shoreham and Brookhaven. No, it wasn't that Weiss wanted them but that he didn't want *him* to have them. Okay. Why?

Shoreham and Brookhaven. What . . . Wait. Wait! The waiting room! Oh, Jesus!

"The waiting room!" Schwartz said aloud, making the woman next to him look up from her Macy's bags.

Schwartz slipped the pieces back into the envelope. Good old Virgil. No wonder Weiss wanted them: these were the blue chips, all right. The poor taste of his pun made Schwartz wince, but he kept smiling.

The woman said, "Pardon me. You shouldn't sit there with an open wallet. This city is full of thieves."

Addison, get off the phone. We have a thousand things to do.''

Addison covered the mouthpiece, forgetting he held a large cheese Danish. "Lenny, is wonderful seeing again the genius of the place. Wait, I finish this little sideline case we're doing.''

"Little *what*?''

"Shh,'' went Addison, peeling the Danish from the phone. "Mrs. Saltzman, yes, I'm following your husband and photographing, catch him so fragrant and—No, is 'fragrant and delectable,' legal term for this no-good bastard husband you got screwing this floozy. Okay. Sure. Good-bye.''

"Addison, pick off the slivered almond, wash the phone and leave, because you're fired. No, first I want to find out where the hell you've been. No, first we're going to leave here for a little experiment.''

Addison was finishing his Danish. "Eshprimen?"

"I could say you said a mouthful, but I won't. Let's go."

Fifteen minutes later, Addison was pulling a shrimp out of an egg roll in front of Luck Joy's Chinese food wagon at the end of St. Andrew's Plaza.

Gerry Santini was delighted with Addison and unhappy with the experiment. He ducked and wove about, blowing on his finger ends as if it were much colder, for Santini, having modeled his street behavior on Jake LaMotta, thought this showed pent-up anger.

"You know Gallagher's probably pointing a big finger down at us right now from his office window."

"Let him point," Schwartz said. "How long will we have to wait?"

"I don't know. A few minutes. Believe me, the searchlights in that pile of pink stone are trained on honcho pathologists like yours truly. You've really stirred something with your old buddy the Wimpkin."

"He wasn't my buddy. You tough middle-class cops are all the same."

"Hey, Addison," Santini said, throwing short half-jabs into the air, "you're already something of a sleazy legend over here. Is it true you have seven wives in Brighton Beach, each of whom knows about the other six and still adores you?"

"Is silly," Addison said, laughing. "I have one Irinatchka and am luckiest man, so good and beautiful a wife with three wonderful baby kids, two girls, a boy, you'll meet. Listen, what kind of scale you need for bidding to supply medical equipment for police?"

"Don't encourage the man, Gerry. The last doctor who did ended with a prostate operation. Addison performed it."

"Boss is joking. I know warehouse in Steinway full of good

first-aid kits, also all sorts little forensics, save police amazing money."

Santini was talking to his pocket. "Let's go. This had better be good, Len."

Addison finished his egg roll and rubbed his hands. "Boy, Police Headquarters. This is going to be good time, I mean, interesting. It shall be interesting."

"Interesting," Schwartz said, looking at the black box on the table. "Looks like a piece of stereo equipment."

"You switch it on and hold whatever you're testing to that little window. If it was too big, you'd point the window at your specimen," said Santini.

Addison, quiet, overimpressed, had his elbows on the table, his chin in both palms.

Santini switched on the geiger counter. "I'm turning up the volume. Hear that?" There was a small distinct click, then a pause of a second, another click, another pause. "That's background radiation, the crap we're stuck with if there are no more Hiroshimas, Three Mile Islands or Chernobyls, or any kind of testing. Lecture's ended. Go on, Len."

Schwartz took the wallet from his pocket, turning away from the table. As he turned back, the clicks increased to a continuous flat buzz.

"You definitely have something there."

"I see. I hear. And this isn't even what I'm testing." Schwartz brought the wallet beneath the table and drew out the stamp envelope. He moved it toward the counter. The counter needle swung up and stuck right off the gauge. The clicks became a louder buzz, thickened to radio static in a thunderstorm.

"Christ!" said Santini. "What the hell have you got?"

Addison had come around to see. "Yes, boss, what is?"

"It's Virgil's ghost. His message is in code."

Codes, codes. Santini was driving them to a medical library. Schwartz kept his eyes shut to think. Addison and his mathematician friend Braverman had been out to Princeton where Virgil had often worked in summers and at special conferences. But it wasn't exactly the university; it was the Princeton site of IDA—the Institute for Defense Analysis, a cold-looking blockhouse of a place, windows only at the top. Braverman knew of it: a Cold War setup that invited pure scientists to do seemingly pure problem solving, the happy coincidence being that problems in pure math were essentially identical to those in abstract cryptography—making and breaking codes.

From Princeton, Addison and Braverman had returned to NYU, where their research turned up links between Cal Tech and IDA, and IDA's links to the CRD—the Cryptography Research Division of the National Security Agency. Addison had noted Braverman "saying NSA so big and everywhere makes CIA look like Cubscoutings." Braverman had suggested that such programs as IDA's at Princeton—SCAMP, Summer Campus, Advanced Mathematics Program—was one way that the best minds . . .

Santini had turned off the siren. Schwartz opened his eyes. He was parking the car between an "Absolutely No Parking At Any Time" and a "Don't Even Think of Parking Here" sign. Addison was grinning.

Addison stopped grinning as they got out. He told Santini he hated hospitals. "Is put me into afraid and tremblings and the sickness into death."

Schwartz said that Kierkegaard had felt almost the same about the New York Hospital–Cornell Med School. Santini said that until he'd graduated, so had he.

Schwartz followed the other two, thinking again of Virgil. Like other top math and linguistic minds in the country, Virgil had been part of a program designed to get scientists used to working for the National Security Agency, not that NSA would tell any of them that there was an interesting problem in numbers theory whose solution would ultimately help get cocaine to the contras. But the military was linked with the NSA code and spying business, especially the Navy. And the Navy, as Carter Hayes had said, had a research station at Brookhaven.

They were in an office by the reading room, with Santini sorting a stack of books and journals.

"Right, folks. I've fiddled my schedule, forced my subordinates and fooled my superiors for the chance to get into even bigger trouble. So here we are where nobody can spy on you, Len. So tell me."

"It came together all at once, just south of Thirty-fourth Street on the IRT. I was looking at the skin flakes in the envelope and—bango—I saw it in my mind: the microphotographs Simpkin had shown me and the ones I'd seen in his PHS waiting room in a journal of radiology. They were identical."

"Okay, here," said Santini, flattening a page. "Here's Kaposi's sarcoma, at a magnification of 130. Up here's the epidermis and all this is the layer of stretched dermis."

"I remember Armand telling me this."

"And it looked like this?"

"Yes. I mean, he said it wasn't a brilliant microphotograph. It was all right for death certification, along with other evidence, but it wasn't of a scientifically useful standard."

"Oh-oh." Santini shook his head. "The supercautious Simp said that?"

"Yes, words to that effect," Schwartz said, wondering if it hadn't been Weiss.

"Well, bullshit. There's only one standard in forensics or pathology for death certification, and that's the scientific standard. That's the firstest principle: without it we might as well call a bullet wound a rope burn."

"Let's see the radiation pictures."

Santini was flipping through a book. "There's plenty here, but I need to—"

"You want find some about same magnification," Addison said. His ordinary excessive enthusiasm had returned once he understood they'd be located in a library rather than on an operating table.

"Exactly. Here. Here's a range of radiation effects at about 130 to 160."

Schwartz looked at the microphotographs, nodding for Santini to turn the pages. "Yes, yes, all this stuff, the big white spaces. This is more like it, like the microphotos I saw of Virgil Hayes."

"Well, don't get too excited. It still could be AIDS. The KS related to AIDS runs very aggressively and often doesn't have the textbook histology, so that this sort of huge vascular space you see in these radiation tumors appears in the KS dermis. Another difficulty is that the spindle cell characteristic of KS is very hard to locate in AIDS-related cases."

"Okay. But, Gerry, if you were trying to *hide* the fact that someone had died of massive radiation sickness, could AIDS KS make a plausible cover?"

Santini began tapping a tango beat with his fingers. "Well, there are these visual similarities. And, yes, what could further confuse matters are the immunosuppressive characteristics of both radiation effects and AIDS, especially if we're talking about extreme, fatal doses of radiation. And that's what I'm damn sure you have in those bits of skin."

"So you think . . ." Schwartz let the idea hang.

"Possible. It's possible. In this particular case it would be much more possible, given the general condition of the body. And the lungs, for example—pneumonia or conditions like it are classical in advanced stages of extreme radiation illness and, of course, in AIDS."

"May I offer contribution, Lenny?" Addison asked.

"Sure."

Addison looked at Santini's thrumming fingers. "Doctor, for arguing, let us suppose Dr. Wimpkie absolutely on straight and level. Is reason why he should *not* consider possibilities radiation death?"

"Sharp question," said Santini, looking to Schwartz.

"Don't look at me: I've taught him absolutely nothing he knows."

"The answer," said Santini, "is yes. There are plenty of reasons why he shouldn't think of radiation. First, it's relatively rare. Second, it's even rarer in police work. Len, how many cases have you run across in your horrible career with the very still?"

"None."

"And another thing, unless you specialize in industrial medicine—which is usually company doctoring to tell the poor bastards that their asbestosis is only a summer cold—you don't learn much about radiation illness. You study it, but only in terms of radiation therapy side effects. And since forensic pathology doesn't involve that . . . Well, you can see the reasons piling up for why Simp or others mightn't think of it. And here's another: since we're seeing more and more AIDS symptomatology these days, it would come to mind quickly, especially given the other evidence of the state of that body."

Schwartz said, "So Simpkin may not have suspected radiation. And any federal type around who did was certainly not going to put the idea into his head, since they wanted a nonhomicide verdict to be able to get on with their investigation. Or Simpkin may have suspected radiation and, for reasons I'm aware of, decided it wasn't worth chasing. Given all the factors, it would have been easy to rationalize his findings. Well, we certainly have a package to present Dr. Simpkin. But there's still . . . "

Santini gave a big dip, finger flourish and let up. "Yes, there certainly is," he said.

"And you know I'll need you, Gerry. You'll be in the nastiness very formally, then."

"What you two talking make me feel so slow in the brains about?" And then Addison understood and said, "Aha!"

Schwartz nodded. "We'll have to move fast. If we start the formal work today, with luck we'll be able to disinter poor Virgil on Monday."

Addison looked at Santini, wide-eyed. "You going to help with this? I got math friend Braverman who help, but you taking big risks. You a braver man than Braverman."

Santini shut his eyes. "Len, this man has been with you too long."

An exhumation order, as Schwartz found, was difficult to obtain at the best of times. This wasn't the best of times: the order pertained to a body for whom exhumation had already been refused, whose next of kin wanted it for reasons which Schwartz was attempting to keep out of the proceedings; and it was an order for which federal intervention was imminent, given the scrutiny that Weiss and agency (CIA? NSA?) were able to bring to the slightest offstage clearing of the throat in this, until now, leaden farce.

So by four o'clock, Schwartz had modified his plans and sent Addison off to the Hayeses with forms for them to sign before a notary. By seven o'clock, Schwartz knew he needed help and left Santini's office, where he'd worked cramped and formaldehyded to make Santini feel helpful in providing this torture chamber.

Schwartz entered his old offices, keeping his eyes down as he passed the staff—part shame, part the shy vanity of superstars. He nodded, said "Hi" and "Fine, fine," and knocked on the closed door.

"Come in, please."

Oh, that "please"! Schwartz said, "Hi, Bob."

Malinowski stood to attention so fast that his desk chair rolled back into the wall. "Sir! Hello. This is . . . Sit down, sir, please. No, here."

Schwartz sat in a chair before the desk. "Your office now, Bob. Your desk, your chair. You're boss."

"Only temporarily."

"You think you won't be promoted?"

Malinowski blushed, probably all over. But that was Malinowski all over: overachieving and underconfident. His one eccentricity was his worship of Schwartz. Schwartz regarded this as a quirk rather than a flaw.

"You'll be promoted. You'll make my rank and more. Well, has Gerry managed to call you in the last two hours?"

"Yes, sir. Len. I know you want me to call you Len. The 'sir' keeps coming out. Uh, not because you're older than me. I mean, you're not much older than me."

"Ten years, Bob. How are things going?"

"Not as well as they would if—"

"Oh, for Christ's sake."

Malinowski was back in his chair. His long, bony hands pulled at each other. "Well, there are no complaints from Deputy Chief Gallagher."

"Good. Anything else from the Deputy Chief?"

"Well, uh, if he's telling us not to give you any help, it's only because he wants you back so much."

"And do you want me back?"

"Oh, you don't have to ask that. You know I do." Malinowski's torso leaned over the struggle of his hands.

"In that case, I suppose you also won't help me on this exhumation process."

Nothing if not logical, Malinowski smiled through the expression of pain at the thought of refusing Schwartz. "Of course I do. I will. I know that, uh, however it may look to Chief Gallagher, you're doing the right thing, um, Len."

Schwartz smiled. He thought of Jake. This huge Polish detective captain was another he deceived. "Bob, listen. Maybe I haven't said this; I should've. I've always been grateful for your confidence in me, even when—maybe most when—I've made fun of it. It's been important."

Malinowski began a hand-pull of denial.

"No, I mean it. I'm worried that your belief in me is too naive, especially now that I'm not your boss. This business needs some faith, I guess, but not naiveté. Bob, I'm not the perfect—"

"I don't think you're perfect, sir."

"You don't know."

"What? What don't I know?"

Bob's look was open, awful. "About the bribe. That investigation business."

"What are you saying, sir?"

"I think you know what I'm saying. Only, I can't say it. Still think I'm always the good guy?"

Schwartz saw it in Bob's hands. The fingers stretched out and curled in, and the hands pressed into the desk like two scared spiders.

"I'm not that naive," he lied. "And I'm Catholic. I believe in human fallibility and in repentance and forgiveness. I mean, for everyone. Look, sir, I sort of speak, uh, stiffly. I know. Not like you and the Chief. I'm trying to say I believe in you because of what you've just told me. Not despite it. So if you have the notes, I'll get someone right onto work on the forms. Gerry's told me

200

enough so that I can present this to Chief Gallagher as procedure involving probable case reopening as homicide. Personally, I don't want the New York Police Department caught up in suppression of justice somewhere down the line. Sir?"

"I'm here, but emotionally I'm still back there with you saying you weren't naive. That's transcendent fibbing. Thanks. Here—the notes and forms. You have my office number if you need me. Don't call me at home if you can in any way avoid it. I'm in a personal constitutional crisis, trying to work out some separation of powers."

Schwartz jumped up, squeezed Bob's shoulder and ran out before either one of them burst into tears.

Outside on Police Plaza, the rain had stopped. The air was colder, seasonably cold. If he'd gotten through that, somehow, with Bob, maybe he could with Jake? Schwartz took deep breaths. He sensed the wind, which veered northwest, sweeping in over the Palisades and the Hudson.

"Lost in thought, or what?"

Schwartz turned. Tom Gallagher had walked up behind him.

"I was just going home," Gallagher said. "Been busy in there?"

Schwartz had no wisecrack. He smiled and slapped the top of Gallagher's right arm. "Yes, very. Malinowski's office is working on an exhumation order for my case. With real cause. Santini's name will appear on it, and there's next-of-kin authorization. I hope to have it pulled together and in chambers by late tomorrow afternoon, with luck and no interference."

Gallagher brushed the hair from his eyes. "I'm not gonna stop it. It's outa my hands now. I don't even have to fight with Collins. Look, I can understand how you want to do this for your clients, professional standards and all. But what the hell are you trying to come out with? Do your clients want to go to court against the government? That's how it's shaping. And if they don't, you gonna go alone? You got a law firm wants to donate to a cause like that? Hey, and that's another thing. What cause? Lenny, I'm not shitting around with you; I'm genuinely curious."

"I don't know, I don't know. There's a lot that stinks here. But one step at a time. Or two, at most. Bob had a good reason: he said something about not wanting the Department involved in suppression of justice."

"Neither do I. But I don't think that's what's up for grabs here. Ah, well, I'm not gonna argue. You got problems enough."

Schwartz turned up his raincoat collar. "Which reminds me, how was dinner last night?"

"Delicious. Kitty made Long Island duckling, the Kraut way, with that red cabbage stuff, you know, and—"

"Give me a break."

Gallagher laughed one of his gentler laughs, something between a guffaw and a burp. "Karen's crazy about you, is my opinion. Kitty thinks she's on the brink of divorcing you. We stayed up half the night fighting about you two. Get it together, will you, for the sake of your nervous old married buddies."

"What did *Karen* say? She was crazy about me? Divorcing me? Both?"

"Neither. She didn't say much, like that. She said she wanted the two of you to get counseling. We said yeah, that sounded right. Then she said she didn't want to talk about you, but being with us made her think of you, she said. So we just had dinner, talked. You know. But over coffee, out of nowhere she starts telling us—telling Kitty, really, like I wasn't there—telling her about the two of you when you first . . . first . . . Jesus, Lenny, she's going on about the first time you two did it. You know, went to bed together. And then about the second time and you telling her how . . . Buddy, I can't even repeat it, about your aunt. I mean, don't misunderstand me; it's no dirty story, nothing like that. It's just that it was so personal I wanted to sneak out. I mean, she wanted to tell Kitty, I understand, like guys will tell each other, you know . . . "

"I know, Tom. Thanks for . . . As they used to say, you'se is a good boy, Denny Dimwit. I'm off now."

"Yeah. Jesus, Denny Dimwit! You that old? Hey, you better bring some warmer clothing over to Warren Street. So long, buddy."

Gallagher slapped Schwartz's shoulder, giving him a good push off toward the Municipal Building. Schwartz looked up to its white wedding-cake top. They hadn't had one. They'd married in a Chicago registry office with only a few university friends in attendance, pissing off both their families. Then they'd all gone for nondescript pizza and beer in Englewood. The next weekend the two of them had splurged at the Pump Room, but Englewood had been better—thick beer foam, milky mozzarella nuptials.

At his office, Schwartz opened a can of tuna, shredded in some lettuce, chopped in a tomato, globbed on the mayonaise, and sprinkled dill and thyme. He mixed it and ate it from the stainless mixing bowl with a spoon, standing looking out the window at the empty street below.

He poured a vodka, drank it neat, called Karen.

"Hi."

"Hi."

"What are you doing?"

"Reading notes."

"How's it going?"

"Fine," she said. "It's going, you know. At this stage it's impenetrable and insubstantial, at once. When I get this into rough chapters, I'll feel better. Are you warm enough?"

"This place is warm, but I'll need to pick up some other clothes from home. I miss you."

"Yes. I'm feeling . . . Me, too. I had a nice dinner last night with Kitty and Tom."

"Yes, I just bumped into Tom. He told me, said you talked about us seeing a counselor."

"Yes. Do you still think it's an idea?"

"I'd like to. I think."

"We can talk about it this weekend. I don't know why, but I found myself telling Kitty about our early days in Chicago."

"Early nights, and Tom was that 240-pound fly on the wall. He told me, in a stumbly first confession sort of way."

"Oh, dear. Are you angry?"

"For that? No, not a bit. How could it make Gallagher's ideas about left-wing Jewish upbringings any more bizarre than they already are?"

"Len, I'm starting to think seriously about your private detective business. I didn't intend it this way, I mean with the separation during the week. But I see it *is* possible for you not to bring home the craziness you did, all that . . . I mean, I think if we could work it out through counseling, we could live together all the time, but . . . God! I'm making such a mess of saying this! I'll try to say it clearly. I really appreciate how, for once, your work is remaining your work, how it's not intervening here. I guess it's tough on you that your work just can't be brought home comfortably. You know. All that . . . Well, maybe what you're doing now is all very different from Homicide. Len? Are you there?"

"I'm here. Smiling."

"Good. Can you bring some salad and vegetables tomorrow from downtown?"

"Sure."

"Thanks. Should I find us some theater tickets or a jazz club for Saturday night?"

"Wonderful idea. Or a concert or anything that looks good."

"All right, Len. Good night."

"Good night."

Later, Addison called to say that everything was set with the Hayeses, but it had taken much more time than they'd thought, and he'd get them to a notary at nine the next morning.

Whatever Carter Hayes might know about his son's massive radiation, Schwartz felt they'd done the right thing by not informing him, them, of what they'd found. Carter Hayes had turned in his son. Carter Hayes seemed to be pressing for an investigation that would lead back to himself as directly or indirectly involved in his son's death. Was that some guilt unconsciously seeking to declare itself?

Schwartz went to bed thinking about his tongue-tied confession to Bob.

At six in the morning, he opened his eyes, remembered the phone call with Karen and smiled. He went out running in a gray mist whose damp air hit his nose and mouth with the hollow smell of just above freezing.

He felt good when the phone rang at nine. Addison was at the Hayes's apartment, saying he was running a little late, but "by 9:30 notarizationizing be in the bag, boss."

So when Malinowski called at ten to say that the notarized authorization had arrived by messenger service, Schwartz assumed that Addison was off on other related chores and "in the bag" was more of his chopped-liver English wordplay. He needed him for the afternoon, when Malinowski thought the orders would be ready to proceed to the courts, and there'd be lots of running and jumping and standing still for both of them.

Just after eleven, Schwartz finished setting up the new and specialized autopsy with Santini, assuming they'd have the body at the start of the week. Then Schwartz called the cemetery office in St. James, out on the Island, where Hayes was buried. He'd explained the process to the director, a Mr. Peters, and was getting along nicely when he referred to "gravediggers." He spent the next ten minutes listening to Peters's lecture on the use of the term "ground staff" for the "somewhat insensitive term *you* used." Schwartz mollified Peters, though he thought that "ground staff" made burial sound like a ballgame.

And this marked the turning point in the day's progress.

At twelve o'clock, Tom Gallagher called to "warn you, Lenny, 'cause I just heard that you can expect a visit from Judge Dubin."

Schwartz had thanked Gallagher not five minutes before the office doorbell rang and to "Come in, please" entered the humbug homburg and dark coat.

"Mr. Schwartz."

"Judge Dubin."

"Leonard."

"Marshall, have a seat. To what do I owe this unexpected ordeal?"

Dubin's face was heavy jawed and forever five o'clock shadowed. It gave a wince of mosquito-bite intensity. "What's the style of your office, Leonard? Bohemian?"

Schwartz looked slowly around. "Bohemian minimalist, I'd say." He nodded toward Dubin's three-piece-suited amplitude. "And your style is still baroque Hasty Pudding."

Dubin shook his head. "You've made a career of pissing on Harvard."

"Yet Harvard burns on."

"Very clever."

"Swift, actually, but you always did need notes to hand."

"Leonard, I used to think I'd get you where you were doing the most damage—in the police force. It turns out to be now that you've quit. And you know something? I find I'm not fussy."

"I don't know what you're talking about, Marshall, but

you've just blown whatever it is because this is all on tape."

Dubin put up his hands in mock horror. His hands were short and thick, and the hair from the back of his fingers showed through. "Let me hear that tape, and I'll leave right now and run an apology in every edition of next week's *Times.*"

Schwartz put his own hands up. "Gulp, you have me there, Judge. I was trying to trick you. Seriously, Marshall, I'm very pressed. I have to run around between seventeen different hard places now, chasing up an order for exhumation."

Dubin said, "I know."

"Gosh, you do? Wow, are you smart, for someone who tried to buy his way into old Harvard clubs and couldn't and so went to Hasty Pudding. Scenery, wasn't it, Dubinsky? Didn't they let you schlep scenery for three years? And then, as they say on the slopes, you dropped the 'ski' and bought your way to class marshal. Marshall the marshal. Oi-oi."

"Leonard, you make me ashamed of being Jewish."

"Marshall, the earth, the clouds, the stars that twinkle in the firmament make you ashamed of being Jewish. That's because you *are* ashamed of being Jewish. You're an Irving Berlin with no talent. And your reproach reminds me of someone named Choochie Richard Weiss, the creep who's written the lousy script you're here with today. He should have known better. You're no good with lines. Schlepping scenery, you're okay. The Pudding knew what it was doing with you."

"All right, Leonard, we don't like each other and never will. But I'm here on business bigger than our personalities. I am not going to let you get this exhumation order because there's a higher justice being served here."

"You mean you're doing a favor for a pal on the Court of Appeals?"

"A bad joke. I've been informed of the national security interest involved. And no crooked private dick, ex-crooked cop, is going to override that. Stop the lunacy now. You're *never* going to get that exhumation order in this state. Of course, if you could rebury the body in another state . . . But that requires an exhumation order, and you are *never,* et cetera, et cetera."

"Thank you, Marshall, and good-bye."

Dubin went to his homburg and black cashmere.

Schwartz said, "And I *mean* thank you. If you thought you could stop me, you would have waited to do it in the courts where it would be sure and public and painful; them that's got four aces doesn't bluff."

Dubin shut the door.

But as the day went on, it appeared to Schwartz that both of them were bluffing, or each held a pair of aces. The process wasn't stopped, but it was slowed to a crawl. Addison hadn't shown. Schwartz waited in a series of dark-paneled rooms where the clocks still went tick-tock or tick-tick. When they said 4:30, Schwartz understood he couldn't get the order until Monday, by which time who knew what smokescreens or radiation shields Weiss would have thrown up.

He'd go to the office. He'd call Karen at home to ask about the vegetables she wanted. Karen. At least he wasn't messing home with this damned business.

"Karen? Hi, darling. What sort of—"

"Don't bother."

"—of vegetables: arugula? avocado? artichoke?"

"Three things."

"Vegetables?"

"First, I've just spent two nasty hours being questioned by the CIA."

"What?"

"Second, they've been talking to Jake at New Haven. He called, very shaken."

"What?"

"And third, you . . . You . . . There's a message for you to go and identify a body—"

"A body? They couldn't have exhumed—"

"At Coney Island Hospital—"

"But—"

"The name is Addison. That's it."

BOOK IV

CHAPTER 1

Schwartz sat with the phone in his hands. His clothes felt skimpy, see-through. He hung up and hugged himself.

He stood, flapped his arms crisscross. As a child, he'd seen a picture from Russian War Relief: a Wehrmacht officer in elegant uniform freezing to death on the Russian plains, a moral picture with its caption "The Season Turns." Now he felt it from the German's point of view, undressing in his little bedroom area to put on two T-shirts, jeans over his chinos, a polo shirt, a button-down and a sweatshirt over that. Then Schwartz returned to the *Ostfront* of his desk, overdressed, awkward, still cold.

He telephoned Jake at New Haven, clamping the receiver to his ear so he wouldn't bang his head with shivers. Jake's roommate answered. Terry was a nice kid, probably not being put through Yale on the proceeds of a cocaine bribe, who told

Schwartz that Jake was out and, yes, he'd leave the message that Jake was to call.

"Sir?"

"Yes, Terry?"

"What's it like now, as a private detective?"

"It's no good. Don't become one when you graduate."

Terry laughed. "No, it's just that you're something of a romantic figure to us in New Haven."

"Just stick to . . . What is it you're studying?"

"I'm still not sure. I've sort of narrowed it down to either epistemology or stocks and bonds."

"Let's talk sometime, Terry. Please get the message to Jake. It's important. Bye."

"I will. Bye, sir."

Yale had a lot to answer. It would take poor Terry years as the stock and bond dealer he'd become to clear his head of all those epistemological snippets. Schwartz put his revolver and several boxes of bullets into his briefcase. What else? Yes. He took a long drink of vodka from the bottle and went out.

He was running to identify Abraham Resnick-Yarmolinsky-Addison's dead body. It was freezing. He was running west on Avenue Z. Freezing. Brrr. Zzzz. When autumn comes, can winter be more than two and a half hours behind? Ode to Avenue Z. Some truth wasn't beauty. That was Keats, not Shelley. Addison was all he had to know. Freezing. He hadn't seen the sky in weeks. What was up there was an orange haze over the street lamps, an electric orange going up into the flat gray skylessness.

At the hospital desk he asked for Addison. The woman told him "Rubin Ward, fifth floor." He didn't argue. The desk never told you "Morgue, sub-basement." You had always to traipse to the ward, the floor nurse, the doctor, and finally . . .

He saw her as he left the elevator. She looked up, peered and stood with a baby in her arm.

"You are he?"

"I'm—"

"You are the boss Mr. Schwartz?"

"Yes," he said. "I'm so—"

She groaned, "Oh, oh-oh. Oh-oh," and began to cry.

Schwartz touched her shoulders. She cried even harder, and her black hair went into his chest. He felt the baby she held at his waist. Her shoulders rocked back and forth under his touch.

Something pulled at his leg. "Mister, they got a candy machine there. Can I have some? Candy? Can I?"

She screamed, "What you say! What you now ask at this time for!" and still in Schwartz's arms she started hitting out with her free arm at the small boy who ducked back around Schwartz's leg, so that Addison's widow kept hitting Schwartz, crying harder with each powerful slap she landed on the back of Schwartz's thigh.

The boy was half under his raincoat. "Mrs. Addi . . . Mrs. Resnick," he began, under her wailings, "I'm so sorry."

"I know. I know. Oh. Is so . . . Oh. So terrible!" She was shouting, crying, screaming the few words, hitting the back of his raincoat.

Schwartz heard a smaller crying behind him, on the floor. He tried to see, turning with the boy clinging to his leg still saying "Candy?" and the mother again clamped onto him with her infant between.

Halfway around, his coat collar twisted into his neck by the woman's fisted grief, Schwartz managed to see a tiny girl in a very flouncy pink dress lying on her stomach on the floor, hitting it steadily with a pudgy hand as she cried in long shrieks.

"Mischa!" Mrs. Resnick screamed at a level so startling

that Schwartz involuntarily jumped back, and the four of them tottered like a totem pole about to drop.

"Mischa, you look, you let Marinachka onto floor like that! You'll kill me!"

She sobbed and wailed again, burying her head in Schwartz's coat. His hand was on the sleeping infant's head. Such peace in the middle of such chaos. Then he felt Mischa let go. The boy went to his little sister on the floor and with his left foot rolled her over. She immediately stopped crying and looked up pleasantly from her nest of pink ruffles.

"Please, Mrs. Resnick," Schwartz said, desperate for some decorum, pushing her shoulder. "Let's sit down, over there. Please."

Crying, she reeled off to the children. She yanked up little Mischa by his arm. Mischa pulled along Marina by her arm, and the four of them danced chairwards together like characters stuck to each other in a folktale. On the other hand, short, stocky Irina Resnick was broad-shouldered enough to have yanked four or forty where she would. She threw Mischa onto a chair and little Marina seemed to fly with him, so that she landed perched, pink and delighted on his lap. Irina with the infant sat down on the sofa with Schwartz. She began to rock and sob quietly.

"Mrs. Resnick, what happened?"

"Marinachka was on floor, so—"

"No, Mrs. Resnick, to your husband."

"You not know? My God! Two inches from home, he crosses Island Avenue and a car is coming and . . . " She stopped in sobs.

"I understand. I'm so sorry. Take your time."

"So this car comes around corner from nowhere and runs him all over and doesn't stop!"

"How awful. Were there witnesses? Did people see this, Mrs. Resnick?"

"Of course people see this. Abrasha see this!" She started crying.

Schwartz saw the logic of the victim as witness to his own death. "That's not quite . . . Have statements been given to the police?"

"Police, yes." She rubbed her eyes with the back of her hand and looked redly at Schwartz. "What for you getting him involved this? All his time he's up to plenty trouble, believe me, plenty funny stuff, but he never gets . . . Never gets . . . " She sobbed. "Excuse, please, Mister, I must to say this."

"I understand, Mrs. Resnick. Of course you have to. But what makes you so sure this terrible thing was connected to what Abrasha was working on with me?"

She looked at Schwartz as if he were a half-wit. "You saying? Of course I'm certain. Abrasha tells me this. How I be certain? You crazy?"

Schwartz dropped his eyes. Addison had lived long enough to . . . He must have died in front of her, in her arms. "I didn't know he . . . Oh, Mrs. Resnick, forgive me. I thought he died instantly."

"What?" She began crying, catching her breath, banging the sofa between them with her fist. "Of course he not die instantly!" She sobbed, caught her breath. "You think? My God, you crazy? Abrasha's not die! He's alive. You crazy? He's in there waiting to speak you. Die dead? You think he dead?" She started to wail.

Schwartz stood.

"Dead? You think he dead I be so calm like this!" she screamed at Schwartz's back.

On the corner bed of the Rubin Ward, Addison lay propped up with his eyes shut, his burly, hairy arms and shoulders rolling out over the strapping plaster around his chest. He looked like a drugged bear in a white barrel. He looked terrible.

"Addison! You look wonderful! You're alive!" Schwartz said, laughing, leaning over.

Addison's eyes opened. "What you think, little hitting and running going waste me, boss? Few cracked ribs, some sprains, bruisy-wooziness, but I got car make—black Cougar Mercury. Not license."

"You think it was no . . . Damn, it's . . . I love you. It's so good to see you alive! I . . . "

"Shh. Is okay. Good being alive. And to see you. Lenny, is no accident. Car coming at me from my sidelong vision and I jump and also seeing car swerving to follow me into curb to get me. I think because of . . . Ooh, hurts. Of snuff information I keep chasing . . . Oh, full of pain, a little. But okay, I got insurances."

"Take it easy. You don't think maybe it was a warning?"

"I think? I think you remember fire on Flatbush Avenue? That kind warning. If they kill you, that's okay. If not, it's warning. Ooh-ooh! I talk slow in short. Breaths. Less chest. Swell. You see Irina? Baby kids?"

"Yes. They're all—sensational. Yes."

Addison motioned Schwartz closer and whispered, "I got police phone written, also notes for you from what I'm up to. There in folder in drawer. Cost two thousand. Don't ask. Two thousand dollars' worth of don't ask, I bought to buy what I write down there from person Anon who see disgusting pigshit snuff show last April. Maybe same one, because . . . You read. See. So don't ask what I buy with two grand. Or who from."

"I won't, Addison. Here?"

"That folder, yes. Take."

"You'd better rest now. I'll get someone to guard you."

"Being silly, boss. Really?"

"Not for you, tough guy. For Irina's peace of mind."

"Aha. Good thinking. Is also kind thinking. Is also clever thinking to protect you from her? She's fabulous woman, yes?"

"Fabulous. I'll stop by tomorrow. Need anything?"

"Psst, you sneak me vodka. Irina thinks no good. Hey, I'm back at work next week."

"Sure, sure. Next week, the week after. Take care." Schwartz patted Addison's rough head and remembered his hand on the infant's, that soft eggshell.

He stopped in the hallway at the candy machine and bought packs of M & M's and took them to Irina.

"Irina? May I call you Irina?"

"Of course."

"Call me Len or Lenny. Here, for the children. You need anything? Any money?"

"Money? No," she said, looking to check on the two older children on the sofa. They were asleep. "Abrasha's good man, give me all moneys I need."

"Fine. I'm going to have some protection for him, a guard."

"Police give this?"

"Sure," he fibbed. He patted her shoulder. "I'll be back tomorrow. If you need anything, call me—in Brooklyn."

He walked to the elevator, convincing himself that if Addison could survive being run over, maybe Schwartz could survive going home.

As he unlocked the door, Karen called, "Len, I wish you'd go." Then there was silence.

She was slumped in her reading chair with a large whiskey, which wasn't her drink. When he went to kiss her she pulled her head away. He pulled it back and kissed her.

"Rough stuff now?" she asked.

"No. Gentle stuff. I love you, Karen. We're going to get counseling together and I'm happy my assistant Addison isn't dead, despite your message."

"I gave you exactly the message I got from someone screaming in broken English."

"That was Irina, his wife. He was run down by a car; he's got some broken ribs. The car's probably in worse shape."

"I don't want to know. If you insist on being here, at least don't bring in the violence."

"Right. What did Jake say?"

"Not much. That someone from the FBI asked about you and said some awful things."

"That's it?"

"Yes. And that he wanted to talk to you."

"Damn . . . Why are you drinking Scotch?"

"It's Irish. I found some Irish whiskey here and felt like getting ethnically drunk. Okay? Don't you, ever?"

"The idea of a Manischewitz high is too depressing. Karen, you used to like me sharing things about my work with you."

"That was before your work began attacking me. Look, that CIA slime had the nerve to show up at MOMA when I was working. Can you believe it? He said the library was too public and made me go out to the sculpture garden. Do you remember the delightful weather this afternoon, the temperature falling out the bottom of the thermometer? And for over an hour—"

"You said two."

"Arrest me! It felt like ten! He asked me about your politics, my politics, Jake's—for heaven's sake—Jake's politics! This is what I mean by your work attacking me."

"What was his name?"

"Wilson. Yes, Wilson. He—"

"Wait. Was it . . . Wait." Schwartz picked up his briefcase to find the Weiss photosheet, but as he balanced it on his knee it slipped, tipped, fell open, and the gun fell out. A box hit the carpet. Bullets rolled to Karen's feet.

"Oh, hooray!" she cheered into her whiskey. "Here's another first from Mister Nonviolent, bringing home an arsenal. What next, corpses at my feet like some damned cat with birds? And does it expect to be petted?"

Schwartz, on his knees, had picked up the gun and was scrambling after the bullets. He started to laugh. He made a little pile of the gun and bullets at Karen's feet. He said. "Pet me?"

Karen hit him on the head with her fist.

He sat. "Pet me?"

Karen slapped his head.

"Pet me?"

Karen patted his head and came down onto the carpet beside him.

"I love you," he said and kissed her on the lips.

She fingered his cuffs. "I like you because you're wearing two pairs of trousers and because you *do* touch me when you say things like that. Think we can stay married?"

"Yes. Please. God, why hasn't Jake called? I left a message with Terry. Maybe it's too early."

"I've called and called, too," she said. "I think Jake will either show up here or lie low for a while."

"How can you be so cool about Jake? Here, this," he said, handing her Weiss's photo. "Was this the CIA man?"

"Yes."

"His name is Weiss. I wonder why he bothers changing it? Anyway, he's trouble and I'm worried about Jake."

"Don't. Jake's my very cool son. He's more sensible than—as the shrink said—either of us put together. Len, you're always nervous about *yourself* with Jake when you say you're worried about Jake."

"Karen, does Jake tell you about his sex life?"

"No. Is that your worry? I assume you give him man-to-man advice."

"Advice? From time to time I scream at him about AIDS. My God, what in hell do kids do these days? Jake says I shouldn't worry. What a world. It's the plague, the thirteenth century. The revivalists are thriving. But I'm a healthy enough fellow. Kiss me."

She did. She pulled away. "Before I forget this Wilson-

Weiss creep. First, I told him the truth and finally I told him to take a flying leap. He kept staring at the Maillol superwoman, and it wasn't aesthetic study."

"What do you think he really wanted?"

"Once I stopped being scared I could see that being scared is what he wanted. So that I'd scare you, do you suppose? He knew the story of your life. It was clear he didn't need my information. I'm helping you again, aren't I?"

"Yes. Hate it?"

"No, not if I can feel better about us. I wish we could make the feeling last for more than forty minutes, though. I don't mean the sex. I mean the friendship."

"Well, we're going to try. But for now, what about forty or so minutes of sex before I make dinner?" he asked, pulling Karen down on the floor.

Karen laughed, squirming, saying "Ouch!"

"What?"

"Darling, it's just the bullets up my ass."

"Oh, God," Schwartz said, scrambling to pick them from the floor.

Karen helped. She put the gun back into the briefcase, picked up the folder and collected Addison's notes to slip in. She glanced at the notes, then began scanning them quickly. "Len?"

"What?"

"What am I reading? What *is* this? This is unbelievable! What . . . Do people really . . . What are you investigating? My God! This is the most revolting . . . "

"Give it to me."

"No, let me finish this."

"Come on, Karen, if it's so revolting."

"Oh, God. It's a description of one of those snuff films, isn't it?"

Schwartz pulled the notes from Karen. "Something like

that. And that's just the sort of thing I'd never bring home. I mean, I brought it home, but it's the sort of thing I'd never leave around . . . Well, I sort of did leave it around, but I . . . " He put the notes into the folder.

They sat on the floor looking at each other. He put out his hand. "You shouldn't have seen it. I'm sorry."

They held hands. Then Schwartz took the folder and briefcase upstairs to the guest room. He'd look at it later. He took off his summer clothes and took off the summer clothes under those. When he returned to the living room, showered and sensibly dressed, Karen was putting down the phone.

"Jake?" he asked.

"Yes. I mean, no, he's not there. Terry's not actually cursing me, but he's hissing promises to force Jake to call the instant he sees him. He says he's left messages at some other likely places. So."

"So, Mama-cool."

"I'm cool. For all you know, I'm doing this for you. I never said I was cool about *you* and Jake. Well, so what do you have to do this weekend?"

"Just staying here with you, as per—"

"Don't take me for a jerk, Schwartzie. Come on!"

"I have to visit Addison at Coney Island Hospital. Maybe I have to chase after an exhumation order because of interference being thrown up by my dear old buddy, the drear Marshall Dubin. Oh, and I'm thinking of breaking into Weiss's office, or what he calls his office. Another ordinary weekend in Park Slope."

"And to think you're not even a cop anymore. Will there be time to go out? There's a nice concert at Symphony Space. Oh, and the car will finally be ready, by lunch tomorrow."

"What's the concert? How much?"

"It's—you know it was a very major sort of renovation or

whatever they call going down into the engine. An underhaul. Under a thousand."

"Speak low, if you speak lucre. A thousand American dollars?"

"It's Schoenberg and Berg, chamber work. You'll adore it."

"If it's under a thousand that means it's over nine-fifty, because if it were under nine-fifty Dave would have said 'not much over eight.' Symphony Space sounds great, but no Yupper West Side eating. It's all so bad: northern Italian food by chefs who've watched too many late-night films from Japan."

"Speaking of which, what are you making for dinner tonight?"

"Fettuccine Noguchi. That's pasta on the rocks with seaweed."

It was steak and frozen vegetables and all right because of the bottle of Hermitage.

Afterwards, they both looked at the telephone. Karen wondered if Jake had maybe gone up to brood with Grandma in Boston. Schwartz thought not, thought they'd better stop brooding about Jake.

"So who are you calling?"

"Bob Malinowski, at home."

After giving Bob details about the Addison hit-and-run and requesting a police guard, when Malinowski made small coughing sounds, Schwartz said he understood very well that he'd have to pay for it. Schwartz apologized for the trouble and hung up.

Karen asked if Bob had been saying "Not at all, sir," and "Thank you so much for disturbing me, sir."

"Something like that. Darling, what can I get for Addison? Fruit or magazines seem so boring."

"Lots of flowers. Everyone loves flowers, but men rarely are given them."

"You're brilliant. Addison brought me some, three million years ago on Flatbush Avenue. Great bunches of dyed baby-blue somethings that had clearly fallen off a hearse, on its way to the funeral of good taste."

Karen smiled over her coffee. "You like him, don't you?"

"I don't know. I suppose. He's like a feral version of me, a manic brother I never had. Do you ever think that because you and I are only children and Jake's an only child that we're, I don't know, really more like three bright, competitive siblings?"

"No." She finished her coffee. "Of course, the odds were for us to have one child, if we had any. I think they were against him being so unspoiled, and I don't take more than eighty percent of the credit. Seriously, you've been . . . " She reached along his shirtsleeve. "Maybe I don't tell you enough how good a father you've been and are. You know, the bribe can't touch that."

"Thank you. Karen? Let's go upstairs soon. I want to show you *my* feral version of me."

She shook her head. "I'll get the wildness from the paintings I study. Right now I need gentleness from you."

"All right. I'll be your soft and cuddly *fauve.*"

Schwartz woke so wound in Karen, arms and legs around, so belly bound to Karen that he didn't want to get up, ever. Home was this warm space between the blanket and the nape of her neck.

Karen turned. "Mmm. What are you doing to me?"

"Musing on you."

"Again? You were so amusing on me last night. Hey, where are you going?"

"It's Saturday morning in Brooklyn. Some guys go out and wash the car, and others go out and break into federal offices."

"I want to go with you," she called, stretching her arms out.

"My cyclonic girlfriend, you shift direction faster than I can change sail or course or whatever you do to keep a metaphor afloat. Besides, it's sort of, aw, gosh, breaking the law and might be, shucks, danger . . . you know, the 'D' word. You said you were going to work on the great American artbook on Russian paintings. Wasn't it 'rayonism' you were going to begin?"

"I'll leave rayonism to duPont. I want to go with you."

Schwartz went to the bed, buttoning his shirt.

"You *have* to love me, Karen. You're telling my sort of joke, now."

"I do. I have to love you. Let me button your shirt."

He bent lower. She unbuttoned his shirt.

This made him forty minutes late to Canal Street. (But who cared? Who cared!)

Schwartz's plan had the advantage of simplicity and the disadvantage of silliness. It involved four stores: two electric, one odds-and-ends, and one used clothing.

From Warren Street, he called the federal office building which he knew was closed and so got the guard at the desk.

"Yes, I know it's closed. Is this John?"

"No, it's Jim."

"Jim, I mean. Jim, this is Fogarty, from Building and Maintenance. You know that construction in the south wing towards Lafayette?"

"Fogar . . . Yes. What about—"

"Has the electrician come yet on that emergency call?"

"What? No, no—"

"Damn it! Listen, Jim, some offices on the tenth floor there where all that work's going on? Well, they had a local power outage there late yesterday. The construction people promised an emergency repairman would be around so everything would be fixed by Monday morning. Said about ten o'clock this morning."

"It's only about a quarter past. That's not really late. Those guys can keep you forever."

"All right. Look, Jim, I'll check back with you later. Associated Electrical," Schwartz said, looking at the shirt and yellow hard hat he had purchased. "They know where it is. But get a good look at the security pass."

"Course I will. I'll be looking out for him, Mr. Fogarty."

"Good. Get back to you later, Jim."

Schwartz typed in the official-looking card, then stamped it. He changed and left his office, thankful that Jim was even simpler than his plan.

He knocked on the glass. The guard came to the door. Schwartz held the card to the window. It was stamped full of federal eagles and words like "Security" and "Temporary" and "Work" and "Pass." He let the donkey jacket fall back so that Jim, a portly fellow of comfortable white mustache, could get a clear view of the electrical tool belt slung on his hips which had cost $32.80.

"Associated?" Jim asked, opening the door.

"That's it. The screwup on the tenth floor, back there," Schwartz said.

Jim had him sign in. Schwartz had written "Steve" and was drawn to make the C for "Canyon," but thinking that would be too crudely comic, finished it as on the card with "-ohen."

"So you know," Jim began, eying his cushioned chair.

"Yeah, down there back of the partitions and then up. Shouldn't take too long."

But in front of Weiss's door, Schwartz experienced a panic, recalling that he had no idea of lock picking and less of electronics, should the door have an alarm. The panic ended in

228

I RVING WEINMAN

his recalling that should anything alarming happen, he was supposedly up there fixing it.

He turned the handle. Locked. It was a heavy bronze knob
and lock plate in a dark wooden door whose top half was frosted,
bubbly glass. He urged himself on by considering that he had to
be nearly as intelligent as the cretins who did break-ins every day.

All right. The door was heavy but didn't appear wired to
an alarm. From the inside of his jacket he brought out the crow-
bar, a piece of equipment he'd considered Jim without the electrical engineering background to understand. Now, if he did this
just right, with this sort of door, he'd be inside neatly and quietly.

He placed the flattened end in just above the knob and
middle of the lock plate. He pulled back. Good, yes. Definitely.
Just another steady, delicate . . .

The doorframe cracked; the glass plate fell in and crashed
to pieces.

Schwartz was standing on tiptoes with his eyes closed,
whispering "Shh! Shh!" to bits of wood and broken glass. Why
was the noise continuing? Was the great roar some special federal
alarm? Was it his luck to have set off some WPA alarm system
built by 312 unemployed alarmmakers who'd show the world how
an alarm could alarm? What the hell was roaring?

It was the pressure in his ears from not breathing. He
opened his eyes and looked down the empty corridor. He turned
the doorknob, and since it still wouldn't open, he put his gloved
hands on the frame and stepped over and through the locked
door.

And marvelous! Everything had been moved from the
front office but its upended desk. At least he didn't have to smash
the door to Weiss's inner office-for-a-day. But in there it was the
same story: flag and photos gone, the desk upended.

A waste of time. Schwartz pulled out a drawer and
slammed it back in. Damn! He pulled out another drawer.

229

Nothing. Another. What did he expect, Weiss's signed confession that he'd framed Virgil? Another . . .

This one stuck. It moved a bit. What was back there? He moved the drawer above it, now to its left. Something was wedged between. A magazine. He got his fingers on it, jiggled the drawer back and forth and drew it out. The cover said only *AMPICS*. Photos of electrical meters? Maybe Associated Electric would . . .

Schwartz turned the pages. He stopped, took a plastic bag from his pocket and put the magazine inside. What remained in his mind weren't so much the ordinary awful naked poses—the swallowings, wallowings, impalements—or even the devices of wood, leather or lifelike painted limbs, but the determined smiles of those women amputees, the triumph of the spirit's sickest parody. What was humanity but such a poor, unforked suffering as these smiling, fucked stumpers?

Putting the broken glass into a bin of rubbish down the hall, Schwartz thought of Addison's notes from the snuff show informant. He thought of C. Richard Weiss enjoying the *AMPICS* photos under those of his President and chieftains, beside his American flag.

Schwartz considered whether Addison might like a small palm or one of those ficus trees that seemed woven, they had such twisted trunks.

Twisted trunks: he put *AMPICS* in its plastic bag into a padded envelope, stapled it shut and sealed it with tape. He made a similar package of the skin flakes in the stamp envelope, labeled both and phoned Malinowski.

"Can you hold these in safekeeping?"

"Yes, sir. Potential evidence for assumed homicide pending exhumation."

"Assumed exhumation. Bob, this is a rotten one-plank bridge you're walking out on with me."

"I'm certain we'll get the exhumation order. I have someone chasing those papers today. I thought it would be better for a serving officer to ring judges' doorbells on the weekend."

"Judges don't have doorbells; they have doormen. And you're right. Thanks, Bob. What about the guard for Addison?"

"You don't know? Addison discharged himself early this morning. The precinct says they'll still have to send some sort of bill for the roster change."

"Yes, sure. Christ, he shouldn't be out of the hospital. Listen, if you need anything from me we haven't anticipated, let me know—even at home, I'm happy to say."

He put the phone down and pulled for a while at his top lip. Then he called Karen to ask how she felt about his sort of working and sort of being home, too. She said she felt all right, in a shaky sort of way.

"As long as you're trusting me, there might be a call from Bob about the exhumation order. Mind?"

She didn't. Schwartz said he adored her for not minding and also for certain matinal unbuttonings. She said "matinal" was a great improvement on "sort of" and the next best thing to having a Latin lover was having a Latinate one.

Schwartz felt like dancing, like checking the phone messages he should have checked half an hour before.

"Boss, is Addison from at home. Sorry aggravate you, but I hate so hospital, the night I spend there kill me with frights. And they are pissed, making sure I sign twenty times say they are not responsible. That's why I want to leave because they irresponsible. But protection, here in neighborhood, don't worry: this place we got defending like Stalingrad. Beside, I do much more work for us from house. And postscript from Irina, boss. She's completely nuts about you."

And then, act of good faith, Addison gave Schwartz his home address and phone number, which Schwartz already knew. The moment after he put down the phone thinking that Addison could be completely trusted, he thought of why he couldn't trust Addison. His circumstances, for one thing: a Russian émigré of

doubtful background and incredible foreground was too easy for
Weiss to pressure. Wasn't he? God, that was the high road to
paranoia, which reminded him to call his friend Ed Ginsburg. As
owner of a bookstore, Ed might know of Sci-Fi Fisher's where-
abouts; besides, he'd been wanting to speak with Ed about—
everything.

"You answered the phone, Ed? It's Saturday, your busiest
day, the day when some of the browsers are readers and some of
the readers are buyers. Is business that bad?"

"I deduce from this garbage that I am speaking with none
other than Leonard Schwartz, boy private eyeball. Well, three
weeks off the city payroll: are you rich, famous, tough at last? And,
yes, there are buyers and, hey, I just sold a collection of Poeiana,
horrible word but big profit, to one of those small colleges in
western Massachusetts we always chuckled at, whose graduates
are doing so much more interestingly than us drab Cantabs. So
I'm feeling very expansive-expensive and can spare about thirty
more seconds to talk with my friend, if, that is, I can bring myself
to stop talking before thirty seconds are up and I don't think I
can. Help. Interrupt! Help!"

Schwartz shouted "Sci-Fi" into the phone.

"What? I don't carry it."

"Him."

"Sci . . . Cy Fisher? What do you want with him?"

"It's private eyeballing, Ed. Where is he these days?"

"He works out of home. One of those enormous old
places in Midwood, not so far from you in Park Slope. He lives
there with his ancient mother and is in the phone book and is
doing well. This after closing Conspiracy Books a number of
years back. He said it was government harassment; I heard the
rent zoomed. Maybe the two were connected. Then he worked up
at Liberation Books for a while, but Cy the Great Leveler has to
be boss, so there was friction and he quit. Listen, it's easy to make

jokes about Sci-Fi, but he's paid his dues. He's a very good person. Eminently unlikable. And—"

"Stop, Ed. This is your interrupter speaking. Any tips on how to get information from him? I remember he had a reputation for being paranoid."

"Cy? Are you kidding? All you do is take him to lunch. You see, no one in his right mind would take him to lunch because his conversation is all about how there are seventeen plots against him, and when you finally get fed up and ask him to prove it, he says the proof is that no one ever takes him to lunch. And all this, you see, while he's eating, being taken to lunch, so that no one ever takes—"

"Anything else? Anything else?"

"No. Yes. If you go to his house, bring gifts of food. A flight of geese, a smoked ox. But eat before you go. *Your* gift he puts into a freezer the size of the Ritz— 'for Mom,' he says. She's ninety-four, they're both thin as rails, so you tell me."

"Good. And how's Ben?"

"He's fine, we're fine. He was just saying how he's missed you, and I don't mean you buying his overpriced cognac. We . . . Note how I'm slowing down? Karen's been in. We've had lunch. So may I, my dear friend, politely inquire what the fuck's going on? You've always been our inspirational straight couple. We know a few others, straight and gay, who've been together almost as long as you two, but most of them are so damn dull. So, what I'm saying, and I know I'm talking faster again, but please don't interrupt, is that if you want to talk or just see me or us and have lunch or whatever, we're here. You and I go back forever, Len, for heaven's sake, to pre-*Love Story* Harvard."

"Thanks, Ed. Things are, even as I listen to you slow down and speed up, getting better with Karen and me. We're dating again! Going to Symphony Space tonight."

"Old atonal home night! So are we. Let's meet and go out

afterwards? I know. You have to come back downtown, so come back to our place for take-out Chinese. What could be more New York than a carton of cooling shredded beef in Greenwich Village?"

Schwartz said it sounded tacky and irresistible, though he'd check it with Karen, and Ed interrupted his thanks by saying that was fine but he couldn't spend all day on the phone. Didn't Schwartz know the store was busy?

He did, hung up and called Fisher.

"My name is Len Schwartz, a friend of Ed Ginsburg. I'd like to talk to you about V. J. Hayes."

"Why? What do you think I know?"

"Over lunch. Is it too late for today, anywhere you'd like?"

"Anywhere I'd like? You'd take me to Windows on the World?"

"No, nor to Four Seasons. On the other hand, I wasn't going to suggest Sammy's, Mr. Fisher."

"So what are we talking here? I want to be precise. I like exactitude, Mr. . . . "

"Schwartz, Len Schwartz."

"I'll call you Schwartz. Len's such a . . . Wait. You're Ginsburg's friend Schwartz the cop?"

"I was a policeman. I'm now a private investigator. If you like fish, Gage and Tollner's might be convenient for both of us."

"I can travel. I tell you what; I'd like to eat someplace new and hip, Schwartz. Schwartz, Schwartz. I'm sure I've met you. A big guy, right?"

"No. Medium. Well, medium-small, for exactitude. But wiry."

"Schwartz, is that a Brooklyn accent under the mother-of-pearl inlay?"

———

The minute Fisher came through the revolving door of Diana's, Schwartz recognized him. Fisher was the only one slouching, looking back over both shoulders, the only one with the short white messy beard and knapsack over a black and white giant houndstooth raglan greatcoat. Schwartz waved.

"Sorry I'm late," Fisher said, ignoring Schwartz's hand to twist breathless from under his knapsack and start on the saucer-sized coatbuttons. "I took a few minutes to do some research on you, Schwartz. The word is you're a clever cop. Private eye, whatever. A lefty. What's that mean for a cop—you won't throw stones at Mario Cuomo? So show me. Say something clever. No, tell me about this place," he said, curving into his chair. "I see fake marble columns and from the address I'd say this was once a decent schmata salesroom. Lots of real flowers and classy diners. That I can tell because they're nearly perfect at pretending they're not staring at me."

"Why should they?" Schwartz asked, staring at the string-bean man wearing a yellow T-shirt with big purple letters: BRING BACK THE NO-SLOGAN T-SHIRT.

Schwartz said, "I thought Diana's met your criteria. Owned, managed and cheffed by post-feminist women, serving a clientele, especially during the week, that's sixty percent successful professional and business women, several of whom, my wife among them, chew thoughts here about how neatly the concept 'post-feminism' does away with feminism. I thought you'd be interested."

"I'm not married," said Fisher. "But I know. I live with my ninety-four-year-old mother and I have a few lady friends, one of whom I sleep with sometimes. But maybe I can't know? Is that apples and oranges, logically?"

"More like apples and apple strudels."

"Okay, Schwartz. Not great, but not bad for a cop. I think

if the food's good enough we might get along. You're in luck, because I don't drink. Just seltzer."

That was just as well. Fisher ordered two hors d'oeuvres, the two that were as expensive as any two entrées. And then, by listening with care to the recitation of the specials, he was able to find the one entrée twice as expensive as the two hors d'oeuvres.

Schwartz ordered a salad and mineral water.

"Fisher—"

"Cy. Nobody I eat with calls me Fisher or Sci-Fi. Here," he said, bending to the knapsack. "Here's a pamphlet of mine I thought you'd appreciate, with that accent. It's a history of local radicalism."

Schwartz took it. It was called "Only the Red Know Brooklyn," and Schwartz knew Fisher had that introductory patter down pat. "Cute title. Thanks very—"

"Two-fifty."

"What did you say?"

"Two dollars and fifty cents. It cost me. They're almost out of print, now."

Schwartz wondered if, between double courses, Fisher would hawk pamphlets table to table. He pulled out the contents of his pocket and found $2.50 for Fisher in the smallest coins, and pushed them across the table.

Fisher took them. "It never fails. *I'm* supposed to be the boor and the schnorrer, and I bring people like you to the limits of their so-called good manners in a few minutes. Hey, this is good, this pheasant pâté. Rich, but good: you should order something more than salad. I like to see people as their veneers peel. You want to know someone, know them pissed off."

"Some dictum," said Schwartz. "Mid-life in Midwood with Mother must be wonderful."

Fisher's mouth bent up so that the white grizzle twisted and shook under his long, thin nose. He was laughing. "My mother is a saint. For her, there is no evil but everyone needs help. She's much crazier than I am. And I don't think she's happy, but she believes in the millennium and she's sticking around for it. Each birthday I tell her, 'Maybe this year, Ma,' and she says, 'I certainly hope so, Sonny,' and we start in on the candles. You know, this lobster stuff in this pastry is very good."

"V. J. Hayes, please."

Fisher chewed and stared at Schwartz. He reached into his knapsack and came up with glasses, put them on and stared at Schwartz again. "So far," he said, "I've gone about blurred. It makes me less nervous; it also makes me hear better. Now I want to see you clearly. How much are you going to tell *me*?"

"I think I can tell you about everything. I figure my 'about' everything and this lunch equal your everything."

"If the entrée's as good as the hors d'oeuvres and your answers are as good as the entrée, I will. Now talk about Virgil's father."

"I know he's a retired program administrator for Brookhaven Labs, but he hasn't retired from the John Birch Society. He's hired me to prove Virgil didn't die of AIDS, as the coroner's report strongly suggests. His motives stink, but he's probably correct on that."

"Uh-huh," said Fisher.

Schwartz sipped water and watched Fisher sop the lobster sauce and bits of pâté with the same large piece of bread, a skeletal Pignatelli. "Cy, you remind me of a very fat man."

"I'm not going to be baited. I don't have time to cook like this at home. That's all. Listen, if I would've asked you for a thousand bucks to talk, you would have given me a thousand. Besides," he looked up with his bent smile, "you're in the middle of telling me what *you* know. So give me VJ, now."

Schwartz said, "There are reasons to suspect that the AIDS business was a cover-up for VJ's death. This, I think, is what it meant to cover: Virgil Hayes woke up one day, thanks to his girlfriend Ann's interest in not having the planet trashed or ashed, to find he was providing codes for NSA cryptography. Imagine his chagrin and delight when some time later, fooling about in his dad's office or with something brought home by Pop, he found he could crack its code—because he'd helped provide it or was just damned clever. And then imagine that he found it concerned something big and nasty about—I'm vague here— some connection between something at Brookhaven and some- thing at conveniently nearby Shoreham which wasn't supposed to be and which, if blown, would be damaging to the nuclear power industry. Somewhere in this, two years or so back, there appeared a CIA or NSA or something agent named something with a W—Williams or Wilson or mostly Weiss. Here's Weiss, that photo, in full frontal nattiness. Recognize him?"

Fisher didn't look at the photosheet. "Later," he said. "Go on."

"I'll skip some things that concern me, not you, things like bending of police rules, a plan involving job favors and bribe providing and, in fact, a formerly reputable chief coroner- pathologist up to the chin he doesn't have in this funny death certificate."

Schwartz looked at the piece of bread he hadn't touched. "Perhaps Virgil Hayes took some vital radioactive evidence. He must have felt he had to take the risk. And I think the terminal illness it produced was used somehow to set up and fake his death. I'm not at all sure of the details. My pet theory, to date, is that Virgil would have told his tale to the world with his deadly proof, but Weiss and company put it about that Virgil was spying for the Russians to neutralize him. And he got the radiation tumors to appear on the friendly coroner's report as AIDS-re- lated Kaposi's sarcoma. Whether Weiss's or the CIA's or the NSA's hand was in any of the other circumstantial evidence of high AIDS-risk activity, I have no idea. That's my story, Cy, and I'm stuck with it."

Fisher nodded.

"So what do you know?"

Fisher narrowed his eyes.

"Fisher, how's your entrée?"

"Great quail. I've never had it before, but I can tell this is very good, because if I'm wrong, good quail would be even better than I think. Optimistic, isn't it? I guess I'm my ma's boy in some ways."

"Well, what's her son's story?"

"He's a nervous sixty-year-old, doing okay now. But the years '69 through '73 were tough for him and Ma when he was in the slammer, guilty of slowing down the killing in Asia and other related crimes for humanity."

"Have I told you everything you know about Carter Hayes?" Schwartz asked.

"Yeah, in effect."

"Then here's something new. It was Carter Hayes who turned in Virgil."

Fisher stopped eating. He tapped the side of his plate. "Yes, yes. Oh, wow!" he said. "Sorry, Schwartz. In times of deep insight I revert to The Who or Janis Joplin."

"Perfectly understandable, Cy. I myself flip back to high school in Crown Heights."

"Yeah. Okay, for the quail and that Carter Hayes bit and your Brooklyn boyhood, I'll tell you. Wait, just let me mop up this sauce here. It's the best quail sauce I've ever had. You really should have ordered some."

"I know," Schwartz said, remembering Ed's description of Cy as a "very good person" and "eminently unlikable."

"Okay," said Fisher. "I was working with Mobilization for Survival when I first met VJ, through that tall, neurotic Ann who got scared off into the arms of that artiste. He's lucky. She's making him famous; she's a great organizer. Anyway, I put Hayes onto the idea that it was more than the luck of LILCO that put Shoreham so close to Brookhaven. I gave him books on the nuclear industry and the power brokers, industry ties with secret research, NSA controls, all sorts of linkages. It amazed him, especially the role of so-called 'pure' science like his own, at that outfit in Princeton. So he became one of the radicals in the movement—first to fasten to the Shoreham fence, first to throw himself in front of bulldozers, lots of short arrests. That sort of thing. Then he dropped out. Ann told me they'd split up and that he was being bugged by the CIA. Shortly after this, I was, too. Maybe NSA. Who the hell knows. That photo? Wilson was what he called himself then. He was the nastiest of the turdheads. Looks something like you. So according to him, VJ was supposedly the enemy. The same old lies. Then VJ calls and shows up late at night with a story so crazy it made perfect sense of some loose pieces I'd been aware of. Working with another smart guy, he'd cracked a code, information he'd gotten through his father. He never said much about the old man. A very loyal son. So I asked him first thing if he was selling information or giving it away. I'm a radical left-winger, Schwartz, but I'm an American radical and wouldn't have anything to do with that shit-eating USSR establishment. VJ's denial was good enough for me. Straightest person I've ever known. Bizarrely honest. I got a theory that's somehow how they got onto him. So we met a few more times in a few obscure places. He was being watched. He'd tell me how it was coming—he said he was working it out with care, with this other mathematician, and they'd found that, as opposed to stated policy . . . "

The waitress came over. Fisher decided finally to have the dessert trolley rolled over and get "little samples" of each, which ended up as two big bowlfuls. Then he concentrated on eating until the waitress had left the coffee on the table.

"If people asked me out to eat more, Schwartz, I think I wouldn't eat like this," Fisher began, wiping a long chocolate dragmark from his chin. "I know this kind of eating might be the reason they don't ask me more, but when they do, you see, I take no chances. Yeah, so getting back to Virgil. Virgil Hayes took chances. Pu-239, plutonium. That's what he found. Against the specific terms the Regulatory Commission had set: no plutonium production at Shoreham. Plutonium, you know, the boom-boom stuff. But wait, listen to this: VJ found that Shoreham, without being officially open, was secretly producing it as part of the NSA experiment at Brookhaven, administered in part by his father. And the purpose of this cozy project was to find ways to *disguise* plutonium production in order to make it at nuclear power plants where it wasn't legal to make it. Nice? An illegal contract including an NSA-controlled section of the AEC. And they'd found a method or two and were starting to produce right under the noses of the Nuclear Regulatory Commission. So VJ understood that nothing could be revealed until he had overwhelming proof. I saw VJ once more, a few months before he died. He looked terrible. I knew the moment I saw him what he'd been up to. He wouldn't compromise anyone else, so when I asked him straight out he didn't answer, but he wouldn't deny it. He'd taken some of the plutonium. What he said was that he now had proof— photo and copies of pertinent documents in and out of code, names of people, and his own notes explaining the coding business. He said he'd thought of giving it to me for safekeeping, but he felt that would be too obvious, which was correct. He said this other mathematician would be the perfect person to leave it with while he chased up the national press and tried to stay a step ahead of those chasing him. I guess Wilson, your bald look-alike, was one of those. And the strangest part, Schwartz, he said this other mathematician was perfect to leave the stuff with because he wasn't even known as a mathematician. A few people in the field knew of him, but he was a nut who'd officially disappeared from the math world when he'd made his way over here from— guess where? The USSR! Ironic? VJ was sure the CIA or NSA never knew about his connection with this person. Just some crazy Russian Jew, some sort of Brighton Beach street hustler. Schwartz?"

Schwartz pressed his hand onto the tablecloth. "Did Hayes give you a name?"

"I think so, yes. A name, a funny name—like someone else."

"Addison? Was it Addison?"

"No. The essayist? No, I'd remem . . . Hey, wait. It *was* literary. That Russian critic, the one who wrote on Dostoyevsky. Whatsit—Yarmolinsky. That's it. The guy was going under the name Yarmolinsky. Schwartz? You okay? I knew you should have had more to eat."

C H A P T E R **4**

S chwartz had immediately gone to the flower district following the belief that when pigs fly and the moon turns all to blood, you mind your own business. On Seventh Avenue he hadn't gone for the palms or ficuses he'd thought of, nor had croton or hibiscus caught his eye.

The cabdriver said, "It's a beautiful red rosebush, buddy. Like a tree."

Schwartz nodded in the backseat and looked into the leaves, little green pig wings around the bloody moons.

"Some weather, huh?" the driver said, helping Schwartz out at Warren Street.

But Schwartz was oblivious to the miracle of a cabdriver— unthreatened, unbribed—helping a passenger.

Schwartz thought, who was Addison? Nothing was what it seemed. Treachery and . . . It was as if Bob Malinowski's large,

2 4 4

open face had started to appear on post office wanted posters.

In the office, the rosetree was wonderful, Schwartz thought, pulling open drawers and looking for evidence of . . . The rosetree was absolutely apocalyptic. For $348 it had better be.

And how could Schwartz use the rosetree to confront Addison at Brighton Beach? Birnam Wood come to Stalingrad? He needed to be bloody, brave and resolute . . .

Braverman! Schwartz's fingers paradiddled the desk. He looked at the letter; no envelope, no West Coast postmark. No Cal Tech colleague, no Braverman. Yet this was perfect college-educated English-high inarticulate. Was Addison's English astounding, or was he a native whose true imitative genius was for phony Russian accents? Could Addison be Braverman? Yes. He'd left all that business to Addison. But *why* should Addison be Braverman?

To feed in the mathematician's information without revealing that he—Yarmolinsky-Addison—was the mathematician. And now the tough question. The fingers rolled, the rosetree faded, the office hushed. For five hundred dollars a day and the chance to survive (applause and oohs from the ego): Mr. Schwartz, why hasn't Addison told you who he was?

But first, this message. Schwartz called NYU and asked for the faculty directory. He said it was an emergency. They said wait and came back to the phone. At this point, Schwartz felt his intended pose as Braverman's brother might lose some credibility since he didn't know Braverman's first name. Wait . . . The letter.

It began, "Dear Bernie." He asked them for Dr. Bernard Braverman, Mathematics. They said there was no one in that department by that name. There was a Braverman in the Spanish department, a Conchita Braverman. Schwartz, sensing this wasn't his brother Bernie, thanked them and hung up. So Addison was Braverman.

And the big question? Why didn't he want Schwartz to know—for good or bad reasons?

A good reason would be that Addison was a Russian émigré who didn't want confrontation with any secret service, though he wanted to contribute what he knew. Or perhaps there was something illegal about his status here . . .

But he'd checked when Addison had first shown up. He was a citizen. Well, another good reason might be general fearfulness, but that didn't seem in character.

And now the bad reasons. The bad reasons came dropping, trickling, white-water roaring through the narrow walls of Schwartz's head. He dialed home.

"How does the car run?"

"I don't know. Good, I guess. No problems so far."

"A thousand-dollar repair job and you've gone fifteen blocks with no serious problems? Remind me to send Dave a tip. Could you possibly come over here, darling, to pick me up? I have something heavy. I could get a cab if—"

"I could continue testing the car, if you think it can stand up to it. See you in half an hour."

Schwartz was at the window trying to smile. That Karen was coming to his office would have two weeks ago, two hours ago, given him such joy. And now . . . He watched two women walking across the street, hugged into their quilted coats. The tip of his nose was to the glass; he smelled the bitter soot of winter, saw the small bumps of ice out on the windowsill.

It wasn't only that Addison was probably working with Weiss to set him up, was probably willing to kill him if so instructed, but that he'd come on so warm and alive and turned out a creature of Weiss's, a homunculus. It was very saddening.

Right down to the fine details. Like Addison's "luck" in getting a good photograph of Weiss. Very clever. And now very clear. Addison was helping just enough for Weiss to see what loose ends of the cover-up were sticking out. And how helpful Schwartz had been in calling attention to the Simpkin collection of post-Colombian police files.

He put water in the kettle. Tea for Karen. There was lemon and sugar. Good.

His hand on the refrigerator began to shake. If Addison were Weiss's man, why not Carter Hayes? Yes, how simple. The entire investigation was set up to once and for all dispose of anything embarrassing to the worshippers of megadeath. They'd waited for the perfect man, L. Patsy Schwartz, with his well-developed network of police and other contacts. Of course there wasn't anyone inside the force. Schwartz was their insider!

He stood at the window again, looking down on the empty sidewalk with its painted footprints. Sometimes they were merely street ads leading to bars or punkish clothing stores. Sometimes they were personal statements, outlined feet, outlined bodies, the urban school of alienation art. Schwartz had seen others, hundreds of crime-scene body outlines. And another kind, the body outlines that appeared each August—the sixth, wasn't it? Body shadows, Hiroshima Day. Disappearances, those shadows singed into memory. And what was the point, here?

Schwartz's palm was on cold glass. What was he going to do? Fight the federal establishment? He couldn't. That was Gallagher's point.

He turned to the rosetree. The point was way too big. He'd focus on a bit of truth at a time, as it showed up.

Karen showed up. He ran to her and hugged and kissed her and laughed. He kissed into her cold, damp hair and put his hands beneath it either side to warm her neck.

"This is so nice! The room, too, Len, darling. And the roses! That's as good a single rosetree as I've ever seen, a bit of Dumbarton Oaks downtown. It's—"

"For you. It's for you. Darling. We'll take it home in the repaired car."

Karen laughed and kissed him and asked if it weren't for Addison. He said that he'd gone to get Addison a strangler fig and saw this and knew, now at least, that it was always for her. She found this hopelessly romantic and very hopeful. She went around the office and into the kitchen-bar saying "very nice" and into the toilet-shower saying "very funky-adequate" and back out through the bed area saying "too cozy by half" so that he had to insist on its pristineness, excluding self-solace, to which she said "poor baby" and smiled, sitting on the bed while he explained that he did want to, yes, very much, "but not here, now, with what's going on."

So she shrugged and they had lemon tea and buttered rusks, sitting at the two desks. And when Karen said, "Tell me," Schwartz ducked into asking if Jake had called.

"He hasn't. He'll be all right as long as you're there when he does. Now tell me. I mean it, but I won't ask again."

So Schwartz thought. Then he told Karen the story of Virgil Hayes with Fisher's amendments and additions in their brutal poignancy. He didn't mention Virgil's documents.

Karen said, "You're right. It's too complicated to see an ending. But couldn't you test some of your ideas by asking your client for, say, a thousand a day? If he's really working with the CIA or NSA and they want you running interference, he'd agree and you'd know."

"If it's official, my asking for a thousand would tip them off and they'd just stop using me. Whatever or whoever's game Carter Hayes is playing, I've uncovered enough so that they'd feel the business has to be brought to some sort of conclusion, with or without me. For example, there's the very official business of an exhumation, which Bob's confident we'll get."

In the car, Karen asked, "Does this mean you'll have to go along pretending you don't know about Addison?"

Schwartz looked in the rearview mirror at Karen. Too tall to stand, the rosetree slanted across her lap so that Schwartz saw not pigs and moons of blood, but a forest grove from which Karen emerged crowned in red roses, Titania of the Volvo.

"You look . . . You look . . . I'll have to think about how to deal with Addison. If he is Weiss's man, he might well know that I know; that's how good their information gathering is. I'll call and put off visiting until tomorrow. Maybe he was hit by people connected with the particular business he found out about. I don't . . . Karen, you look so wonderful back there. Getting you the roses was the best thing I've done for you in—"

"The next best. You're going to do the best when we get home."

Oberon nodded and signaled a left turn.

That night at the concert with Karen, Ed and Ben, Schwartz thought of Karen's face in the backseat woods and, later, her face beneath his, looking out from its thicket of dark hair. He'd held her tight after making love. Then he'd pushed up from her and stayed on locked elbows.

"We're trying so hard," he said. "It's frightening."

"It is," Karen said. She paused. "What do *you* mean?"

"It shows how bad things still . . . how close we are to the edge."

"But you were happy just now!"

"I was. I am. But . . . "

"And you were happy to see me in your office."

"Yes, yes, when you came in it . . . It's . . . " Schwartz lowered himself so that he stretched full out over Karen. He spoke in a whisper into her hair.

"This is what I've always dreamed of, the political and criminal, and this is the biggest thing I've ever touched and the only reason I've been allowed a peek in is for *their* convenience. They've set me up, I can tell. This is it, the nuclear gangsters with the authority of the state. The joke is that I need police resources, but even if I were still there, the police wouldn't touch this case. That message was clear from the start. And worse than that, Karen, I've had to get information from the same sources I took the bribe from. I've had to. Can you hear me?"

"Yes," she whispered back without moving.

"And that part of it is like pulling open your own scar and poking back into the wound. I've had to. It's the only way. I thought . . . It has me deeper into their debt. We all know it. They're delighted to do me the favor. I've come back for more. They owe it; it vindicates their morality, though 'morality' is a funny word for what they have, that code of ice."

Schwartz came out of his reverie and joined the audience applause.

In the intermission he huddled with the other three behind the orchestra. He had to talk. He saw he was boring, embarrassing. He had to.

"It's always the woods for me, that Schoenberg wind quintet, but I don't know if I ever heard it when I was a kid and we drove up to the Catskills. Of course, it's conventional, the horn and bassoon associations with the classical hunting motifs, but I'm in the backseat of the Pontiac looking out the window into the shade and light slanting across the rocks and through the pines. Like the flute's the leaf ripple, the horn is something or someone moving through the bassoon shadow, way back. Wind and light. And I'm the kid in the car who can't take it in fast enough, can't possess all that flashing, so I keep turning as if by looking far enough ahead I could hold it all. I keep asking my poor mother to shift her position so I can see farther up the road through the windshield. But the distance is too much, the perspective is just solid wall or indistinct. The best way was to throw my head backwards, like this, over the back of the seat, so that I was looking out the rear window upside down and could roll my eyes to either side, like the last movement of the quintet. Yes, yes, Ed! I see you smiling your 'poor pretentious bastard' smile. But it's true. I mean, the point: the repetitions and variations of that rondo were my light caught and recaught, echoing backwards out the pouring-backwards window of my father's Pontiac, caught receding, of course, only as I lost it. Does anyone understand what I'm saying?"

Karen pulled her arm tighter around him and said, "Relax."

"Ed?"

"All I did was ask you what you thought of it."

"Ben?"

"I used to like that piece."

After the concert, the four of them walked out arguing. Ben said, "I'm not saying that. It was fine. But only an hour and ten minutes of music is a rip-off."

Schwartz disagreed. You could concentrate perhaps that long, certainly no longer. Ed said it wasn't the length but the sameness of the two pieces that bothered him. Karen thought it was brilliant, following the wind quintet with the Berg chamber concerto—musically and in scoring, historically because Berg had finished it just a year or so . . .

They were staring out at the street through the open foyer doors at snow. It was snowing. Around them others were saying, as they themselves started to say all at once, that it must be a record swing from hot to cold, crazy. Someone said radiation. Someone said, "Gone with the ozone."

They walked out onto Broadway. The sky was pewter-purple, and the flakes fell small and gray. All around them were people with heads thrown back, eyes shut, with open mouths and tongues stuck out, playing taste-the-snow, like children, like taking soiled, cold communion.

CHAPTER 5

Schwartz first thought he'd woken because of the wonton that had lain at the bottom of his soup like a mine. But he saw the telephone and went downstairs to call.

And hung up before its first ring. Jake wouldn't be there. Jake was . . . Maybe he was with a girl, a girlfriend. They didn't talk about that enough—safe sex, AIDS, abstinence. Was he kidding? Kids used sex as a form of communication. Convincing them of AIDS was like trying to explain that saying "Hi" was lethal.

It was cold. He'd have to wait for Jake to call. Let Terry sleep soundly through the night, dreaming the epistemology of thirty-day options, the dance of the bull with the bear.

He went to the dining room and pulled back a curtain. The snow was lighter now, a few flakes blowing down to join the tarantella on the sidewalk. Still no sky above, no taurus, no ursa, no moon.

Schwartz's depression on waking at eight came from the checklist in his head. To visit his battered friend he required the following: warm clothing, flowers, candy for the children and his stubby gun in case he had to kill him.

Karen didn't have to ask. He saw her angry smile over the orange juice and said, "Be back by lunchtime." He left Addison's address on the telephone pad.

He stopped at the bottom of Prospect Park South for candy, at a store on the Italian/black border where the white proprietors were loud, cheerful and wary, yelling "No more?" when Schwartz stopped piling bag on bar at twenty-five dollars' worth.

And the morning continued heavily at the stop for Sunday flowers—the truck stall by the gates of Greenwood Cemetery, the vendor in thick blue parka and black gloves pouring milk-brown coffee from his thermos as Schwartz selected this and that pre-wrapped bunch of chrysanthemums, zinnias and asters, cold star flowers in cellophane.

Then, candy and flowers on the seat beside him, gun in its holster snug and uncomfortable, Schwartz drove down to Brighton Beach under a sky the flaked gray texture of chipped ice. He tried taking comfort in the fact that he hated his gun, had a custom-fitted safety on the .38.

He turned off Neptune onto Brighton Sixth, wondering what R could mean after Addison's address. This? A sign by the driveway: R meant rear. Schwartz parked out on the street, took the shopping bag of candy and armful of flowers, and walked down the driveway whistling "My Favorite Things" until it turned left and became a major alleyway between and behind houses and backyards and turned right and narrowed and opened onto Addison's Stalingrad. Kremlin. Addison's castle.

Schwartz stopped and smiled. It *was* a castle. It even said

CASTLE'S STORAGE in peeled gold wooden letters that ran the two hundred feet across the building up at the third story, beneath the crenellated roofline. And below the CASTLE'S C and the E of STORAGE there were, instead of windows, decorated arrow slits. It was a turn-of-the-century warehouse that somehow survived within the later zoning, great-grandfathered. Schwartz knocked and rang the bell and knocked.

Leave it to Addison. The place was dumpy and very charming. Almost, Schwartz thought, smoothing his holster bulge, disarming.

"Is you, Mr. Schwartz! Come in, come in, come in," Irina said, bustling, a big smile and a laugh as Schwartz gave her the bag of candy and some asters.

"These other flowers are for Abrasha. How is he?"

"He's fine. Terrible. I mean is wrong he's not still at hospital, but he's like bull, strong as bear, so he get well here and more relaxing. Come, come."

They went through a hallway of the big apartment. The walls were hung with painted wooden bowls and spoons, shawls and rugs and prints from Russian fairy tales with Folkine princesses and firebirds.

"In here is Abrasha. I make some tea or you like coffee?"

"Tea, thank you," Schwartz said, knocking on the open door.

"In, in. Good morning, boss. Wonderful you come. My spirits much stronger even without vodka you couldn't bring."

Schwartz was in a bedroom thirty by forty feet long and almost twenty high in which Addison lay propped on a small hill of pillows on a four-poster fringed with bright Afghan hangings. There was a very large vanity table and mirror with a chair beside it. And that was all the furniture. The rest was clothes on cushions, clothes on the floor, clothes over hangerless dress rails, painted wooden boxes, knocked over piles of books and a stereo system between two banks of speakers fit for a Yankee Stadium rock concert.

Addison was chuckling and groaning at Schwartz's expression. "Ohh, hurts when laughing. But so, what you think?"

"Something like the Ali Baba roadshow comes to Strawberry Hill. Here are some flowers, Addison. I'd thought of something grander—palms, a rainforest—but I had too rich a lunch, yesterday."

Schwartz dropped the flowers at the bottom of the bed so that they covered a pair of woman's underpants. That Addison, torso strapped, ribs cracked, was still enjoying sex enormously— Schwartz's reading of the ordinary rumpled emptiness of those underpants—made him glare with rage at Addison, who now pulled the flowers up and was pulling them from their wrappings. The underpants had come up with them, but Addison had eyes, indeed wet eyes, the bastard, for only the flowers.

"How you knowing, Lenny, big rough man like so much pretty flowers? You are very fine, sensitive boss. Thank you so. So. Yes, take chair from over there."

Schwartz dropped the clothing onto the vanity and brought the chair beside the bed. "I knew about the flowers," he said, sitting, "because your wife told me. So much for my extraordinary sensitivity. I'm more interested in your extraordinary range of knowledge. You know how I've always been threatening to discuss it? Addison, Steele, The Spectator; not the Ali Baba bit, of course; you'd know Scheherazade's stories better than I. But, Addison, 'Strawberry Hill'—how would you know that?"

Addison put his hand out, frowning. "I don't say I know that. What's matter?"

"Do you? Do you know that?"

"Yes, I know. Is Walpole, Gothic revival. Yes. Is some crime to know?"

"I'll tell you what's some crime: it's—"

Irina followed her knock with a large lacquered tray of glasses of lemon tea and plates of bread and jam. "Here is everything. Is sugar and butter, but we take sometimes just jam, sometimes no bread under but eat, you know, spoon of jam. This I make. Plum jam is not bad."

Addison looked at Irina. "Is magnificent jam," he said. "Irinachka, you please excuse us for is important detective discussion."

"What is tears?" she asked, jumping to his side and dabbing at his eyes with a paper napkin.

"Is only from laughing in cast. From, you know, cracked rib-ticklings."

"Go it easy," she said, leaving. "Go it easy. Mr. Schwartz, you say hello, you got time after to Mischa. He's so wanting to thank you for all—"

"I will, Mrs. Resnick," Schwartz said to the closing door.

"You should be calling her Irina, Lenny."

"Yes? Well, what's in a name. Irina, Addison, Resnick, Yarmolinsky, Braverman. Yes, what's in a name like Braverman?"

Addison shifted his position and winced.

"Oh, very good, Addison, the way you use the pain to cover your reaction. If there is pain. If, I mean, there was any hit-and-run at all."

"What is the hell in the matter with you?"

"Braverman is the matter. Or, to be perfectly correct, the nonexistence of Braverman is the matter."

Addison's right hand moved beneath the sheet. Schwartz drew the .38 and pushed off its safety. "Don't move."

"You gone nuts!" said Addison.

Keeping the gun pointed, Schwartz drew back the sheet. Addison's empty hand lay on his thigh. Schwartz directed him to lift his leg. There was no gun, nothing. "All right, there's no gun.

There's also no Braverman. I checked at NYU. And don't make up amusing stories about him."

Addison shook his head. "You are right I am making up Braverman, getting someone to write letter so to be authentic lie. I apologize, boss."

"Why invent Braverman?"

"I can't tell you, only I promise is not for any bad reason. Please, Lenny. Please believe. Is for good reason, but I cannot explain. Is way of getting to you information and protect—"

"Your own ass. Yes, I might have found your being the Yarmolinsky who helped Virgil break the code too much of a coincidence."

Addison asked, "Is all right I have tea?"

"Yes, with no tricks."

"What tricks? I make move it hurts like hell."

"Really?" Schwartz asked, leaning toward Addison. He hooked two fingers over the strapping.

"Please, Lenny. I understand you angry, confused. But put away gun. Irina get crazy she see this."

Schwartz leveled the gun at Addison's stomach and tugged down sharply on the strapping.

Addison screamed, clutching his side. The glass of tea spilled over his thigh. He bent forward to rub the burn but screamed again with the pain it brought his ribs.

"What is yelling going on?" Irina cried, entering. "What, oh my God, what is such . . ." She stopped and began cleaning up the tea.

Schwartz put his gun in his jacket pocket.

"I . . . I spilled. Oow! Irinachka, sorry. I spilled tea and burned—"

"Yes, you are big fool! And what for you make bandage loose? You are crazy man! You want not get better so you stuck here drive yourself and me too crazy?"

"Sorry, Irinachka."

"Mrs. Resnick, is someone looking after the children?"

"Sure. I have mother, sisters, in-laws . . . Yes."

"Please, sit down here," Schwartz said, standing, backing from the bed so that she wouldn't be aware of the gun in his pocket. "Mrs. Resnick, I have some questions to ask. They're very serious and your husband isn't answering. They have to be answered. You understand? Serious, important questions."

She looked at Addison, who shook his head.

"I shouldn't pay attention to that now, Mrs. Resnick. Is your husband or was your husband a mathematician who called himself Yarmolinsky?"

"No," she said.

Addison groaned and said, "Yes. All right. Yes, as you know I am Yarmolinsky who is mathematician."

Schwartz thought. "Addison, you know this means I'll have to arrest . . . bring you in to be arrested."

"What?" screamed Irina. "He is of course not this mathematician! Abrasha! Tell him truth. Now is no longer good to . . . Mr. Schwartz, he is not this Yarmolinsky."

"Don't listen her, boss. Is me!"

Schwartz bent to Irina. "Who is Yarmolinsky?"

"He—"

"Irina!" Addison threw himself forward to reach her, caught his breath with pain and clutched at his strapping. Tears ran from his eyes.

Irina stood and helped him to lean back into the pillows. She spoke Russian into his ear. Schwartz heard him say, "Nyet! Nyet, Irina!"

Then she motioned Schwartz to follow her out. It seemed a dumb thing to do, but everything else seemed dumber. So he followed.

She opened the door onto an enormous kitchen full of

freezers and refrigerators and two full restaurant ranges and ovens. There was Mischa, chasing another boy around a long table at which were fifteen or twenty people, from old grandmothers to infants in arms.

Irina said, "Please, Mr. Schwartz, who you want is—"

"Run, Anatoly! Run!" came the shout from behind Schwartz. A gray-haired man pushed away from the table and seemed to vanish behind the stoves. Then Schwartz saw the staircase and ran around the table.

Mischa lunged for his leg. "Mr. Boss!" he shouted. "Thank you for candy! There's lots!"

"Not now, Mischa!" Schwartz snarled, stopping to pry off the smiling giant limpet. He saw Addison collapsed in the doorway with a small crowd attempting to lift him.

The door at the top of the stairs opened to a pitch-dark hallway. Schwartz found the light switch. At the other end of the hallway a door was closing. Schwartz ran down and through it and found himself in an unconverted warehouse.

He steadied himself on a pile of boxes and listened. The noise down to his left stopped. That was the way to go, but the light was so dim in here it showed only the outlines of piles and stacks and the longer shadowed strips of passageways. He moved to the left and stopped again. Footsteps came from his right. Other people had come up another way.

Schwartz considered the stupidity. This wasn't Stalingrad. This was Brighton Beach and these were ordinary people. "Listen!" Schwartz called. "I don't want to hurt anyone. I only want to find someone called Yarmolinsky. But I have a gun, and if my life is endangered I'll use it to defend myself. So, please! Please, let's just go—"

His words were lost in an enormous crash. He drew out his gun and turned, sour, drenched, dilled. His feet crunched on the pickles. Damn it! They'd lobbed a two-gallon jar of dill pickles at him. That could have hurt! He began moving off, and ran into—something big! Schwartz jumped and stopped. He pulled his .38 away from Big Bird just in time. Stuffed animals. All around him big stuffed creatures from Sesame Street. Ali Baba's cave. And there was another opening to the left, up there.

He put his head around. Nothing. He stepped out. He rolled. He put his foot out. He rolled on the other one. Balanced. Rolled, rolled and fell hard on his ass in a clatter.

Crazy. Bats! He'd fallen onto, into, five dugouts full of baseball bats. He used one to push himself up, holstered his gun and walked, feet scraping the floor, pushing away the bats. So Addison had a deli and sporting goods repository up here.

Shadows up ahead. Machinery? Schwartz crouched. Someone was behind the machines. He saw shadow movement and heard a click and another and another of machines turned on.

Something flew by his shin. And now by his waist and now his head. Baseballs, pitching machines! Shit, and the count was two and one and he couldn't see. Three and one; that was definitely wide. He'd swing on the next.

The good thing, he knew as he sunk to his knees, was that these machines didn't pitch faster than about seventy miles an hour, so he'd live. He fell very slowly, it seemed, onto his face, thinking there'd be a huge bump, a bump the size of a baseball, on the side of his head. On the other hand, he'd be on first base when he came to.

And this seemed to happen immediately, as Schwartz's next thought was whether it would be scored as a hit batter or, since he'd been beaned on the three and one count, a base on balls. He began crawling toward the three pitchers' mounds.

There was a crash behind him, as of a baseball hitting a large jar.

Schwartz stayed below the line of baseballs until he came to another left-hand passageway, just before the machines. He stuck his bat into it. Nothing hit at it or chopped or banged or sliced it. He rubbed his head and crouched around the corner. He'd use the bat.

Things began coming at him from behind, from back there. He knew that because somebody was actually calling out, "Back here!"

They were throwing . . . throwing . . . Ouch! Schwartz touched his hair. It was sticky. Blood from the beanball? He licked his finger. He was bleeding pistachio halvah? No, it was being thrown, thunking down around him, exploding in soft splinters.

Jesus! A five-pound chunk hit next to his toe. But he wouldn't be drawn back there, the way they wanted him to go. He saw the strip of light where they didn't want him.

At the door in a tornado of halvah, Schwartz lifted the bat and swung. The door smashed open. Squinting through pain and pistachio, Schwartz faced the man who'd bolted from the kitchen, whom Addison called "Anatoly." It was difficult to tell if he was a mathematician. It was easy to tell he was an archer, the way the longbow was drawn back and the arrow pointed steadily at Schwartz's heart. Schwartz considered the bat against the arrow.

"At best, I'd foul it off," he admitted and dropped the bat. He put his hands up in the air just to show there were no hard feelings.

There were. An arm squeezed around his throat and at least seven other arms pulled back on his two, and thirteen feet tripped him so that he was on his back with the population of Odessa kneeling on his chest. Six inept hands took his gun.

"Friends, leave it like it is. Don't fool with the little gizmo over the trigger," he said. He hoped someone understood him.

The gray-haired Rubin Hood stood over him. He slacked the bow and removed the arrow. And in good, though accented English, he said, "I'm very sorry, sir. I panicked. My name is Anatoly. I have used the name Yarmolinsky, and I am the person you wish to speak to. Please," he said to the others who got off, got up from and generally unhanded Schwartz.

Yarmolinsky, a lean man who looked sixty and sorry, helped Schwartz up and showed him to a bathroom where he could clean himself.

"Here is your gun," he said as Schwartz came out. "Please don't blame these people. Let's go downstairs. They're good people, really. And the best of them is my brother Abrasha."

$\mathsf{H}$is brother? Keep holding the ice to the bump."

"This long after?"

"Yes. Don't be such a baby and stay still. Tell me about the brother," Karen said.

Schwartz, on the living room sofa, felt very cozy and slightly dizzy. "I was still suspicious, but they sat me down at the kitchen table and showed me documents: photos of Anatoly at the Institute of Science in Moscow, papers by Anatoly Resnick in math journals. And then Anatoly told me he'd fled Russia because he'd become an antinuclear activist there. That must have been gutsy, because their pro-nuke brainwashing is even stronger than ours. He showed me a *Manchester Guardian* article that mentioned him. He was in serious trouble and out in Vienna for a math conference, facing who knows what prison or madhouse sentence when he returned. So he didn't. He jumped west. But once he got here he was nearly debriefed to death. And he was courted—he said 'hounded'—by our science-war establishment. And that's when he decided to drop out to Yarmolinsky and to his younger brother's clan castle in Brighton Beach. But he found it hard to stop witnessing to the truth. He was still too scared to protest directly, but he advised local antinuke groups, and that's where he met fellow mathematician Virgil. And, of course, when the math-cryptography problem came up, Anatoly felt he had to help. But then . . . Karen, this is too cold."

"So take it away for a minute, big baby!"

"That's better. Yes, so when the CIA started in after Virgil, Anatoly was naturally very frightened and kid brother Abrasha swore to protect him."

"But how did he manage to learn you were on the case?"

"Well, I would have used him for any large-scale case. But it was just luck. Of course, as Addison admitted, he had been keeping up with the developments, looking out for Anatoly. So he knew as much as I did, at the start. Ah, but the papers."

"What papers?" Karen asked.

"All the evidence of criminal conspiracy Virgil had taken from Brookhaven and Shoreham. I didn't tell you about the papers before because I thought I knew where they were, with Addison, who now turns out to be Yarmolinsky-Braverman-Resnick's brother. But now that I don't know, again, I can tell you."

"Oh, security. I get it. But only because I've been married to your double-talk for so long. Put the ice back on."

"Anatoly said Virgil was going to leave the papers with him but changed his mind and said he'd found a much better place—with Robert Mondavi. Anatoly couldn't figure that out. That's what Virgil intended."

"With the wine maker?"

"Or in a California vineyard or in a wine cave or in the

back of a liquor store anywhere between Cal Tech and Princeton. It could mean anything. There are no obvious trails. Oh, and Virgil never spoke about having taken the plutonium. But, like Fisher, Anatoly was sure he'd had a lethal dose of radiation. And then, beaned or not, I ended up with a jolly breakfast party and bizarre argument with Addison about his faked expenses with the nonexistent Braverman on their nonexistent Princeton trip. During that time Addison was doing some uninspired moonlighting on a wronged-wife case, hanging around Sheepshead Bay restaurants and photographing people known to me as 'Saltzman the bastard and his floozy' as they made goo-goo eyes over the scungilli. Addison won the argument, but only by agreeing with me that had the lights been on in the warehouse I would probably have doubled on the second pitch deep to left vacuum cleaners. We don't need one, do we?"

They didn't. Nor did Schwartz need the special treat, next morning, of Santini's taking the helicopter controls over Garden City. The helicopter flown by the same police pilot was bad enough; with Santini flying it was for the first ten minutes something like a shakier and louder version of the big hill on the Cyclone at Coney Island. But when the pilot smiled an extremely impressed smile, Santini settled down and followed directions. And through the throb-throb-throb of the rotors and the beat-beat-beat of his head, Schwartz praised Malinowski, also on board, on obtaining the exhumation order despite the interference of Weiss via a certain powerful judge with whom Schwartz had the misfortune to room for his first freshman term, which to this choppy day corroded his memories of Harvard Yard.

Twenty minutes later, they landed at St. James Cemetery. Mr. Peters walked from his office to meet them.

Schwartz's contribution was a hissed "Don't call them gravediggers," to Santini and Malinowski as they produced the documents. This done, they drove to the unbroken grave, Peters showing them the way.

As they started to dig, Schwartz walked off. He wasn't officially here anyway. He found a stone bench and sat with his head bent, lumped side up.

It was a cold gray morning in a cold gray cemetery. From his cocked angle, even the grass in its morning frost-melt was fine pearl gray. He didn't visit his parents' graves. He thought of his parents, but visiting two stones among a hundred thousand others wasn't memorial.

His father had told him, about three years after his mother died, that he'd seriously thought about having a seagull carved on her gravestone rather than a Jewish star.

Schwartz had been amazed. "Dad, you mean *you* also thought of her—of them—as the 'seagull sisters,' not just the Seigel sisters?"

His father rumpled his hair, something Schwartz usually squirmed from. "What, boychik, you think that was *your* original idea?"

"I really did."

"Before they married, everyone knew them as that."

"Dad, you miss Mom?"

"Oh, boy, terribly. Terribly," his father said, and kissed his cheek.

"Dad, did you like . . . I mean, did you think Aunt Celia was pretty, sort of?"

His father shook his head and laughed. "Pretty? She was beautiful. I had a crush on her—before I met your mother. I tried to date Ceely first, but couldn't. Understand, Leonard, Rebecca was no consolation prize. I just happened to meet her like that. I loved her. I love her. I'm glad I didn't go with Ceely. Maurie and her, they were right together, I guess."

"Did she give Uncle Maurie a hard time?"

"What kind of a . . . Well, you're seventeen: why the hell shouldn't you ask? I think they gave each other a hard time. They were both a little crazy. But they were a couple, and if I believed in an afterlife I'd think they were still screaming at each other, wild about each other, bringing a breath of bad air to heaven."

A breath of bad air: Schwartz remembered how he'd thought about the phrase. He looked up. Would he himself like to be buried in a place like this?

Beside a low pile of dark earth, Santini was motioning to him.

Schwartz walked over. It was such rich brown-black earth it looked edible, like moist chocolate cake. Pretty cemeteries didn't matter; there wasn't enough land left. Ashes were best. Maybe, since you were like ninety-three percent water, they'd find a way to boil you down to a gritty soup and freeze you, a little ice cube, and drop you in deep space, absolute zero, your own super-conductor.

Santini whispered, "See that? We're in luck. As good a casket as you can get. Minimizes decomposition. Although what we're looking for has a half-life in bone of over a hundred years. Did I tell you his parents wanted to be here? I advised them not to come."

"Absolutely," said Schwartz.

They watched the casket wiped clean and loaded into a low van. And then, in Peters's car, they followed it back to the lawn before the chapel and office, where Malinowski, Santini and Peters signed and exchanged copies of documents and Schwartz helped load the casket into the helicopter. It was very heavy, but that was solid bronze, not frail Virgil.

The flight back was subdued and cramped. Malinowski's assistant, Williamson, had to sit on the casket; Malinowski and Schwartz's seats had to be folded down so they sat backs to the front seatbacks. Santini was all doctor now.

Schwartz pulled himself around, kneeling, and yelled into his ear, "What's the setup at the hospital?"

"Superb! Ten minutes out, we radio and they'll be waiting by the pad. Then it's on to the trolley and down to the path lab. And there we'll have Forman the radiation expert, and Jean Garber, who's seen more AIDS close up than we have stubble in the mirror, shaving. And then there's yours truly and two young smarties from my department. And first-rate technicians and all the right equipment."

"Impressive."

It was. As Santini had said, they were met as the engine cut, and within ten minutes the casket was on the lowered trolley by the dissection table. Everyone had met, the papers had been inspected and the videotaping, Malinowski's good-bookkeeping idea, had begun.

There was a moment's panic when Santini thought they weren't going to be able to get the casket open, but one of the technicians ("Thanks, Larry. Jesus, Larry, you saved the day.") came up with an ordinary wrench for the latch screws.

Everyone else circled around. Schwartz was too head-achey excited. His lump had settled to a small, fierce tom-tom. He'd get a look at Virgil soon enough. He could see him now, in his mind: bare, forked, blue and gold . . .

Schwartz heard the gasp.

"My God!"

"Oh, Jesus!"

Schwartz looked around. They were all professionals used to such sights, not first-year . . .

"Sir?" said Malinowski, making space. "You'd better take a look."

"I intend to," Schwartz said. He looked into the open casket, said, "Excuse me," and ran to the phone.

It answered. "Judge Marshall M. Dubin's offices."

"I know the judge is too busy to take this call, so would you please leave this message: The judge, as usual, was right. We have not been able to exhume Virgil Hayes. This is because nothing's in his coffin but a hundred or so pounds of cement."

"And who shall I say called?"

"Dubinsky's roommate."

BOOK V

A drunk sat soiled at the bottom of the subway stairs, a blotch-faced white man, smelly, with his hand out, his eyes fixed at foot level of the passersby. He started speaking when they'd moved several steps away, so that his "couldyagiv" was muttered into emptiness, at which point he'd track and stop, as other pairs of feet passed by. And again his broken reflex began, "Ygotsome" at vanished Capezios or Weejuns.

Schwartz watched this man's perfectly wrong timing and put some dollars in his hand.

He'd promised Karen that she and Jake wouldn't get into trouble: that this was because he wouldn't be able to get Weiss into trouble was an insight Schwartz kept to himself. He'd run out of luck and into brick. Walls. Perfectly wrong timing.

The note in his pocket had reached him an hour before via "Manhattan Speed," the express rider jumping, shivering, singing in the doorway, the personification of Manhattan speed and probably crack, whereupon Schwartz himself had metaphorically jumped and shivered, reading: "Fruit and vegetable information today at 4:30. Pizza Heaven. 6th and 42."

Pure longshot, pure Montanares and too late.

Schwartz found a free four inches of stainless steel and clamped a glove to the pole as the train doors closed. The investigation might be closed today or the day after tomorrow because, according to Malinowski and Santini and a note from a Judge Dubin's apprentice, Washington was about to say: "That's enough now, boys and girls. This is too important for police to touch." And without the police, what did Schwartz have?

Too much, damn it. Lots of facts and bits of skin, an intensely witnessed empty casket and the mystery mathematician of Brighton Beach, Virgil's papers without the papers, and Gallagher's maxim: "Sometimes, the more you know, the less you have." And all that the nuclear midnight-men had to do was keep telling their lies.

Shit! Schwartz slapped the pole. The hand below his belonged to a bag lady who gave him a terrible stare and turned back to her *Wall Street Journal.*

Schwartz knew he was in trouble. A citizen of a country defended by C. Richard Weiss who counted on help from Juan Montanares to better serve Carter Hayes was in real trouble.

At Thirty-fourth Street, Schwartz felt hot in his coat and scarf and gloves, but by the time he took them off it would be time to put them on and climb into the freezing fog. And that slight tickle at the back of his throat was no joke.

Schwartz crossed Forty-second Street toward Pizza Heaven, one of those corner speed-eaties crowded and screaming even when empty, stools set too close to keep you moving, six-inch eating ledges with pepper and oregano jars so oily they had to be gripped in both hands.

And it looked especially crowded because there, two
stools concealed under his drooped buttocks, was Pignatelli. He
was chewing, his right hand moving from the stack of pizza slices
in his left with a slick slab toward his mouth. Tomato sauce
dripped onto his shirt.

Pignatelli did something strange: he smiled. "Mmm," he
said, wiping his mouth with the back of his hand. "Hey, Schwartz.
Guess you weren't expecting me."

"I wasn't, but now that you're here smiling, I understand."

"Hey, the pizza's not bad here. Want some? On me, I
mean."

"No. I'll bet you'd even apologize for giving me such a
hard time a few weeks ago in Junior's—and afterwards?"

"Schwartz, honest to God, I'm very sorry about that. All
that. Please. Listen, Lenny—"

"Schwartz."

"Schwartz, sure. Look, please, I don't know who you know
so well, but I don't want to fuck with them. Some very important
Family people told me to deliver this message or . . . Ah, never
mind." Pignatelli shook his head.

Schwartz loosened his scarf. Even with its doors wide
open, the place was hot with the crowd and the ovens.

"Deliver the message, Piggy." Schwartz pulled napkins
from the holder and blew his nose. Of course, the start of a cold.

Pignatelli wiped his mouth and forehead. Red oil streaked
over his eye. "Okay. Last April, a place on Riverside Drive. Your
man caught it there, but he wasn't brought by the organizers. Man
called Wilson, a regular show follower, supplied him. But it
turned out to be a setup. Your man was almost dead on delivery,
and after the show there was federal trouble. They think Wilson
was FBI. The snuff show organizers who survived been interested
to meet him since. That's it."

"Piggy, you're full of shit," said Schwartz, going to the counter for an orangeade.

"Hey, Schwartz, why didn'tya ask me? Get me a couple of Cokes, willya? Big ones. You don't have to pay. Tell them they're for me and—"

Schwartz came back. "No. Piggy, I don't like your message. You must have it all wrong."

"Schwartz. Look, Schwartz, please. Please. This ain't an argument. You ask me to tap fucking dance for you on this fucking counter, I'll try to fucking tap dance. But, please, my business is not to fuck up messages. I'll give it to you again, word for fucking word. I'm giving you what I got, I swear to the Holy Virgin Mother," Pignatelli said, lifting his hand. A string of mozzarella swung off the end of his thumb. He ate it. "Scuse, Schwartz, I'm thirsty. Hey! Mario! Couple big Cokes over here!"

Schwartz asked, "Who'd you get this message from?"

"Guy named Alvin. He said you can find out more through your friend. That's the whole message. Honest to fuck, Schwartz."

"Well, maybe I'll say you gave me the message all right."

"Thanks. Listen, no hard feelings. About Junior's or anything else after. It wasn't me. I don't give those sort of orders, y'know. I don't get involved."

"Not even enough to warn me away from my own barbecuing? And what do you know about the hit-and-run job on Addison?"

"Nothin'! Nothin'. I don't know. I'm sorry about that other, Schwartz. I didn't . . . They don't tell me. Please give me a fucking break. Please. Nothing personal. I mean it. Say, you hear the one about Diana Ross and George Burns?"

"You mention that joke once more, I'll tell my friend that's *all* you told me," Schwartz said, sweating, wrapping the scarf around his neck and walking out into the cold. He sneezed.

He blew his nose into the remnants of the napkins.

Twenty feet before him the air was a muffled white gray. Ice fog. Carter Hayes was ice. His response on being told of his son's missing body had been, "There's probably a very good security reason for the body not . . . At any rate, I'm thankful for Mrs. Hayes's sake that we weren't there."

At the subway entrance Schwartz looked back to the food bar. Lights were broken at the end of its sign. It flashed PIZZA HEAVEN. PIZZA HEAVE. PIZZA HEAVEN. PIZZA HEAVE.

Schwartz watched Gallagher pull the wrapper from the long cigar. He walked to the wall. This was the photo that always held him: Gallagher and the archbishop on the sunny steps of St. Patrick's. Before that marmoreal opulence, the archbishop, white mitred, surpliced white, looked as lacy-filigreed as the cathedral. Tom loomed, proud and uncomfortable. A bold man for most seasons, here he was square stanced, feathered in vest, tie and jacket, his chest pigeon-puffed as usual. But there was the sun's hard reflection on his forehead as if he were caught in the beam of God's Patrol Car and smitten, cat among the doves of God, the actual city pigeons just out of sight in the clipped photograph. He was masquerading as the burly saint, Patrick, to be sure, for wasn't Tom also in the way of driving the snakes from this granite isle? And what were those snakes after all but homelier dragons such as English George was always lancing at so airily?

"What are you looking at, Lenny?"

Schwartz turned. "Iconographic fantasies. Like reading those smoke signals you're sending up, if it *is* you, hot dog, under the mustard gas."

"It's me. It's my cigar and my office and my nerves. You realize I talked to Don Phillips for forty minutes in there? I mean, you know Don, he wants clear arguments, proper cause, procedural detail, safety. Safety, Lenny! And I'm winging it. You say you told me everything, and I'm dumb enough to believe it until I get into the Chief's office." Gallagher swung his feet off the desk and sat up.

"I didn't say 'everything.' I told you I had to protect my sources," Schwartz said, angry because he had to protect *himself* from his sources.

"Yeah, well, if only that was all you skipped. So I get in there and feel like a damn fool, but I have to keep going, what with honest Don giving me his time and sitting there taking notes on my bullshit. You get me, Lenny? The Chief of Detectives of the City of New York is sitting there taking notes in his own hand on this malarkey I'm spouting about plutonium, snuff shows, rogue NSA agents, and a—I can't believe I said it—a Russian mathematician hidden in a castle in Brighton Beach! Can you imagine how I felt?"

"Like in that picture with the archbishop?" Schwartz closed his eyes and saw an emerald cross.

"Are you nuts? Don't bother answering. You're into one of your daydreams."

"No, I'm here. I'd love to see Don's notes, especially for the part of the lecture on Betty Simpkin. You didn't leave out the bit about her offer to mud wrestle, did you?"

"I didn't give any wiseass details. I think I put it like, uh,

'And, Chief, there was, er, an episode in which Mrs. Simpkin attempted to compromise Inspector Schwartz." Gallagher blew smoke and chuckled.

"What did he say?"

"He said, '*Ex*-Inspector Schwartz.' "

"Ah, yes. But he must be interested if he's having me hang on here for his answer."

Gallagher smiled. "You wanna know his real interest?"

"Silly me. I forgot to ask He who Knoweth All."

Gallagher snorted smoke through his nose. Schwartz squinted down a pencil to make it a lance.

"Snuff-show producers. Don's been after them through Homicide and Vice and Drugs for four years now. If we could promise him even a half day, four hours, even, in advance on the location, he'd buy it."

"It'll probably be half an hour, an hour at most, in advance. That's the word from my sources, and I have to go with it. I can't make other promises."

"Yeah, yeah."

Schwartz pulled a tissue from the box. Maybe he wouldn't get a cold. Sure, like maybe Weiss didn't know he'd been fingered.

The phone rang. Gallagher put up his hand and said, "Send him right in." He stood and began stubbing out his cigar.

Don Phillips came in jacketless, sleeves rolled up, tie loose. "Tom, Len," he said.

"Chief," said Gallagher.

Schwartz said, "Hi, Don."

Gallagher gave him a look.

"Relax, Tom. I'm not his chief now. Haven't seen you out on Long Meadow all fall, Len. I've had to throw the football around with guys way too young and fast. Great workouts, terrific depressions."

"Well, I've been busy setting up this PI business, and . . . And there's been the weird weather—from swimming to hockey in three weeks. And some personal business. You may have heard."

"Only generally. Hope it works out for you. Well, to business."

Gallagher pointed Phillips to his chair.

"No, you sit there. I'll back off from the remains of the campfire on the desk," Phillips said, sitting down, as did Schwartz, across from Gallagher.

He looked at the long legal pad across his lap and tugged the end of the gray mustache at the corner of his mouth. "Tom's told me your story, along with the input from Santini and Malinowski. It's a puzzler. I've just been on to the legal commissioner and the D.A.'s office for advice. And I have to say, especially to you, Len, that while the personal rantings of scum like Judge Dubin mean nothing to me, I'm advised he's probably right in saying we won't be able to touch Weiss for anything connected with Virgil Hayes, including the empty grave. At most, if we can catch him with his pants down, and maybe I'm being literal, we may be able to embarrass him into stop pulling our files. Am I making this clear?" he asked.

Schwartz nodded. It was clear.

"And Tom, for the record: To whatever extent we act on this, and you know I'm damned interested, the department will not be involved on any account concerning the matter of Virgil Hayes and Charles Richard Weiss, a.k.a. Dick Wilson, a.k.a. Chuck Williams. Unless, of course, it develops that there's a material case for murder in which he's a suspect. But so far none of the real or reported or suggested evidence indicates that. Is *that* clear, Len?"

Schwartz nodded. It was all too clear.

Phillips, a round-faced man whose color was just the

brown side of cordovan, was smiling. "Don't look so damned offended. If we go for the organizers, we may well have to round up a lot of other people there and perhaps take photos and videos. I know Tom will pay his usual close attention to those details. So you'll probably get something on Weiss; that is, if, as you say, he's due to show up there. Tom, you'll be in charge of the operation, but Sarotta's office will supply personnel from other units concerned."

Gallagher scratched his jaw.

"Yes, Tom, you'll have to report to Peter, but he knows my interest, so I expect him to be very cooperative, as I know you *always* are with the Assistant Chief."

Schwartz stood and walked to the window. The morning's fog had thickened. It could be snow hanging there, near suspended in the thick, cold air. "I don't see what I am in this."

Phillips still looked amused. "Officially, you're an outside contact. Unofficially, we're depending on you as we would if you were still with us, short of giving up your life, of course."

Schwartz blew his nose. "Thanks for small considerations."

Phillips said, "The people I think are running this can't become suspicious of our involvement. They are crazy dangerous and always heavily armed. We'll have to be very careful. You'll keep in touch through Tom?"

Schwartz looked at Gallagher, who nodded and said, "Yes, Chief, and through Malinowski. I'll take him and Williamson. You mind if Schwartz is at the briefing?"

"Not at all," said Phillips.

"I do," said Schwartz. "Tom or Bob can tell me what I need to know, but from now on I'm staying the hell away from this place. As a matter of fact, I'd like an unmarked car and a clever driver to get me out, say, to Penn Station."

"You going somewhere?" Gallagher asked.

"Back to my office three blocks from here, but hopefully unnoticed."

Phillips stood, Gallagher stood.

"See, Chief, in or out of the force, Lenny's the same neurotic mess."

Phillips put his hand on Schwartz's shoulder. "We want you back, but Tom can get along without you."

"Thanks, Don."

When the door closed, Gallagher said, "You take a pretty casual line with him, don't you?"

"What am I supposed to do?" Schwartz said, and blew his nose. "We play football in Prospect Park. He throws perfectly placed bullet passes that sting the hell out of my hands. I get back with welts on my chest. I hate it. We have a good time. And our kids played Little League and City League ball together. Should I stand to attention in private conference? What the hell am I even saying this for? I'm not a cop!"

"Yeah, yeah. Shit, this cigar is ruined and I promised myself to keep it down to one a day."

"It was one a week, and I'm off. I'll be in touch."

"Ask Lizzy out there, Sergeant Thibault, to drive you. She's a great driver. And it was one a week, once, weeks ago. What's up with you and Karen?"

"Superficially better," Schwartz said, picking up his coat and scarf. "The ego hits the fan a week from Monday when we go to a counselor."

"What are you scared of?"

"That the counselor will listen to us for about four minutes and tell Karen the answer to all her problems is to leave me."

"They work that way, those counselors?" Gallagher asked with wide eyes.

———

Schwartz closed his eyes and opened them again. Sergeant Thibault swung off Thirty-third into the Penn Station jam. He said, "You're a good driver." He hadn't said much else, half thinking, half watching how she'd move very fast across lanes in the traffic gaps and near-run red lights and check to see if anyone kept with her.

She said, "Thanks. You drive much?"

"Some, when I partnered Gallagher, but the department came to an arrangement: they paid me a bonus if I didn't drive. You haven't been with Tom's office for long, have you?"

"Six months. I used to see you come in. Heard the shouting through the door. This all right, here?"

"Fine, Sarge. I like your style. You have a good boss."

"You know it. Bye."

He nodded and walked off.

"Hey! Hey!"

Thibault was waving. "You'd better get in. It's a message for you from Captain Malinowski."

"Sir," came Malinowski's voice clearly, "can you hear me?"

"Of course I can hear you. Why should the police radio network suddenly fail because you're on the line with me, Bob?"

"No reason. I have sort of a terrible message. Mrs. Hayes . . . Irene Hayes, sir. She died about two hours ago. Looks like suicide. She took a massive dose of sleeping pills last night. Her husband called the ambulance when he couldn't wake her this morning, but she was DOA. They've just brought Mr. Hayes back to their apartment."

"Thank you, Bob."

"Yes, sir. Sorry."

"Thank you for calling me back, Sergeant Thibault."

"Sure."

Schwartz went into Penn Station. The usual bunches of

homeless drunks huddled in its bland perimeters. The duty cops
might hustle them along each half hour or so but wouldn't kick
them out in such bad weather.

Irene Hayes hadn't been killed with kindness. Carter
Hayes hadn't killed her that way. She'd killed herself, of course.
He imagined her pale hand reaching for the emerald on her
throat. No, that was someone else's jewel, the dragon-colored
cross. Hers was a ruby, pigeon's blood.

Get in quick so the cold don't get in," said the driver, the black window closing over his black hat.

"Thank you," added Montanares. "Lenny, heh. Can we sit here and talk?"

"We'd better drive around. I'm not saying I'm under so-phisticated sound surveillance, but they told me to see someone about my heart murmur," Schwartz said. Montanares sat in a pile of fur—mink and ocelot and bear and fox. Schwartz supposed his socks were baby sealskins.

"Ramon, drive out to Greenwich and up to Canal and then back here," said Montanares. He switched off the intercom. "You must be confident if you're cracking jokes."

"When I crack jokes I'm nervous."

"Scared?"

"No, Juan, nervous," Schwartz said, rubbing his nose to

keep from sneezing. The car's heater was set to August, Death Valley.

"So, Lenny, looks like this very sick character Weiss will come along to the little party."

"As long as he doesn't think it's in his honor."

"Lenny Schwartz." Montanares said the name looking straight ahead. Then he was silent, a small smile on his face. "Are you going to kill this man?"

"No, I'm a private investigator. And I wouldn't if I were still a cop. Cops have a thing about that."

"I haven't noticed."

"Well, Juan, perhaps there's been some provocation. I hear stories of your business involving the use of slingshots and even BB guns. I have to take off my coat."

"I think you'll kill him. I know you, whatever you say. Take off your coat, sure. It's cold out there. Usually I don't go south until November, but now, this is much too cold. Unhealthy. But I'm staying around to see this thing through. For you, Lenny."

"Touching. Why are you being so nice?"

"Lenny, Lenny. One reason is because you have the *cojones* to ask me such a question, even though you're afraid of me. I like it. Not many family men have this. This is why, one reason why, I don't have a family. Besides, I'm too dedicated to my work. It wouldn't be fair. All right, of course there are other reasons. I'm staying to collect money. These show people owe me money. They should make a few hundred thousand on this and they owe me that *as interest.* I'm like the banks with the poor countries, except I'm not going to roll over anyone's debts."

Schwartz sneezed.

"You see? Why live in such a climate? I'm going to be very honest. I want to impress you with what I can do so that you'll join the business and come south with me. For your family. It's better to be the wife and son of a rich man. You could have a beautiful house in Miami and you would travel. Have you been to South America? No? Believe me, an educated man like you would find Colombia and Bolivia beautiful and fascinating. Maybe you know that I employ some ex-policemen. They're good but, really, not in your class." Montanares stopped, the same half-smile on his face, but now he turned from his perfect right profile to half smile at Schwartz.

"I don't know, Juan. Last time I was in Miami Beach the Concord Cafeteria had closed and I couldn't even get a good game of gin rummy." Through the one-way glass, Schwartz looked at the sky and river, two pieces of flat steel.

"Jokes? All right, I understand. I wanted to ask. I also want to ask if you're still a police officer, Lenny."

"I'm not."

Montanares turned back to show his perfect profile. "I don't want to embarrass you by asking questions about the police help you're getting. But now I want an answer without jokes. Would it be safe for me to be at this show?"

Truck horns were blowing on Canal Street. "No. They don't know about you, but you shouldn't be there."

"Correct, Lenny. Lenny Schwartz, the man with the correct answer. You get a prize for that: the little affair is at Western Cold Storage, tomorrow or the day after. You'll get a call. You know, I hear your business is political."

Schwartz sneezed. He wiped the sweat from his forehead.

Montanares looked straight ahead as he spoke. "Politics is bad. It's full of crazy men, professional liars. You aren't listening."

"Of course I am, Juan. This is your big hot car and you have my undivided attention. Would you have your driver stop here, please, at this corner. Thanks."

"See if you can shut the door quickly. And the job offer stands. I think you'll take the job. I think you'll kill this man,

Lenny Schwartz," said Montanares and burrowed deep into Fur Hill.

Schwartz's nose was running into his pulled-up scarf. Montanares knew everything.

Schwartz was shivering, sneezing, wondering how to put off calling Carter Hayes. He drank a small glass of syrupy iced vodka and then three cups of hot tea. He took three aspirins and called Addison, asking if the assigned officer had introduced himself.

"Yes, but what for you make me feel so fraidy-cats before my complete family?"

"Here's what for: you and your First Halvah Lancers are defenseless, and I don't want to be distracted by having to rescue you or be compromised if they used you or any of yours as hostage. Oh, and I haven't quite worked out who pushed me under that ball. The officer has orders not to let you leave your moated dacha, Abrasha. So watch your ribs and be your brother's keeper. Bye."

Schwartz put on another sweater. He felt lightheaded. No way around it—he'd have to visit Carter Hayes.

Forty minutes later, Schwartz blew his nose in front of the apartment door as the bolts were drawn and the latches pulled and turned.

"Come in," said the tall, thin woman quietly. "I'm Barbara Morton, Carter's sister. I just got in from Troy."

"Yes. Sorry, Mrs. Morton. I'm Mr. Schwartz."

"He's in the sitting room. If you could please pay your condolences and leave, it would be so considerate. He asked . . ."

"Of course."

Carter Hayes was standing neatly by the mantelpiece in gray suit and white shirt and red-and-blue-striped tie, staring at the parquet floor.

Schwartz went toward him to shake his hand or make

some contact but found he couldn't, the man was radiating such coldness. Two steps from him, Schwartz went into a sneezing shiver-fit.

"Sorry, Mr. Hayes. I mean, I'm very sorry about Mrs. Hayes."

"Too much for her. She couldn't understand, you see, not finally," Hayes said, his eyes still down.

"It must have been a terrible shock, the news about the exhumation and . . ." Schwartz mumbled off into his damp handkerchief.

"She didn't understand. In some ways she was not a thinking person. You see, I didn't just blurt out that Virgil's body wasn't there. I very carefully and completely explained why they didn't want to have Virgil buried."

"Why? What do you mean?" Schwartz asked. He felt his head float off toward the window. He sank into an armchair.

"Schwartz, it's far too late for polite silence. In one way, I suppose the NSA thought it was being kind with that disease story. They thought, should we ever find that Virgil wasn't there at St. James, we'd be able to think it was for public health safety reasons."

"What?"

"Yes, I know they do bury AIDS dead in ordinary ways. But those of us who understand the disease for the degenerate . . . They'd suppose we would want to believe them." Hayes turned to the empty fireplace, putting a long gray hand onto the mantel. "At any rate, this is all beside the point, since we know the real reason for the empty casket is that they would not allow a traitor to be buried on sanctified American ground."

Schwartz looked up. He stood and walked to face Hayes by the cold fireplace. The man was not foaming at the mouth, nor did his tongue loll. Schwartz shivered and sneezed. But the man was anyhow a mad dog.

"This was how you broke the news to Mrs. Hayes?"

Hayes nodded slowly, looking down. "Yes, she wouldn't understand. She had this stupid belief in Virgil's innocence despite all the evidence. Right until the end."

"No," Schwartz said, "not quite to the end. You seem, finally, to have disabused her of that belief. How *economical*, Mr. Hayes. Virgil's grave turned out to be empty, so you pushed your wife in." Schwartz's nose was dripping.

"Mr. Schwartz, I believe we have nothing further to discuss, unless you have something to report in your professional capacity."

"I do. Virgil *was* a health hazard—a radiation hazard. He was so full of plutonium you could have set him on the Shoreham plant and seen him from Brookhaven in the dark. But his body wasn't taken for health reasons. They took it because it would have blown the elaborate lie of Virgil's being a Russian spy. Oh, Virgil spied—on some traitors: you and the plutonium project team you ran for the NSA, against the law, against your country, to put it in your terms. So there it is, in one way like you wanted: Virgil wasn't a traitor, Virgil didn't have AIDS. And if that's now unprovable, it's because of you and people like you."

"Don't—"

"Keep quiet, Mr. Hayes. I'm no longer working for you. You owe me nothing because you've paid in advance. But I'll stick with the case, for a little while longer, all on my own." Schwartz found his hands trembling. He walked away.

"I'm sorry I hired you. I should have hired an American, not a Jew."

Schwartz turned and went back to Carter Hayes.

"Mr. Hayes?"

Hayes lifted his head. Schwartz slapped his face. His head snapped back. A plate fell from the wall. Hayes was holding his face in his hands.

"My condolences," Schwartz said. He smiled at Mrs. Morton, blew his nose and left.

Back at Warren Street he left the mail on the desk until after his hot shower and a change to dry clothes. A rent bill, a plain envelope . . . Inside, the same green-bordered sheets, the same long-tailed bird in the camellias.

> *Dear Mr. Schwartz,*
>
> *What will have happened when you read this is in no way your responsibility. You have acted honorably in what had to be an impossible set of conflicting demands and prohibitions. But for me, caught between my love for my late son and the wish not to hurt his father—a hurt which I believe would literally kill him—there is no point in going on. But I want to go feeling I have vindicated my beloved Jimmy, who was too dedicated to the good of all others for his own good.*
>
> *Please identify yourself immediately upon receipt of this note to Mrs. Harriet Pearson, Safe Deposit Department, at the Fifth Avenue branch of the Bank of New York. I know you will do the right thing with the materials Jimmy entrusted to my safe-keeping. Thank you.*
>
> *Irene Hayes*
>
> *Please do not tell Carter that I held these papers.*

Schwartz looked at the small, neat handwriting. Right to the end. And her faith in Virgil. But if they learned of her death . . .

Schwartz phoned the bank and got through to Harriet Pearson who said, yes, Mrs. Hayes had been in a few days ago and the box was waiting for Mr. Schwartz upon proof of identity. Schwartz said he'd be right there.

It was a gross figure of speech. The cabby said they could go up the West Side Highway or maybe go West Broadway and up Sixth Avenue or—"Either way's got its problems. What do you think?"

Schwartz thought fastest was best. Fastest.

"Oh, fastest? If you want the fastest, we'd better get over onto FDR. Longer, but faster. Oh-oh, but you want Fifth and Forty-fifth? There's always problems up there with all the Midtown Tunnel traffic. So you want—"

"You to start. Go. Do it. Make the car move forward. Please. Good. Can you please go faster?"

"Listen, friend," the cabby said, slowing to a stop to concentrate on the conversation into the rearview mirror, "I don't want to get in trouble with the law."

Schwartz flashed his Visa card and said, "Police. I'm the law. It's okay."

"Oh, in that case," the cabby said, gunning the car from thirty-one to thirty-seven miles an hour, only twenty miles an hour slower than any other cab along the river.

Schwartz told the driver to turn off at Thirty-fourth Street. The cabby agreed that wasn't such a bad idea but wanted Schwartz's opinion about attempting Times Square. Schwartz told him they could go up Park Avenue. The cabby wondered if Schwartz had taken into consideration that they'd end up way above Forty-fifth, that is, if they wanted to try to avoid the traffic on Forty-second. What did Schwartz think?

Schwartz thought he might weep. Two blocks from the bank the cab was slowed for the first time in heavy traffic.

"See what I mean?" said the cabby.

"Keep the change," shouted Schwartz, leaving the cab as the cabby began a long question about why Schwartz didn't want to be taken to the door.

It was the bank he'd ducked into when being tailed from the Algonquin. It was very grand and Alexander Hamiltoned. He showed identification to Mrs. Harriet Pearson, who smiled, showed him to a leather wing chair and returned in three minutes with a sealed Robert Mondavi wine box.

And it was that simple. Schwartz stood outside, sneezing, with the evidence in his arms. He yelled to a cab, "Take me to—"

"Hey, friend, it's you again! We going back downtown? How should we . . ."

Schwartz was running.

When Cannonbury came downstairs, Schwartz saw him through the papers he was sorting in the box.

He peered at Schwartz. "Did you run up here from Police Plaza? You're soaking wet and sneezing and shivering and where the hell have you been for over a year? I didn't even get first grab at those two fair-to-middling stories you were involved with. If they were better I might have been really angry."

"I know, John. I'm making up for it now. This box. I asked for you and Feldman and I'm glad it was you who's around. This box," Schwartz said, closing and thumping the box on the counter. "A terrific story in here, an NSA–CIA plot to discredit the exposure of an illegal secret plutonium-hiding project between Shoreham and Brookhaven."

"It's never been in the peacies?"

"The what?"

"Come over here, sit down," Cannonbury said, taking Schwartz and the box to the chairs. "The peace newspapers."

Schwartz slumped in the chair. "No. It'll be a *Times* exclusive."

"It already sounds highly improbable. But I promise to take a serious look."

Schwartz felt feverish. He dropped a hand on Cannonbury's sleeve. "These are the only ones. Can you make two copies of everything, immediately? Send them express, one to Captain

Robert Malinowski at Number One PP, and the other to Sandeman at the *Voice*."

"You mean in case I can't touch it, it might be weird
enough for Sandy?"

"Yes, and I also mean safety in numbers, in case your
copies disappear."

"Hey!" Cannonbury frowned. "This is *The New York Times*.
Things don't disappear *from* here; they disappear *to* here. But I'll
take care."

Schwartz wrote out Malinowski's name on the top of the
box.

"Any more action to follow on this?" asked Cannonbury.

"Plenty, but it may be rough, and I can't protect you
because I'm not a policeman anymore."

"What? That itself's a very tiny story."

"Let's try to keep it off QXR for a while longer. I'm now
thinking that being a private investigator is more and more a trial
run—in a kangaroo court."

"It's still Schwartz, the metaphorical detective." Cannonbury lifted the box. "If this is good I'll try to use it, but only if
it's really hot."

Schwartz thought about radioactivity. No, paper and film
wouldn't be hot from being touched by Virgil. "Can you really get
those copies and have them delivered today?"

"Certainly, old bean. How's KW?"

"Wonderful. Hanging in with me. Just."

"A glutton for metaphorical punishment. Give her my
best and bye-bye."

Outside, Schwartz stopped a cab, took a close look at the
driver and collapsed in.

Now, after the running and getting and taking, he knew
the *Times* would find it too legally close to the line. Something
like the police department, that way, the old establishment *Times*.

And Al Sandeman at the *Voice*? He'd make, if anything, a witty, overstated piece of it, the upshot of which would be seventeen letters to the editors comparing this to the Rosenbergs. And that would be that.

By Fourteenth Street, between sneezes, Schwartz was dripping with anger. Virgil should have given this immediately to all the peace press networkings in the country. Virgil had been a good and honest man and, damn it, a dope!

C H A P T E R 4

Schwartz's way to cure a cold was to irritate it to death. Drug it, overdress it, sweat it out, outrun it. He was now on lap seven around the World Trade Towers, over five miles, and his calves had begun to loosen, but his fever was still slow-simmering so he figured another seven laps should bring him to a rolling boil and convince the cold he was a lousy host.

Even with most of their height lost in freezing fog, the World Trade buildings were still Ultimate Bulk, so that the few figures he passed strode thinly, animate Giacomettis. And Schwartz saw himself running around and around in a fever, the allegory of his own frenetic aimlessness, his impassioned loitering.

At least he'd called John Cannonbury to add that if the *Times* couldn't use them, Virgil's papers should go to the peacies. His legs felt good, as if he'd already forced the head cold from

297

them. His ankle was better, his calves were loose, thighs warm, tendons stretching nicely and no groin strain.

And of course the start of an erection. Always with fevers, rising with his temperature, from childhood the swollen glans with swollen glands, with teenage mumps the painful lumps under the sheet, only one of which was his hand. Think serious thoughts.

The nuclear lies and swindles. Maybe some good would come of this. That terrific antinuke postcard: WHITE MEN IN TIES COMPARING MISSILE SIZE.

It wasn't his fault, this thing between his legs. The running was rubbing him the wrong way. He was a white man running around and around and around the biggest, thickest, tallest erections . . . Little White Lenny. In the morning they'd find all that was left of him—a small pool of sperm on Liberty Street.

At Warren Street it was clear that the cold had fallen back only to regroup. Schwartz, showered and rebundled, defended with two cans of beef bouillon heated to boiling, dusted with pepper and chug-a-lugged, mug after mug.

He was the mug. Schwartz struck the cutting board and cried, "I will not serve."

His heart thumped. Could it be that Virgil Hayes hadn't been stupid, had been stuck? Hadn't released that material, not because it proved his father a law-breaking chauvinist but because it proved him to be a Russian spy? And that Schwartz had been serving Carter Hayes all this time to keep Weiss off his trail? No, no.

Schwartz took three aspirins with a glass of vodka, put on his overcoat and sat on the edge of the bed.

And Weiss? Weiss had gotten rid of Virgil—in his own sick way—as an embarrassment to the secret U.S. establishment. And then had he hung around at first curious and then highly suspicious of Carter Hayes? Schwartz turned on the radio. BGO was playing Ornette Coleman; the music seemed simple compared to these thoughts.

And wouldn't the John Birch Society be the perfect cover for a Russian spy? Was this true or was Schwartz now as mad as Carter Hayes and his sick ilk, for whom, eventually, all life became a commie plot?

He'd ask Karen. He didn't care if the phone was tapped. He'd ask the tapper.

He called. He told Karen he had a cold and loved her. She told him to stay warm. He told her his problems with the Hayes family—the dead, the just dead and the technically living.

"You're crazy, Len. If Carter Hayes was so incredibly dedicated a spy he never would have risked stirring things up by demanding Virgil's exhumation. I think Virgil was genuinely good and honest, and in not revealing his findings right away, a very big jerk."

"You're right. I'm crazy. Delirious. I'm going to get better."

"And be home when?"

"Within . . . When . . . I can't say. Soon. Has Jake called or anything?"

"No, not yet."

"Karen?"

"What is it?"

"Wish me very good luck."

"Oh, my God. I mean, of course I do. Good luck. Oh, it's this sort of . . . Very good luck. Of course. Take care of yourself. I hate . . . I . . . Good night."

He was soaked with sweat. He drank a quart of orange juice and went to the bathroom and peed. Then he drank two large glasses of seltzer and began piling the comforter with clothing and finally a twice-folded carpet from the floor. He put the aspirin bottle by the tissues on the bedside table and brought two seltzer bottles and the big glass pitcher filled with half water, half orange juice. He took four aspirin and, pulling off his slippers, pushed himself doubly clothed under the mound of the comforter and clothing and carpet, exhausted.

In no time he was wide awake and awash in sweat. Then he tried to hold back his pee so that he could remain warm. He thought of the event toward which he reeled. If Montanares thought he was going to add to the evening's merriment by killing Weiss in front of all assembled, then they'd let him in armed.

He couldn't stay in bed. He elbowed off the coverings and ran to the toilet. If only he could get back into bed before he froze. If only he could stop peeing within the next twenty minutes.

He ached and shivered back in bed. He slept. He woke and drank. He shut his eyes. Double crosses. Weiss didn't count; he would or wouldn't be there. The organizers could double-cross him on that. But would they double-cross Montanares? Sure. And what if Weiss had found out and struck a deal with them? Maybe the deal would be to lure Schwartz there and nail him in return for federal immunity or a free drug run from Air America? And Montanares? If he felt he couldn't own him, why not set him up, get rid of Schwartz as some sort of submoral irritant? How many double crosses was that? Schwartz fell asleep.

He woke. He hadn't even considered the possibilities of "disappointment"—he wouldn't say "double cross"—from Phillips and Gallagher.

Schwartz peed. He froze. He stripped and took a hot shower and put on sweat clothes and a pair of ski socks and got into the cold wet bed and slept.

Light. The bell was ringing. He went aching to the door. They could, any of them, just come on up and come on in and kill him. "Yes?"

"Coffee and blueberry muffin."

"What?"

"Sid's Coffee Shop. Come on, you ordered it," the woman's voice said.

Schwartz opened the door. "Liz?"

"Yeah, can we talk?"

"There," Schwartz said, "for security," taking the bag and leading Thibault to the back of the loft.

"What's happening here?" she asked. "You having a garage sale on your bed?"

"No. I've got a cold and—let me put on a coat," Schwartz said, shivering, noticing he'd been standing with an erection in his sweatpants like a little tentpole.

"There's really coffee and blueberry muffins for you and me in there," she whispered to Schwartz's back. "Gallagher's set me up waitressing for Sid. It's a great cover for messages, but it's a lousy job. Sid's is primitive."

"Not pribitive. Sid's stuck in 1947."

They drank coffee. Schwartz didn't want his muffin.

"I should have got bran," Thibault said. "Then there would have been a choice."

Schwartz nodded. Thibault was a nice, direct person-sort-of-cop, like he'd once been. "Doesn't matter. Message is today or toborrow, at Western Cold Storage, a meat warehouse up for sale on Seventeenth between Tenth and Eleventh. Maybe Tob can take a look from the old West Side Highway, but I think the organizers' people will already be watching."

"Okay," she said, finishing her coffee. "I'll be back for your 10:30 coffee break."

"Corn buffin, please," he said.

By 10:30, when Thibault returned, Schwartz had managed to change the wettest bedding, rearrange the covers, shower and fall back into an aching aspirin-daze. There was nothing to report. "But could you get a thin protective vest for me?"

When Thibault put her head in just after noon, Schwartz was on the phone, his hand motioning her in. He nodded, said, "Right," and hung up.

They went to the bedroom area. "That's it," he said. "The vegetables will be delivered tonight. I'm being picked up at eleven. Nobody should tail me. I mean that. I'm trusting that this ride and its company will get me in there armed. Speaking of that, where's the vest, in the corned beef sandwich?"

"You sound better and the jacket's there," she said, hitting her midsection with her fist. It made a flat "clack." "Wait. I'll get it."

When Thibault was in the bathroom, Schwartz was marveling over the corned beef sandwich—four inches of corned beef from old half-inch Sid's?

"What's gotten into Sid? What a sandwich!"

"Sid? Are you kidding?" Thibault said, dropping the vest on the bed. "Sid threatened to fire me when he saw me making it. I told him he couldn't because I didn't work for him, but when I said it was for you, he softened. He told me you're the greatest detective since Philip Marlowe."

"Are you in on this tonight, Liz?"

"Yes."

"You married?"

"Was. Two great kids and, thank God, a great mother and dad and two sisters. You?"

"A son and a wonderful, outraged wife."

"Yeah, I know. I half couldn't blame Ray, my husband. I three-quarters could. It's crappy comfort to know it happens the same way to brass like you. I hope it works out. Gallagher's already got people looking for likely observation and entry points up there. When's showtime?"

"Midnight, earliest. Probably one or two. Liz, I don't

know your background, so don't be offended if I keep wondering about you and the very rough crowd, crazies, actually, who'll be ushering and selling the popcorn tonight."

Thibault swallowed her bite of chicken sandwich. "I'm okay. I can look after myself. I won't be back after this. If you want me for anything I'll be at Sid's until about 2:30 then I'm going back to Number One to get some sleep for tonight."

"I'll see you," Schwartz said, walking the short, slight woman to the door. "Liz? How okay are you, really?"

"This is embarrassing. Let's say . . . Could you handle Chief Gallagher in a fight?"

Schwartz thought. "No."

"I could. Oh, he wants to know if we're to know you there."

"Not until I give the signal."

"Do we know it?"

"It goes: 'It's me, Schwartz! Help me, Gallagher, you bastard!' It's an old signal. Tom will recognize it."

They nodded as Thibault shut the door. She could take Tom Gallagher in a fight and Schwartz could barely lift his corned beef sandwich.

But he put on two scarves and a hat and an overcoat and crossed City Hall to Nassau Street and was very pleased with his purchases from two sporting goods stores for only seven hundred dollars. Another expense was the relapse caused by the outing. Still, he was as ready for the night as he was going to be, barring the miracle of full recovery in the next seven hours.

Then he was out of juice and seltzer, but the first three local stores he called wouldn't deliver. The fourth said it had to be an order of a hundred dollars or more, and Schwartz, too weak to argue, ordered a dozen seltzers and the rest of the hundred in orange and grapefruit juice. And giving them the address and twenty minutes to deliver, he hung up, depressed.

But he cheered up as he watched the kid yank the stacked hand truck, bump, bumpety-bump up the stairs.

"Here's five bucks for you," he said, as the pink-faced boy put the last of the three boxes behind the kitchen counter. "And a hundred and two-fifty for the drinks. Aren't you too young to be working? Shouldn't you be in school?"

"Naw, I'm eighteen. I graduated last year," said fresh face, who looked fourteen. "So, you the private detective, like it says on the door, private investigator? What do you have to, like, you know, do to become one of them?"

"Well, I went into it from the police. That's pretty good training. You interested?"

"Police? Yeah, sure. I could dig that, becoming a police-man," he said, folding the money and watching Schwartz put a roll of cash back into his pocket. "Hey, mister, wanna score some coke?" he asked, with a look worthy of any aging cherub by Bellini.

"Get the hell out of here!" Schwartz yelled, giving himself an instant sore throat and a worse headache.

"Stay cool," the boy said, shaking his head at Schwartz's outburst as he pushed the hand truck through the doorway.

What was happening to the culture? The privileged were using epistemology to corner the market, and the others wanted to work their way into the police by dealing drugs.

Schwartz filled the small refrigerator, drank five glasses of mixed orange-grapefruit-seltzer and decided against more aspi-rin, trying not to think why. He lay down sick, guilty of the world he'd helped Montanares create, where choirboys delivered news-papers or crack with the same sweet market enthusiasm.

He woke at 7:30. He peed. He felt better. He checked his accounts, finding he had more than he'd thought. And what if he had twenty or a hundred thousand more? His life would still be in the cold killer hands of Montanares and some sadists he had yet the pleasure to meet.

Still, he felt better. He set the alarm for nine and slept.

It rang. He felt worse. Very bad. A terrific dryness was in his head and throat, a soreness when he breathed, in his lungs and through the surface muscles of his back and sharp in his weak right kidney and a dull grinding in his groin.

Time for reality. He couldn't take more aspirin because if he were shot he'd hemorrhage. In his shaving kit he found the very strong painkiller prescribed last summer and put two on his desk by a small glass of water.

Then he showered, rubbed himself dry as hard as he could and began the ceremonial donning of space-age ski tights, metallic undersocks, straps under the insteps. He was an aluminum-nylon toreador. And then ordinary heavy socks, ordinary bulletproof vest, a shirt and a humdrum shoulder holster and, yawn, old .38 Special loaded and laid next to the heal-all tabs on the desk. And pants and the black track shoes that might in the dark seem fashionable. He'd leave the jacket until later. The jacket was just to hold a box or two of bullets.

Then Schwartz buttered two round rusks and brought them on a plate to his desk and sat down to wait.

His head fell to his chest. His mother was motioning to him. It was Aunt Celia. She pointed to Jake, who stood with Karen behind the Seigel sisters, their backs turned on him.

The alarm? No, the phone. Oh, Jesus, was it all off? "Hello?"

"Hello? You're not Mr. Addison? You Mr. Schwartz?"

"Yes, but Mr. Addison's not here."

"Listen, tell Mr. Addison, will you, that Saltzman the bastard is back with me and I'm giving him one more chance, but I was wanting Mr. Addison to hang on to those discriminating photos in case the bastard gets any ideas of picking up with the floozies again. And so maybe your boss could take something off the bill, like he said if I didn't win a divorce he'd refund all my money? Well, I don't expect all—"

"Yes, yes, Mrs. Saltzman. I have it all down here for the boss: You're back with the bastard, discriminating evidence, ideas about floozies and a nice discount. Good luck and good night, Mrs. Saltzman."

Schwartz hung up and fell asleep.

C H A P T E R 5

Schwartz lifted his head. The horn was blowing. He swallowed the pills, put the gun in the holster, and put on his jacket and overcoat. The stairs were soft rubber sinking under his feet.

Outside, he took a deep breath and pulled open the limo's back door. There was a heavy cloth to push through.

"Quick," said Roberto, sitting on the jump seat.

"He's closed it," said Montanares from the endangered species section of the back seat.

"No, he's right, Juan. I must have lowered the temperature in here to a hundred and two. Good evening."

"Lenny Schwartz, funny man. You know Roberto."

"Yes."

Roberto nodded.

"And Julio, sitting up front with Ramon."

The car drove off. Julio, to Roberto's tap on the glass, half turned and nodded back. Montanares's furred arm emerged from a bearskin. Roberto handed him a silver tube and silver pillbox. He took two short, hard snorts. His business. Schwartz didn't want to be nosy.

Montanares said, "Roberto and Julio are the best protection."

"Why bother to need it? I mean, why are you going? I gave you an honest warning, yesterday."

"Say that I want to protect my interest. I've promised protection."

"For a few hundred thousand dollars? You? Have you lost your money or your mind?"

"*Esta bien*, Roberto. Be careful, Lenny. Roberto and Julio sometimes come to my defense too fast. Never too slow. They don't know how this directness in you is a quality I appreciate. Up to a point, Lenny, up to a point. Would you like a hit?"

"No, I talk too much already. Besides, I'd have thought tonight would be exciting enough."

"I don't toot for tonight. It warms me, warms my thinking, helps me forget a little about this terrible cold. You understand, the cold for me is a mental thing. Like this heat in the car? Down south, I'm warmer in much lower temperatures. Here, I know that everything outside in every direction is cold. I'll confess something to you, I trust you. It's a fear I have, a dream I keep getting that I'm alone in the center of a space so large it could be the universe. And it's so cold and I can't move my naked arms or legs. What would you call that, Lenny? You're very intelligent. What would you say that is?" Montanares pulled the bearskin and a silver fox rug tighter to his shoulders.

"I'd call that the truth beneath the furs."

Roberto pushed the palms of his hands down on his thighs. Roberto was of medium height and build and had, the good word was, survived a cocaine massacre and staged two others for his master.

Montanares sighed and resumed his small smile. "Let's leave it. We're only disturbing Roberto, who in some ways is more sensitive than we are. Listen, you know I don't need the few hundred thousand. If I wasn't there in person tonight I'd still get the money, but I would lose the respect of my debtors. That would be a big mistake."

"How old-fashioned, the last of the personalized businesses."

"Yes, personal. It has to be because we all sell exactly the same products. But I wouldn't say it's old-fashioned: these people I see tonight will pay me in the next two years over four million dollars."

"If they survive."

Montanares turned forward into full profile. "Exactly. A reason that I'm going."

"Just the four of you?"

"Three. Ramon is my driver. But others will be there. Besides, Lenny, you're going to play a part in the success of the evening."

"Juan, I keep telling you not to count on me."

"I know," said Montanares, sinking down into the furs. "But it happens to work out that way. What are you carrying?"

"One .38 and extra bullets. That's all." Schwartz sat back, shut his eyes and wondered how they'd set up the entrance security.

By the fire escape. As the limo slowed, Schwartz looked out to see people walking the fire escape stairs to an entrance door at the top. At street level and on each landing, men stood ready to check and frisk and bounce. From the fifth floor, "bounce" would be literal.

"Look, Lenny, there's also security up on the old high-way," Montanares said, watching him.

He looked. It wasn't anyone he knew or would want to.

"But we don't have to climb in this cold."

The car turned into a loading bay off Eleventh Avenue and stopped behind two generator trucks from which cables ran up over the platform into the meat warehouse.

"The second truck is for me—power for more heating," Montanares said, draping the fox rug over himself and nodding up to the front.

Julio sprang from his door and pulled Montanares's door open as Roberto held the bearskin and fox to Montanares's fur-coated shoulders. By the time Schwartz slid out, Roberto was motioning to him from a small side door.

Then the four of them were in a small office, crowded with two others who were introduced as Alvin, a tall blackbearded man, and Ahmed, a short wide-shouldered man whose crewcut belied the very Sikh regimental beard and saluting mustache. What also crowded the room were the three electric and two kerosene heaters blowing and smelling and heating away, as well as an expanse of white tablecloth over a desk and the six vast crystal glasses around the two double coolers crammed with bottles of champagne.

Ahmed, in his jacket with its sleeves rolled up and yellow shirt unbuttoned down his hairy chest, explained: "Weiss should arrive at the party around midnight, Mr. Schwartz. It's important you don't let him see you until you're ready. We'll set that up."

Schwartz nodded. Alvin poured Dom Perignon and Montanares, warming, stripped to the full-length mink coat over his suit and proposed "Mutual success."

Alvin said, "Juan, you stay here as long as you want. By the time things get going upstairs there'll be a lot of people, and it will be nice and warm up there. We've got almost all the extra power and heaters upstairs."

"And how does the business side look, Alvin?" Montanares asked.

"Very, very good, from early response. We think the gate could be over three-fifty. Hey, Ahmed, look at that smile. I told you Juan would like that."

"He certainly did, Mr. Montanares!"

Schwartz was nervous. And he was stupid with it: he'd drunk off this huge glass of champagne on top of those pain-killers.

No sooner had he realized this than he became very light-headed and sensationally relaxed. High, really. And no sooner was he high than he realized how he was to fit into Alvin and Ahmed and Montanares's frolics. He would provide a little extra frisson by snuffing Weiss. So they thought. And, Schwartz wondered, trying to sniff the last of his champagne, as an encore, why wouldn't Montanares or even Ahmed Ben-Evolent snuff Schwartz?

Schwartz was giggling, tickled by the champagne bubbles. And then, why shouldn't Montanares & Organization make everyone's evening by murdering Alvin and Ahmed & Co.? Make the survivors' evening, that is. Tickled to death, that was.

Ahmed and Alvin were asking him to come upstairs now. He was bowing yes. Montanares was lifting his head to Julio, who knew a headlift from a handsaw and was joining them.

Schwartz put his head back in. "Juan, everything okay?"

Schwartz saw Montanares's uneven high nostril seem to soar into a wink from an eye so bright it seemed like the teeth in his smile which, after all, seemed part of his nodding. "Yes. Heh-heh. Lenny Schwartz."

The stairs were wooden; Schwartz's feet were leaden. Up above, under a purple lightbulb, Julio held a radio to his mouth.

Schwartz, who had been climbing the stairs for an hour and a half, realized he'd reached the second floor. Had they put a dash of bitters or a splash of lysergic acid in his drink?

Then he walked into the party. What was all the fuss about? Seventy-five or a hundred people were dancing to a disco or drinking at two bars or sitting at tables, talking. It was a very nice, very ordinary New York party, and Schwartz knew his fears were merely bitter, free-floating anxieties, angostura in the malted milk of life. On the other hand, why were there cages set about the room containing half-naked dirty boys and girls?

Schwartz, dizzy, decided to sit rather than faint.

"Do you mind!" said a pleasant though sharp voice beneath him.

He said, "No, not at all. Make yourself comfortable under there."

The voice pushed him up. He wanted to ask her how she'd managed to get beneath him on the chair without his noticing, but here was Ahmed the skinhead.

"Ah, hide and Sikh, my host."

"Excuse us, please, boys and girls," he said, and led Schwartz across the room to where, at one side, scaffolding stood with mounted spotlights.

"Sit behind there on that box, sir. You won't be seen. This area is going to be roped off. That's the show area, just there. Do you want something to drink, Mr. Schwartz?"

"No, I'm fine, thank you, Ahmed."

"Just keep low and out of trouble. The lighting people won't bother you."

Schwartz nodded. At the bottom of the nod he found the most wonderful valley floor and soft grass with a stream to sleep by.

A wiry man with dreadlocks was holding his shoulders. "Sorry, man. I must knock you wi' lights."

Schwartz looked up. This was a pleasant-looking young man with long dreadlocks. What the hell was he doing here? "You know what kind of a party you're lighting? What's your name? Mine's . . ." He stopped and said, "Dan."

"I Kino. Yes, sure, man. It's a rich man's party an' I clear tree hunred, man. That's what I know. Twice what I make usual."

"I mean, Kino, do you know what's going on here to-night?"

"I tole I get money, I don' botha, man, wi' what goes down. I no fool, man. Tell you look out dere, look what you see? I tell you, you see tree hunred, four hunred 'em walkin', dancin', so you tink dem live. But dem dead, man, dem joombie dancin', man. Dis Satan's, dis a joombie jamboree!" said Kino, turning back placidly to check the swivel action on his lights.

Schwartz shook his head. What was he doing here? He was sitting on a box and had bullets in his jacket pocket. He felt under his left arm. He had his gun. He whispered, "Me, Karen, Jake . . ." and when he said "Jake" he remembered what he was doing here. How could he stay awake?

"Kino? Could you wake me when the show starts, if I'm asleep?"

"Shu-ah, man."

Schwartz pushed the box back. He leaned against the wall. Overhead were rows of meat hooks. It figured. He nodded off.

He was shot in the shoulder. He grabbed at the wound. It had toes. He was holding a sneaker.

"Dan! Man, I have to kick you from up here to get you wake again."

"What? Yes. Thanks."

Schwartz followed the lights to where they played over the cages. Kids! Why should such young kids want to hurt themselves like that? It was awful, pathetic, a rock band tossing hunks of raw meat in and the kids fighting over it, ripping off each other's rags.

Schwartz looked away from the mess. And the band played on.

He looked for Weiss. At least five hundred people now. Plenty of *jeunesse doré,* quite a few Dorian Grays, and more than a bit of smoke, coke, crack, smack and back there by the bar C. Richard Weiss.

Cool, cool Choochie, with a pretty woman, too. Oh, Jesus, Betty Boop! What next, Dr. Armand Simpkin seated at the orgy in a three-piece suit reading *La Revue des Deux Mons*? No way to warn her without being spotted. Maybe she'd separate from Weiss, go to the ladies' room? Maybe she didn't want to be warned? Choochie was drawing her attention to another cage.

It was more of the same: raw meat and all-in fighting and, he supposed, sex. And it was certainly nasty, but it wasn't a snuff show. Schwartz looked at his watch: 12:30. What did he think he was waiting for? Weiss's most embarrassing moment? Maybe. And then? Well, if the department did its thing . . . He went to the windows, but they were painted black.

Ah! And there was a scene to warm the cockles of your trigger-finger muscles: Ahmed seeing Choochie and hugging him. Bowing to Betty and, yes, kissing her hand. And here came laughable, affable Alvin, paying his respects. Did Alvin think they were his last respects? He seemed to be urging Weiss and Cousine Bette to view the proceedings in the cage.

Then Ahmed and Betty left Weiss talking with Alvin at the bar and walked over to a cage. The earsplitting band played on. People danced. Ahmed did a by-the-numbers twist, but Betty— oh my, did Betty bop, did Betty Boop!

Schwartz's ass was sore. He had to pee. But that meant going across by the bar. He stood and turned to stretch. There was movement behind the stage curtains.

A crash and applause. Then another band came on in white tie and tails. Women and men. Maybe he could pee back in that dark corner. No, too many electric cables.

He watched Weiss leave Alvin at the bar and go to Betty and Ahmed. Alvin came over to Schwartz.

"Told you he'd show. Here's your DP."

"Forget the D, I want to pee."

"Go back in that door, there. It's a broom closet with a sink. Hey, you know who you remind me of?"

"Weiss?"

"Yeah, that's right. You related? Is this some sort of family feud?"

"Does Montanares want you to ask?"

"Sorry. None of my business. Julio tells me that Juan's on his way up with Roberto. I hope it's warm enough."

"Where's Julio? I didn't see Julio talking to you."

"Right here. I got Julio in my pocket," Alvin said, tapping his gold jacket. "I've got to go backstage."

Radios. Everyone had two-way radios. All it would take was an accidental turn of frequencies for Bob Malinowski to ask Ahmed if the police sharpshooters had enough hot coffee. Great. Thoughts while peeing in a sink before dying for not murdering someone.

Schwartz emerged from the closet to a drumroll. An act, a veritable act. Schwartz went to his box seat. A very good view, too, it had of Weiss at a front row table. And there was Roberto arranging some extra gas-jet heating for Juan in the mink, in the pink, over by the bar. What would it mean if, say, Weiss said hello to Montanares? Would it mean Weiss and Montanares had done a deal? It would mean good-bye to Schwartz.

Now the band was playing mystery music. The curtains opened.

A scene, a pretense of story. Schwartz looked at Weiss, whose eyes were intent on the stage. A supposed brother and sister and his male friends entered the living room set. Schwartz looked at his black running shoes. Nowhere to run. His head seemed to bob just above the surface of consciousness. Now the crowd was cheering. What, a gang-bang? Schwartz heard the whip. Weiss was staring, nodding. Betty's eyes were down on her drink. Schwartz looked at the stage. The man was hitting his supposed sister. She was chained to the sofa.

Schwartz began to draw the .38 but let it go. This wasn't it. This was vile and violent but it wasn't snuff.

Big applause, closed curtains. Weiss was scowling, explaining something to Betty, whose eyes widened. She shook her head. Weiss laughed. The tuxedo band struck up; people rose, went to the bar, started dancing.

And Schwartz found himself fallen off his painkiller. He was champagne dry, aching-assed on a box in the near dark and angry, understanding how these shows worked, how it would go from rough to cruel to crueler through dreamy drink and yummy drugs and the heartbeat music pumping so that when murder came everyone would have dumped the right to protest— knocked it down, knocked it back, shot it up. And up overhead was Kino, witnessing the devils Euro-USA had loosed on the world for four hundred years come back to drag their masters under at the joombie jamboree.

Weiss was dancing with kissing-cousin Betty what Schwartz as a teenager had called the "dirty boogie," updated but still the same old strut-thrust, hands on the ass in the clinches and sliding away over her breasts to hold hands and rock backwards, backwards, knee to knee, back to back and belly to belly.

Maybe police videos were catching this. Maybe this would be embarrassment enough. Enough for what? For Weiss to say of course he and his cousin liked to go dancing, poor kid, and Armand Simpkin not only knew but had given them some pocket money for ice cream sodas afterwards?

No, Weiss would have to be scared to death, to just short

of death, to admit anything of interest. Besides, if Schwartz played his hand now he might tip the police setup, tip his own head off, if Ahmed and Alvin and Juan depended on him and Weiss for . . .

Video? Was Montanares going for a video of Schwartz killing Weiss as a way to own him? Thank God Montanares was an unknown factor to Gallagher and Phillips. Not exactly inconspicuous, though, the man in the mink by the bar in the blue-red half circle of four gas-jet heaters. Why all this swagger from Juan?

Schwartz's cheeks flushed, his chest went cold. It was for him. Montanares was the peacock, bird of paradise, hellfirebird to dazzle and seduce Schwartz. Schwartz tried to think of any New York police officers with as much rank as him who'd gone over to the criminals. He couldn't. What a catch he'd make! He didn't like the marriage metaphor.

Juan had warmed, was taking off the fur. A black silk suit and white silk shirt and even from here the emerald cross showed, pulsed green in the gaslight.

How many men did Juan have here besides Julio and Roberto? Five? Ten? All with automatic weapons. There'd be a massacre. All right, not exactly a massacre of the innocents, but these people, too, were citizens . . .

When would something happen? He shifted on his seat. "Kino," he whispered up, "when's the next act?"

"When they band stop and they a fanfare, man."

Now Montanares was talking with two beautiful women, showing them the cross. Soon, no doubt, he'd have them on their knees praying to those sacred emeralds the Incas took from the earth, that the Spanish took from the Incas, that Montanares took from the Spanish; Montanares, cocaine conquistador.

Schwartz shut his eyes. He had to stay awake. He opened his eyes at the drumroll. A trumpet fanfare. There was Betty, at a table halfway back. Where had Weiss gone? Gone? The curtains opened. Schwartz rubbed the sleep from his legs and leaned forward.

On stage were three crucifixes, on two of which were a naked man and a young girl. They looked bored or drugged, or both, and kept shifting their feet on the small crosspieces supporting their weight. A man done up as a Roman soldier leaned against the empty third cross. Then three men in loincloths came on with whips, and Schwartz looked away.

Across at the bar, Montanares was still talking with the women.

Whistles, cheers and boos came from the audience. When the sound of the whipping stopped, Schwartz looked at the stage. Two more soldiers in plastic armor dragged in a blond-bearded man wearing a sheet. Schwartz was about to turn away when a flash of light from one of the soldiers caught his eye. It came from the steel of a real broadsword and it was brandished by C. Richard Weiss.

Schwartz stared down at the electric cables by his feet. What was he supposed to do, threaten Weiss with citizen's arrest for offending public decency? For blasphemous bad acting? And even if the police had someone in here videoing, why couldn't Weiss say he was working undercover and claim immunity "in the interest of national security"? And could Montanares really believe he'd kill Weiss?

He heard screams of pain from the stage, loud slaps. He looked. The two had descended their crosses and were slithered into the writhing pile of sex on the floor. Centurion Weiss strutted around the bodies slapping at them hard, two-handed, with the flat of his sword.

Schwartz looked down at the big, crowded space. Some people were standing, some on tables, to get a better view. He couldn't see Betty. He hoped she was hurrying home to Staten

Island. And there was Montanares motioning to Schwartz to look at the stage.

Weiss held up his sword. He was smiling, sweating. "There's a Roman custom that only one of the prisoners shall be crucified," he shouted, well into his role. "Who shall it be?"

The bodies on the floor disentangled; two soldiers held the Christ figure by the central cross. Someone in the audience yelled, "Snuff 'em all!"

Weiss laughed. "No, just one. Shall it be her?" he asked, pointing the sword at the girl.

"Too young," said a few of the people on stage.

"Him?" Weiss indicated the man who'd been up on a cross.

"No," said one of the other men, "he's a wimp. He's already dead."

Weiss went to the figure held to the central cross and put the tip of his sword between the man's legs, slowly lifting the sheet. "In that case, it's—"

"Crucify the Jew!"

Schwartz looked across to the speaker. It was Montanares. Again in a loud, clear voice he said, "Crucify the Jew."

Schwartz looked to the stage and understood. Weiss hadn't. Dragged down by the other men, he was saying, "Okay, okay. Stop fooling around and let's . . . Come on! Stick to the script. Cut it out!"

Montanares smiled over at Schwartz, and Schwartz remembered Cal Anderson's chilling homily about the best snuff shows always being surprises to their victims.

He had to look. Yes, now Weiss had begun to understand. He lay held down on the floor, stripped and spread-eagled as the sexual abuse began. He screamed. He was hit in the face with his own broadsword. He started crying.

Schwartz backed from the light scaffolding into the shadows. Hundreds of faces stared at the stage. Montanares was looking for Schwartz in the shadows. What did he want? Of course. Of course he knew Schwartz couldn't kill Weiss. But if he didn't, he'd have to stand by and witness his murder. That's what Montanares knew—how Montanares could get the moral edge and, so, own Schwartz.

Now Weiss was screaming. They'd stood him up and bent him over . . . And whoever planned this—Alvin, Ahmed, who-ever—was taking a very thorough and personalized revenge.

Schwartz ran his hand through his hair. His scalp was wet and cold. If he went for his gun he'd be shot before his hand left his jacket. He was supposed to wait for his cue.

Weiss was screaming, "I'll kill you all for this! Enough! Enough! Let's just—" Schwartz shut his eyes as the fists came everywhere at Weiss.

From overhead, Kino said, "Hey, Dan. Hey, man. Take haht. Wha for you be so sad? Dem *all* dead meat, man. Dem no soul!" He swung his legs to another perch on the scaffolding.

Schwartz looked up. "I don't have your faith."

The central crucifix was down and Weiss was held to it. A soldier came on stage with a tool bag from which he drew a sledgehammer and six-inch spikes. He held them up to the audi-ence. Someone called, "You nail him, handsome." Soiled, bruised, Weiss was sobbing.

Schwartz began to shake. If he waited for his cue and let the show go on, he'd belong to Montanares. He looked at the tool bag on the stage, like the tool bag of the man who'd died on Worth Street. Like Schwartz's death. Doing nothing, knock-kneed, was his death.

He drew out the pistol. Montanares shook his head and raised his finger. And to make it gem clear, he lifted his crucifix at Schwartz and smiled.

Schwartz shook his head, and to make it street clear to

Montanares he lifted his left hand and raised his middle finger.

But he couldn't walk. Weiss was screaming and there was still time, but Schwartz couldn't walk. He grabbed the scaffolding and pulled himself.

They'd turned Weiss with the crucifix so that the audience could get a clear view of the hammering, so there was still time but he couldn't, his legs still couldn't he was so afraid, could hardly drag his feet over the cables running up and over.

Schwartz tugged Kino's sneaker. "Get down. There's trouble."

"Where is trouble, man?"

Schwartz waved the pistol.

"Ah, yes, thank you, man," Kino said, jumping down and running into the shadows.

Weiss was screaming. Schwartz backed two steps and began shooting cables. Sparks flew with the first shot; a screaming panic started with the second. Schwartz shot again: bulbs burst, and the sightline between Schwartz and Montanares was lost in the chair-tipping screaming stampede toward the doors. By the fifth shot—Schwartz's, for now there was other gunfire—the only light came from the gas-jets.

Schwartz crawled up to Weiss and put the reloaded .38 to his mouth. "If you thought you've already had the worst inside you, think again, Choochie."

"Oh, thank God, Schwartz," Weiss cried, unaware of the gun.

Schwartz tapped Weiss's teeth with the barrel. Weiss got the point. People ran by. Schwartz pulled at the ropes around Weiss's hands, working him back toward the scaffolding. Then Weiss was able to roll up and ran crouched with Schwartz back to the ozone reek and sharp smell of burnt rubber. Glass was breaking. Schwartz could make out nothing in the blue-orange light across by the bar. A woman's high heel kicked his cheek.

He pushed Weiss down under the scaffolding and held the gun that he'd never fire this way to Weiss's head. "Weiss, I don't even have to ask the fucking questions. Talk."

Weiss, bleeding, sobbing, stank of sperm and shit. "It was—"

"Wait," Schwartz said, pushing at Weiss's ear with the gun. The loudspeakers from outside couldn't be made out in here. Schwartz knew they were saying that the building was surrounded. A few brighter types had deduced as much and were sitting down again, waiting for the night's Armageddon with good champagne.

"All right. Now."

"Schwartz. Lenny. Yes, the spy business was a plan to discredit VJ. Of course. He was becoming a big pain in the ass, even though we got the plutonium back from him. Shit, I'm cold. You know he would have died anyway from all that radiation. You know that. It was a way to . . . What did it matter, a snuff show, anything, in his state? I was in charge of security for the entire project. Yes, to find ways around those ridiculous NRC prohibitions. Please. Don't let them get me again. They're on to me, you see, from . . . They're getting even."

"They don't get even, Weiss. They get rid."

"Just get me out of here, Schwartz. Please. I have documentation on this. I'll do what you want. Get a hearing. I'll testify to Congress. I promise."

"Sure, the Bill Casey School of Promise. What happened to Virgil last April? What?"

"Like this. Shit, I feel—"

"Like what?"

"Damn it, he was crucified."

"Crucified!"

"Yes, like this. Damn it, just get me out of here. I have to get attention. To wash. You understand?" Weiss reached for

Schwartz's arm. "I have to clean myself. I'm scared. Lenny, they were porn actors. They have . . . I don't want to get AIDS." Weiss began crying again.

"Are you bleeding there?"

"Yes."

Schwartz crawled off. Weiss wasn't going anywhere. "Excuse me, folks," Schwartz said to the stoned occupants of a nearby table.

"Here, Weiss, champagne. Just do what I say."

Weiss followed the instructions.

"Look at this, Julio. The Good Samaritan, Lenny Schwartz. Heh, heh."

In the flashlight beam, Schwartz's .38 looked quite forlorn. He dropped it. "Keep up with the Dom Perignon douche, Weiss."

"Isn't he smart and good?" asked Montanares. "Look how he dropped his gun and avoided all those holes in his sports jacket. And look how he cheers up the guy there, with a bottle up his *culo*. Lenny, your coat and my rugs are down in the office. Let's get them. We'll take Mr. Weiss. I need him. And you. For a while. Isn't that so, Julio?"

"Yes."

"Roberto?"

"Yes."

Schwartz saw the machine-gun barrel bisect the flashlight beam as Julio lifted it to Weiss's chin.

"Up," said Julio.

"Yak, yak, yak; that's all you ever do, Julio," Schwartz said, standing. Roberto's automatic was pointing his way.

"We'll walk behind," Montanares said. "First Weiss, then you, Lenny. That door behind the stage. And go easy on the joking. I like it, but Roberto and Julio don't have such a good sense of humor."

They went through the door, the flashlight moving across whips, flails, dildos, leg irons, leather masks. Schwartz muttered, "Ah, the green room."

Two flights down they met a waiter, panicked, running up. The sight of Weiss naked did little to calm him.

"Go back down," said Montanares to the man.

Looking up at two machine guns did even less to calm the waiter, and he continued running up, saying, "Lemme by, lemme by," turning his shoulder to squeeze past.

When Julio shot him, the man gasped, shook his head and kept turning his shoulder to squeeze by. He fell to his knees and slumped forward on his face, the shoulder still moving as if excusing his way into death.

"See, Lenny? Julio gets nervous. I warned this man to turn back."

"And I warned you not to come here, Juan, but you turned up anyway."

They went downstairs, led by the trembling, naked Weiss.

"Well, I'm like you, Lenny. I have to be where the action is. At the bottom we take the door on the left and cross the floor to the opposite door."

"I can't," said Weiss.

Schwartz pulled open the heavy door. They moved through a space full of pipes and hanging meat racks.

"And how do you plan to get out of here, Juan?"

"A private way. And you and Weiss being along should help."

"Until Julio got nervous, you didn't have to worry about

going quietly to the station. You'd have been out in a few hours. Or have you been up to more naughtiness when I wasn't looking? Well, don't count on my presence. The police might think I'm your associate, and there have always been plenty of them who wouldn't mind taking a shot at me at the best of times."

They'd gone through another door into a small passageway. They faced another door.

"It's sad, Lenny. Now you'll never be my business associate. But there's Weiss. Weiss, are you politically important?" Montanares asked.

Weiss, enough ego intact, whimpered, "Yes, of course."

"Juan," said Schwartz. "Listen, I haven't lied to you yet. This man has so fucked up everything that now his own people at the CIA or NSA as well as the police would be delighted to put him permanently out of the way."

"That's not so," said Weiss, making a remarkable recovery in smoothness and assurance, for someone naked and dripping in the dim light.

"Julio," said Montanares.

Julio kicked the door open, jumping in with the gun fixed to fire. He said, "Okay."

"Blabbermouth."

Montanares laughed. "Lenny Schwartz. I'm sorry. You do amuse me. I really wanted you to work for me. Anyhow, I promise to end you quickly."

Schwartz followed Weiss into the office. Candles still burned on the tablecloth. Bottles were still in the coolers. And also on the desk, at its far corner, sat a woman with her back to them, legs crossed, drinking champagne.

She turned her head. "Oh, shit, can't anyone get a quiet drink around here?" She wore a black leather miniskirt and black net stockings and a low-cut, red-beaded tank top.

"What are you doing here?" asked Montanares. "Who are you? Where's Alvin and Ahmed?"

"Who? Oh, I know Alvin. He's neat. I don't know. I was in here with Freddy, my date. He went out to piss. Oh, yuk! Isn't that the guy from the show?"

"Out, *puta!*" said Montanares.

"Hey, wait a minute," she said, jumping off the desk and smoothing her little skirt. "Doesn't that mean something dirty in Spanish? I have a Spanish girlfriend, well, she's really Puerto Rican but she calls herself Spanish, and she—"

"Quiet!" said Julio, stepping toward her with the gun.

"I'd do what he says, young lady," said Schwartz. He turned. "Juan, now that we have our overcoats and furs, I'm as ready to get out of here as you are. Later we'll talk, or I can plead about other details, like my life. But now, if you know a safe way out of here we better move before someone really starts shooting and the whole place goes up."

"Roberto," said Montanares, tapping his pocket.

Roberto gave him the radio. Julio directed Schwartz and Weiss in back of the desk. Schwartz pointed to the tablecloth and to Weiss and then pinched his nose. Montanares nodded, but Roberto got to the candelabrum and coolers first. He almost smiled as he shoved the tablecloth to Weiss, who made a rough toga from it.

"Alvin, it's Juan, from your office. Over."

Schwartz heard something coming back into Montanares's ear.

"Right down. We have Weiss and Schwartz for insurance."

"What's your name?" asked Schwartz, wondering where on earth in that outfit a radio could hide.

"Lizzy Thibault. What's yours?"

"Len Schwartz."

"Come, Lenny," said Montanares. "I will say to the end of your life I admire your style."

"Her?" Julio asked.

"No, too many. Julio, don't." Montanares draped the bear and fox over the mink.

"You heard the boss, Gabby," Schwartz said, following Weiss. "Bye, Lizzy. Some other time, maybe. We seem to be off or down now." He thought, please let the walls have ears and please let them be the big ears of Tom Gallagher.

They turned into the large meat room they'd crossed and went to another door. Julio opened it and pointed down. Montanares shone the flashlight. They went down one and then down another long flight into a sub-basement passage filled with pipes and ducts. Montanares shone the light ahead. It showed more of the same.

"Down here and to the left," he said.

Schwartz felt the cold and damp hang on his face.

Julio moved slowly in the lead, gun ready in the wavering light. Then, after Montanares, came Schwartz and then Weiss and then Roberto, covering with machine gun at the rear. Drops of water fell on Schwartz.

"You know, Juan," he whispered, "I almost want to apologize to you for saving Weiss. It wasn't personal, I swear. If it had been Weiss chuckling and you being crucified, I think I would have loused up Weiss's fun."

"Yes, great style," said Montanares.

"You think that's something, Juan, wait till you see this cask of amontillado I have down at the end of the passage."

"The humor of nervousness, Lenny?"

"Of scared shitlessness, Juan. Aren't you scared?"

"No, I'm chilly, which makes me uncomfortable. And feeling sorry to lose you but looking forward to Miami. Julio! Careful around this corner. The door is twenty feet along. They'll be in there."

Schwartz waited as Montanares moved up to give Julio light. He held the flashlight around the corner pipes, and Julio leaped into a firing position. Then Julio disappeared. Montanares followed.

"Roberto," came Montanares's voice.

Roberto said "Go" to Weiss and Schwartz.

Schwartz yearned to tell Roberto this was no time to stand around just *discussing* matters, but he went forward quietly and around, as he heard a door open and some noise.

Roberto said, "Wait."

Then Montanares put his flashlight and head out the door and said "All right."

Schwartz, then Weiss, then Roberto went through the door marked "QF."

"Jesus D. Christ, you took your time," said Gallagher, as police, a gun in each of Roberto's ears, took the gun Roberto set on the floor very gently.

Schwartz put his head down and took deep breaths. He looked up. Gallagher in a camouflage flak jacket looked like a Pershing tank.

Roberto and Montanares joined Julio, Alvin and Ahmed, lying face down, arms and legs spread, on the wooden floor.

"Did Liz tell you, Tom?" Schwartz asked.

"Earlier. When we got Alvin and Ahmed, the Chief's particular interests."

Weiss had come to stand with them. "Chief Gallagher," he said, putting out his hand.

"Don't shake it, Tom. It stinks of mortality and Dom Perignon and worse."

Gallagher's eyebrows rose. Schwartz nodded.

"Get this goddamned suspect down on his face on the

floor," Gallagher shouted. "Don't you jackasses know anything but how to shine those flashlights in each other's faces?"

Two policemen put Weiss down. Gallagher was on the radio. There were six policemen besides Gallagher and about seventy-four thousand pipes, walls and ceilings solid with pipes.

Gallagher said, "Lenny, Lizzy says there's a gunfight going on. A lot of unarmed people in the middle. Know how many men would be involved?"

"Ten to twenty, total, I'd guess. Juan?"

"Gentlemen, you can ask my lawyer."

Schwartz thought it uncooperative but stylish, especially since Montanares lay shivering in just his suit. "Have you frisked his fur coat?" he asked.

"Yes, sir," answered a young policeman.

"Then let the man put it on again. He's got a special health problem called Miami."

"Lenny," said Gallagher, "didn't your church teach you that being evil to evil is being good?"

This was more faith Schwartz lacked. From the floor he heard, "Lenny Schwartz. Heh. We're not through, yet."

"I think we should move," said Gallagher. "Lenny?"

"Yes. There may be as many as twenty up there, or coming down, armed more or less like the kibitzing kids here. We should move. Tom, I don't have a gun."

"You didn't even take that safety with the toy gun attached?"

"I took it. I took it, damn it, but I lost it. Anyone have an extra .38? I have bullets."

"Here, I do," said Gallagher. "Okay, you, in front with me, then one behind each of these sleeping beauties who should get up now. Get them up! Then two covering behind. Not you, Lenny. You get the fun and safety of sticking with Weiss, because you're a noncop. Okay. Let's get lined up in that hallway. Be quiet and follow orders."

They moved out into the passageway.

"Okay, now slowly forward."

There was a burst of gunfire. Bullets ricocheted off pipes. Gallagher went down and then everyone went down.

Schwartz called, "You okay, Tom?"

"Yeah, yeah. Where the—"

There was another burst, mayhem in the narrow passage. Schwartz squirmed back to the police at the rear. They began firing into the dark. The shell casings could maim everyone.

He heard Gallagher's "Get up here!" and understood. Schwartz said, "You two, up there. You come back here with us three so that we're surrounding and protecting the prisoners. And put out that flashlight."

Gallagher said, "We're gonna move ahead up here and you guys go back down to the other end of the corridor."

"Now listen," Schwartz said to the three policemen at the rear. "Don't fire behind you. Fire only when returning fire, and don't wave your barrels wildly. This is a tiny space. Go on." Schwartz tapped the shaking arm. Kids.

"Thank you, sir."

"Sure. Go." It was, he knew, three-quarters irrelevant, but hopefully what he'd said had calmed them.

There was firing behind them.

"Not our concern," Schwartz yelled. The man two away from him let loose a nervous blast of automatic fire into the dark.

And that brought answering fire, which had everyone blasting away and the air choked with cordite. A casing singed the side of Schwartz's hand. Then there was silence.

"Lenny?"

The power came on before he could answer. Forty feet

back down the lit corridor a gunman lay in the pool of his blood. Schwartz asked if everyone was all right.

"Tom? We're all right here. One of the bad guys looks dead."

"We're okay up here and— What the hell!"

Schwartz looked around. Between the two groups of police, only Julio and Roberto remained.

"Jesus," said one of Gallagher's group, "that must have been the sound I heard between the shooting. They must have gone back in there," he said, pointing to the "QF" door.

Gallagher ran to it. "They locked it from inside. It's thick as hell. Let's just leave them in there for a while. You two guard the door, in case they decide to come back out and are armed. And don't anyone tell me you searched them. You also guarded them, didn't you? Let's go."

With lights and caution, and with stepping around and over the bodies of the two other gunmen up ahead, they made it back up to the office, where Malinowski met them and had two officers take the now handcuffed Julio and Roberto outside.

"Whatever you do," Schwartz warned the accompanying police, "don't let those two get talking."

Malinowski reported that Sergeant Thibault was up on the top floor, attempting with others to talk the remaining gunmen from their guns. Two hundred people were still up there hostage.

"Malinowski," said Gallagher, "why are you making this report to Mr. Schwartz the private investigator?"

"Sorry, sir. I thought I was looking at you. At both of you. I . . ."

"Take two men and see what's happening downstairs," said Gallagher.

When the door closed, he told Schwartz he wished he had someone as good and loyal.

"You do. Liz Thibault. She's good, and I'm *trying* to get her to like you."

"Ha-ha. Wait." Gallagher spoke into the radio. Then he listened. "Damn. Okay, I'll be in touch."

"What?"

"They got them to surrender their weapons, but one crazy bastard wounded Lizzy before throwing down his gun. They think she's not badly hurt. Can you imagine, only she gets wounded? I tell you, no one else can talk guns away like she can. Jesus—"

The door burst open. "Chief Gallagher. Chief Phillips says it's over, upstairs. Thibault has a superficial arm wound."

"Great. Thanks. Tell the Chief we'll be right up with the heavyweights."

The officer left.

"Tom? That room downstairs was where Montanares was going to meet the others to get out. There must be a hidden way out from—"

"Not any more. Don't worry; we pulled the plans of this place from the City yesterday and sealed up every escape route, including that one in the quick-freeze room."

"QF—quick freeze? And the power's on!"

Schwartz ran through the door, across the hall and through the opposite door. He stood in the hum of the cold storage room, its pipes already frosted. He ran back.

"Tom, come on! How quick does it freeze?"

"I don't know. Quick, like it says."

"Come on, Tom! Downstairs! The door, the door was locked!"

Gallagher ran after him. "Shit, they pulled it shut and locked it. We didn't."

"Shit! Shit!" Schwartz shouted, jumping stairs. He ran down and down and stopped as he turned the corner of the subbasement passageway.

Corpses were covered. Malinowski was scratching his chin. "Sir? It must have jammed when they locked it. We tried to shoot it open and it only jammed worse."

Gallagher puffed up, looked at the quick-freeze door and yelled, "Jesus Christ, Bob, have someone shoot that thing open. Not three damned .38 bullets! Yell to them inside to stay the hell away from the door and have someone fill that latchplate with automatic fire. Fifty rounds, at least. Come on!"

Everyone not involved moved around the corner.

Gallagher pulled Schwartz aside. "What is it?" he asked in a whisper. "You look sick as a dog."

"You don't understand. Montanares is crazy afraid of the cold. Phobic. You couldn't have known."

They covered their ears against the heavy blasts of automatic fire.

"So?" Gallagher said when it stopped. "Big deal. A cocaine boss could be . . ." He stopped and touched Schwartz's arm. "He's your contact."

Schwartz looked down. "Damn it, if he were only that! If he's dead, I'm . . . His organization knows I was here. I'm . . ."

Then Gallagher understood who Montanares was. "Oh, Jesus. Oh, my God. Lenny. I never would . . . I didn't . . . Shit!"

Schwartz walked after the running Gallagher.

"Get out of my way!" Gallagher yelled, staring at the smoking, blasted door. He backed to the opposite wall and plunged at the door with his shoulder and crashed and fell half through as it shook open. Icy air rolled over him like more smoke.

"Are you all right, Tom?" Schwartz asked quietly, trying not to see inside, not yet.

"I think I busted my shoulder. Maybe not. Get in there." Gallagher pulled himself up onto one knee and yelled, "No one's to move *near* this door until we come out. That's an order."

Then, through the rolling ice mist, Schwartz saw, so that

when Gallagher stepped toward it he was able to put his arm out and say, "No. Don't Tom. Let's look first. It froze too quickly but not quickly enough."

Alvin and Ahmed were neatest, sitting against the pipes, their legs straight out. Their faces were frost-whited so that the single bullet holes just above and between their staring eyes looked darker than they actually were. The run of blood had frozen halfway down Alvin's nose but had gone down into Ahmed's ice-tipped mustache.

Weiss, however, had been able to move. He lay five or six feet from the wall on his face, his right arm stretched before him. Was he attacking? Making supplication? The posture, the blood through the back of the tablecloth toga: Weiss in death had the appearance of a murdered Roman senator, an irony that Weiss in life, like his masters, was too mean-spirited to understand.

"Lenny, it's freezing. Come on, let's—"

"Wait."

Perhaps they hadn't searched Montanares or his coat well enough. Perhaps the .45 had been hidden in the room as part of the escape plan. Anyway, there it was in Montanares's hand, in Montanares's mouth, in what was left of the once near-handsome face of Juan Montanares. Inner space was outer space. He understood. Better that quick hot ending than his ice-isolation.

Weiss's blood. Juan must have dipped his finger in Weiss's blood to write out that death sentence in clear red-black letters on the frost floor: LENNY SCHWARTZ.

Schwartz shivered. Tom would feel better doing it himself. "All right, Tom."

And rubbing his right shoulder, Thomas Gallagher broke a prime rule and changed the crime scene, destroyed what wasn't but might have been vital evidence by pushing the blunt toe of his black boot back and forth into the blood and frost until it was just SCHWARTZ, then WART or maybe ART and then nothing but a pink-orange smear in the slush between two corpses.

They came out as Don Phillips arrived. Officers stood to attention or got busy.

"I'm sorry, Chief," Gallagher said. "Your snuff-show gangsters are dead. So's Weiss and the drug dealer Montanares."

"You all right, Tom?"

"Yessir, just bumped the shoulder getting in there."

"Len?"

"Just catching cold again. Don, Montanares was my contact on this. What happened in there was gangland: Alvin and Ahmed owed Montanares a lot of money. And Weiss, well, Weiss just put himself in the way, thanks to his nasty tastes. The cold drove Montanares crazy. He probably killed Weiss just for fun. I'll make a full statement through Tom's office."

Phillips said, "Damn. I wanted them. Still, it's quite a haul, what with the fifteen or twenty live fish we have upstairs. Quite a haul. Thank you, Len. Above and beyond the call . . ."

"No, it wasn't. But I did see Weiss engage in unlawful activity tonight, Don, and if your people want to seize any papers of his in evidence, that would be very good. Understandable if you can't. And I'll see that the big fellow, here, takes care of his shoulder."

"Right. Well done, Tom."

"Sir," said Tom.

Outside were lights and ambulance jams and the reporters they ducked from. Three blocks down on Fourteenth Street was Tom's blue Lincoln.

"You sure you can drive?"

"I can drive. My shoulder's sprained, nothing more. Kitty can look after it better than any damned hospital. Let's just sit here and let the car warm up for a bit."

"Sure."

Gallagher was staring out in front of him, wet cheeks beneath his eyes.

"Tom, forget—"

"Lenny, I can't tell you . . . You know I never would have in a million years, if I'd known. But I didn't know, I didn't know. Jesus, I haven't thought for years who, you know, *who* it could have been."

"Sure. Tom, if there's any fault here it's mine, because I never told you. I always thought I hadn't the guts. But then, at my place a few weeks ago, I knew it wasn't you I was afraid of. I was afraid for Karen and Jake. If you'd have known, even if you didn't mean to, there'd be twice the chance that they'd know, that he'd know. And now . . . Remember 'The Life of Riley'? Bendix saying 'What a revoltin' development *dis* is!' "

Gallagher laughed. He wiped his eyes. "I still owe you. I can't just do nothing while they . . . Shit!" He hit the steering wheel and winced at the pain it gave his shoulder. "Listen, after I drop you off, I'm coming right back to those thugs of his and I'm gonna warn them that if you even catch another *cold* after this, it's war and they're dead. I'm gonna make sure Montanares's entire organization knows it. They don't want that kind of trouble."

"Sure. Great, Tom. That's what I need. Thanks."

Gallagher grunted and drove Schwartz to Warren Street where he said he wanted to clean up before going home.

As Schwartz got out, Gallagher leaned across the seat. "You're full of shit, Lenny. All that thanking me and 'That'll do it.' We both know that if they want to—"

"Stop it, Tom. Stop driving both of us crazy! Just get back there and do what you said you would. I told you the truth. Jesus. Good night."

"Yeah, sure. Good night. You gonna come back to the department?"

"Don't know. I'll think about it—with Karen."

"Great. Couldn't ask better. Bye, buddy."

He was washing his face. Even with the grime off, it was a very worried forty-three-year-old face. Even Montanares had seen the trouble in his face. And Tom had seen through his beau geste lies. They could kill him. They'd have to kill him, just for the symmetry of it—*coca et decorum est.*

He threw the bullets into the drawer and put the roll of money in his pocket. He'd go home. Home. He wouldn't wake Karen. He'd sleep downstairs on the sofa. He put a fistful of tissues in his coat pocket and ran down the stairs.

He'd find a cruising cab, a limo, anything. What was that up there? Clouds? He hadn't seen real clouds for weeks. And was it thawing or was that the million-dollar long johns?

No cab, no cars, no nothing around City Hall. Schwartz was down in the subway waiting for anything that came along. There, a rackety old RR. He was so tired he fell asleep across three seats the moment he sat down.

He woke. Had he passed his stop? God, only Rector Street, two stops from City Hall. He looked up. Handholds on the old subway, meat hooks. They'd kill him unless enough of them felt good riddance of Montanares.

So tired now, the train finally crawling, screeching down and down, down under the river, those purple tunnel lightbulbs under the river. Down. Here was the deepest part and now began the pull going up.

The RR so late at night pulling up under the East River like a cog railway at the bottom of the world. There it was, now. Up. And up.

In three days or four days if they didn't kill him, he and Karen would start the marriage counseling. What did it mean? Fine. Anything. He'd talk about Maurie, Aunt Celia, Karen in

Chicago. Jake. Marcia Wax. Maybe Cicero and Virgil. Up.

Virgil, poor old VJ. Brilliant and honest, a fine man who'd blown it by sitting on it. Maybe Cannonbury would use it. Maybe he'd get it to the peacies.

Peace. He wanted peace. But when he spoke or worked they were for war. What was that, a psalm? And where had Lizzy hidden the radio?

It was Brooklyn now. Going up into snoozing Brooklyn. If you could lift the lids off the wood-frames and brownstones and projects and apartment houses and castles by the sea and look into all those rooms and all those sleepers . . . Such sleep. Such an amount of sleep! What happened with such sleep?

Union. The union of true . . . Union? Schwartz sat up. What line? The RR?

Union and Fourth. He lunged out of the train. The door stayed open; the train was taking a snooze in the station.

Schwartz ran up Union Street. Up Union Street Schwartz ran, up Park Slope, up the slope he could hardly move. The faster he ran.

He stopped. Deep breaths. There was something he'd forgotten to tell Tom.

Tom? Karen? There. Seventh Avenue. Up slowly now. Up the last sloped blocks up slowly sloping home.

He took deep breaths up on the slate before his door. Quiet. Just very quietly and not disturb.

The door swung open without his touch. It knew him, a magic door—

"Len?"

"Karen? Karen, why are you up, darling?" He pulled her to him and hugged her. Her hair. He felt her anger.

"You're all right. You smell of . . . That's gunpowder, isn't it?" Karen pushed him back but held on to him.

"Yes. But I'm all right. Everything's all right now."

"We've stayed up talking."

"Who?"

"Jake's in there. He came back tonight. He's waiting for you to talk to him, to explain."

"I—"

"As best you can."

"Now? Like this? I can't even stand. My eyelids are—"

"He's waiting."

Schwartz looked into Karen's eyes. He couldn't see them. He imagined them. "Yes, sure. I'll be right in. I just need a few breaths out here."

Karen went in. The door was open.

Overhead, a mass of cloud broke up, and once again Schwartz thought he saw the stars.

Irving Weinman was born in Boston. He was educated there and at Trinity College, Dublin, and Cambridge University, England. He has been a university lecturer in English and divides his time between London and Key West, Florida. He is the author of *Tailor's Dummy* and *Hampton Heat,* both available from Fawcett Books.